CRIMEU~~~

TOTALLY P~   ~

A Murderous I~   ~ogy

**************~   ~*******

Murderous Ink Press

CRIMEUCOPIA
TOTALLY PSYCHO LOGICAL

First published by Murderous-Ink Press
Crowland
LINCOLNSHIRE
England
www.murderousinkpress.co.uk

Editorial Copyright © Murderous Ink Press 2024
Base Artwork by Marius Moisa (aka Maru) © 2023
Cover treatment and lettering © Willie Chob-Chob 2024
All rights are retained by the respective authors & artists on publication
Paperback Edition ISBN: 9781909498563
eBook Edition ISBN: 9781909498570

Acknowledgements

To those writers and artists who helped make this anthology what it is, I can only say a heartfelt Thank You!

And to Den, as always.

Contents

Welcome To The Minkey Haus....
(An Editorial of Sorts)

Totally — adverb: completely; absolutely. Used to emphasize a clause or statement. "He/She is totally bat-shit crazy!"

Psycho — noun: an unstable and aggressive person. "Don't you know? My ex is a total psycho!"

adjective: exhibiting unstable and aggressive behaviour. "There's some kind of psycho nut job on the loose out there!"

Logical — adjective: characterized by or capable of clear, sound reasoning. "His/Her *logical* mind? Are you nuts or something?"

But are all psychos 'nut jobs'? Or, given the chance, could they show that their actions really are totally logical? At least, from their perspective that is.

Laurie Stevens opens this visit to the Minkey Haus, by landing us on *Shelter Island*, and putting a twist on the expression 'holiday snapshot' — before Jesse Aaron explains all about *The Emptiness of Eternity*.

A short walk down the corridor brings us into the *Sunroom*, where we find *Patrick Ambrose* talking about drinking popskull and Uncle Lyman's exploding chickens.

And over by the doors leading out into the grounds you can find *Stephen D. Rogers* as he sets the *Snare of the Fowler,* while watching on, *Wendy Harrison* smiles and assures us that *It's Nothing Personal.* But, do we believe her…?

Through the door and following the path down to the river we come across *Jan Glaz*, making notes about her *Last Case Scenario*, and even cross paths with *Brandon Doughty*'s *Beachcomber* (who, apparently, isn't all sun, sea and insanity), before we find *Elena Schacherl*, who admits it's not the first time she's been *Lost in Fish Creek Park.*

Back in the, er, relative safety of the Haus, *Joyce Bingham* stops to ask *Have You Seen Rebecca?* – and beside her *Jeff Somers* gets in touch with his feral side by talking about how his *Teeth Can Hardly Stand*.

Going past the reception desk, we head into the cafeteria, where *Glenn Francis Faelnar* keeps saying the clocks are all wrong and that in his reality *It's Twelve Midnight at Haley's Diner* — before *Douglas Soesbe* moves in to see if he can get you to take pictures of himself and his *Trophy Wife*.

Up at the thankfully padded Naugahyde and Formica counter *Carol Goodman Kaufman* assures us that it's all *Skin Deep*, and we're pretty sure that *Daniel C. Bartlett* also knows Uncle Lyman, because he wants to tell us just *How Easily Things Can Explode*.

Over at the far table, *Richard J. O'Brien* is playing a variation on Spin the Bottle, only he calls it *Let My Pistol Decide My Fate* — which we readily take as our cue to leave for more, hopefully safer, places.

As we pass the reception desk again, we find *David Bradley*, writing everything down and, for whatever reason, keeping score in his *Ledger* — and just before we head on home we're met part way by *Kamal M*, who keeps asking the question no one seems capable of properly answering for him: *Who's Moz?*

So, with the door firmly shut and locked behind us, we can rest safely in the knowledge that the Minkey Haus is now closed to visitors — the access securely triple-locked and bolted of a nighttime — before lights out at 22:00.

Of course, locks can be picked and security measures can be circumvented…which will be the next items on the list of problems to solve, once we figure out how we can get out of this straightjacket….

As always, with all of these anthologies, we hope you'll find something that you immediately like, as well as something that takes you out of your regular padded cell comfort zone — and puts you into a completely new one because, in the spirit of the Murderous Ink Press motto:

You never know what you like until you read it.

Shelter Island
Laurie Stevens

"I know you're having an affair with my husband."

My best friend Lela doesn't appear angry as she addresses the girl who lies under a cabana on a chaise lounge. You'd have to fight me off from throwing the tanned little bitch into the hotel pool.

Lela sits with a rather blank face on a chair next to the girl, who appears to be in her late twenties with dark eyes and waist-length brown hair. "I know you and Richard are sleeping together, so let's not keep up the charade."

My heart dies in my chest. Lela has yearned to have this confrontation with her husband's mistress for weeks, but, being a shy, timid thing, she couldn't get up the guts to do it. She and I practiced this scene repeatedly so she could say her peace. Lela, the unimposing wife of Richard Sarnow, usually hovers unseen in the background while her blowhard husband hogs the limelight. Richard is the senior partner at Sarnow, Appel, and Polski, a La Jolla criminal defense firm I call SAP. Rightly so.

His mistress, Nereyda, works for him. When Lela sat on the chair beside her, Nereyda's skin, the color of a mocha latte, went more latte, and I imagine she's a bit short of breath. The frothy piña colada in her hand sweats condensation that wets her clenched fingers.

Meanwhile, I stand sentinel a couple of feet away and suffer the sun to beat on my hatless head. Under the cabana, Lela says, "You've been more than a law clerk to Richard for months now, haven't you?"

"What are you talking about?" Nereyda's nervousness deepens the Spanish in her accent. "Mr. Sarnow and I—"

"I'm here to say that you can have him."

The scent of coconut and vanilla drifts past my nostrils as another tanned, bikini-clad young woman strolls by. Does she, too, work for SAP? I'll bet Richard, the Senior SAP, purposely hires young female law clerks so he can ogle them. Maybe that's why he books the company retreat each year at Shelter Island. Here, on this strip of sand connected to the mainland of San Diego, he can lounge at the hotel pool and stare slack-jawed at the bodies of his clerks. I'm here because my best friend needs moral support this weekend.

Lela inhales deeply. "Richard says he wants to save our marriage, but frankly, I don't believe a word he says. He knows as well as I that our marriage is over."

"Mrs. Sarnow—"

"Call me Lela. You're sleeping with my husband. The least we can do is be on a first name basis."

"I'm not doing what you think."

Lela glances at me for help. I give her an encouraging nod. *You can do this*, I silently tell her. *Show them how brave you've become. Show them you've got guts and won't wimp out like they expect you to do.*

Lela glues her eyes to Nereyda's. "I have photos from a private investigator. You have a mole next to your right nipple."

Bravo, I think. Well-delivered. I want to clap my hands but refrain from doing so. Instead, I step under the cabana because the sun is bleaching my dyed red hair.

Nereyda regards me in fear. I'm a tall, red-headed, athletic-looking gal, most likely descended from Vikings, so maybe she thinks Lela hired me to kill her.

"This is my best friend, Shelly," Lela explains. "I'm going to stay in her room tonight. That way, I don't have to play the fool while you and Richard sneak around behind my back."

Nereyda shivers under the warmth of the sun.

I focus my gaze on the harbor. What a tough thing to do in such relaxed surroundings. A sailboat skims past. A gull flies overhead. Shelter Island isn't actually an island but was once a sandbar in San

Diego Bay, visible only at low tide. From what I read in a hotel brochure, in 1934, workers built up the bar using material dredged from the bay. Now, Shelter Island hosts a variety of hotels like this one, Halia Kai, and has a distinct Hawaiian feel with the sunshine, the blue ocean, and the Polynesian-themed restaurants.

The group in the next cabana over closes the curtain between us. Maybe they sense that something serious is going down. A small refrigerator hums next to me and has a basket on top filled with packets of corn nuts and candy. My stomach rumbles. If there's food around, I want it. Typical.

"I know you two have been carrying on for at least a year," Lela tells Nereyda. "I believe Richard loves you because I see how he looks at you. He used to look at me like that." She reaches for a striped hotel towel and hugs it to her chest like a shield. "Anyhow, last week, I told Richard I wanted a divorce. He argued against it, although I don't know why."

I watch my friend's desperate eyes travel to the pool, where a slick of oil coats the water. "Three children," she murmurs. "We have three wonderful children. Did Richard tell you one is in medical school, and the other two are finishing college? I'm sure he did. He likes to brag about them. I never wanted to break up my family, but I can't do this anymore."

Lela refocuses on Nereyda, on her smooth, velvety skin, the rich chestnut hair, and the girl's flawless body. "I guess I can understand why he cheats. I know I don't look the way I used to, but neither does Richard."

At that, I can no longer keep quiet. "He's a fat turd," I yell.

Lela widens her eyes at me, and I shut my mouth. I promised her I'd hang back, but it's hard. I've always been the bolder of us, the delinquent in high school when she was the valedictorian. During school, Lela befriended me. Maybe she admired my big mouth because she had trouble speaking up. Her demure manner and softness attracted me in a more-than-a-friend way, but I kept my crush to myself. I had to. I didn't want to scare her away. When we grew older,

Lela fell for the smooth-talking, ambitious Senior SAP, a decision I tried to talk her out of. Meanwhile, I never married any gender but used my big mouth to work my way up from a sales rep to a sales manager at a software firm in Laguna Nigel.

Lela uses the towel to wipe tears from her eyes, and I quit thinking about myself.

"We built a life together," she tells Nereyda.

"And he shot it to pieces," I pipe up again. "Richard's always had to play the big shot lawyer with his fancy clothes and fancy cars. He's an insecure little asshole."

"Shelly."

I wave a dismissive hand at young Nereyda. "You're welcome to the flabby jerk."

"Shelly." Lela regards me with those calm doe's eyes, and I leave the cabana before I spout off again. I loiter near the Jacuzzi, which is crowded with bathers. The mist from the spa hits my face and feels surprisingly cool.

Lela stands up and puts a hand on her lower back. Like me, she's pushing fifty, and we don't exactly spring up from a sitting position anymore. *She gave Richard the best years of her life.* I cluck my tongue. Shake my head. *This is how he repays her.*

Lela reaches into her purse, hands something to Nereyda, and says, "He's all yours." Then, she walks over to me. As we leave the pool area, I put a sympathetic hand on her shoulder. We head toward her room, but we don't talk. I know she's grieving.

"If you want to cry, cry," I tell her. "If you want to scream, scream."

Lela, however, does neither. She simply walks along next to me in silence.

When she opens the door to her room, my mouth falls open in disgust. "Are you kidding me?" I step onto the brown carpet and survey the place. "He booked you into this cave? Why is it so dark in here? Why would Richard take a crappy room on the bottom floor?"

My temper rises. I storm across the room to the floor-to-ceiling plantation shutters and push them open to reveal a dirty sliding glass door. The view is an up-close wrought iron fence covered by a hedge. I put my hands on my hips. I'm so mad I could spit.

"Well, at least you don't have to see the parking lot. I hope nobody's brakes go out. You'll end up with the fence and a car in your bed."

Lela lifts a suitcase onto the bureau and says, "Richard claims all the other rooms were booked. He said that since this event is for the benefit of his employees, we have to take the worst room."

I wave away the dust motes flying in the filtered sunlight. "So, Richard put you in this dungeon while he plans to flit off to Nereyda's room, which, I'm sure, has an ocean view. He's got some nerve." I peer through the dirty glass and the hedge beyond. "You know, there's all kinds of creeps walking the boardwalk at night. Any one of them could easily jump this fence and get in here." To make my point, I jiggle the sliding glass door. "Look at this! One shove. That's all it would take." I bend down and pick up a pole on the track that keeps the door from opening. "*This* is the lock. Unbelievable."

Lela's shoulders droop as she shuts the case. "It doesn't matter. I'm sleeping in your room tonight anyhow."

My heart goes out to her. I walk over and take Lela in my arms. Rocking her lightly, I whisper, "Sorry. I don't mean to give you a hard time. This must be horrible for you. It's his loss, Lela. Remember that. It's Richard's loss."

Her hands clutch my shirt. "You've always been there for me, Shel. I appreciate you coming to help me through this."

"What are friends for?" I pull away, reach into my shirt pocket, and hand my room key to her. "You'll like my room. It's two floors above, and we can see the water." Something occurs to me, and I sigh. "The hotel had better rooms, Lela. I was able to book mine. Richard just wanted to make you feel worthless again. Why else would he accept a room off the parking lot?"

She nods in defeat. "I know."

"But his days of dishing out psychological torment are over."

"I know that, too."

Lela shoulders her purse, I carry her suitcase, and we walk to the door together. When Lela opens it, we find Richard standing before us. He ogles me in surprise and nods to the suitcase.

"What are you doing?" he asks his wife.

Lela visibly shrinks next to me. "I'm spending tonight with Shelly."

"What do you mean, you're spending the night with Shelly?" He scowls at me. "What are *you* doing here?"

"I'm here because someone has to be a friend to Lela. God knows you aren't."

Richard puffs himself up, the all-powerful *SAP*.

"Can you give us some privacy?" His arm pushes the door wide, and I step into the hall with Lela's suitcase. He shuts the door in my face, but I put my ear against the wood to listen.

"Lela, honey," I hear Richard say. "What's going on here? Were you actually planning on leaving me tonight?"

"You give me no choice, Richard."

"Please, baby. I brought you on the retreat because I thought we could mend things between us."

"With Nereyda here?"

I hear Richard mumble something, then a slight scuffle and Lela says, "Let me pass, Richard."

"No." His voice becomes whining. "Just give me one more chance. Please. I have plans for us this weekend. Tonight, I thought we'd order in room service and talk it over. I need you, Lela. I want you."

"Do you want me, Richard, or my inheritance?"

In the hallway, I wait for Richard's response. My heart pumps so hard that I put a hand on my chest.

Then, Lela says, "I know things have been lean, Richard. I know you've overspent, and now the firm is in trouble. Maybe if you weren't supporting a wife and a mistress you'd have more disposable income. I guess selling your Bentley never crossed your mind. I'm leaving. Nereyda can deal with your financial crisis. I don't want anything from you, but you're not getting one thing from me. Not my inheritance or, if I die, that million-dollar life insurance policy you took out on me last month. I'll be calling the insurance company as soon as they open tomorrow to have you removed as my beneficiary."

"But I'm breaking it off with Nereyda," Richard pleads, and I can hear the desperation in his voice. "She never meant anything to me. You're my wife and the mother of my children. Please don't break us up. Give me this chance to prove myself."

"No."

"Why do you think I brought you here on the company retreat? I wanted to show Nereyda that I'm back with my wife. I mean it this time. I know I've been bad, but I can't lose you, Lela. Please. If you don't feel any different in the morning, then leave, but give us both tonight. Please!"

I sense a profound pause. *Oh, no. Don't do it. Don't cave in.*

"Sweetheart," Richard says, "We've been through so much together. I promise you, things are going to change."

"You won't be with Nereyda?"

God, Lela's voice sounds so weak.

"I won't leave your side," Richard assures her, "except to buy some fine champagne from the liquor store down the street. I want us to celebrate new beginnings tonight."

Outside their door, I shake my head. This isn't the first time Lela has floundered under Richard's lies. He's a former litigator and knows how to convince people he's sincere.

I push off the door and stand in the hallway, numb. A moment later, the door swings open. Richard grabs the suitcase, takes it inside, and closes the door on me. He doesn't even grace me with a look.

My sigh fills the dank corridor with its ugly print carpeting and musty odor. There are better hotels on Shelter Island, and I wonder why Richard chose such a cheap one. Lela's right. He must really be having money problems. With nothing more to do, I have no choice but to return to my room.

Room service arrives, a wet piece of garlic chicken with dry rice complimented by a Mai Tai. I down the drink and eat the bruised maraschino cherry and the chunk of canned pineapple speared by a paper umbrella. At least the hotel makes a strong drink. My crush on Lela has never served me well. I always thought that maybe she felt something mutual, but apparently, she'd rather love a cheating jerk than me.

After placing the meal tray in the hall, I move out onto the balcony to watch the sunset. Boats bedecked with fairy lights drift past. This hotel's saving grace is the view of the harbor from the upper floors. I look down to the rooms below and try not to think of what Richard is doing to woo Lela back into his web.

Taking a seat on the white plastic balcony chair, I rest my feet on the matching plastic table, which is warped and wobbles. Still, the balmy night air soothes my broken spirit. An hour goes by. Maybe two. Maybe three. I lose track of time as I gaze across the bay at the lights of downtown San Diego. I'm sure Richard and Lela have long finished their 'romantic' dinner by now. When my butt finally hurts from sitting so long, I stand up and stretch. I'm about to head inside when Richard's voice fills the parking lot.

"Okay, sweetheart. I'll be back in a jiffy with the bubbly."

I look over the balcony to see him cross the lot to his Bentley. He gets in, starts the engine, and drives off. The sliver of the moon over the dark water cuts my heart. Lela and Richard have rekindled their romance, and there's no reason for me to be here. I consider leaving when, suddenly, the door to my room opens, and Lela enters with her suitcase.

"Whoa, what are you doing here?"

She puts a finger to her lips, sets her case on the bed, and crosses to my balcony. I step outside and stare at her in surprise.

She grips the railing, surveys the parking lot, and goes still as a statue. Lela appears to be waiting for something. I, too, take hold of the railing and wait. It's almost midnight, and the grounds are quiet.

A few minutes pass. It's getting chilly, but Lela remains stock-still beside me. Watching. Waiting. For what? I don't know.

Then, a male figure wearing a black tracksuit and a ski mask crosses the parking lot toward the hotel. Lela gasps. To my astonishment, the masked figure disappears into the hedge affronting Lela's room. The foliage draping the fence moves, and a swish of black fabric bounds over the fence.

"Oh, my God! That dude just hopped your fence!"

I back up into my room to search for the house phone. "We've got to call the police." Panicked, I grab my cell, which is closer. "I told you those first-floor rooms were ripe for a robbery. We've got to alert hotel security—" My eyes glimpse Lela's suitcase.

"Wait." I pause. "What are you doing here? I thought you and Richard…"

I'm at a loss for words, but Lela's dark eyes give nothing away. At that moment, I hear the firecracker sound of a pistol shot.

My breath stops in my throat as I creep to the balcony. Squatting low in fear, I look over. Sure enough, the ski-masked figure jumps the fence and races across the lot to get swallowed up in the dark.

Lights go on in nearby rooms. Some curious souls creep out into the lot. I imagine many more people are like me, crouched in their rooms in fear.

"Lela," I whisper. "You could have been shot."

Down below, two hotel security guards arrive and circulate the parking lot on foot. One talks into a radio. I can't make out what he's saying because my mind is racing. In the distance, sirens approach.

"I hope you don't mind me staying with you as planned," Lela says.

"I don't understand. What are you doing here?"

Two headlights light up the activity in the lot. Richard has returned. A security guard holds up his hand to the Bentley, and Richard rolls down the window.

I can't hear the exchange between them, but Richard parks erratically, exits the car holding a champagne bottle, and looks anxiously in the direction of his first-floor room.

Two police cars screech into the lot and light the place up with flashes of red and blue. The area fills with hotel personnel and curious guests holding up cell phones to record the moment. One of the police officers inspects the hedge in front of Lela's room. Two other officers disappear inside the building. I watch Richard speak to the officer inspecting the hedge and then race inside.

Lela tugs at my sleeve. "We should go now."

"Someone broke into your room!"

"Richard is there. We have to go."

Lela and I take the elevator down and find the hallway crammed with people chattering anxiously with each other. A detective arrives, accompanied by more officers, and they brush past us.

"Oh, my God, Lela." I take a deep breath. "You're lucky you decided to leave when you did."

"Luck had nothing to do with it."

"What do you mean? How in the world could you predict a burglary?"

"It wasn't a burglary."

I face her and lower my voice. "Are you saying…?"

"I'm saying Richard planned to kill me tonight."

That sinks in.

Lela searches my eyes. "Do you understand, Shelly?"

"But how did you know?"

She offers me a sardonic smile. "The life insurance policy he took out on me last month? The fact that I have a large inheritance that he can't touch if we divorce? The invitation to come on this retreat when he's never wanted me to join him before? I asked you here in case my hunch was correct. Then, when I saw the room with its easy access to the parking lot, I knew tonight was the night. You were right. Richard wouldn't normally book a room like ours. Before he left to get the champagne, I saw him take the pole from the track of the sliding glass door and hide it under the bed."

"My God." I swallow hard. "I can't believe this. I knew Richard was a cheat, but a killer?"

"Oh, I seriously doubt that masked man was Richard." Lela looks down the hall toward her room. "Remember, Richard is a criminal defense attorney. He's met a lot of scumbags in his career. I imagine it wasn't too difficult to find someone who would accept payment to stage a break-in-gone-bad."

I'm stunned, but then my blood begins to boil. "Okay. Let's go in there right now and tell the police that Richard tried to have you killed tonight. He's going down for attempted murder."

I begin threading my way through the people in the hall, but Lela takes my arm and holds me back.

"How can we prove that, Shelly? They won't be able to finger him personally for the crime. He's got an alibi, remember? He went out for champagne and, no doubt, picked a liquor store that has video surveillance. As to hiring someone, Richard's experience defending criminals has taught him how to cover his tracks."

"So, we're just gonna let this go?" I gape at my friend. "You're going to let him get away with trying to have you murdered?"

Lela takes my hand and leads me toward her room.

As we approach, I hear the unmistakable sound of sobbing.

A uniformed officer stationed at the door glowers at us. "Stay back." He then orders another officer to "clear the hallway."

Before they can shut us out, before the officers push us away, I peek into the room and see Richard kneeling on the ground. He's crying over Nereyda, who lies dead before him. Blood runs from a hole in her shirt.

The officer yells at us to leave, and Lela takes my hand and leads me down the hall toward the elevator. During the ride up, I stare at Lela.

We walk inside my room, and she goes to the balcony where the night air ruffles her hair. In the distance, the lights of downtown San Diego twinkle.

"Before I left to come here," she says, "I called Nereyda and told her I was leaving. She and Richard were free to be together, and she might as well come down. I don't know if you recall, Shelly, but at the pool I gave her a key to my room. I guess she wanted to surprise Richard." Lela smirks. "He was surprised."

I join her on the balcony. "I didn't know you had it in you, Lela."

In response, she puts her hands on my shoulders and kisses me full on the mouth. Smiling into my eyes, she says, "It took me a while to find out that I did."

The Emptiness of Eternity

Jesse Aaron

I want you to listen carefully to what I say. Every word counts. I have waited eighteen years for this day and waited an eternity for this moment. This is the only time that matters. Everything else was the waiting.

I wipe my hands on my pants. The trigger and the stock are covered in my sweat and gun oil, creating a beautiful rainbow of swirling color as I look down the barrel at the reflected sunlight. It is a beautiful day, and it makes me think that some higher power knows that this is right.

I prepare my sight picture on the doorframe, just as I practiced. I remove the clip and slap it back in. I can't have any jams. I get ready to cross the street. Yesterday a killer came home, and today he will die.

*****

My foster parents are good people. Since I was three, I knew my parents were gone. I didn't really understand why or how until I got older, but I was always lonely. Once I was old enough, I started reading the stories and viewing the videos online. My foster parents never hid it from me, but any time we talked about it they became uncomfortable. I finally just decided to stop bringing it up.

As I got older, I missed my parents more and more. All around me my classmates and friends had parents and brothers and sisters, and I had no one. I have one uncle, but he lives far away, and he made it clear he wanted nothing to do with me. Even though I lived in a nice house and had lots of toys and pretty much anything I wanted, I was still alone.

Slowly, like a malignant cancer, the loneliness grew, and then transformed into rage and finally a calculated vengeance. There was something inside me that drove me to my parent's killer. I began following any news about him and finally decided I was going to kill him. He had taken everything, so I was going to take it all back with a bullet.

As I matured, I became a quiet person. Many described me as reserved. Some said I resembled a tall, dark, and handsome prince. My looks never really mattered to me. I had other things to think about. Once I had the plan set in my mind it provided me with a kind of temporary peace.

I had a mission, and so I directed all my pain and longing for my parents towards the plan. I did well in school. I never had too many friends, as there did not seem to be much point in developing close connections. The plan was my deepest and most sacred secret, and it gave me power.

I knew it was important to protect my plan, so I have always said the right things and I have worn the right clothes. Inside though I was waiting. Waiting for this day and this moment. Every day of my life has been a play in which I filled the role of the diligent and thankful child.

I always did well in sports. It has always been important to me to be physically fit. I knew this moment would come and I had to be ready. After today I can eat what I want, and I will no longer worry about being the ideal person and looking right.

I have asked myself how it will feel, and what would I do and who would I become. There is no answer. My stepfather always told me I would find my way in my own time, step by step. If only it were that simple. My entire life has consisted of getting to this moment, and after it is over, I don't know what will be left.

I only have flashes of my real father and mother, and I can't really remember their last day. I just remember what came after. The emptiness, being alone, wondering what my life could have been, missing all those moments I could have had, wanting them to be with me so badly I could taste it on my tongue like the metallic flavor of blood.

And then knowing all along that this animal, this piece of human waste took that. He took it all in the flash and pop of four rounds of cheap ammunition. I had pictured it in my mind over and over. I could clearly see him walking up to the counter and buying the tools of death without a thought, as if he was purchasing a carton of milk.

The bright flash of light created by the trailer door opening kicked me back into the moment and I knew what I had to do. He was coming outside on his way to work. I had been watching him from a distance for weeks, and I knew his routine. I stood up and walked quickly towards him, rifle tucked neatly under my arm. He didn't see me right away and that was good. Even an extra second could give me the time I needed.

He was looking at the sky, squinting into the sunlight. Now that I was close to my life's obsession, I felt slightly disappointed. Somehow, I felt he should be ten feet tall, with massive arms and legs as wide as tree stumps. Now that I was close, I could smell him, and he stunk of sour milk and booze. His hunched over form stuck out in a small round belly and he only had random patches of thin hair on his square head.

He had a bent scarred nose and stubble on his chin that was peppered with flecks of white the color of old bone marrow. He was wearing a stained white t-shirt and tan cargo shorts. I could see his arms and his legs were thin, countered by his stomach.

I realized that he was an old man. I could plainly see he was weak and out of shape and that the world had passed him over long ago. He looked down from the sun and finally saw me, and when I locked my gaze on his milky blue eyes, I could see he was already mostly dead.

But behind the atrophy was some small spark. It was still there. The killer he had been still looked out at me laughing, pointing the finger at me, mocking me and my entire life of wanting and pain. I have never forgotten the moment I first saw those eyes look into the camera.

I was ten years old, and my foster parents finally allowed me to view the news footage of my parent's killer. As he was being led away by the police he looked directly into the camera and smirked. It was the first time in my life I had seen real and pure evil. The memory came back to me in a rush, and I had a stark reminder of why I was here. I raised the rifle.

He stepped back and raised his hands.

"What is this, another YouTube stunt?"

His voice was high pitched and had the annoying whine that a lawn mower makes as it wakes you up on a Sunday morning. I clamped my teeth together as I felt the rage pour out through me into my hand and vibrate down the barrel of the gun. It felt like I could propel the round with all my volatile hate and pain that had been sitting in my stomach for eighteen years.

The Bastard was smiling at me.

"What's a sissy like you doing with a gun? I bet you can't even fire that thing. The kick will knock you down and you will cry and beg for a real man to help you."

Now he was openly mocking me! My hands began to shake. I had to clear the anger. I needed to be calm to make sure that he suffered before he died. I moved the barrel down from his head to his groin.

The smile left his face as he realized my intent. I kept the gun pointed there, and then briefly, just for a couple of seconds I felt my stomach tighten as the first small seed of doubt sprouted in my belly. I hesitated. I realized I might not want to do this.

Now that it was real, it seemed less satisfying, and the hollow darkness that had dominated my life seemed to only grow larger. At the final moment I had a jolt of clarity that this might solve nothing.

Then, in a flash, his hand was on the barrel of the gun, and we were struggling. Back and forth the barrel went, up and down, left and right, as we continued the struggle that would determine who got to live. He was much stronger than he looked, and for a few moments I thought I would lose and that he would add my soul to his sickening tally.

As the barrel moved back and forth, I could see his body for a second and then he would push it off to the side. There was not enough time to center in on him and fire a kill shot. Now I knew I had no choice but to finish this.

I squeezed off two shots that went wide and pinged into the side of the trailer. We kept up the struggle, and as the barrel moved back and forth rapidly, I felt two more shots jerk the rifle. This time there was no metallic sound. I realized that during the struggle he must have been hit. He let go of the barrel and fell backwards. He sat on the ground, smiling up at me.

I took a few steps back and leveled the barrel on his chest. There was a long pause that felt like the eighteen years I had waited for this moment had all rolled into one flash. I briefly let go of the trigger and put my finger on the trigger guard. I was still deciding.

The blackness within screamed at me to do it, but there was another part of me that knew it would solve nothing. Then he smiled, and I saw the pure disgusting arrogance come to the surface, like a pimple that needs to be popped. I saw the same malevolence and absolute evil I had witnessed in the video of his arrest eighteen years ago and I knew he had not changed.

I put my finger back on the trigger and left it there for an eternal moment. Then I felt something in me collapse. I could not finish him, I could not do it and no longer wanted to. He was sitting in a pool of his own gathering blood. It was over, but nothing had changed inside me. The emptiness was still there, but now I had added another level of violence to the rotten layer cake that made up my soul.

I stood over him and looked down at my life's obsession. He was still alive. I had some questions before he was gone. I put my foot on his stomach and he grunted.

"Just so you know. Just so you know why. I've been watching you my whole life. On the news, and then when they let you out of the mental institution. Waiting, waiting for this moment. And the most important part is that you know. You must know who and why.

Eighteen years ago today you killed my parents. For no reason. It was a nice day in the park, just like today. I was three. I don't remember much, but I was able to watch myself online. I saw you kill forty-three people that day. Forty-three lives, multiplied by all the other people you touched that day. If you add them all up, it is a small city.

I just want to know one thing. Why? You never gave a clear answer. I watched all your interviews, and I read all your published letters. Why did you do it? Why did this happen? Why did it happen to me?"

Tears were streaming down my face, each one like a marathon runner, straining to reach the finish line that was my chin.

With a grunt he smiled as blood seeped down below him and formed a small pool around him like a liquid pillow. He continued to smile and said nothing. I quickly realized he was not going to answer, and I knew it no longer mattered what he said. As he stared up at me with that idiotic smirk, I realized I was staring into the abyss that is random violence and suffering.

The truth hit me in the stomach like a medicine ball and then made me tremble. There was no answer. There is no explanation for evil. It just exists, and sometimes it lands on you.

I pulled back the rifle and laid it on my shoulder. I made my way back up the hill across from his trailer. I thought that this moment would change me. I thought that it would provide an answer, but all it did was create another space in my soul. It was still a deep black well with no end.

I realized the ultimate truth that there was no magic and there was no way to heal the pain that flooded my being. Violence and death only make the hole wider and deeper. There was no satisfaction in this moment. Only emptiness and a feeling of dark inevitability that I would never heal.

I would never be the normal happy person I had pretended to be through all those parties, games, and school dances. That man never existed and never would. He was an illusion created to get me to this moment, and now that it was gone there was nothing left. What do you become when the rage and anger have dissipated? What is left after the cold and swift action of violence has been perpetrated on another human being?

As I collected the last of my things, I began the wait for the police and the media to show up. The sound of the shots had drawn attention and I could see other trailer doors opening. I knew it would not be long. I sat down on the hill facing the trailer and his body and stared up at the bright blue sky. It seemed to go on forever and I felt myself float high up and fade away into the sunlight, like a lost balloon, never to touch the earth again.

Sunroom

Patrick Ambrose

Mama Kat says I've got Uncle Lyman's genes. Like him, I grew up guzzling popskull and huffing gasoline. And like him, I've got a green thumb and can grow damn near anything—from heirloom tomatoes and vanda orchids to potent Spoke-County Screambud. Lyman and I even spent time in the bughouse.

But Uncle Lyman blew up chickens. Decades ago, from the rooftop of Kat's log barn, I saw him fasten dynamite to a rooster and collapse into hysterics when the bird exploded.

That's where he and I differed.

"I'm no sick-o," I say aloud, shaving, free from the scrutiny of nurses and orderlies. A gaunt, weathered face stares back from the mirror. Through my other's gaze, I sift through trapped memories. An institutional stench of antiseptic, body odor, and stale decaf eclipses the fresh scent of shaving cream, and I drift back to the dayroom couch in Chestnut Grove Psychiatric Hospital.

Astrid checks vitals. She adjusts the blood-pressure cuff on my arm with slender, agile fingers. Shimmering raven locks trickle down her cream-colored blouse like spilled ink. Her sandalwood scent relieves me from the locker-room stink of confined men.

Patients line up at the dispensary window. From the end of the queue, Floyd Farnsworth watches us. I glare at him. He looks away.

I ponder my foam slippers.

Astrid lifts my chin and glowers.

"I could get fired for this," she whispers, slipping me Percocet tabs. "You'd better make 'em last."

I nod. *Claro, muñeca*

"You gotta get your head right, Nolan."

Her demand dissipates into faint echoes. Her image fades into my reflection.

From my boom box, Jimmy Ruffin wails about broken hearts and broken dreams.

I slap on aftershave, grab my sport coat.

I need distractions.

*****

At Purgatory, a boilermaker slows racing thoughts. Erv, the owner, keeps to himself. Aside from him, there's nary a soul in the place.

Until a plump ass plops down on an adjacent stool. Sheriff Hubert Corley. He orders coffee to go. He adds lots of cream and sugar.

"Nolan," he grunts.

"Hubert," I mutter.

He squints at me.

"Couple fellers at the office wanna talk to you."

I swig beer, meet his narrow gaze. "What about, Hubert?"

He sips coffee, appears thoughtful.

"Let's take a ride," he growls, rising from his stool.

*****

The barren, nondescript room contains a pockmarked wooden table and four stiff-backed chairs. The "fellers" wear grey-flannel suits. State guys, I suppose. Hubert fills a Styrofoam cup from a coffee dispenser.

"Compliments of the Spoke County Sheriff's Office," he says, handing it to me.

"Nolan Brundage?"

The man is handsome, twenty-something and well-built with mahogany skin that almost glistens. But he's not sweating.

"I'm Special Agent Wilbright. And this is Special Agent Sturridge," he says, gesturing at a burly, frowning redheaded dude. "We're from the State Bureau of Investigation."

He pauses, smiles. "Astrid Dearborn? That name ring a bell?"

"Yes sir," I answer.

"Ms. Dearborn hasn't been seen in nearly three weeks. She's not returning calls either."

Acrid steam spirals from my cup. Astrid's features seem superimposed over Wilbright's inquisitive expression—a unique conglomeration of lines and angles. Black eyeliner and magenta lipstick accentuate her high cheekbones and narrow chin.

"I wasn't aware she was missing," I say.

"Missing?" asks Sturridge. "Who says she's missing?"

Wilbright studies me. I deadpan. Or, at least I think I do. But maybe my forced expression is hemorrhaging guilt.

"In what capacity do you know Ms. Dearborn?" he asks.

"She was a nurse when I was hospitalized."

"Was a nurse?" inquires Sturridge. He whistles through his teeth.

Heat crawls up my neck. Perspiration pops from my forehead.

Wilbright sports a poker face. "You're referring to Chestnut Grove Psychiatric Hospital?"

I nod. *Big 10-4, G-Man*

"How would you describe your relationship with Ms. Dearborn?"

Our eyes lock. "Cordial."

Sturridge sighs. "You're not being truthful with us."

He unfolds a square of paper. "Remember this?" he asks, sliding it across the table.

Astrid's note. I thought I had flushed it.

I hand it back. "Never seen it before."

"That's funny," he quips. "It was found in your room the day you left the hospital."

"Must've belonged to Gus, my roommate."

Sturridge glares.

Wilbright scribbles into a pocket-sized notebook. "Have you and Ms. Dearborn made contact since your release?"

"A few times."

An eyebrow raises. "Your relationship with Ms. Dearborn evolved."

"You could say that," I reply.

He frowns. "Why didn't *you* say that?"

I force a grin, shift in my chair. "I thought your initial question applied to when I was a patient."

Wilbright looks annoyed. "When was the last time you saw Ms. Dearborn?"

I rewind to the last place we were seen together. "About a month ago. At Bishopville Public Library."

"The date?"

"It was a Friday afternoon. Last week of June."

Wilbright wanders over to a calendar pinned to corkboard. "That would be the twenty-fourth. What were you doing at the library?"

"Research for an article."

"You're a writer?"

"Yes sir."

Sturridge titters. "In other words, you're unemployed."

"Underemployed," I clarify. "I also teach history classes and grow organic vegetables. I sell my produce locally."

Sturridge harrumphs.

Wilbright scrawls. "What did you and Ms. Dearborn talk about at the library?"

"The usual. Work, movies, what we're reading."

"Did she mention plans to leave the area?" he asks.

"No, she didn't."

Wilbright hands me his card.

Sturridge scowls. "Stay within shouting distance."

*****

I still see her that night she disappeared. The vibe is weird. She's shut in her bedroom, and I'm in her den watching YouTube videos about fungus-gnat control. An hour passes. I press my ear to the door. Her cadence flows through thin plywood.

"Yes. I see. Yep. I'll have them. OK. I'll be right there."

When she's done, I step into the room. She holds a gun. What appears to be a .38.

"Where'd you get that?" I ask.

"Used to belong to my father. He was a cop."

"How long have you had it?"

"Longer than I've known you."

I sigh. "I didn't mean to pry."

She scowls at me. "Then don't."

But I can't help myself. "What's going on, Astrid?"

"None of your damn business," she snaps. A tear runs down her cheek.

I should back off. Instead, I press on. "You in trouble?"

Her hands shake as she feeds rounds into chambers. She closes the cylinder, inserts the revolver into her handbag.

"Please talk to me," I plead.

"I'm going out," she croaks. "Lock up when you leave."

Her car starts. Wheels crackle on gravel. The engine's purr fades as her taillights disappear into the nighttime fog.

On the bedroom floor, a suitcase filled with her clothes. Beneath the bed, a black canvas bag contains her laptop.

I grab the laptop, suitcase and remaining ammo. She'll want these. I'll have one last chance to reason with her.

But she never came home.

*****

"Any morbid thoughts?"

That's Dr. Morley's usual opener, unless I spill from the get-go. Today, I'm distracted. Edgy. I can't stop thinking about Astrid.

"No," I reply.

"You seem preoccupied," he says, leaning forward, feigning concern like a true professional.

Be honest, my gut tells me. "I'm worried about Nurse Dearborn. She seems to have disappeared."

He leans back. His demeanor sours. "You stayed in touch with her."

I nod, slightly.

His lips tighten. "We certainly miss her here. Any idea where she might be?" he asks, stroking his salt-n-pepper goatee.

"Not a clue."

He raises his chin. "Were you two romantically involved?"

I shake my head.

There's a long pause. Dr. Morley's Freudian pose. He hopes I'll pop off about Astrid. But I've got something else in mind.

"My memory slips in class," I say. "I lose my place in lectures."

His head tilts to one side. "Anxiety?"

"Must be. And the Dean's gonna observe me next week."

He hands me samples. "Take one of these an hour before class. Let me know if they work for you."

Bingo. Xanax.

*****

I rewind, and reconsider — I should've called 911 the next day, when her car was missing from the driveway. When my texts went unanswered and my calls went straight to voice mail.

To unwind, I toke up some Screambud.

I bottom out. Bitter pills deliver. A double-dopamine surge dials back dread. Pleasure fills mental space, flows in waves.

Reality check: I'm sitting on evidence. And it's too late to come clean.

Once again, I rummage through her suitcase. Her clothes exude her sandalwood scent. I sift through sundresses, shorts, sandals, a few blouses, underwear, one pair of white cotton slacks. There's nothing in her pockets or laptop bag. Nothing on her machine except a web browser and the Office suite.

A pile of clothes, a wiped computer.

All that's left of her.

*****

Prowlers.

Marked, unmarked.

Danger. Excessive Heat.

First Priority: Launch "Operation Liquidate."

I unload remaining product, sodium lamps, hydroponics.

Sayonara, Screambud.

Next Objective: Grow more legal stuff.

*****

In the sleepy town of Bubbling Well, Professor Norman Cobb hosts an orchid auction. Plant nerds gather.

Floyd Farnsworth sits in the front row. I stay near the back. I can't handle a head full of Floyd.

Dr. Norm spews auctioneer babble. Bidders offer homes to cattleyas with trumpet-shaped labellums and dendrobiums sporting thick canes.

A lofty brunette brushes by. She's just won a bidding war over a miltoniopsis in full bloom. My eyes settle on her sun-bronzed shoulders, exposed by her backless lavender dip-dye top. The full Carolina sun lends her locks a coppery sheen.

Sauntering back with her plant, striated ridges ripple down her sculpted thighs to slender, tanned feet in Birkenstock sandals. Sunlight glints off the wisteria lacquer adorning her nails. She points at the folding chair beside me.

"Is that seat taken?" she asks.

The pungent, earthy scent of patchouli envelops me.

"No ma'am. It's all yours."

She slides onto the chair. A flower grazes my cheek. Sketched on its lavish burgundy petals are brilliant white circles and squiggly lines radiating from bright-orange amoebic-shaped blotches.

Her eyes glisten. My chest tightens. Fragrant petals envelop my nose.

"Take it all in," she croons. Her sharp, oblique features resemble Astrid's.

That flower's rosy scent, her welcoming eyes, and the exquisite contours of her face course through my brain's circuitry.

Norm's patter reverberates, captivates. Other orchid genera appear on the block — vandas, ascocendas, renantheras. Bidders babble.

She scrunches up her face at a brown pseudobulb among an array of healthy ones. A single blemish on an otherwise perfect plant. I sterilize my multi-tool with my lighter. My hand shakes as I hand it to her. She severs the bulb and notices my name engraved on the blade.

"Nolan. That's nice," she says. "I'm Iris."

Her manicured thumb presses into the parched sphagnum moss anchoring her plant. "I'd better get this lady home. What are your plans, Nolan?"

My thoughts derail. Her question lingers, unanswered.

She leans closer. "I'll repeat the question," she whispers, her face so close I can taste her warm, minty breath. "What are your plans, Nolan?"

"You see that?" I ask, pointing at a tall, gangly plant with a couple dozen alternating leaves running up the stem. "I'm taking that *renanthera imshootiana* home."

Her fingernails graze my arm. Her hand settles on mine. A wedding band encircles her ring finger.

Biochemistry ignores social mores.

"I've got a full wine cellar," she explains. "And I'm less than a mile away. Your orchid might be comfortable in my sunroom."

I sputter nonsense.

We exchange business cards.

Hers reads: *Iris Mendelssohn*, Landscape Design. There's a phone number.

When I look back at her, she's nearly ten feet away, moving briskly toward a white Mini Cooper in the parking area. Like Astrid, she struts — a limber, sensual swagger conveying confidence and spontaneity. A curtain of indigo hair obscures her face, and I'm no longer certain it's Iris. The sudden change in hair color — from brunette to black — befuddles me. Must be the natural light, up to its usual mischief, transforming everything it touches.

Sunrays pierce the clouds, illuminating her wavering tresses — now, brunette again — as she tucks herself into the driver's seat.

Natural light, delusion — uncanniness explained.

*****

Footsteps crunch the gravel behind me.

"You avoiding me, Nolan?" a raspy voice inquires.

It's Floyd. He wears an irate expression. An SLR camera hangs from a strap around his neck. He carries a black canvas backpack. He ignores my outstretched hand.

"I know you saw me back there," he insists, eyes narrowing. "Bet you figgered I'd blow your chances with that chick."

"She's not a 'chick,' Floyd. She's a woman. And a lot prettier than you."

He ponders my point.

"OK," he mumbles, grim-faced, agitated. He tugs the brim of his cap emblazoned with the Shaw's Nursery logo. Stringy, straw-colored hair frames his worn demeanor.

"What you doin' here?" I ask him.

He grins. "Mr. Shaw gave me the day off."

Mr. Shaw also punched the crazy bastard's ticket to the bughouse. Earlier, that same day he landed in the hospital, Floyd led kindergarteners and senior citizens on a silent tour of the nursery. His guests took a pointless, meandering stroll through acres of plants and learned nothing about them.

"I didn't know you fancied orchids, Floyd."

"I don't," he replies. "I was hopin' to meet a woman here."

"How'd that go?"

"Not good, seein' that I'm talkin' to you. But I took pictures of the flowers before everyone arrived. Mr. Shaw needs pics for his website. I'm gonna throw my hat in the ring."

I gesture toward his camera. "Let me see your pics."

He grimaces. "I wanna go through 'em first," he mumbles, scratching an X in the gravel with the toe of his boot. "I could use a drink."

I hoist my lanky renanthera. "Gotta get this girl home, Floyd."

His eyes widen. "You mean *woman*, Nolan. You keep belittling her like that, she'll never bloom for you."

*****

I surf. I visit Facebook, LinkedIn, Pinterest, then cross-check her name with orchid message boards.

Iris Mendelssohn is off-the-grid.

Her name appears in a wispy, lavender font on white fragrance blotter. A familiar scent tickles my nose, mostly patchouli with hints of sandalwood. Almost Astrid. Close enough to send me back to the Chestnut Grove dayroom for movie night, featuring Spike Lee's *Malcolm X*.

On the screen, Malcolm addresses a crowd in Harlem. Patients stand and raise clenched fists. Gus, my roommate, spews rapid-fire Spanglish to applause. Others join the cacophony — a fusion of multilingual banter resembling a chorusing brood of cicadas.

Orderlies rush in and subdue rowdy bugs with Haldol. Amid the chaos, a folded paper square lands in my lap.

It reads, "Hall Bath. Now."

I scurry down the empty hall and slip into the dark, single-occupant restroom. I welcome the warm pressure of Astrid's silky hands cradling my face as her mouth closes over mine.

Iris's card flutters from my hands and lands at the center of my keyboard. Block-print letters on the keys surround the elegant script that spells out her name.

*****

I pop Zannies.

I review lecture notes.

The class: World Civilizations II.

Subtitle: The World Since 1650.

Translation: Life After Descartes Shit the Bed.

First day, summer term. The course is overenrolled, so the Dean moved it to an auditorium that seats close to a thousand. There's still lots of empty space, students scattered everywhere.

From the dais, I sift through my syllabus projected onto a large screen. My roster mostly consists of early-college students. High-school age. It'll be difficult to wander the vast auditorium to ensure they're not imbibing internet waste.

I do OK. The Zannies boost my confidence. But as I'm wrapping up, my peripheral vision catches the sharp contours of an angular face, framed by wavy chestnut locks. She sits in the very back, far-right corner. Her penetrating stare pokes and prods, searching for a way into my head.

"Excuse me, ma'am," I say, brushing past a line of students with questions for me.

She doesn't respond.

Afternoon sun pours through skylights, enveloping her features in a blinding glow. Light flickers, strobe-like, as a series of ghastly expressions bear the reversed black-and-white tonalities of a photographic negative.

"Professor Brundage?"

I turn to meet the gaze of the male student at the front of the line. He's in his early twenties, wearing a torn Ramones t-shirt.

"Sorry," I say. "I got stuck in the Age of Reason. Thanks for bringing me home."

That earns a laugh.

I glance back in the woman's direction.

Her seat is empty.

*****

Floyd chugs beer.

On the bar between us is a seedling tray. In each cell, a reddish-purple stem hoists two oval leaves.

"Doesn't look like spinach," I say.

"That's because it ain't a true spinach. But Mr. Shaw says the mature leaves make a nice salad. He says they have an earthy taste. Like mushrooms."

A wiry dude with spiked hair sets a rocks glass in front of me. He fills it to the brim with single-barrel rye. "Compliments of the lovely lady," he says, with a nod toward the other end of the bar.

All I see is an unoccupied stool. And a few bills beneath an empty wine glass.

The screened entry door slams shut. Through the wire mesh, a copper-colored French braid bounces between naked shoulder blades.

David Allan Coe roars about riding shotgun with the ghost of Hank Williams.

Floyd gestures at the tray. "Mr. Shaw says these Malabar spinach plants can grow up to eight feet tall."

"You're kidding."

"Am not," he snaps. "You want 'em?"

"I'll take a couple."

"Thirty bucks for all of them," he says with a wink.

"For thirty bucks, those beanstalks better climb their way into heaven. And take me with 'em, too."

Smoky rye burns my throat. He slides a hand mirror across the bar. "Look what's beneath the tray."

In the refection — pills, wrapped in cellophane, taped to the bottom of each seedling cell.

"They're tens," he says. "You're gettin' 'em half price. The spinach is free."

"Where'd you get the Percs?"

"Wrong question," he drawls.

He downs the rest of his beer and smiles, exposing crooked teeth.

"But there's more where them came from, Nolan."

*****

I brood.

Writer's block. And I've got three days to deliver three thousand words on venomous snakes in the Carolinas. My screen stays blank until lunchtime when I finally head to the Piedmont Tavern.

Outdoors, I enjoy a cold brew and summer breeze. My memory sifts through impromptu encounters with coastal-plain pit vipers. I often met them on hunting trips with Grandpa. Inspired, I crank out a thousand words.

Something metallic clinks on the patio. It's a set of keys lying next to sun-bronzed feet with lavender nails. In Birkenstock sandals.

I glance up at my reflection in the lenses of cat-eye designer sunglasses. Lavender lip liner accentuates a radiant smile.

"Iris," I whisper.

Sunshine glints off her silver belt buckle. The natural light gives her lengthy locks a purplish tint.

"I've missed you, Nolan." Her shades slide down her nose. Red-rimmed eyelids surround glimmering hazel pools. She adjusts her glasses, picks up her keys. A tan line encircles her ring finger.

My heart jackhammers. My guts twist, and my surroundings spin, sucking me into the vortex of a mental storm.

Thoughts tumble, breaths shorten. Pheromones collide. Hers and mine.

"You feel it, too," she murmurs, touching my cheek. The moist pressure of her hand flips a switch, stops the swirl.

"I could give you so much, Nolan," she purrs.

*****

I wait.

A week passes. She doesn't call.

I Google supermarkets in Bubbling Well, and then visit the town, pushing grocery carts through the aisles of every store, hoping I'll run into her.

But I don't.

I consider contacting Dr. Norm. Maybe he'll give me her address, and I'll surprise her with an orchid?

She's married.

So I down a double rye.

Halfway through my second drink, she calls.

*****

Her stone ranch home has a slate-tile roof. Ancient live oaks shade most of the front yard, but the southeast corner gets plenty of light. Ideal for a sunroom.

An engine roars. It's a generator, beneath a canopy, with a heavy-gauge cord that enters the house through an open window.

I stroll past her white Mini. The front tire is flat.

She poses in the doorframe, wineglass in hand, her eyes glistening through a tapestry of tight curls dangling just above her shoulders. A bare foot rests on a tire, which she nudges forward.

"Could you give this lady a hand?" she inquires as the tire bounces down the steps. "I'm not sure where I packed my jack and lug wrench."

I consider calling the auto club. But I've gotta show my chops.

I grab my jack, tire iron and a can of spray lubricant from my trunk. I change the tire.

In her living room, on a glass coffee table, flickering candelabra cast dancing shadows on the walls. Aside from a distressed leather couch, the other furniture is covered with dusty bed sheets.

"I hope you don't mind the candles," she says. "The electrical wiring in this house was ravaged by squirrels. I'm having it all redone."

She removes a bottle from a cooler and fills wineglasses. "Cold rosé. My go-to summer drink."

Glasses clink. The wine is fruity with a subtle, bitter finish. Across from us, a portable air conditioner, powered by the generator, struggles against summer heat. Beside the front door, oak shelves protrude from the stone wall. Polished agate bookends contain an array of Gothic classics by Elizabeth Gaskell, Shirley Jackson and others.

On the couch, a single cushion separates us. A rotten odor wafts by.

Her nose crinkles. "There's no tellin' how many rodent carcasses reside in these walls."

I gesture at the covered furniture. "You just move in?"

"Yes," she murmurs, glancing down at her hand, ring-less, no tan line, with lacquer-free nails.

I swallow hard. "I had hoped to see your sunroom."

She pats my cheek. "In due time."

We polish off the bottle.

Anticipation resonates. Bare toes touch my thigh. She wears an inquisitive expression as she lifts my chin and traces my lips with her thumb. She kisses my throat. Her subtle, earthy scent morphs into muskier notes.

"Follow me," she says, rising from the couch.

She saunters toward a stone arch in the southeast corner where the hardwood floor meets flagstone. As I amble over, objects in the room shift in and out of focus. She disappears into what appears to be a hallway, and I follow her into darkness. The sudden dampness of soaked air seems similar to being submerged in an inkwell. Fumbling for a light switch, I touch slick, algae-covered stone. Using the wall as a guide, I press on.

"Iris?"

There's a slight echo. Warm breath tickles my neck.

"Right here," she whispers from behind. Her icy fingers thread with mine, and she drags me further into frigid blackness. Rounding a corner, light bleeds through the translucence of a glass door. She releases my hand and enters the sunroom wearing nothing but a towel.

Thick, humid air engulfs us. Moonlight pours through the ceiling and three glass-paned sides. A stone wall to my left completes the enclosure. Against the wall stands a mesh table, populated by an assortment of plants, including her miltoniopsis. Straight ahead, a seven-foot rectangular flowerbed rests on concrete pillars. The raised bed contains no plants, just topsoil. A hint of that putrid smell floats by, then disappears, followed by a spicy, floral aroma. Iris drops her towel, snatches off my shirt. I slip off shoes and baggy cargo shorts.

She shoves me backward, bare-bottomed, into the dirt. Astride my hips, her weight shifts forward, sinking my elbows into the soil. I close my eyes. Maroon spider webs crisscross my lids. She nibbles my ear, and there's slight sting, like a paper cut, on my cheek just above the jawline. Colorful kaleidoscopic patterns fill my vision, and for a moment, I'm weightless, as if I'm hovering over a meadow. An electrical current buzzes through my nerves and veins, as moving images sift through my brain — me, lying in a trench amid gunfire as a luminous iridescent haze appears over the horizon. Like a floating cloud, the greenish fog approaches, enveloping me. I choke on fumes and taste death, but cannot will myself awake.

Absent from her grip, entombed in a reeking oblong box, there's the thump-thump of a hammer, sealing its lid, and I enter a yawning black hole.

*****

Bright sunlight sears my shut eyelids.

Cocooned in damp loam and a cadaverine stench, I extract myself from the coffin and open a window.

Skeletal remains of plants clutter the table. Withered leaves and petals litter the flagstone floor.

A gentle breeze carries the aromatic sweetness of gardenia blossoms and breathes life into dead stillness. Body parts of plant corpses swirl in a grotesque death dance among my scattered shoes and clothes.

I brush dried dirt from my backside and slip on pants. My fingertips are rusty brown. In my pockets: my phone, my lighter, wallet, and keys. But my multi-tool is missing.

I backtrack through the hallway. An infusion of dry air has left the rockwork merely damp, and inching along, my hand against the stone, I turn the corner and enter the living room guided by sunlight.

My body quivers.

The candelabra have disappeared. Dusty sheets cover the couch and coffee table, and the bookshelves are empty. The generator, air conditioner and cooler are also gone.

In the adjacent kitchen, I pass a wrought-iron prep table with a butcher-block top and catch a whiff of carrion. Opening a window doesn't help because the odor seems to be leaking through a wooden floor hatch. The trap door is unlocked, and once I open it, a hellish stench erupts from the bowels of the house.

The waning glow of a key-chain flashlight accompanies me down creaking stairs into a dank basement. To my right, a moldy wooden bookcase contains an assortment of nonperishable items — canned soups, bottled water, tins of tuna, and sardines — along with a wind-up alarm clock and a half-empty bottle of bourbon.

I follow the flashlight's dim beam along the wall till it reaches a joint-compound bucket. On it, there's a candle and a lighter. I ignite the candle. Its flame flicks shadows on a sofa bed, unfolded, where something lies beneath a crimson bedspread. I snatch off the covers.

It's Floyd Farnsworth, naked, with a crushed skull. His right hand is missing. And there's a tourniquet twisted around the wrist of that arm.

Piled up, at the foot of the bed, are his clothes. I rifle through his pockets. His wallet contains the usual items: driver's license, credit cards and some cash. But tucked inside a sleeve is a folded square of pink paper with a header that reads: Doyle T. Morley, M.D.

It's a blank sheet from Dr. Morley's prescription pad. But Floyd couldn't have gotten this from Dr. Morley.

I hear Astrid's voice though the hollow core of her bedroom door:
"I'll have them. OK. I'll be right there."

I see Floyd's crooked smile, accompanied by his granular drawl:
"There's more where them came from, Nolan."

Did he see Astrid slip me Percs in the dayroom? That would be enough leverage to convince her to swipe scrip pads. A simple ward-stock audit would cost Astrid her job.

Floyd got what he wanted.

And made Astrid disappear.

*****

"There's no record of anyone with that phone number," Wilbright says, sliding Iris's scented business card across the table. "And there are no landscape designers in the Carolinas who fit that description you gave us. What's with the canned food in the basement? Were you squatting there, Mr. Brundage? Or maybe Mr. Farnsworth was?"

Exhausted, depleted, I gaze wearily into his eyes. "I wasn't squatting there. I can't speak for Floyd."

Wilbright's eyelids flicker. "You knew him."

"We were acquaintances."

Sturridge leans forward on the table. "That house is owned by the bank. It's a foreclosure. Hasn't been occupied since the housing bubble burst in '08."

I sigh. "I suppose that explains the generator."

His face reddens. "What it doesn't explain is the corpse in the basement. Or Mr. Farnsworth's severed hand, buried in a raised bed that contains traces of your blood. By the way, where did you get that scratch on your cheek? From a struggle with Mr. Farnsworth? Things don't look good for you, Brundage."

Wilbright clears his throat. "Let's get to the point," he says. "Is this yours, Mr. Brundage?"

He pushes a clear plastic pouch across the table. On it is stamped "EVIDENCE." The bag contains a multi-tool, blade extended, displaying my name.

"Could be," I say, trying my damnedest to remain cool. "Where'd you find it?"

Wilbright smiles. "Where'd you lose it?"

He slides a larger evidence pouch across the table. "Maybe this'll refresh your memory."

The L-shaped tire tool shines, except for socket end, stained rusty brown. Not mine. Floyd's body had been in the basement at least a couple days before I arrived at the house. Before I had used my tool to change Iris's tire.

Wilbright wears a grim expression. "That lug wrench caved in a man's head. The socket end is awash in Mr. Farnsworth's blood. The prying end is covered with your prints. It was found in your car."

My mouth is bone dry. "I need to speak to a lawyer."

Wilbright gestures toward a push-button phone. "You can tell your attorney that you're under arrest for the murders of Floyd Farnsworth and Astrid Dearborn."

"Astrid Dearborn?"

Wilbright shakes his head. "You're not denying you killed Mr. Farnsworth."

Sturridge snickers.

Wilbright smirks. "We found Ms. Dearborn's suitcase, clothes and laptop when we searched your home, Mr. Brundage."

Sturridge grins. "Things just got worse for you, asshole."

*****

They had bluffed about Astrid. But Floyd's murder got pinned on me.

My attorney went all-in on a nut-job defense after I got charged. During my trial, a parade of medical experts testified, including Dr. Morley. Prior prescriptions for atypical antipsychotic drugs bolstered my case and convinced the jury that I was not guilty by reason of insanity.

My lawyer insists he did me a favor. "Parasites inhabit real prisons," he told me. "You couldn't do the time, Nolan. You'd get passed around the joint, wearing Kool-Aid for lipstick."

But Duck Creek Forensic Psychiatric Center isn't a resort. Most everyone in here is a serial killer, serial rapist or both. And I'm one of the few patients who refuses to surrender his commissary purchases to Wombat Reynolds. I broke a chair over his head for that privilege. Wombat isn't crazy. He gamed the system to get in here. And I got conned by a ghost.

Iris Mendelssohn hung a perfect frame on me. And she doesn't even exist.

My attorney speculates that a number for a pre-paid phone was listed on her business card. After she called me, she must've destroyed that phone. The following morning, she probably used another burner to dial 911 and report a disturbance at the house. Her timing was perfect. I ran right into the cops when I opened the front door.

Next to my bed, on a nightstand, is a wooden picture frame with its glass removed. To most, the frame is empty. But my gears turn when I stare at the mounting board and see two young women, mid-twenties, with striking features and long, wavy hair — one brunette, obviously Iris, and another whose darker tresses awaken a painful familiarity.

Astrid never mentioned having a sister. And her spartan living accommodations, bereft of personal memorabilia, provided no insight into her past.

I focus on their faces. Eyes glimmer like snifters of cognac, illuminated by candles. Those alluring gazes hover over high cheekbones separated by elegant, sloping noses. Full lips surround perfect teeth. Unable to sustain the image any longer, I return the frame to my bedside and fixate on the hairline fissures in the plaster ceiling.

I struggle to explain why I'm here. But one thing, in particular, haunts me — Floyd's blood on my tire tool. Because I'm acquainted with only one person adept at drawing blood and preserving a sample. A blood sample that could later be used to douse my tire tool.

Nurse Dearborn.

Snare of the Fowler
Stephen D. Rogers

"Are you picking up what I'm putting down?" Sometimes it wasn't enough to be clear. Sometimes you had to make sure, just to be sure.

"I heard you, Boss."

"I didn't ask if you heard me. Is that what you think I asked? Is that what you heard?"

"No." Dixon broke eye contact.

"Are you sure?" When someone like Dixon showed weakness, it was time to probe, time to discover how deep the rot went. "Prove to me you were listening. What did I ask?"

"If I picked up what you were putting down."

"Exactly. I asked that particular question because that's what I want you to do. I want you to pick it up. I want you to feel the weight. I want you to put it in your pocket and never forget it's there until you finish the job."

"You want me to find the girl."

"She's a woman and she's dangerous." Flaherty pointed at Dixon. "Remember that."

"I will."

Flaherty snorted. "You will. Future tense, as though you're not thinking that now."

"I misspoke, Boss. I know she's trouble. That's why I'm here."

"Find her." Flaherty took a long, deep breath. "Find her and put her down."

*****

The Drunken Sailor was a twelve-unit motel on Route 28, the seventh place she'd tried and the first that accepted cash. Probably too much to hope they'd spend it fixing the sink.

Kylee padded naked out of the bathroom, her skin still damp from the shower, her hair newly brown.

In the movies, characters on the run either hid behind sunglasses or completely transformed their appearances as though the process wouldn't require a team of experts. Kylee didn't have access to a makeup department, and she wasn't stupid.

She sat at the table and didn't grab her purse. Decision time.

A drop of water landed on her thigh, and after staring at it for a second she squashed the bead flat with her thumb. Continued pressing until her flesh turned white.

Flaherty was going to kill her.

That's just the way he thought.

Kylee reached into her purse.

Pulled out the phone she bought when she stopped for hair color, hiding hers in the trashcan outside the convenience store amid empty coffee cups and losing lottery tickets.

Once she made the call, there would be no turning back.

She'd run. Already there was no turning back.

Kylee pressed the numbers.

✴✴✴✴✴

Ryan left the newsroom, nodding at the people he passed, not slowing his stride and inviting conversation. Get this over with as soon as possible.

Gambling wasn't a problem until you made a bet you couldn't cover, until you made a bet you couldn't cover and then lost. That's when you had a problem. That's when you needed a friend.

Sometimes that friend needed a favor.

Just information. That's all Ryan ever gave him. Nothing secret, nothing confidential, nothing that would harm the paper. A heads up, a preview, a peek. Nothing that wouldn't became common knowledge as soon as the story appeared.

No harm done.

In fact, what he did might even sell an extra few copies, generate a few extra page views, and his bosses certainly couldn't complain about that. Everybody wins.

Outside, Ryan walked across the street and kept his back to the building.

The few old-timers still remaining probably read lips.

Ryan scrolled through his contacts and pressed the only person identified by a single initial.

The phone rang once before someone answered, "Yeah?"

"This is Ryan, from the Boston paper. I need to talk to Flaherty. I've got something he's going to want to hear."

*****

Dixon frowned as he crossed the Bourne bridge. Being told she was on the Cape saved him some time, but being told the motel room number? Made the job too easy.

What happened when Flaherty decided anybody could do what Dixon did? What happened when an up-and-comer took Flaherty's place, when a new boss with a fresh perspective started crowdsourcing jobs in order to cut payroll?

The internet changed everything.

Dixon swung past the state police barracks and continued down Route 28.

Flaherty didn't need Dixon's tracking ability if anybody with access to cell tower logs could reveal someone's location within a foot. Flaherty didn't need Dixon's loyalty when anybody hired anonymously online didn't know enough to cut a deal.

If Dixon stopped providing value, he'd be retired, retired in a way that would ensure he would never spill the information he'd gathered over the years.

Dixon swung around the next rotary past signs for the National Cemetery.

With the internet, "Find this woman" became "Go to this address and kill her."

Flaherty didn't need Dixon. He needed a VPN that masked his location and cryptocurrency that masked his identity.

Any moron found online could follow GPS directions.

Dixon sighed.

*****

Kylee ripped open the package of panties: pink, purple, and gray. Selected the third and pulled it up her legs. Strange to put on something she'd never washed, but before she reached the strip of motels, she'd stopped for a complete change of clothes.

Not a disguise. Dressing differently wouldn't fool anybody, and she needed something more than a cheap disguise. Warriors prepared for battle.

While she had never thought of herself in those terms, Flaherty would see to it that she did, just before he made it plain she'd lost.

Kylee settled the new bra over her breasts and fitted the clips with her other hand.

Flaherty took everything personally. Viewed everyone as an opponent. Saw every move as a threat.

Kylee had left. Ergo, she had or would betray him.

His response would be automatic. Find her. Silence her. Contain the damage.

Kylee had no choice but to prepare for his arrival.

She bit through strands of thin plastic to remove price tags from the blouse and jeans.

Three pairs of panties because that's how they were sold. Other than that, a single change of clothes.

Even then, she didn't think she'd be lucky enough to see holes develop in the panties, colors to fade from the blouse, scuff marks to appear on the sneakers. Entropy took time that she didn't have.

Kylee slid on the blouse. Pulled on the jeans and tucked in the ends. Bent. Stretched.

Stuffing the tags and packaging into the room's plastic basket, she buried the outfit she'd worn when she arrived at the motel, the outfit she'd worn when she'd run from everything she'd ever known.

She stayed leaned over the basket for a long minute, staring at the debris that circumscribed her last day, struggling not to puke out her guts.

*****

Ryan strode into the newsroom only to be accosted by his editor.

She crouched to look up into his face. "Where were you?"

"Following a lead." She raised an eyebrow, and he retreated from the implication. "I thought I had something, but it didn't pan out. You know how it goes."

"We're short today. That's how it goes."

"A mixed blessing."

She placed her fists on her hips and huffed. "Make some calls. Nudge the recalcitrant. I need inches. Feet if possible."

"Will do."

"I'm serious. No drama too small. Individualize the details and make it large."

The worst kind of news. The kind of news that didn't give you a buzz, the kind of news that wasn't news. Chasing a word count instead of a story.

She touched his arm. "Get out there, Ryan. Make it happen."

"You got it, Chief." And off she went.

Time was, he loved this business. Loved sifting through the lies, searching for the nugget. Every new day concealed a different set of stories, stories that he blasted out of rock.

Once upon a time, anyway, until he realized there was no longer anything "new" about the news. Instead, he just kept uncovering the same ugly truths, the same tawdry secrets committed by people who didn't understand they themselves were only pale copies.

The highs got lower and lower until a new high took their place.

The fall of a card, the roll of a die, the twist of a wheel.

Human history repeated itself. Every administration. Every organization. Every relationship. The same exact mistakes and foibles, repeated with numbing clockwork.

Unlike the only place where the odds were known but the results unknowable. Until he himself made it happen.

Ryan glanced at his phone.

He could be at the casino in forty-five minutes.

*****

Recalling the symbols displayed on the diamond-shaped yellow sign just passed, Dixon wondered who decided which lane closed — the left or the right — when two lanes merged into one.

Who had the power to declare which path came to an end?

Along this stretch anyway, the choice seemed arbitrary. To his left, forest along the median strip kept northbound separate. To his right, nothing but a ditch and cut-back trees.

Close the left lane? Close the right lane? The verdict affected no one except the lone traveler.

Dixon snorted. People made big bucks signing off on that kind of order.

Which lane? How many of each sign were sitting in storage?

He flexed the fingers of the hand on the wheel.

Meanwhile: the body. Hide it, stage it, or fake it to appear an accident? Was the killing a message, and if so, how was that message best delivered?

And then the median strip separating northbound and southbound traffic disappeared, and Route 28 became a single road snaking through the wilderness.

From four to two to one.

Dixon had to guess what Flaherty wanted. Had to deduce what kind of killing would produce that result. Dixon's judgement. Dixon's call. His fault if anything went wrong.

Dixon's experience. A point to remember, a point in his favor.

The road that curved through woods straightened as it entered a residential section, houses that could have been built by the Pilgrims, carving out enough land to farm as if the soil wasn't rocky and watered by salt.

Then residential became a bit more commercial. A gas station. A lawyer's office. Signs for the hospital, always good to know, just in case.

An intersection.

Dixon tapped his brakes. Stopped the car as the light changed to red. Listened to the engine yearn.

*****

Kylee checked herself in the hotel's mirror, verifying that that her new clothes met the standards of propriety, confirming that nothing that should be covered was exposed.

Only then did she call her father.

"Daddy?"

The line hummed. After a moment, her father interrupted, "I didn't expect to hear from you again."

Kylee turned from the mirror. "I was thinking about you earlier."

"I wasn't aware you did that: think."

Kylee closed her eyes, squeezed them tight until she saw stars. "Remember that revival we went to on the Cape? I must have been seven, maybe eight. The time a herd of deer—"

"What do you want?"

"Just to say hello."

"Then say it and go. I have messages to write."

Kylee scratched the inside of her right arm to distract the twitch.

This had been a mistake, but then it would have been a worse mistake not to try. If things went badly today, she didn't want to die knowing their relationship had ended in silence.

"The thing I remember most about the deer was the way they looked back and forth between us, waiting to see which of us would feed them first. I almost cried because I didn't have any popcorn left. You told me not to be a glutton."

"They wanted to determine who offered the bigger threat so they knew which way to run. 'Deliver thyself as a roe from the hand of the hunter.' Proverbs 6:5. You'd know that if you read your Bible."

"I really think they were just hungry. They probably smelled—"

"Genesis. 'And have dominion over the fish of the sea, and over the fowl of the air, and over every living creature that moveth upon the earth.'"

And was this conversation so very different than silence? "I didn't call to argue with you, Daddy."

"'Therefor I will not refrain my mouth; I will speak in the anguish of my spirit; I will complain in the bitterness of my soul.' Job 7:11. I am not arguing. I am stating fact."

"Daddy, did you learn nothing from what happened?"

The line hummed.

"I loved your mother."

Kylee reached up and pinched her lower lip. Reached higher to tug her ear. "Proverbs."

"Do you really have the temerity to quote the Bible?"

"Proverbs. 'The tender mercies of the wicked are cruel.'"

Kylee moved the phone from her face and hit "End."

*****

At the exact moment Dixon saw the sign for The Drunken Sailor along with the additional advertisement: "Vacancies," his phone rang.

He glanced at the screen to check for an update.

His daughter.

Dixon pulled into the next entrance and parked. Not live parked, parked, and cracked the window before answering.

"Hey, Cupcake."

"Dad, I really need your advice. I'd ask Mom but you know she never liked Megan and so whatever Mom says, it's not what she thinks I should do for me, it's what she wants me to do for her."

"Did something happen with Megan?"

"I don't know Dad. That's part of the problem."

"I'm listening."

"There's this boy. Ingrid told me he's sort of interested, and because Megan is my best friend, he asked her if I was with anyone. She told him 'yes,' even though I'm not."

"Are you sort of interested in him?" Ingrid. Dixon couldn't remember meeting a friend with that name.

"I don't know, Dad. I barely know him. But I might have had a chance to know him a little better if it weren't for Megan. Why would she do that?"

"Did you ask her?"

"I can't accuse my friend of sabotaging my future."

"While I can't speak for Megan, if she did want to keep the two of you apart, there might have been a reason."

"Like she doesn't want to share me."

"Or maybe she knows something negative about this boy. Maybe Megan is afraid there's a good chance he'll betray you. She might have been looking out for your best interests."

"Hmph."

"Cupcake, it seems to me that you're talking to the wrong person."

"Ingrid wouldn't lie."

"I meant me; I'm the wrong person. The only way you're going to learn why Megan did what she did — assuming she actually did do what Ingrid said — is to talk to Megan."

"And say what?"

"'Hello. Can you believe what happened in French?'"

"She's not even in my French class."

"Whatever. You're best friends. If she believes you're in danger, she's going to say something about the guy."

"Maybe."

"If you talk for a while, and she doesn't mention him, you could always say that Ingrid heard something strange."

"Megan hates Ingrid. It goes back to a second-grade birthday party."

"Then maybe what Ingrid said didn't happen. You can ask Megan, or you could ask the boy."

"Dad!"

*****

Kylee froze as the knock echoed.

She couldn't breathe, and if she couldn't draw a breath, she couldn't cross the room, couldn't open the door, couldn't discover who waited on the other side.

She hadn't heard anything until now. How could anything have happened?

Maybe it was room service. She barked a laugh, and that broke the tension enough that she could inhale. Exhale. Inhale. Pad towards the door.

She looked down at her bare feet. Had she never put on the new sneakers, or had she pulled them off after the call to her father?

Kylee leaned against the door. Laid her ear against the smooth surface. "Hello?"

Waited for the bullets to punch through the door and into her, tearing as they tumbled.

"Special Agent Williams."

Kylee removed the chain with shaking fingers, twisted the lock first the wrong way and then — after the door wouldn't open — correctly.

Backed into the room with her arms wide, her palms open, still ready to get what she deserved.

Special Agent Williams entered and closed the door. "We got him."

"Flaherty."

"Well, not yet. Guy named Dixon. You know him?"

"I should have realized Flaherty wouldn't fall for the bait. I thought his ego would be so bruised—" Kylee sniffed. "I should have known I didn't mean that much to him."

Her legs no longer able to support the weight, Kylee dropped onto the bed.

"He cared enough to send his best." Williams licked his lips. Thumbed towards the bathroom. "Do you mind if I get some water?"

"There are some plastic cups next to the television." Plastic shaped like cut crystal, ready to celebrate.

Kylee leaned forward to brace her elbows on her new jeans and lowered her face into her hands.

She expected to die here today. She thought it when she arrived. She thought it when she called the FBI. She thought it when she heard the knock at the door.

Flaherty killed people. Flaherty had people killed.

She should be dead.

Williams returned, took a final gulp, and placed the empty cup on the dresser, the thin plastic rattling until it landed flat.

Kylee looked up. "I should be dead."

"No, I would have too much to explain." Williams smiled. "I know I told you — earlier in the room and before that on the phone — that we would protect you and stop Flaherty." He cleared his throat.

Kylee rocked back. "Yes?"

"While I knew we could protect you, I didn't really expect he himself would appear today. Men like him don't. That said, we knew someone who would pass along a tip, and we can use him — and Dixon — to get to Flaherty. In the meantime, you're going to disappear."

A trap that sprang in slow motion.

And while the jaws took their sweet time, she moved from motel room — waiting for the knock on the door — to motel room, stuck in a snare of her own devising.

It's Nothing Personal

Wendy Harrison

The last time someone tried to kill me, it was hotter than hell in an Afghani desert and they used an IED to do it, so it was nothing personal. This time, though, it was different.

I showed up for work early and touched the sign over the door for good luck, the way I did every day. "DeLuca's Gym." That's me. Dani DeLuca. When I left the Army, I used all my savings to open this place, a safe haven for the girls and women in my old neighborhood. It had been a struggle to turn my dream into reality, but I loved every minute of it.

I headed for the free weights to get in a workout before anyone else showed up. I froze when I heard a sound coming from my office. No one should have been there. No one else had a key.

Slipping past the weight rack, I picked up a dumbbell bar. Even without weights on it, it could do damage. I hoped I wasn't bringing a dumbbell to a gun fight. With any luck, it was just a neighborhood kid looking for something to sell for drugs. It wouldn't be the first time. I pictured the Beretta M9 I had brought home from my last tour. I was sure it was locked in the small safe behind my desk. Not helpful, but at least it wasn't going to be used against me.

When I reached the open door of my office, I sneaked a peek around it. A man dressed in camo had his back to me as he tore open my desk drawers.

"Looking for something?"

He jumped and spun to face me. He wore gloves and a ski mask.

"Really? A ski mask in Florida?"

"Where is it?"

I sidestepped as he ran at me. "Where's what?" It was an honest question. I had no idea what he was after.

I knocked the bar against my side to make sure my grip was secure. I was ready when he rushed me again, hands raised to grab me. I yanked the bar upward. He gasped when it connected with his chin. I took advantage of his distraction to use a side kick to knock his feet out from under him.

As he hit the floor, I straddled the intruder and reached for the ski mask. It looked as if all the years of weight training and boxing that I continued even in the hot deserts of Afghanistan had paid off. But it didn't stay that way. His hand connected with my left arm, and he twisted it until I thought my elbow would snap. I raised the bar in my right hand but before I could use it to adjust his dental work, he shoved me off him and scrambled out the office door. I debated chasing him. Giving up wasn't in my nature, but my elbow was screaming for attention so I let him go.

I took an ice pack out of the freezer in the little kitchen next to my office and wrapped it around my aching elbow. At least it was my left arm. I could still function with my right. I hit speed dial on my cellphone.

"Detective Hendershot."

"Hey, Linda. It's me." That was enough of an introduction, even if caller ID hadn't given it away. Linda was my best friend since we were kids. Getting each other into trouble was our idea of fun growing up. "We had a break-in."

"Oh no, Dani. Are you okay?"

I described what happened. "Nothing's broken. I'm just confused." I told Linda what the masked man had said. "I have no idea what he could've been after, but I'm hoping he won't be back. I'm sure it wasn't as easy as he thought it would be."

Linda laughed. "I'm sure not." She said she'd come by to take a report but unless there was a way to ID him, I knew it was going to turn into just another unsolved burglary in the neighborhood.

It turned out that I was lucky. My elbow was just bruised, and I was able to hide the injury from the girls that came to the gym. My first priority was that they felt safe under my roof.

A week later, I was surfing the local news online as I cooled down from a workout. I always looked for any news that might affect the gym, but I wasn't prepared for this particular headline. "Luther Wallace joins governor's race."

I stared at the photo that ran with the article. Lieutenant Luther Wallace, with his sleek, blond wife next to him, their arms raised in a hoped-for victory sign. LT. My CO in Afghanistan. The man who saved my life the last time someone tried to kill me. It was a day I had been trying to forget for years.

LT was in the lead truck in the convoy that day, on a broiling August morning. I was behind him in an up-armored Humvee. The sudden explosion from an IED knocked me out for a few seconds. I was trapped in the burning vehicle and bleeding everywhere from the shrapnel that had torn into me. Suddenly, LT was pulling me out through a window, like toothpaste squeezing through a tube. He dragged me to cover, somehow returning fire the whole time. I was the sole survivor from the Humvee that day, and LT was my hero…until he wasn't.

The phone rang and brought me back to the present. "DeLuca's Gym." Silence. "Hello? Can I help you?" I was about to hang up.

"Sarge?"

I knew that voice, no matter how much time had passed. "LT?"

"It's been a while. Sorry I haven't stayed in touch. But I've been hearing good things about the gym and wanted to congratulate you. I remember how much you wanted it."

"From what I hear, you're getting what you wanted, too. I saw the news. Governor?"

"Yeah. Who would've thought? Tell you what. I'd like to get together. Talk about old times."

I knew which old times were on his mind. After the IED attack and a stay in the hospital, my wounds healed, leaving a path of scars that workout clothes couldn't hide. I volunteered to return to duty anyway. I felt I owed it to LT, to be there for him when he needed me. But one day, I saw something I shouldn't have and everything changed.

*****

I was in a supply storehouse, tugging at a carton of phone chargers on a top shelf, when the shelving wobbled. From the back of the shelf, a lockbox flew toward me and then broke open as it hit the concrete floor. I started to gather the papers that flew out of the box when I realized what they were. Bank statements in LT's name. Invoices for large shipments of fuel. It was no secret that military bases had become hot spots for thieves. Fuel and weapons were disappearing at a staggering rate. LT was the last person I would've suspected. I knew I should report him, but I owed him my life.

I emptied the box and stuffed the documents in a large envelope. I put the empty box where I found it and went to LT's office. I walked in and closed the door behind me. He looked up and pointed to an empty chair.

When I told him what I found, he argued with me at first. I didn't know what I was talking about. I had it all wrong. It took a while, but when I held up the envelope and pulled some of the documents partly out, he shut up. I could see him thinking about the best way to talk his way out of it. He begged me not to turn him in and promised he would stop.

"If you don't, saving my rear end won't save yours."

"I get it. I'm done. I swear." He stopped. "But I want that." He pointed to the envelope.

"No way in hell." I glared at him. "I've already sent copies to a safe place, so don't get any ideas." I had no second thoughts about lying to him. I was pretty sure my life depended on it, but the shock and regret on LT's face seemed genuine.

"I would never hurt you, Sarge. Never."

I agreed to keep my mouth shut, but I had no idea if he would keep his side of the bargain. When I was scheduled to re-up a few days after we had our talk, I knew it was time to pack it in and head home.

*****

The sound of his voice brought it all back. I was sure I knew what he wanted.

"No need to get together, LT. We're good." I hesitated and then added, "You can call your goon off."

When he asked what I was talking about, I said, "We're done here," and disconnected the call. I didn't believe in coincidences. The break-in now made sense. I didn't blame him for worrying about me keeping his secret. I'd worry, too, if I were in his place. But I couldn't forgive him for sending a thug after me.

I made another call. "Linda? Any word on the guy I chased out of here?"

"Sorry. Nothing new."

"Didn't think so. I have something to ask, but you have to promise, no questions."

Linda didn't like it. "What have you gotten into this time?"

"That's a question. Let's try again. Okay?"

"All right. Unless you're calling to confess."

"Confess to what?"

She snorted. "I don't know. With you, I can't assume anything."

"Very funny. Listen, do you still have that envelope?"

It had been years, but Linda knew right away what I was asking. "Of course. Why?"

"I need to be sure it's in a safe place."

"My safe deposit box safe enough for you?"

"Thanks. That's all I needed." I hung up before she could ask anything else. All that mattered was that she still had the envelope I had given her for safekeeping when I got home. She had raised an eyebrow when she saw what I had written on it. "To be opened in the event of my death from other than natural causes." But for once, she had known better than to ask why the drama.

After the call with LT, I was determined to forget about him and focus on the gym, but I found myself following his campaign online. As I studied photos of meet and greets and campaign rallies, I started noticing the same figure showing up, always near the candidate. At first, I thought he was a bodyguard. The guy was big, and it made sense that in these polarized times, LT might have wanted someone there to protect him, although the LT I knew would've been able to handle himself without a hired hand to do it for him.

One morning, I was reading an article that identified the faces in the photo that ran with it. The second person from the left was described as Owen Thorne, LT's campaign manager. I had been wrong. The big guy wasn't a bodyguard. As I studied the face, I realized he looked familiar. As I was leaving Afghanistan, there was a new transfer into the unit, a Sergeant Thorne to take my place. The word was that he was a friend of LT's. I met him once, briefly, but I was more focused on getting prepared to go home than on making a new friend.

Staring at the picture, I was sure Owen Thorne was the former Sergeant Thorne. He must've stayed in touch with LT during the years after they had left the service. For Thorne to have a position high in the campaign meant one of two things. He could do the job and LT trusted him, or he had something on LT who couldn't say no to him.

"Boy, am I getting cynical."

"Talking to me?" Sharice, my young assistant, stood in the doorway to the office.

I looked up. "Sorry. Talking to myself. Do you need something?"

"I wanted to let you know I'll be late tomorrow. Exams."

I began mentoring Sharice when she was given a choice by a judge. Boxing classes at the gym or getting locked up in a juvenile program. She became my part-time assistant and was about to graduate from high school at the top of her class. My favorite success story so far.

"Just make sure you pass."

She smiled. She knew how proud I was of her. She walked to my desk and looked over my shoulder. "Who's that?"

"My old lieutenant. He's running for governor."

Sharice pointed at the screen. "I mean that guy." Her finger was directly over Owen Thorne.

"His campaign manager. Why?"

"I'm sure I've seen him in the neighborhood."

Thorne wouldn't have any reason to be around the gym. Time spent in a community like ours that was supporting LT's opponent would be a waste of energy. I tried to match my memory of Thorne in Afghanistan with the man who almost broke my elbow. Too much time had passed. They did look roughly the same size, but I wasn't even certain of that.

"Let me know if you see him again," I told Sharice and then heard voices coming from outside the office, near the front door to the gym. One of them was male. Men weren't barred from the gym, but they were rare. Occasionally, a jealous boyfriend of one of the girls showed up, making sure she really was taking boxing lessons and not cheating on him. I'd lecture him on trust and control and send him on his way.

As Sharice and I hurried toward the sound, I slowed when I saw LT, standing near the weights, deep in conversation with several of the girls. I stopped and listened as the kids chattered over one another, explaining their training for an upcoming boxing tournament. LT was asking questions about the equipment they had and the workouts they were doing. When there was a break in the give and take, he looked at me.

"That's enough, girls," I said. "Back to work."

LT shook hands with each of them and wished them luck. As they walked away, he turned to me. "Can we talk?"

My first instinct was to tell him to get the hell out of my gym, but instead, I pointed toward my office. He followed and took a seat in front of my desk.

"I couldn't leave it like that. On the phone. What did you mean, my goon?"

I was sure he already knew what happened, but I answered anyway, describing the break-in and my injury. "Nothing like in Kandahar, but I could've done without it."

"And you thought I had something to do with it? I told you back then I could never hurt you."

He seemed to mean it. Besides, if anything happened to me, his secret would be out. He'd be crazy to risk it.

"The guy was looking for something, and it was right after you declared for governor. Two plus two still equals four. Tell me, who knew what you were into in Afghanistan? And more important, who knew about me?"

"The only one who knew about you and what I did was my wife. I felt I had to be honest with the woman I was planning to marry. I told her what I had done and how you let me walk away. But no one else. I can't believe Greta would've told anyone." His tone was somber. "She has plans for me, all the way to the White House. She wouldn't jeopardize that with gossip."

I was starting to feel sorry for him. He had confided in me back in Afghanistan that the pressure was on him to join the family law firm and then aim higher. I wondered why he picked a wife who would pile on with the rest of his family.

"It's been quiet since the break-in. Maybe there wasn't a connection after all." I didn't believe that, and I could see he didn't either.

LT asked for a tour of the gym. When I had shown him around, he said, "It's amazing what you've been able to do here."

"Thanks. We've been lucky with grants, and I have a board that does its best to raise money. We make do."

"You do better than that." He looked around. Young girls were laughing and working up a sweat with the weights and in the ring. "You should be very proud of yourself." We shook hands at the door.

"Don't worry, LT," I said, "I still have your six."

I started to relax and not kick open the door to my office each day. My elbow healed, and my focus returned to my job, part of which included monitoring the school grades of the girls in the grant program.

A condition of their membership in the gym was having passing grades, and reviewing copies of their school reports was part of my post-workout routine. I was making notes one morning when Sharice tapped on the doorway to get my attention.

"You need to come out here. Now."

I followed her to the open front door. A short but muscled workman in a green uniform stood there with a clipboard. I walked over to him.

"You Danielle DeLuca?" I admitted I was. "Delivery. Sign here." He pushed the clipboard toward me.

"I didn't order anything. What's this about?"

The man grinned. "They said I should tell you this is for the girls."

"What is for the girls?"

He gestured for me to follow him. Parked at the curb was a large delivery truck with "National Sports Equipment" written on the side of it with the familiar logo under the words. I knew about them. A high-end sports equipment company. Way out of the reach of a business like mine.

"Don't worry, lady. It's all paid for. Tell us where you want it, and we'll get it set up."

"There has to be some mistake. Who sent you?"

Before he had a chance to answer, a Lincoln Town Car pulled to the curb in front of the truck. The driver jumped out and pulled open the back passenger-side door. A blond stepped to the sidewalk. I could tell her clothes cost more than I made last year. She was followed by a man. A very large man. I recognized both of them from the online photo. It was Greta Wallace, LT's wife, and Owen Thorne, his campaign manager. They came toward me, and Greta held out her hand. "You must be Dani."

"And you're LT's wife."

"Please call me Greta." Her smile revealed perfect sparkling teeth. They went well with the large diamond earrings.

I turned to Thorne and offered my hand to him next. "And you're Owen Thorne, my replacement back in Kandahar."

Thorne still had a military haircut and erect posture offset by a very expensive suit. "You remember me?" He was struggling to sound friendly. Hard work for him.

I wanted to ask if we hadn't met in my office a couple of months ago, but I still wasn't sure he was the intruder. "Our paths crossed when I was mustering out."

His eyes assessed every word. Was he looking for a hint that I recognized him from a more recent encounter?

I turned back to Greta. "Can you tell me what's going on?"

"Luther told me about your work here, with the girls. My family has a foundation that funds worthy programs. We have a process, application, review, that sort of thing, but Luther felt it would be a shame to wait for all the paperwork. This way the girls will have everything they need to get ready for that tournament coming up."

I felt Thorne's eyes still on me, waiting for my reaction. Didn't the man ever blink?

"I don't know what to say."

Thorne tried to be helpful. "You could say you're grateful. Like for when the lieutenant saved your life."

Subtle he wasn't. I knew this was a bribe, no question about it.

"Now, Owen, that isn't necessary." Greta turned to me. "I'm sure the girls will make good use of the equipment. That's what matters."

That and keeping my mouth shut as I already promised LT I would do. I wondered if he knew about this. Could he have forgotten who I was and how I'd react to this kind of pressure?

Before I could refuse, Greta told the delivery men to start unloading.

They rolled dollies loaded with giant boxes into the gym. Greta suggested I check their contents and direct the men where to place them. It all felt unreal. When they finished assembling all the equipment, Sharice and I found ourselves standing in the Rolls Royce of gyms, with all new weight equipment, cardio machines, boxing gloves, even shirts and shorts with the name of the gym on them. The girls were going to be over the moon when they walked in after school.

When everything was quiet, I sat at my desk and stared at my phone. Should I call LT? It was hard to believe his wife would've done this without his knowing, but she and Owen did seem to be running the show. He answered right away. Maybe he had been waiting for me to thank him.

"Sarge? What's up?"

I told him why I called. He didn't say a word until I was done, but I could hear his breath getting shorter and shorter, a sign this wasn't something he expected to hear.

Finally, he said, "I had nothing to do with this. I told Greta about the gym and the girls. I said maybe in the future, I'd see if you were interested in applying for support from her foundation. I know what you must be thinking."

So the bribe came from Greta and Owen. I was right. They were calling the shots for LT, maybe to an extent he didn't realize. It seemed they wouldn't stop at anything to make him governor. Anything. Like sending someone to steal from me, someone who wouldn't hesitate to hurt me? My thoughts were racing. Did Owen decide to provide his own muscle? What stake did he have in this? He was in Afghanistan when I discovered the fuel thefts. Could LT have had a partner? That would give Owen skin in the game. If LT were exposed, Owen likely would be, too.

"Owen made it clear why the equipment showed up, not that I needed him to spell it out. I'm glad you weren't behind it." I realized he was now the only one I believed. "This will mean so much to the girls. I couldn't say no, but I meant what I said. You have nothing to fear from me."

"I'll take care of it. You have my word, although I know that may not mean much right now."

The afternoon went as expected. There were ecstatic reactions from the girls and time spent going over how to use the new equipment safely. The shirts and shorts made them feel like a team, a sign of belonging to something in a way most of them didn't have anywhere else in their lives. By the end of the day, when I locked the door of the gym on my way out, I was hopeful LT would keep Owen and Greta out of my life.

*****

The boxing tournament was only a week away. The past month had been busy. I didn't realize the attraction the new equipment would have to women who wouldn't normally have ventured into the 'hood. Sharice had posted pictures on social media, and membership grew. She was enjoying teaching lunchtime boxing lessons for the new members. Donations started to climb. I began to worry about being in over my head, but Sharice recruited some of her friends to volunteer to help out. It all felt too good to be true, and of course, it was.

I was in my office at the end of the day, trying to get through the increasing paperwork, when Sharice appeared in the doorway.

"Something happened." Her voice trembled.

"Take a breath."

"That man is out there."

"What man?" But I knew the answer before she explained.

"The one in the newspaper. The one who came with Mrs. Wallace."

"Owen Thorne." It wasn't a question. "What did he do?"

"I thought someone was following me."

"Today?"

She shook her head. "For a while now. I figured it was my imagination. But this time, he stopped me outside the gym and told me to give you a message."

"Did he hurt you?" I half rose from my chair.

"No. He grabbed my arm to make me stop and talk, but it didn't hurt. He said you knew what he wanted and he wasn't going to wait any longer. He gave you until tomorrow."

"Or what?"

"Or your dreams would go up in smoke."

It was a serious threat. The gym had smoke detectors required by code enforcement, but the old warehouse was grandfathered on sprinkler requirements. It wouldn't have been hard for Owen to find that out.

"He gave me this card." She held out her hand. It was a business card engraved with "Owen Thorne," followed by a phone number.

"Where is he now?"

"I don't know. I yanked my arm away and came inside. I locked the door, just in case."

I promised Sharice I'd take care of it and told her to wait by the front door for me. When she was out of sight, I opened the safe behind my desk. I took out my 9mm M9 and checked to be sure it held a full clip and a bullet in the chamber. With the gun at my side, I walked to the door and unlocked it. I stepped outside, but no one was there. After I looked up and down the street, I waved for Sharice to join me.

"Go straight home," I told her. "And don't worry. It isn't you he has a problem with. I'll take care of it."

"I'm not worried." Sharice smiled. "I know how to handle bullies." I decided not to tell her this wasn't the kind of bully she had faced in her troubled past, and I watched as she jogged out of sight down the street.

My call to Owen was short. "You win." It hurt me to say it. "I have what you want."

"I knew you'd see it my way. I'll be there tomorrow."

"I don't want you anywhere near the gym. I'll meet you at midnight tomorrow by the pavilion at Lakes Park. And then I never want to see you again."

"No problem with that, Sergeant." He made it sound like an insult. "This was nothing personal, you know"

Sure. Nothing personal. Only a threat to everything I had worked for, to the people I cared most about. It was time to take care of business. I made one more call and then I was ready.

*****

It was nearing midnight. I stood in a patch of grass at the edge of the lake. The park was deserted at that hour, which is what I had counted on.

The sound of footsteps on the gravel path came closer. I felt a breeze that stirred the edges of the water in the lake. I slowed my breathing as I saw Owen.

"Stop right there," I ordered.

"Sure, Sarge. All I want is what was in the lockbox, and I'll be out of your life."

Did he really think I bought his act? He wouldn't feel safe as long as I was still breathing. I raised my left hand, a fat business envelope in it. "I'm going to put this on the ground and back away. Get it and leave."

Keeping my eyes on him, I put the package down in front of me. Before he could take a step, another figure came up behind him. As Owen turned to see who it was, Luther walked into a patch of moonlight. I wasn't surprised. When I called him, he had insisted on coming to help me deal with Owen.

I saw Owen raise his arm, moonlight glinting on the weapon in his hand as he turned away from Luther and toward me. I calculated the trajectory of a bullet that would take out Owen and miss Luther, but before I could fire, I heard a shot. Owen fell forward and hit the ground, his back covered with blood.

"LT?" When he had said he would help me with Owen, I didn't expect he meant he'd shoot him in the back. "I had it under control." Not really. I knew that if he hadn't shot, I would've had to. I guess I owed him my life again.

LT shook his head. "He was a loose cannon. When he botched the search of your office, I knew he had to go."

He pointed his gun at me. "I'm sorry, Sarge. I'm really sor…."

The shot rang out before he finished the sentence. But it was my shot, not his. "I'm sorry too, LT. But, you know, it's nothing personal."

Last Case Scenario
Jan Glaz

New York City 1988

Henry Walker's wife, Suzie, lifted their puppy, Ansel, out of his cozy bed and shoved the unsuspecting pet into his unwelcome arms. "Henry, don't forget to kiss poochie," she begged. Henry didn't have time for smooching poochie. In fact he didn't have time or an urge to smooch his wife. But he did both.

He should've left a half hour earlier, however, wifey never failed to detain him. 'Oh Henry, don't leave yet, fix this, do that'. Most days she'd gab about nonsense, her high pitched words trailing behind him up until he entered the garage, sat in his car and gassed it to freedom.

It was a forty minute trek to his sanctuary, his true home, a place where he ruled. As he navigated jammed intersections he realized how tedious life had become. Suzie was his third wife and there were signs pointing to divorce three. He was aging, his hormones were receding, he no longer craved the sexual companionship or aggravation that went with entertaining a woman on a daily basis. He scanned his withered face in the rear view mirror, and it agreed with his mental state. What if he'd had children? In his 20's he underwent a vasectomy because his nature lacked fathering. His career in the field of law enforcement became his child, and at 62, the child had advanced into the role of Detective Chief Inspector.

His home scene vanished the instant he closed his office door. From an unshaded window a stream of cloudy sun cast a wedge of light on figures strung across his desk. He sat down and fingered them. Snaps of a young woman found in the trunk of a stolen car. It was difficult, even for a seasoned DCI, to scrutinize someone's final hours.

Henry laid each image side by side in rows of three. The woman's body was alluring even in death, long legged, a tiny waistline beneath a pair of sumptuous breasts. There'd been wide coverage of the incident in the news media. He opened a folder and released the coroner's report. It listed information the public didn't have privy to. The female had been bludgeoned, gang-raped, and mutilated with invading knife wounds. Blood, instead of mother's milk, oozed from one of her breasts. Teeth marks clearly administered by more than one brutal mouth flanked the entire surface of her bluish skin. Worse, she'd been used as a bathroom. It wasn't hair spray that matted her golden strands into a web.

Henry's eyes riveted on the surface of her delicate face. Bits of dried blood caked her parched lips like grotesque lipstick. One close-up revealed a faded, fixated eye. It stared at him between a strands of jumbled hair. The eye appeared to be scrutinizing him in an effort to communicate the horror it witnessed.

As attractive as she must have been, she was now but a shattered replica. The ugliness and evil side of his job sickened him, even so, he felt destined to provide society and himself with answers. The task gave him a sense of spiritual fulfillment that religion failed. The young woman had been identified as Brooke Evans. Various other prints lifted from the stolen vehicle were from the car's original owner, the rest were unidentifiable.

Police knew Evans had recently moved to New York from California. Fingerprints confirmed residence in two other states, Illinois and Indiana. Brooke's short life had racked up a number of DUI's. A revoked license had been reinstated after the purchase of red Ford convertible from a dealership in Harbors End, California. The whereabouts of that car remained a mystery.

Her toxicology report noted high alcohol levels and traces of drugs. Henry assumed she was earning dough as a hooker, maybe dealing drugs and something went bad. As was his habit in murder cases, he bowed his head and mouthed a prayer for the victim.

Soon to retire, with aspirations of winging it as a private investigator, Henry was mentoring three police officers, Sarah, Jim, and Mike, to the rank of homicide detective. Estimating this murder an easy solver for the trio, he planned to keep them busy tracking leads. Authorities had linked her to a New York address and he'd requested a search warrant. He wanted to *personally* and *solely* ravish her living space, as not to have his interns botch evidence, which he was certain would be the case with rookies. He assembled his detective paraphernalia and traveled to the slummier part of town.

As he climbed five rickety levels, he couldn't ignore the obscene graffiti splattered across walls. Brooke's rental building strengthened his hooker presumption. Upon entering her apartment the first sight that hit him square in the face was a battered doll, a kewpie, thrown on top of a waste container. On closer examination it had been more than a toy, it had been a fancy décor telephone studded with teeny jewels, maybe genuine, maybe not. The dolls damaged eyes were positioned enviously underneath a dated wall phone. After photographing the scene he bagged Miss Kewpie.

On a counter adjacent to the wall phone an answering machine was blinking, insisting on being heard, he obliged: 'Hello Brooke, this is Steve Lowe from the Waldorf Astoria, I'm pleased to inform you that we have a wait position available in our elegant dining room. I've set up an interview for tomorrow at 10 a.m. in my office. I hope you can attend. Congratulations!'

Henry jotted the date of the call, the time and message into his notepad and then confiscated the answering tape. He'd been mistaken, his victim wasn't a hustler. Evidently, she arranged for a position at the grand Waldorf Astoria Hotel, and was to appear for an interview. He would venture to contact Mr. Lowe to probe the how, when and why, of Brooke's job opportunity at his posh hotel.

Walker continued to rummage around the apartment, snapping pictures, jotting clues, and lifting prints in case a murderer or murderers had been with her before parking her on the road. In a closet, buried deep behind rags and soiled clothing, he stumbled upon Brooke's emotional treasures, the focus of her decrepit life hidden out of sight protected by a plastic bag. Inside the bag a crucifix had been placed, like a gift bow, on top of tied newspaper articles. Inked circles framed her favorites. Could she be tied to the clippings, or was she a nut who liked to save sad happenings? Henry at that moment, in his heart of hearts, believed there was much more to Brooke Evans then drugs or sex.

It was late, he'd missed dinner again, not good when you're juggling your marriage. As he locked the door of the apartment, a shiver ran through him, it was a shiver he was familiar with. Brooke would soon take up a sizeable chunk of his life. At that thought, he zig-zagged off the home trail in favor of one of his favorite bars to wrangle a few ginger ale's and a hunk of cop camaraderie, before his expected face-off with Suzie. The prospect of untangling this case put him in the mood for a few stiff ones, but a promise is a promise and he was in enough trouble already.

*****

Lounging in Henry's office recliner, Jim, a lanky inquisitive young man, busied himself reading and shuffling through findings collected from Brooke's dwelling. As soon as Henry swung into the office, he questioned him.

"Out of state newspaper clips, evidence?"

"Did you notice the dates and locations?" Henry said. "They're spaced out unsolved deaths. If what I suspect is true she may have been a female serial killer, they sometimes stop killing for years and then something triggers them, upsets their psyche, and bang, someone else is dead."

"Why spend time and effort on a supposed killer who's dead?"

"First class investigators investigate assumptions, you never know what strange ideas will lead to a top notch conviction."

Jim began fingering the remnants of the kewpie phone and while doing so a wedge of metal tumbled to the floor.

"What's this?" he exclaimed, as he rescued a 3 x 3 inch packet from its interior.

Henry rushed over. "We'll need to get that to a lab. Case in point, if I'd have sent any of you to her place, would a broken phone have been part of your catch?"

Sweating profusely, Henry wiped the sweat from his secretly overfed cheeks with the back of his hand. Why would she obscure a pack of drugs to that extent? He was undressing her life layer by layer, for him the process was akin to lovemaking. "We're going to back track Brooke. Contact Mike and Sarah, tell them to meet us here tomorrow, 10am....sharp."

The following morning Henry pulled into his office earlier than usual. He needed to ponder which rookie to send where and formed his decisions just as Jim entered the office. Sarah, a mid-aged cutie with three funky shades of hair that reminded Henry of an artist's pallet, trailed a few steps behind. Mike, a burly independent type, strolled in fifteen minutes late.

"Mike and Sarah, you two are headed to California. Jim, I need you to track down clues in the Midwest. Chicago, her birth place, but mainly Indiana. Our gal may have been busy butchering someone when she was a wee-teen."

After his newbies scurried out, Henry grabbed a tweed scarf, an expensive import from Sweden that his second wife paid oodles of his money to buy for his birthday. He dragged the grim reminder twice around his neck and then popped a fedora over a path of grey hair that still lived atop his head.

A cab was waiting.

On his ride to the Waldorf, Brooke's misty eye peering at him between tangled tresses, took residence in his mind, Soon, every inch of her danced inside his inner vision until the whole of her consumed him. He knew of police detectives who chatted about a particular murder case haunting them. Today, he joined them.

He was early for his appointment with Lowe, never the less, a short willowy blond, decked out in a female version of a man's suit, escorted him into Steve's chamber. His den of operation was laced with fine furnishings. The man himself was seated in a chair that had been upholstered in dizzying swirls of brocade. Something women would appreciate, women who may have been attracted to a handsome impeccably dressed resource manager.

Steve, around thirty something, was engaged in a phone conversation. He pointed and Henry sat down to further estimate his prey, a man whose powerful gaze beamed an intelligence his boyish face lacked. Not to be missed, a perfectly coiffured bushel of dark wavy hair, certainly the envy of many a man. There was an absence of frames: No wifey, kiddies, or attractive sweetheart. His calculations were interrupted by Steve's voice, a firm mellow tone that smacked of practiced professionalism.

"Detective Walker, what a shame about Ms. Evans. Thankfully the police were able to identify her or she'd wind up an eternal Jane Doe."

"Well, there's more," quipped Henry, "we have clues that haven't been broadcast. I suspect she wasn't an average garden variety female."

Steve's lips curled into a waifish smile. "Oh… what do you mean?"

"She may have been dangerous. A threat to society. I'm not at liberty to say anything else, but since she's dead any risk to others has died with her."

"Henry, you're insinuating she was a psychopath? We had a brief interview, that's it. By the time she arrived from California the job had been filled."

"If your time with her was that brief, than my line of questioning's hit a dead end. The woman died of asphyxiation. Even if the culprits didn't intend on killing her, she's gone. Brooke Evans may not have been their first homicide. I'm fishing for bigger fish."

Steve opened a drawer and handed Henry a copy of Brooke's resume.

"As you requested. Hope it helps. I'm ashamed to admit that she was definitely coming on to me and I was definitely interested."

Steve produced a folder, and flipped through it.

"Job applications. Each came in before hers. I interviewed over thirty eight seekers, male and female, and hired five. I placed the remaining on a waiting list. They all had better fine-dining experience then she did, but when a position opened, I passed over the best, and called Brooke Evans."

Henry stood and they shook hands as a parting gesture.

"Well Steve, I had Brooke chalked up as a drug addict, an alcoholic, and she was. I tagged her as a prostitute, that she was not, but in a sense, yes, she used sex."

"Ms. Evans impressed me as a clean cut career girl burdened with a healthy hormonal appetite. She swiveled her hips when she walked and sat so her skirt raised a bit too high. Upon leaving she offered her hand, when I obliged, she held mine and gave it a lengthy squeeze. I mean… she was definitely coming on to me."

Henry taxied back to his office, all the while tossing Brooke's sensual character across his years of sleuthing. Her saved newspaper clippings were no longer random treasures. He now held in his hands her job history, it matched her souvenirs. His well-crafted intuition was baking up a psychopath who sculpted spiteful antisocial behavior into murder. And that crucifix? She had a spiritual consciousness, one that lived by its own satanic rules.

*****

His blossoming spies had unearthed a bevy of tidbits. Jim had performed a bounty of scouting. Brooke was illegit, no dad, no siblings, mother died in an asylum when she was in her teens. A frequent saga among sinners. Flashing an image lifted from Evan's driver license at local stores and restaurants gave birth to a call from a man whose guilt prompted him to confess.

Henry deemed it was time for a pow-wow.

At their team roundup Jim played a taped interview from his tipster:

"This voluptuous young woman offered herself to me. At the time I was employed at a garden center she visited, I also side-jobbed as an exterminator. She never gave her last name, called herself Gale. She wanted to kill big rats and didn't want the variety poison we sold at the center, I didn't ask any questions. I was hungry for intimacy, as I was having a long dry spell with my then wife. We met up. I gave her a generous amount of what she longed for, and visa-versa."

Jim broke in. "We can tie Brooke to that newspaper death at the 'Capricorn Steak House'. I'll bet that guy croaked like a rat. He was a short order cook who died of a supposed heart attack. But later, after a sting operation, police discovered that the cook had been involved with selling drugs to minors, enlisting them to sell, plus he profited from child pornography."

"Just as I suspected, our Brooke *was* a vigilante!" Henry produced a foot long wooden crucifix from the evidence box.

"Jim, take a close look at this. What do you see?"

Jim's eyes traveled its length and width, he flipped it around a few of times and passed it to Mike and Sarah. They stood with blanks on their faces.

"C'mon! At least one of you budding dicks should have spotted the clue."

His team continued to fondle it, until Henry swiped it out of Mike's hands.

"It's worn." He paraded the object in front of their baffled eyes. "Here… here… and here. Discoloration caused by a pair of frantic hands from the worst kind of killer, a God worker. Religious fanatics often meld into the mainstream disguised as upstanding citizens."

"Man, Henry, you're right on!" exclaimed Jim. "I bet she's linked to the clipping of that fast food guy in Indiana, it's a similar MO. When she was seventeen she accused Pete, the owner of 'Burgers n Such' of rape, which he denied, saying it was revenge because he fired her for giving away food to guys she was fooling around with, and because he withheld her week's pay. Police sided with Pete. About two years later a delivery man discovers Pete on the ground next to a box he'd been unloading, his head bashed in. Police didn't find a weapon. Due to the rape charge, they questioned Brooke and let her go for a lack of evidence. After Pete's demise police receive anonymous tips that Mr. Pete solicited sexual services of underage girls and boys from a pimp. When that news was released, a bevy of rape accusations against Pete came in."

Henry sponged a cigarette from Mike's desk. He'd promised his wife not to touch a pack of cigarettes, let alone smoke one. However, Brooke Evans was having an adverse effect on his honesty. His next words were cradled in puffs of forbidden smoke. "Ironic, it seems killers, unknowingly killed a killer, one that would've been almost impossible to stop. In a twisted evil, Brooke's death may have saved lives. But we still have to sweep her murderers off the streets."

After Henry snuffed his cigarette into an ash tray, he gave his protégés a stern expression, "You guys, didn't see that, right."

"If Suzie asks, I'll say I never saw your hands curled around any illicit objects," Mike laughed, and then with a cavalier gesture, he tossed his and Sarah's California findings, but they missed Henry's desk. While he plucked down to snatch the folder off the floor, Sarah interrupted and delivered unwanted news.

"Henry, I'm leaving the force."

"Seriously Sarah, this is my last case scenario and your last opportunity to step into this field as one of my top disciples."

Sarah flashed an engagement ring. "Ethan popped the question, marriage and motherhood with one condition, he wants me out of the PD, an either or situation. We've been tangling over it for years, and he won."

Mike, unphased by her personal dilemma, broke in.

"Henry, Sarah and I dug up another body at Brooke's California job, the one previous to applying at the Waldorf. Today that place is defunct, it had been converted from a vintage ship to an upscale restaurant that hugged the shoreline, known as "The Bountiful". Miss Brenda Dixon the hiring manager, who no one ever suspected owned the establishment, died suddenly. I ran down one of the Bountiful staff, a head manager. He claimed there was rivalry going on inhouse. Rita, a server hired at the same time as Brooke, felt uneasy around our mystery girl because Brooke came off as vindictive and antisocial. Rita was promoted around the same time that Brenda was preparing to can Brooke like chopped tuna. Brooke was still on board when Brenda, a picture of perfect health, becomes ill, goes home and dies. Poof! No Brenda, no Bountiful, but shades of poison. Problem is, if Brooke did Brenda in, it doesn't fit your vigilante profile."

Sarah disagreed. "True Mike, boss Brenda hadn't committed a crime that would've been punishable by our justice system, however, past records indicate that she'd been firing waitstaff for decades in an unjust manner. Hiring's had to sign a legal document agreeing to abide by outlandish rules. To enforce them the boss enlisted trusted spies, who she rewarded financially. Brenda, though attractive, was an old maid, without close relatives or intimate friends. She had a reputation of getting her jollies off by chopping heads."

"Henry paged through Sarah's research. "I don't see any of what you just said in your report?"

"When I wrote it I wasn't aware of her modus operandi, or I'd have listed it. Last night, Rita, a long standing manager rang me."

"I'm glad this came up! It's a most valued lesson. Whether in teamwork or individually, log every detail, every thought, and every hunch that has bearing on a crime. Whatever pops in thy heads! Sarah write it in today. Now, about the employee legal doc."

"Brenda forbid staff to date regular customers, and she often favored one server over the other, allowing them to work prized events and parties that garnished big tips. I couldn't fester up the actual employee contracts, which may have other 'do or be fired' quarks."

"Congrats! Each of you have accomplished what I required. With this information we may be able to bring justice to the name of Ms. Brenda Dixon, and that Capricorn cook. That find that Jim accidently rescued from the doll has been analyzed." Henry opened a drawer and lifted the results in the air. "Ricin!" he shouted, "now we have info about the weapon and a confession from the guy who supplied it! If the victims were not cremated, we can unearth them for an autopsy and bam closure. But not for Brooke."

Sarah walked toward the door, and turned and waved. "I've finished detailing my file Henry. Next time I see all of you I'll be wearing a veil… expect invites."

Inwardly Henry's gender bias didn't wish her well, he detested would be career females who prioritize marriage and motherhood.

"Well guys, any ideas?" asked Henry.

Dead silence reigned, prompting Henry to offer a route.

"Our victim chained to liquor and drugs arrives in New York without contacts. Mentally put yourself in Brooke's druggy shoes. What would either of you do? Me? I'd ask around. Naturally, she'd first prowl closest to her living quarters. I noticed that the vicinity where her body was parked is not that far from the hard part of town where gang wars and drugs are the norm."

Henry strolled over to a wall map hanging behind his desk and pounded his fist on a portion of it. "Police have labeled this entire section 'crime incorporated'. Digging up criminals by visiting bars is my specialty. Our target is Stan's Place. It's known as a biker hangout. Brooke's remains were in a stolen vehicle. The owner of that vehicle had his car jacked while he was partying at Stan's the night Brooke disappeared. I'm certain someone will remember a girl as sensational as Brooke walking into a bar like Stan's unescorted. Don't laugh! I've decided to infiltrate the place, incognito, as a biker. Previous to joining the NYPD I was a member of Hells Angels. I'll play the part perfectly, no one will ever suspect that I'm the great 'Henry Walker' a man who's solved every crime that ever flew into his coup?"

"Gee's that's dangerous, Suzie's sure to object. Maybe I can do it for you."

"Thanks Mike, but no, this one's my baby, my last baby. I can almost taste the satisfaction."

Soon after Mike and Jim left, Henry got down to business. He scoured the yellow pages drifting through second hand shops for biker's gear and bike dealers for a weathered Harley. Next, he called Suzie and warned her of another late arrival.

As he entered his car to go bumming he realized how he didn't like going home to either his wife or Ansel, as for the pooch, the Chihuahua was feisty and considered him a rival for Suzie's affections. Too often Ansel would stage a biting attack, until Suzie commanded otherwise.

*****

Henry called a taxi and then picked up a used Harley. He cycled over to an empty lot to practice wheelies. It didn't take long for him to can that idea, and he headed home. Suzie was sure to ask questions about a motorcycle stuffed in their garage. While thinking up explanations, he yanked a tarp over it and entered the house.

"You smell like cigarettes," complained Suzie, before he could apply his usual peck on her cheek. Gratefully, Ansel was busy in the yard ferociously barking at cars, people or anything else that moved.

"I can't help it dear," he lied, "it seems everyone I was in contact with today had contributed to the financial success of the cigarette industry. It's only odor, I didn't smoke any."

"Well, get out of those cloths. I'll have to take them to the cleaners." In a huff, she walked towards the dining room. "I cooked up your favorite Mexican dish, with a side of homemade low-cal dressing! You must've gained five pounds since last week. I warned you about eating junk food on the job."

He'd have to chuck down whatever Suzie stashed on his plate. She made a habit of giving him the exact amount she calculated he should eat to maintain his weight, which was never enough. He had to smoke on the sly, fill his belly on the sly, and lie to her in the open. So much for marriage.

After dinner Suzie readied herself for a church rendezvous. He'd bargained himself out of attending any of her pious adventures by promising her to quit smoking. Before they married she professed his habits didn't bother her, it was propaganda. And that's precisely why he never felt guilty about telling her the untruths she craved to hear.

A car horn beeped and Suzie rushed downstairs, blew him a kiss, and left to join her friends. In his study he pondered facts. He realized it wasn't the first time a car had been hijacked from Stan's, but it wasn't carjacking he was most interested in — it was drug activity. Weekends people were armed with paychecks. There would be sellers and takers. Henry planned to watch the place for the next month or so, shoot photos of comings and goings, whatever it would take to fan out Brooke's rapists.

His team had interviewed local low lives for clues about gang initiations and criminal activities. All in all, his junior investigators compiled a list of suspects, drug dealers, prostitutes and pimps. The bulk of names were staring at him screaming to be screened. They'd have to wait because the next day Henry would disappear and Wyatt, the lead character in the film *Easy Rider*, would emerge.

Suzie was snoring up a storm when Henry, earlier than usual, crept out of bed. From his hiding place he dug out a pair of tight denim jeans and a vintage moto shirt. He zipped his puffy chest inside a black leather jacket adorned with death-defying skulls. After opening the overhead door, he unwrapped the chopper, seated himself, secured his 'American Flag' helmet and began revving the motor. Suddenly! like a living nightmare, Suzie, in her jammies, hair askew, saliva dripping from her lips, came running towards him.

"Get off that thing right now!!! Have you gone bonkers, you'll kill yourself!"

Without answering, his alter ego, Wyatt, lowered the helmet visor, floored the Harley, and sped out of the garage. On his ride to work, rock music blaring, he noticed himself in the cycle mirrors — youthful, ruthless and ready to rumble.

That evening Stan's stake out was a wash. He was exhausted and left the hangout around 3am. Topping off a bad evening, on his ride home he had a near miss with a semi-tractor truck, his rusty Harley scathed the payment and his pride at the same time. Shaken, he continued home, anxious to swallow a handful of aspirin.

The second he flicked the kitchen light, he saw it. A furious hand holding a red marker had scrawled on a slab of poster board:
EASY RIDER THIS TIME YOU'VE GONE
TOO FAR!!! DON'T TRY TO CONTACT
ME, CONTACT A LAWYER!
All Suzie's belongings, including Ansel, were gone.

*****

Each weekend at Stan's Henry smoked like a fiend and drank ginger ales. Whenever he consumed alcohol it led to trouble, to romance, marriage, or extra marital affairs. At the club, to whoever would listen, he fostered questions, sported Brooke's image as his missing girlfriend, danced with whacky females and cycled home. One night after swinging he discovered Sarah had left him a voice mail. He called, but she didn't pick up, so he messaged her to stop by his office in the morning.

"Ethan and I split," Sarah complained, as she approached Henry's desk. "I've been restless, and hard to live with, the proverbial fish out of water. He attributed my mood swings to quitting the force and broke our engagement. I'm heartbroken, I can't convince him that he comes first, maybe he doesn't?"

"So, you want in again, is that it? Good timing. I have an assignment tailor made for you. I'm betting that Brooke, being new to New York and known to drink and drug, pulled into Stan's Place. The stolen vehicle she'd been trunked in was snatched from Stan's bar. My theory is someone may have told her where she could buy stash. We need that someone. I've been haunting the place as a bad old biker, that stint has failed. It's time for a fresh approach. That's where you come in."

"I talked to Mike, he told me the Evans murder has toppled your marriage."

"My marriage has been toppling itself since it began. Suzie was my final run; as the saying goes three strikes you're out. I'm out, finished with romance, forever! Our head macho police chief is aching for glory. Sarah if we crack this, add a drug lord to the mix and it makes the press, yours' truly will exit his career with notoriety, plus a hefty bonus and the three of you will be guaranteed a jump start to a grand future."

Henry lit his fifth cigarette of the morning and puffed adolescent smoke rings towards Sarah. "I'll have a car fit with California plates. You'll enter Stan's as a copycat victim, named Sally. We'll begin our decoy replay next week."

Several weeks into Henry's charade Sarah reported that one of Stan's ex-bartenders came into the club. She introduced herself to the ex-tender who was sitting at the bar making short notice of tequila shots on ice.

"Hi, Sally here. I couldn't help overhearing you tell the bartender you tended bar here awhile back."

"Yeah, I did, my name's Lucy."

Sarah pulled a snapshot of Brooke.

"My sister's missing. She once mentioned Stan's. I don't want police involvement. I'm doing my own leg work. She's an alcoholic and has a drug problem. I need to take her to rehab," Sarah whisked away pretend tears. "All I have is this photo."

"I lost my youngest brother to drugs, so I feel for you." Lucy walked behind the bar to a brighter scoop of light. "I think I did see her. She told me she was in pain, needed a fix."

"And?" Sarah questioned.

"Hmm, I told her I understood. One of our regular customers was known to have connections. He drew a map with directions on a napkin."

"Can you remember who he was? Maybe sis is living close by or even selling drugs herself?"

"I can't recall his name, it was unusual, a drum comes to mind. He'd be easy to spot in a crowd. A young muscular chunk of man, a frizzy redhead, tall, close to seven feet."

Henry was delighted. "If anyone can weasel information, it's you Sarah. We now have a major break. Whenever you go clubbing at Stan's I'll arrange for a squad to stay in the vicinity. If the redhead drum name visits the bar, tease him the way Brooke would, hint at needing a fix, and then get to a phone. Jim, Mike, I, and a few rugged officers will buzz in."

"Henry, I'm frightened. Maybe word got around that I'd been questioning. Being the guinea pig testing your history repeating theory is one thing, asking me to be the bait that catches a prized murderer is another."

"You'll be covered, protected… I promise."

Mike jumped in with his take. "Could be after molesting Brooke the gang stopped procuring at that location all together."

"No way," said Henry, "an illegal operation doesn't keep buyers information, they can't call them and say, 'Hey we're in hiding cause we killed a customer, so go get your drugs someplace else'. The culprits believe they've gotten away with murder, probably have before. They'll be back!"

*****

Red Headed Bongo

Bongo was distraught because things had been shaky. One of their gang members ratted to police about operations. The stool Pidgeon's breech spread like electricity on a hot wire, and Bongo was ordered to curb all drug activity.

The moon was pushing to full; he was high and cruising around, longing to cause pain. Bongo related his desire to his stepdad. Old cigarette burns, dad's favorite punishment, were nestled inside Bongo's tattoos. He hadn't rocked at Stan's for a spell. He'd hijack a vehicle from their poorly lighted parking lot, and then enjoy a night of dirty work. On Saturday's the joint was always jamming with activity. Hot music, hot chicks, lonely chicks, and desperate chicks hankering to make out with a sexy redhead cockerel.

Under the dark vault of night Bongo pulled into Stan's lot and parked on a grassy slab of ground sheltered by trees. Before entering the building, he examined the herd of parked cars and caught a California license plate attached to a blue mustang. The sight triggered a past adventure. What a delicious night that was, a wanton stranger he and the boys had the pleasure of violating. He thought, 'maybe the car belongs to a dame? Nah, I ain't been lucky lately'.

In the club he zeroed in on Sarah (Sally) dirty dancing with two gents at once. When she went back to her table, Bongo asked her to dance, but she said she had to make a call. When she returned, she told him she had to leave.

Bongo offered, "I'll walk you to your car."

To his surprise, they stopped at the California vehicle. He said, "Have good night." When Sarah turned to key the car door, he cranked his arm around her neck. "Not a sound or your dead."

Sarah froze. She was wearing a skimpy top with a plunging neckline. The redhead retrieved his switchblade and let the tip of it sink in under her left breast. Blood trickled from the cut; drug crazed Bongo licked it.

Sarah's brain screamed, 'where's the cops, where's the team, where's Henry?' And then her mind shifted gears. She applied sex to buy time and whispered in his ear.

"I love this, let's do more painful, dirty, stuff."

Bongo was taken off guard. He wanted rebellion, fear, terror, instead he got a sadistic, piggy woman, the kind he could find anytime, anyplace. Yet, she was too easy to pass up.

"I love to kill you," Bongo whispered back.

During the choke hold Sarah had dropped her keys, he picked them up, opened the door and tried to shove her flying limbs into the car. Instantly, a maze of twirling lights blinded him and a swarm of police closed in pointing guns at his head. It happened so fast, he dropped Sarah and she jumped free.

Bongo was wrestled to the ground and cuffed.

Sarah, the wannabe detective went berserk when she saw Henry playing the hero. He pulled up on his motorbike a few minutes after Jim and Mike rushed out of a squad car. All three tried to calm her. It didn't happen. She ranted, "That nutcase could have cut out my heart!" And then, she smeared blood from her still bleeding chest onto Henry's face.

"It was a twist!" he shouted, "we never expected a kidnap in Stan's lot. You called me and said you were with the redhead and hung up."

Mike pointed to the east end of the lot and said, "There was a surveillance car parked in a niche over there. They were waiting to follow your car home, or wherever. At first the cops thought you were chatting with one of the guys from the bar. It took them too long to figure the danger you were in. We're all very, very, sorry Sarah."

At the police station Bongo squealed like a greased pig sent to slaughter. Narcotic agents rounded up the gang's kingpin and their stash. Later, nine female bodies attributed to the gang were unearthed.

In the end the eccentricity surrounding victim Brooke Evans and her now substantiated poison slayings, plus a suspected 'Pete' the Burgers n Such butchering, led Henry and his protégé team into fame. The complexity of it set off a media frenzy with buzz towards a movie script. Henry fantasized the actor who played "The Man with no Name" in the film "For a Few Dollars More" as Detective Henry Walker.

A retirement party was held in Henry's honor. He pocketed a nice bonus, among other accolades. Mike and Jim received promotions and began their snooping career with a batch of cold cases. Sarah quit the force and reunited with Ethan. The couple staged an extravagant wedding: Henry was not invited. Divorce number three resulted in Henry listing his home for sale.

*****

"How about one for the road?" Mitch the bartender queried. "It's on the house. I've a backlog of ginger ale," he laughed.

"Thanks, but I'll call it a night. I'm apartment hunting in the morning."

As he stood up and began walking towards the exit, a voice trailed behind him.

"You're Henry Walker, aren't you? I saw you on television. The Brooke Evans case."

Henry spun around. "Yes Ma'am, I'm *the* Henry Walker… now retired."

The woman was a youthful, vibrant, curvy bombshell, with shoulder length hair the color of pricey Champaign. Their eyes met, his dark as midnight, hers like violet stars.

"Lisa Scott, nice to meet you Henry."

"You're a fan, are you? How about I buy you a drink."

"Normally, I'd take a pass, but who am I to decline an invite from *the* Henry Walker."

Once seated at the bar, Mitch approached, winked at Henry and asked, "For the lady?"

"I'll have a margarita," Lisa replied.

"One margarita and one ginger ale, coming up," Mitch confirmed.

"Mitch, can the ale, make mine a double scotch and soda." He turned to her. "Tell me about yourself, interrogation is my specialty."

"Real estate is mine. Earlier, I met a client and his wife for dinner here. I was leaving and you were a few steps ahead of me."

Lisa reached into her bag for a business card. Henry's keen eyes spotted a pack of Virginia Slim cigarettes. Taking her card, their fingers touched. He felt a hormonal stirring that he would have bet a million bucks died decades ago.

"What a coincidence, I'm in the market for a home and an office. Can we meet up tomorrow?"

"I have a full schedule but I'll shift it and see you about 11:00 a.m."

Henry gulped down the Scotch and flagged Mitch. "I'll have another round."

Beachcomber
Brandon Doughty

Anne felt relief when she opened the door. White noise filled the silent claustrophobic void that had surrounded her during the four-hour trip to the beach house. Paul, as always, played an audiobook during the drive. The book negated conversation, unless, she was willing to suffer the annoyed finger jab at the pause button, and subsequent, "huh?" that followed from her husband if she deigned to speak. His current listen was an economic text that even Adam Smith would have skipped. She tuned it out and swore she could feel literal pressure building between her and Paul during the trip. The door finally offered pressure relief.

The Texas coast was not always the most inviting. Instead of the soft coastal breezes of some beaches, today Galveston offered an angry hiss of surf and a frigid wind. The sky was bleached white like an aged sheet, singular to the horizon. The only defining feature was the bright circle of white where the sun struggled to provide a diffuse light.

Anne and Paul silently paced the area around the house. She stretched and enjoyed the smell of salt in the air and constant buzz of wind in her ears. It offered the conversation Paul no longer provided. She glanced at him while he looked around. His face was blank and he absently played with the ring on his left-hand.

The beach house — an online find by Anne — matched the color of the sky. It almost glowed reflecting back the hazy light cast by the white-out sun. A three-story shoebox set on its side; the ground floor was mainly open picnic space broken up by regular support columns. The only exception was an outdoor shower sporting trellis walls for privacy, which was attached to the back of a locked garage — Paul made sure to complain immediately when he learned the Tahoe had to remain parked on the limestone driveway. Anne knew the picnic area, obviously laid out to protect against the brutal Texas heat and sunburn, was unlikely to be used considering it was fucking freezing. *In March,* she silently protested. Normally the temp would already be on the steady rise to the high eighties by this time of year.

Behind the house a sandy trail led to a wooden path that bridged to the beach. The website claimed only residents in the homes on this stretch of beach were welcome to share this section of shoreline. The small sea-grass covered hills and bramble were nothing so grand as to be called dunes, but it was nice to see the bridge over them.

On the far side they saw a shining sign next to an old steel-barrel trashcan that might mark the high tide line. Neither Paul nor Anne could read the sign from this distance, but she assumed it read the standard *Don't Mess with Texas* message.

"Not bad Annie," Paul said.

"I know, right? I mean it looked great online, but come on, besides the cold and this hazy sky it's amazing. They claim it's a private beach, and look at that: A perfect shot right to the ocean, nothing in our way but bridge and sand." She couldn't help smiling.

"Gulf," Paul replied. "Not ocean."

"Huh?"

"This," Paul gestured to the coastline, "is the Gulf of Mexico. The *Texas* coast, so *not* the ocean. Just the good ol' oily Gulf of Mexico."

"Whatever. You know what I meant." She decided to take his jab with equanimity and move on. A Paul lecture was sure to ruin her good time just as it started. Anne could not remember the last time they simply enjoyed a trip or good time together. After two years married — seven as a couple — along with twenty new pounds, she questioned if Paul was still on her team. She had watched him grow more distant and protective of his phone this year. Worse, he seemed to think she hadn't noticed. If he was cheating, what was the point? They didn't have kids and nowhere near the kind of money that required an army of lawyers to settle. Why add insult to injury by cheating before deciding to just split up? *If he wanted to leave then fuck him*, she thought.

Maybe. Anne waffled, unsure if she was ready to accept that idea. Perhaps she was imagining things. "I'm gonna head upstairs and check out the inside. If you wanna to grab the cooler and go ahead and bring it up."

"Upstairs *to* check out the inside. So much 'and' Annie. Jeez." Paul grammar-policed her automatically. "*I* thought we might walk out to the beach real quick, but sure."

Anne saw his conflict. On the one hand Paul wanted to be put out by her request but on the other he knew it made sense unpacking first. She could put away food in the fridge and he could add more beer to the coolers. Although, she considered, it was cold enough outside that the coolers might be superfluous.

The stairway up to the second floor had lattice-work similar to the outdoor shower. It minimized the wind and sand on the steps. It also protected the helpful little sign posted on the door from being ripped off:

Welcome!

We hope you enjoy your stay on Galveston Island. Please remember these hints and property rules to make your stay great.

HINT #1: *The door sometimes sticks. Jiggle the key in the lock while turning clockwise. It'll loosen. (We promise.)*

As rental rules signs went, Anne admitted, this one was a winner. She jiggled the handle for a moment then the key turned. Pushing open the door required effort. A pressure hinge, like those found on business doors, wanted to pull it closed automatically. She presumed the hinge protected the entryway from sand buildup. Anne reminded herself to come hold it open for Paul before he got close to the door with the cooler.

A swirl of sand snaked around the door jamb into the house and distracted her from calling a warning about the door. Anne followed it and found another note on a wall next to a key rack:

HINT #2: There is a broom behind the front door. Sweep the entry regularly to prevent sand build-up. (It happens fast making for a grainy, uncomfortable stay. Trust us.)

Anne nodded, impressed. She took a few steps into the house. The storm shutters were closed and the darkness held a mix of smells. Anne inhaled the bland musty scent of an unused closet, but hiding just under the stale odor was a sweet tinge of dampness. She associated the aroma with water and wood. Not altogether unpleasant.

Her eyes adjusted, and in the gloom she made out a large living room, with a flat panel television on the opposite wall. She stepped further inside. To the left a kitchen and dining area. A bedroom to the right of the living space was attached to a bathroom that also opened on the hall where she stood. Up a set of stairs leading to the third floor she found three additional bedrooms, two more bathrooms, *and a partridge in a pear tree.* Anne laughed, admiring the size of the place when something slammed into the door below her. BOOM!

"Shit!" she cried, then ran down to open the door so Paul could haul the cooler inside.

"What the fuck Annie? There isn't enough landing out there to set this thing down. Are you trying to fucking kill me?" He huffed past her, eyes glaring.

"Shit, sorry hon. I swear I even told myself to stay close and warn you about the door. I got distracted looking at the size of this place. And this is just the first floor." Anne tried for contrite, but Paul's attitude made it hard for her to feel much guilt.

"Yeah great. Can we turn on some lights in here?" He banged the cooler down behind the couch.

"Could you put that over by the fridge so I don't trail water across the floor moving stuff?" Anne asked, her remorse quickly turning to frustration at Paul's shitty attitude.

"Yeah whatever. Can you get some fucking light in here? *Please*?" He lifted the cooler sure to give Anne a full eye roll. He moved the cooler closer to the fridge dropping it harder than necessary to underscore his annoyance.

She ignored this and moved on.

Anne found a line of switches by a door that led to the back patio. The owners had helpfully labeled each switch with its function. She hit the toggles for 'Dine Shutter,' 'Living Shutter,' 'Kitch Light,' and 'Door Shutter.'

After some grinding vibrations the first floor filled with murky white sunshine and light from the bulbs over the sink and food prep area. The automated shutters pleased Anne. Previous rentals she'd stayed in required a metal tool to manually open the shutters. Slow, tiring work.

"Wow," Anne said. "This is awesome. Even with the haze it's beautiful. I love this wide-open shot to the oc…" she paused, "the Gulf."

Paul scoffed and walked over and put his arm around her waist.

"It really is good. And look at that fence there on the side. It's like those beach fences in Jaws. All those times in Rockport I never stayed in a place with that type of fencing. I've always associated it with my dream beach house because of Jaws. Great job Babe."

Anne smiled at the the old soubriquet, a relic of the past when they first became a couple. She knew the movie, but didn't have the energy to tell him she had no memory of some fence. Paul played it at least once a year near the end of May during their regular summer party. He went to the trouble of getting a projector and screen, so he could play it outside by the pool.

She knew just one line and expected it any second.

"She's got black eyes, dead eyes, like a doll's eyes." Paul grinned looking at his wife, to confirm she got it and remembered the line. Anne gave the required smile. He'd been using the line since their first date.

Anne's eyes were a dark brown. Only in the brightest light could you discern where her pupils ended and irises began. Paul insisted they made her unique, and were part of what he loved about her. Anne didn't appreciate the idea that he thought she had soulless, pitiless eyes. Dead eyes, indeed. *I'm a caring nurturer, goddammit,* she thought. Although, in the pale light the look she gave Paul, just then, certainly lacked any warmth.

With the moment ruined, Anne opened the door to the deck. Cold wind whipped as they stepped out. The white-blank of sky, grey water, and icy breeze gave her a sense of melancholy. Not in a bad way, though. It was more like the feeling she got reading a Larry McMurtry novel. Beautiful in its own way.

Paul broke up her reverie. "Man, that wind isn't kidding around. It's so cold. Colder than a well-digger's ass," he laughed. "And just a week before spring break. The damn weather is all over the place. Did we bring coats?"

Another classic Paul move. He packed his own bag — based on Anne's lists to ensure he had everything — then drove them down from Austin to give him a sense of control, but truth be told, Anne managed the trip, from searching, to booking, to checking weather forecasts and packing the essentials required for the beach *and* cold weather. Were she less magnanimous she might have prepared herself, but left Paul to his own devices.

"Yes, I grabbed our hoodies. Probably enough, but just in case I grabbed our Patagonia's too. They're good as windbreakers which could be useful in this gale." Anne enjoyed the chill so changed subjects. "Look. We can see the waves coming in," Anne tilted her head, "and you can hear them break on the beach."

"Yeah, I hear it," Paul Acknowledged. "Very nice Annie. Pretty good view."

He shivered and turned back to the door. "I'm freezing. I'm going in. You know if it stays like this, we can just dig a hole and keep our beer chilled with ocean water."

Anne did not correct him.

He walked back through the open door. Anne followed closing it behind her. When she turned away she heard it squeak and glanced back. The door was creeping open again. Millimeter by millimeter the door slipped from the frame then blew wide again. Anne caught it, reclosed it and threw the deadbolt to keep it closed.

Paul said, "That's good to know. We'll need to keep it locked when we're not out there. Not sure what to do if we're all sitting out there. We don't want to leave it open to blow sand and salt all over the place."

Anne agreed. The door staying open also conflicted with 'Hint #1' from earlier. "Yeah, they should put a hinge on it like the front door."

"Almost fucking killed me!"

"Again, sorry about that. We'll need to note that the door wouldn't stay closed on its own to the rental company."

"Yeah, yeah. Let's check out the rest of the place," Paul said cracking his first beer. "Then I'll go unpack the rest of the truck, if you'll unload the cooler to the fridge."

"Sounds like a plan. Do we know when the others might show up?"

"I don't think anyone is coming down until tomorrow afternoon so we'll have to suffer alone tonight," he smiled. "Dave and Kristi have their anniversary dinner tonight so they'll be driving down after Dave recovers from his hangover. Larry and Ash didn't think they could swing the cost and bagged out." He turned up the beer and downed it in just a few gulps.

Anne nodded. This place wasn't cheap and she knew that Ashley had recently lost her job. Part of the reason Anne even allowed Paul to invite others was to offset some of the cost. This place was cheaper than some of the others, but there was always a price to stay right on the beach.

"And Shelli said she might pop by sometime." Paul said reaching down to grab another beer. "I think she was already planning to be in Corpus visiting her mom so she might stop by if she leaves early. She even said she'd pay extra for one of the big bedrooms. Help offset missing Ash and Larry."

"Oh," Anne said, her voice even. "I didn't realize you mentioned it to Shelli? Won't she feel like a fifth wheel? Or is she bringing someone?" She squeezed her hands behind her back digging deep crescents into her palms with her nails.

"Ah, you know Shelli. She'd have fun at a funeral. Don't know if she's bringing anyone. Not sure I'd dig that anyway. Do we want some guy we don't know tooling around the place? Stealing or breaking shit?" He walked down the hall keeping his back toward Anne as he said it.

Anne knew it was to avoid looking her in the eye. In a magically reasonable tone she said, "Okay. Well, there's more than enough room either way. Let's check out the rest of the house."

*****

After getting settled they headed to the beach.

"A walk only," Paul said. He made it clear he did not intend to swim considering the frigid temperatures and wind.

The wooden bridge took them over what they jokingly called the dunes, but was really nothing more than a little scrub of sea grass and thorny bramble. And some trash. The coastal winds, famous for their ability to rip away plates and bags not properly weighed down, showcased their chaos here on the Texas coast. They saw plastic grocery bags and foil lined packages in the greenery, caught on thorny vines and driftwood. But overall, the area was much cleaner than other beaches they'd visited.

At the end of the boardwalk they found a hard-packed strip of sand. It was a road, built by use, where design was likely added later. To the right they saw red 'Wrong Way' signs, and to the left were '15 MPH' signs. Steel-barrel trashcans lined the road every twenty feet or so.

"Road must be for the trash truck to collect in the middle of the night. Explains why it's so clean." Paul said. Anne nodded her agreement as they continued walking.

Near one of the barrels, on the other side of the road, they saw the sign from earlier. It was the only one that faced the houses. Clearly the sign was built to inform those headed *toward* the beach not those walking *along* it. They laughed reading it because it was more direct version of the old *Don't Mess with Texas* signs that once lined the highways across the state.

ITEMS LEFT ON BEACH WILL BE REMOVED

"They are serious about keeping this place clean," Paul said. "Did I tell you? When I was leaving to grab the rest of the luggage there was a sign on the back of the door that had rules on it? Not hints but *rules*."

Anne laughed. "Yeah, there were some on the fridge too. The hints were there, but these were specified as Rules. Capital 'R.' What did you find?"

Paul, described the rules written on the back of the door.

RULE #1: *DO NOT leave items on the beach overnight. Items left on beach will be gone. (Seriously gone forever.)*

RULE #2: *Absolutely NO ANIMALS PERIOD. (Trust us, again.)*

"Between the signs and those fucking rules they seem really hardcore on keeping this joint clean. And I'm sure we're about to see a *No Dogs on Beach* sign. If we do then, and *only* then, I'll finally agree you were right." He shook his head, "It still seems fucking stupid either way: No dogs. It's a goddamn beach!"

Anne turned her head to the ocean, away from Paul, and gave a rueful smile, remembering how Paul fought her about bringing the dog on the trip.

*****

"Of course we're bringing Molly Dog. Why — for fuck's sake — would you not bring a dog to the fucking beach? It's moronic! You..." he'd paused just before dropping an argument ending, new argument starting, c-bomb and recovered with, "you know it."

"Well, it's not my decision Paul. *They* put it as one of the rules on their site: No animals of any kind. They're not trying to single you and Molly Dog out. We couldn't bring a cat or a hamster either." Anne tried to stay matter of fact about it. Keeping calm and explaining things clinically helped keep Paul from going further off the anger cliff. "They could end up giving us bad reviews. That could keep us from using their site in the future, and they seem to have the best rentals."

He threw another fit the day before they left when he had to drop Molly Dog, their chocolate lab, at the pet resort. In the end it was the risk of bad reviews and loss of rental options that allowed her to talk him off his pulpit. She knew he cared more about how others perceived him than how his own wife felt. Anne's opinion — beyond booking travel — didn't seem to carry much weight with Paul these days.

*****

Now here, walking the coast he picked up his argument again. "I refuse to understand why they won't allow dogs. And so far, I haven't actually seen a no pets sign on the beach." They continued down the shore with room for a third person in between them.

"It is what it is I guess." Anne said without reaction to his blanket refusal to accept or acknowledge rules set by other people or apologizing after seeing no sign of other dogs on the beach. There were a few people out, but no animals at all.

"I also wish it wasn't so cold," Paul said.

"It doesn't seem as bad here next to the water." Anne said trailing her bare feet through the surf. "I'm not too cold."

"Jesus Annie, we're wearing hoodies. Of course it's going to be warmer," Paul replied. "But it's still cold. Cold as a witch's tit, my grandad would've said." He laughed at his joke before continuing, "I can't feel my feet anymore. Let's turn around. I can't walk back without feeling my feet."

Anne remained silent. She turned with him, but stayed close to the water, enjoying the surf as it foamed over her feet. She walked, head down, eyeing little pin holes that sprinkled the beach close to the water.

As they shifted back up toward the boardwalk, Paul noticed some larger holes in the sand near the makeshift road.

"You know," he began, "these are made by Ghost Crabs."

Anne nodded, resigned. Paul loved to give a lecture.

"You rarely see them because they can blend into the sand. There are more of them at Padre than here, but they've got 'em here too."

Anne asked "How do you know there are more in Padre if you rarely see them? Perhaps they're just hiding here?"

"Because I fucking read it in a magazine," Paul replied, missing her joke, "or maybe online. Who knows anymore?"

"Is it normal for the holes to be so" she paused, "straight? Symmetrical? They're in a straight line."

Paul looked again, and saw she was right about the holes running parallel to the beach-road on the gulf side. "The fuck do I know? Maybe it's some type of beach aeration. Always trying to say I'm fucking wrong. Jesus."

Anne shrugged, at a loss of how he'd been able to take offense to a simple question. She continued toward the bridge, leaving Paul to his crabs.

He stood for a bit longer, shook his empty beer can then dropped back for a jump shot into the nearby trashcan. The wind caught it, blew the can off course missing the receptacle. He cursed. In protest, he left the can rolling in the sand and headed back to the house. They obviously had beach cleaners. Let them pick it up.

*****

It was late. Paul was drunk. But, to be fair Anne had also been in her cups. Not to the level of her husband but happily loose. That was before mention of the fire.

They had shared a bottle of wine with dinner; red of course. "It's too damn cold for white wine," was Paul's thought on the issue. As they cleaned up, Paul glanced as his watch a second before his phone started ringing. Anne popped another bottle of wine and listened to the slurred one-sided conversation.

"Beach house. Beach bum number one speaking." Paul laughed into his phone. He held the device to his ear rather than tap it to speaker or use an ear bud.

"Yeah, hey man…

"Not bad. Made it in about four hours…

"Yeah, pretty cold, but we took a walk on the beach. Annie kept her feet in the water most of the way but you know…" He laughed hard.

"Yep, Annie has ice in her veins. You called it man. This place is fucking huge dude. When are you….

"Oh. Oh man, that sucks. Both of you huh?"

Anne drifted away from the conversation, happily floating on a cloud of red wine. She thought, *another one bites the dust.* They might get a private weekend after all. Although, so far, their alone time had not proved very romantic. She was disappointed not to use more of the big house, but consoled herself with the other benefits of their now oversized abode. They could try *christening* multiple unused rooms. Or since the beach had actually been semi-private, maybe they could have some *private time* on the beach. Anything to up the romance factor.

"Yeah, maybe a fire down at the beach or something. A fire and Annie can keep me warm my man. Yeah, later bud." Paul finished the call, leaving his phone on the counter, and explained that after dinner both Dave and Kristi had gotten sick. "They might try to make it down for the last day, but don't count on it. What a buncha pussies."

Anne ignored the last and said, "Gotcha. I thought it sounded something like that. Well, we'll have the place to ourselves. That'll be fun." She smiled at him. "What was the last bit about a fire?"

Paul stood, walked over to counter and grabbed a bottle of Tito's he'd brought for morning bloody marys. "With no one coming I won't need as much of this as I thought for the mornings." He laughed and took a swig directly from the bottle. "I'm gonna go build a fire and sit out on the beach for a while. Contemplate life and whatnot. We can bring a blanket and… snuggle."

He looked at Anne with what she assumed were supposed to be bedroom eyes, but his drunken droop just made him look confused.

The wine had lowered her inhibitions so she tried to be funny. "I'm down for a good snuggle if you can *rise* to the occasion." She even bit her lower lip to show she was being sexy playful. Then continued responsibly, "But let's skip the fire. It's already past eleven. By the time you got it setup it would be midnight. Or later considering both our conditions right now. You know, we could just snuggle here." She hoped her smoky tone might temper the *don't play with fire* message.

Paul hung his head, and set the vodka bottle on the counter. For a moment, Anne thought her message might reach him. Until he looked up at her, anger burning in his slitted eyes. Why was it, he could convey his anger so much better with an expression than his desire?

"Of course you wouldn't want to go fuck by a beach fire. When was the last time you wanted to have real fun or do anything sexy for me?" He slammed his hands on the counter, careful not to hurt the vodka. "You fucking black-eyed bitch." Then he laughed. A harsh bark.

He stalked to the couch to tower over her. "What do you tell a woman with two black eyes? Nothing, she's already been told twice." He swiped his hand toward the table rather than toward Anne, but she flinched back anyway. Paul grabbed the bottle of wine and took a big pull. He smiled bloody wine-stained teeth.

"Flinching like I'd fucking hit you. I've never hit you. I'm going down to the beach to build a fire. And I'm going to sit there and finish this." He held up the bottle of wine. "And *this*." He grabbed the vodka in his other hand and walked away.

It was true, Anne admitted. Paul had never hit her. Scared her? Yes, scared her a number of times. When he wasn't drunk, Paul admitted he sometimes had blackout anger when he drank, but justified it by saying, "I'm all bark and no bite."

Anne heard him fumbling with the front door until it finally opened.

"Try not to burn yourself," she said, knowing it was pointless sending the warning anyway.

"Like you care."

The door slammed. It might have been the spring hinges.

Anne sighed. Dimmed the lights and went out on to the deck. The wind had died off. She could hear the surf and her husband muttering and cursing downstairs while banging God knew what around. She watched him pile items out near the boardwalk. Some wood — purchased just for the occasion — his wine and vodka, and a beach chair still in its shoulder bag. He disappeared as he searched for something else under the house.

Anne returned to her thoughts. His words hurt just as much as his hands would. Better — for him — the bruises they left were invisible to their friends and family. No need for physical strikes when her essential-self bruised at every verbal slap. She hated herself for being so passive during these assaults. Always trying to compromise. Paul never checked his tone. He was in a good mood or irritated, period, and wore that feeling with pride. Why was she trying to save something that he never appeared to care about?

Paul had found his quarry. He stalked back to his pile carrying lighter fluid. He really was going to hurt himself.

"Please be careful," she called. He replied by shooting her the finger before turning away again.

Why? She walked back inside closing the door and fell on the couch.

Why put up with it? With him?

The questions chased her into sleep.

*****

BANG!

Anne woke with a start wondering where she was for a moment. Her head throbbed with the wine headache she would suffer tomorrow. For now, it was just a low warning of things to come. She called Paul's name, but noticed the patio door open, grains of sand building tiny dunes on the tile. The wind must have kicked back up, and she had forgotten to bolt the door.

When she moved to close and lock it Anne saw the small flicker of a fire down on the beach. She thought to call him but saw his phone still sitting on the kitchen counter. She picked it up planning to take it down to him and it woke when she lifted it. There were two unread messages on the screen

BRT early tomorrow.

Maybe we can send her to the store so you and I can swim. The final message ended with a smiley face, an eggplant and a peach.

They were both from Shelli Bradley.

Anne almost threw the phone but thought better and replaced it on the counter. She threw on her hoodie and shoes. *Fuck him.* She was leaving. He could ride back with his swimming partner. She packed her stuff not caring if she forgot anything.

Starting the truck, the dashboard clock lit with the time 3:30. She threw her bag in the passenger side. Anne paused, breathing hard. She wasn't going to leave without telling Paul it was over and that he could go fuck himself. Or Shelli. She didn't care which.

She crossed the boardwalk and the little beach road headed toward Paul's makeshift camp. The moon shone bright. Today's haze having finally disappeared left the sky a dome of stars, raising hope for a beautiful day tomorrow. Not that Anne would see it. Not from the beach anyway.

Paul had laid out his wood in a three-by-three pit. The small fire kept consistently lit by a little breeze that freshened the embers regularly. The wine bottle was plugged in the sand, neck first with cans circled around it like an alcoholic sundial. He had trekked back to the house at some point while Anne slept to bring the extra beer. Paul sagged in his chair facing the water. His head lolled to the left, hand wrapped around the handle of his Tito's bottle.

"Paul." She yelled from behind. He did not stir.

"Hey asshole," Anne walked up behind him and shook the chair.

He stirred and mumbled something.

Anne said, "What? I couldn't hear you… you jerk." Her voice caught as tears welled in her eyes. She shoved the chair forward. Paul, still struggling for consciousness, fell forward smashing his wrist into the wine bottle and scattering his beer cans.

"Ow. What the hell Anne." Paul lifted his face out of the sand, tried to push himself up, but his wrist couldn't hold his weight and he fell to his shoulder almost into his fire pit. "What did you do to my wrist. Jeez-sus."

"I didn't do shit, but I hope it's broken. I'm leaving Paul and fuck you." Anne stood shaking with anger unsure of what else to do besides leave. She kicked sand at him like a child, scoffed at herself, and walked away wiping tears from her eyes and sniffling her snotty nose.

Paul struggled to a sitting position and tried to focus on her. He was so drunk, but assumed this — whatever *this* was — would, of course, blow over like everything else. Unfortunately, he couldn't concentrate right now. His wrist might be broken. If it hurt this bad now, it was going to be misery in the morning. That needn't have concerned him.

"What'dya mean leaving?" His words ran together as he tried to get his mind and tongue aligned again.

Anne reached the first step of the boardwalk and turned. "Your girlfriend will be here tomorrow so you can talk her into giving you a ride." Tears welled in her eyes again blurring her vision.

"*You're* my girlfriend you dumbass."

"I'm your goddamn wife you drunk!" Anne started stalking back toward his camp but stopped when she noticed something in the sand. She saw movement in the crab holes along the side of the road. Paul had claimed they were crabs, but he didn't *know*.

She saw a flash of green. What if they were baby sea turtles? Oh, she thought how sweet that would be to see them hatch and head to sea. A little bright spot in a miserable trip. But she recalled there were normally laws and signs and even crime scene like tape to protect sea turtle nests. You couldn't touch them. She quickly jumped back to the wooden bridge on the top step to ensure she didn't hurt or touch the little hatchlings. The thought of turtles saved her life.

"Yeah, yeah, yeah. Wife whatever." Paul mumbled to himself struggling to stand in the sand. He managed, barely. Then he almost fell again trying pick up the overturned chair. When he steadied himself standing up he saw Anne staring. "What the fuck are you looking at. Go if you're going. Stop gaping at me."

But she wasn't looking at him. He followed her gaze to the beach road where something grew out of the crab holes. Not one of them. All of them. And it wasn't crabs…or turtles.

Green globes grew out of the holes. Differently sized and not perfectly spherical they bulged and pulsed like boiling skin. The moon gave them a pearlescent sheen like melted balloons, but they were not hollow nor empty. These things looked like they had mass. They oozed and bubbled out of the holes growing larger and more bulbous. With a SLURP, they were out. All of them at once. They popped out of the holes landing with a jiggle like Jell-O.

Seen out of the ground, Anne had a singular thought: They looked like boogers. Massive, disgusting balls of green mucus about a foot in diameter. Tumorous growths moved over each one. The entire blob pulsed and jiggled constantly. No eyes, nothing to distinguish a head. Not a spec of sand on any of them either. They were disgusting but perfectly... clean?

Everything after happened fast. Brutally fast and terrifying.

Half of them surged toward Anne the other half toward Paul.

No, that wasn't quite right, Anne decided. They weren't headed toward *her* but toward the houses, while the others sped toward the water. Watching those that surged toward her, she saw the goo-balls part around the boardwalk and rejoin their line under the bridge. She watched them in horror and awe.

They did not move *over* the grass and scrub but through it. The vines and spears of grass passed through the gooey balls. She saw the skin of the orbs stretch and then snap back from a plant and rejoin its blobby body. Anne observed little tails as they moved. This made her think of massive green sperm and without warning she puked over the railing. Her dinner landed in the scrub behind one of speeding balls of goop.

The ball nearest the boardwalk reversed direction — the tail disappearing then shooting out the other end as it sped toward the area below Anne. As it drew closer, she watched in horror as a mouth appeared. Goo clung to both the top and bottom of the gaping hole like a shoe pulling gum off pavement. She watched the thing swallow her upchuck and the gummy mouth disappear like it was never there. The vomit was gone, but not a single branch missing or broken, not a blade of grass harmed. Anne looked out seeing the same thing happening to the plastic bags and wrappers they had seen earlier in the day. It was all *eaten*? Anne couldn't decide if that was the right word, but the trash, like her regurgitation, disappeared with nothing more than a crinkle of foil chip bag. The globs were almost silent, generating only a soft susurrus through the scrub, no louder than the waves rolling on the beach.

As the moving loogies reached the end of the dunes, where the powdery sand separated them from the foundation of the houses, the blobbers reversed direction and sped to meet their brethren headed to the ocean. She noticed when they reached the sand again, they left little trails with their tails like rake lines in a Zen Garden.

Headed toward the ocean!

"Oh shit." In her fascination, she had forgotten about Paul. Anne turned and screamed, "Paul, lookout!"

*****

While Anne watched those headed toward the houses, Paul stared at the balls of snot wondering what they could do. If they came for him, he would just step on them and pop them like the balloons they were.

He believed that, right up until he watched one of the green slimes wrap around the sign they had seen that morning. It pulled itself over the five-foot sign like a sock and snapped back to its spherical shape as it passed it, leaving the sign and pole brilliantly clean, shining in the moonlight.

ITEMS LEFT ON BEACH WILL BE REMOVED

Paul started running toward the water.

He looked back, saw three of the jelly beasts melt through a piece of driftwood. One of them then opened its maw and swallowed a plastic sand bucket. The mouth gaped, the dripping strands of goo melting into the plastic as it closed over the bucket swallowing it whole. The green blob took on the shape of the bucket for a moment like seeing a body under a sheet and then it was the goop once more, returning to globular form. Paul kept running, almost to the water line.

He heard "Paul, lookout," and turned to look again. His drunken run had left a zigzag through the sand, as if he were avoiding gunfire. He had forgotten all about Anne. Her voice reminded him and he saw her standing there on the boardwalk. She was so far away, in his thoughts and reality. *Whatever.*

Just as quickly his attention returned to the slimes. He watched as they reached his camp. One took the shape of the wine bottle, somehow swallowing it whole even beneath the sand yet not disturbing the grains at all, leaving only a flattened pristine area with a tail trail behind it.

At the same time, another opened its mouth to consume one foot of the overturned chair. Paul gaped as the leg of the chair continued into the goo, stretching its green skin. Two feet now covered by the gummy maw, and then the blobstrosity started to envelop the seat and arms. The goo continued to stretch and consume the chair. For a few seconds the thing resembled an old green sofa chair, rounded at the edges as whatever internal process worked to consume the beach chair. In a few moments the green slime returned to its regular size and moved on to one of the nearby beer cans, while its mate took on the shape of a Tito's bottle.

They avoided the fire, circling it but not moving to consume it. So while the line of blobstrosities was almost unbroken there was a six-foot gap near Paul's pit where they had split to avoid the flames. He thought this was his moment to get past them and silently thanked Anne for her distraction. He would never have thought to run toward the houses without her calling his name. He stopped, pivoted and ran toward the gap in the line of beachcombers. Fueled by adrenaline and drunken thoughts of grandeur Paul moved with what felt like a glorious runner's stride.

Anne saw his actual movements. He ran in a lurching jog, leading with his gut and taking only foot-long steps toward the blobbers. She was afraid to watch but couldn't turn away.

To his credit, Paul realized he couldn't make the hole in time and saw it didn't matter anyway. They hadn't been avoiding the fire, but circling it like an army. They opened their gummy holes as one and connected at the center making a tent over the blaze. For a moment, the flame glowed orange-green like an evil jack-o-lantern before going black, suffocating due to lack of oxygen. The tent collapsed with a sizzle and a few wisps of steam. The blobstrosities separated and reformed their line. Nothing remained to show there had been a fire except a few blackened sticks of wood that could be mistaken for driftwood.

Paul understood he'd been mistaken, again. He thought he needed to find a hole, but these things were only a foot high. He played basketball at least once a week at work. He could just jump over these fucking things. He drew a calming breath. The blobs surging for him in their line. He drew another breath then exhaled as he stepped with drunken mistiming, intending to launch off from his left foot over these boogers.

*****

Anne watched, horrified, as Paul tried to step on one of them. She hoped it would pop but, of course, it didn't. In a flash a goopy hole opened right where Paul's foot stepped and he fell six inches *into* the thing. Or into the sand, it was impossible to tell. He screamed but used his right foot to push off again into a little leap. The jerkiness of the motion shook the thing off his left leg, but what was left could no longer be called a foot. It looked like someone had whittled his leg at the ankle leaving a rounded end like a peg-leg without the wood.

It was a partial success. He lifted into the air over the rest of the blobbers. Unfortunately, he stuck the landing — literally. He landed with his nub first, sticking it in the sand like a spear. With this forward momentum abruptly stopped from below he took a massive header into the sand. While we like to believe the sand is soft and giving, when Paul hit, his nose shattered from the force and as his lungs expelled his breath through his broken nose. A blood explosion blasted the area around his head. He lay there looking like a fresh mob execution.

Appalled at the thought, Anne noted that Paul had been right: He couldn't walk without his feet. He failed with just *one* foot missing.

She also realized he had gotten past the blobbers.

But it didn't matter. Not only was Paul unconscious, but as with Anne's puke, the blobs changed direction instantaneously. She watched as one of them opened its maw and stretched up Paul's right leg, the body extending like a python swallowing a deer. Paul woke as he was consumed and started struggling but the slimes learned as quickly as they moved. Three others shifted to help clean him up; one for each of his other extremities. They met in the middle, and for just a moment created a green clay sculpture with a human head. Then his head popped off and Anne watched it roll toward the ocean with more blobbers chasing after. They consumed Paul's head, regained their line then continued their cleaning ritual back toward water. Not a drop of blood left behind.

Anne observed as they swept over the last of the beach and dissolved in the water. Dissolved? She wondered if Paul would have been safe if he'd only gone and waded in the water. She collapsed to a sitting position and started crying. Or laughing even she wasn't sure. Anne calmed herself staring at the sand and surf. The wind was gone and all was quiet except the waves lapping the shore. Anne suddenly recognized it had been this quiet throughout the entire situation. Anyone listening had no reason to think anything had occurred beyond two people fighting or perhaps playing a game.

The beach looked pristine, showing little trails like rivulets of rain down a window. *Brushed clean*, Anne thought, her face still streaked with tears. No, not tears this time. It was sweat. She removed her hoodie and laughed. The weather had finally warmed up. She watched the sunrise then returned to the house shutting down the truck on the way. She needed a nap.

*****

Anne woke on the couch to knocking. The living room blazed with sunlight. She checked her phone. It was 11:30 in the morning. She couldn't determine if she was impressed or disturbed that she'd gotten almost four hours of uninterrupted sleep after watching her husband consumed by large globs of snot that same morning. Anne decided she felt pretty good. A burden lifted for her. And, since that sounded passive, she promised herself to be more assertive moving forward. Promised to remove her own barriers in the future.

The knock came again. She called, "Be there in a sec."

On her way to the door, she tapped Paul's phone and saw a string of messages, but only read the most recent.

I wish you'd answer me. Running late. Be there soon. BTW bringing Bart. This one ended with a kissing face emoji.

Anne opened the door patting down her hair. "Oh, hi Shelli. Paul mentioned you might be coming out. Glad you made it."

"Hi Annie. Oi, looks like I woke you. Sorry about that. Do you want a little time to cleanup? I can go run on the beach. Hang with Paul. Whatever." She gave a toothy smile like a chimp showing dominance. She also tugged at a leash.

"No I'm fine, just a little catnap," Anne replied. "I'm thinking of doing this with my hair all the time." She patted her head again, then looked down with a smile. "Who is this little guy?"

Shelli pulled the little corgi roughly by the leash again to get his attention. "This," she said, "is Bart." *Jerk.* "He's my devil dog." *Jerk. Jerk.* "Never listens."

"Here let me take the leash. Come on little buddy," Anne spoke softly to the dog and he ran into the house tail wagging.

"Oh. Okay, I guess. Paul told me there was some rule about no dogs allowed, but that it was dumb and I could bring him if I wanted to." Shelli gave another predacious smile, which Anne ignored in favor of scratching Bart's head.

"Yes," Anne said. "It's a silly rule. We didn't bring Molly Dog but she's so much bigger. This little guy is a button." She grinned at the dog as he turned circles in the sand by the back door. Anne thought maybe it was time for Molly Dog to get a playmate. There would be more than enough room for another dog without Paul's stuff.

And speak of the devil.

"Where's Paul?" Shelli asked.

"He went out early today. He and a guy he met on the beach yesterday chartered a fishing boat. But he'll be back tonight." Even Anne was impressed with the speed of the lie.

"What? I've been texting him since last night and he never answered."

Shelli's smile dropped and eyes widened. She realized what she had just admitted, but Anne did not react. She just looked at Shelli and smiled. It didn't reach her eyes.

"Yeah, we spent most of the night on the beach. Our phones were up here so we didn't see any messages. Paul was so revved up for the fishing trip he decided to leave his phone today too. But he told me to expect you and take care of you."

"What about his watch though?"

"We don't have cellular on our watches, so we have to be by our phones to get messages. The batteries died while we were out on the beach. When I came in this morning I was bushed; never thought to check my phone before sacking out."

"Oh. Okay." Shelli looked non-plussed.

"Hey, brighten up sunshine." Anne said. Her smile grew larger — so many teeth. Her eyes were pits. "He wants us to hit the beach tonight. He mentioned having something special for both of us. I think we might be down there overnight. And if it's anything like last night it's going to be wild." Anne winked.

Shelli returned the smile, weakly. The offer sounded intriguing, but something about her eyes. Shelli wondered if anyone ever told Anne she had black eyes. Kind of dead and unnerving. If she had asked, Anne could have told her that Paul shared that thought. Shelli and Paul shared a lot that weekend.

Lost in Fish Creek Park
Elena Schacherl

Glenna's husband slunk into the kitchen, rubbing his deep blue eyes. He toasted some bread, slathered apricot jam on it, poured his coffee then sat down across from her.

Why do I continue to be so attracted to him when I know what a jerk he is? She waved her fist at Andrew and shouted, "Get out you asshole and don't bother coming back."

He slammed down his mug. "You silly bitch. What's with you now?"

"I dropped by the clinic yesterday, and Jody told me all about the two of you. You cheating bastard."

He twisted his mouth and shook his head. "Bollocks. Why should you believe her?"

"Because this isn't the first time, is it?" She leapt up, rushed over to him, raised her hand and smacked his face—her hand throbbed in pain.

Andrew flinched, sprung up from his chair, stretched to his full height of over six feet, grabbed his briefcase and bolted away. Glenna rebuked herself for being upset at his departure. *Why should I care where he's going? Or whether or not he plans to leave for good?*

*****

After a tiring day at the accounting firm in Calgary's Beltline where she worked, Glenna finished the audits due that afternoon, contacted her clients and went home early. At a quarter to five, she shuffled with relief to their two-storey house overlooking Fish Creek Park. Her elderly next door neighbour Karen—a widow since last year—stood in her front yard, clearing the thick layer of leaves discarded by her birch trees. She waved to Glenna.

"Hi Karen," she shouted then scooted inside.

In the kitchen, Glenna slung her jacket over a chair and sat down, expecting her husband any minute. But by 5:30 p.m., he'd still failed to show up. And no sign of their dog Rufus either.

Glenna scrambled over to the fridge, lifted out a chilled bottle of Riesling, poured herself a glass and carried it to the family room. There was leftover lasagna, so thank goodness, she wouldn't need to make supper—she could relax while she waited for Andrew.

Slouched on her navy leather recliner, beside a bookcase packed with the mysteries she loved to read, Glenna savoured the sweet, cool wine. On her lap, Peter Robinson's latest book lay open. She flipped through the pages trying to figure out where she'd stopped reading last night. *Damn it. I forgot to use a bookmark again*. Nevertheless, she definitely preferred real books to e-books. After figuring out where she'd left off, she gladly escaped back into the story.

Before sitting down, she'd turned on her iPod and was now listening to "It Ain't Me Babe". Bob Dylan's music always resonated with her and usually cheered her up, though not this time. And despite having hoped the wine would calm her down, she remained extremely anxious about her missing husband.

After reading for a while, she texted Andrew—over and over again—but to no avail. She shifted in her chair and wrung her hands. He'd never been gone on his dog walk this long before —never. Although she couldn't count on his fidelity, she could always rely on Andrew to keep a consistent routine. When he got home from work at five every day, he'd take Rufus to the park, and without fail, return by six o'clock. Today he must have gone early, so he should be back by now. And if Andrew planned to not come home at all tonight, Rufus would have greeted her at the door and she'd have had to take him for a walk. Besides, if he wouldn't be here for supper, he'd let her know.

Every evening after his stroll, Andrew would return with Rufus who raced after him toward his food dish. "How you doin' luv?" he always said. His affectionate nature bugged Glenna, knowing how badly he treated her otherwise. Did Andrew take her order this morning to never come back seriously? She'd only meant it as a threat, trying to get him to behave.

She first suspected her husband's recent betrayal when she intercepted a racy text from Jody, the curvy young dental hygienist from his clinic. Yesterday, when Glenna dropped by to confront Jody, she chose a time when she knew Andrew wouldn't be around, because he was meeting their son for lunch. She'd been pleased to hear he was getting together with Jim, since normally they didn't get along.

Their son went to university after high school but dropped out after a couple of years. Now he worked sporadically in construction, barely earning enough to support his family. Andrew kept insisting he finish his degree, but Jim remained adamant that he wouldn't.

Jim had dropped by to see her last week after a bike ride in the park. Sipping on an iced tea, he'd said, "Thank god Dad isn't here. He came by my place the other day, and as usual, gave me a hard time." Jim clenched his hand and pounded his fist on the table.

Glenna sympathized with her son, but was astounded at his degree of anger. Although she herself became infuriated with Andrew after she had lunch with his mistress the other day.

*****

When Glenna had arrived at the dental clinic, Jody stood at the front counter, chatting with the receptionist. Glenna stepped back and listened for a while. They were discussing meeting at a pub after work. *I wonder if they'll ask Andrew to join them.* She approached the dental hygienist. "How'd you like to go out for a bite to eat?"

Jody cringed. "Okay. I was about to go for lunch anyway." She slipped off her white lab coat, revealing a low cut black tank top over a pair of snug stretch pants. Glenna winced.

Soon they sat together in a nearby East Indian restaurant. Glenna had picked this place because Andrew had an ulcer, so she didn't have to worry about bumping into him here. But now she was sorry to be having lunch with Andrew's lover. Although it was safer to be away from the other clinic staff, and despite the enticing aroma of spicy grub, she'd lost her appetite. Yet Jody gobbled down her curry.

"Are you originally from Calgary?" Glenna asked.

"No. I was born and grew up in London, England. My parents immigrated to Canada when I was a teenager. I regretted moving here until I discovered the mountains. Love snowboarding. I'm looking forward to another winter."

"Really? Not me. Snow's not my thing. And are you married?"

"No, not yet. But after all, I'm only thirty."

She was twenty years younger than Andrew! "So you're British like my husband." Glenna crossed her arms across her chest. "And what do you think of Andrew?"

Jody raised her eyebrows. "What do you mean? He's my boss."

"I believe he's more than that. The other day I saw a message you sent him that suggested the two of you are having an affair."

"Then I guess there's no use denying it." Jody grimaced. "We've been seeing each other for months."

Glenna's voice cracked. "And where have you been meeting?"

"We've spent time at my place as well as in Fish Creek Park. But Andrew claims your marriage has been on its last legs for years."

Glenna clasped her cheeks. "You thought you'd help finish it off, did you?"

"Sounds to me like you don't need my help." Jody wagged her middle finger at her, sprang up and dashed outside.

Glenna wiped her eyes with her napkin and paid the bill. Returning to her car, she tried to console herself. *At least now I know my suspicions about Andrew aren't a fabrication.*

*****

Glenna set down her empty wine glass and slid her book onto the teak end table. She got up, drifted over to the living room and out onto the balcony. Leaning over the railing, she gazed down the hill at the park. White spruce filled the foreground, farther back was the balsam poplar forest with its yellow-tinged leaves, and in the background, the snow-covered Rocky Mountains. Occasionally she joined her husband on his walk, so she knew the route he always followed. *Silly me. As if I could see him from this distance. Yet he must be down there.*

She trudged off the balcony and back to the family room. After reading a while longer, she checked her cell phone. Hell, it was 6:30. *I should call Greg. Surely my policeman son-in-law could help.* She tapped his number into her cell. When he answered, she said, "I'm calling because Andrew's been missing since five. Something must have happened to him."

"Really? You shouldn't worry. He's been gone for less than two hours," Greg said in an annoyed voice. But he didn't know about the terrible fight they'd had this morning nor how

committed Andrew was to his routine.

"How stupid of me to think you'd help," she replied and ended the call.

Unable to stand the tension any longer, Glenna decided to go look for Andrew. First she left a message on the kitchen table, letting him know where she'd gone and asking him to contact her. Glenna grabbed her jacket and raced out.

Breathing heavily, Glenna crossed the street and clambered down the precipitous slope that led from their house into the park, her eyes darting in all directions. Chokecherry and Wolf Willow bushes appeared randomly. It'd been quite a warm fall day and hadn't cooled off much. Maybe Andrew had just wanted to enjoy the remnants of summer—after all, it wouldn't last much longer. Glenna took off her jacket and tied it around her waist.

When she reached the main path running past the park office and Annie's Café, she wandered by dry fescue grass interspersed with purple loosestrife, growing alongside the walkway. Glenna had learned about this invasive growth when she'd volunteered for the Friends of Fish Creek Park last year. It'd been a wonderful learning experience and a distraction from her rocky marriage. With dusk approaching, she appreciated the gas lamps lining the path. And as usual, she admired the artistic garbage can adorned with pelicans and a Canada goose, and behind it, the coyote statue. But no sign at all of Andrew. Damn it. Where was he?

The usual plethora of mothers pushing strollers and brightly clad bikers whizzing by were mostly absent, likely gone home for supper. A barking dog on a leash bounded toward her. It was a cocker spaniel, not their precious Rufus. Alongside the path, towered white spruce and balsam poplars with gold-tinged leaves, blowing in the breeze.

Glenna stopped to greet two young women passing by, uniformed Park Watch Stewards. "Have you seen any dog walkers?" she asked. "I'm trying to find my husband who's with our
Siberian husky." They frowned, shook their heads and took off.

After resuming her search, Glenna soon halted at a wooden bench, bent over and read the plaque: "Loving Artist and Rebel". Nice epitaph. She could definitely relate to it. Glenna considered herself a rebel—she always fought for what was right. And although painting was only a hobby, she longed to become an artist someday. Plunking down on the seat, she yanked out her cell and opened her text messages—nothing.

Glenna stifled a groan. Tightness crushed her chest, as she recalled this morning's argument. Despite her rant earlier today, she wanted her husband to stay, but only if he stopped fucking around. Clutching the metal arms of the bench, she shuddered as she reflected on why she'd kicked him out this morning.

It wasn't the first time Andrew had a serious flirtation. With his broad shoulders, intriguing British accent, thick, curly black hair and twinkling blue eyes, women always found him attractive. They were also charmed by his quirky sense of humour.

She often teased him about this. "You should have been a stand-up comedian not a dentist," she'd say.

"You're the funny one," he'd reply, grinning.

Recalling her lunch with Jody, Glenna wondered how her marriage could possibly last. The threat of it ending led her to woefully remember when, decades ago, she'd first met Andrew. After she'd graduated as an accountant, Glenna had taken a trip to Northern England with her best friend Diane.

They'd known each other for ages, having gone to Western Canada High School together. And after she got a degree in journalism, Diane found a job at a newspaper in Calgary. After all these years, they could still spend time together, although it'd been a while—she missed her. *I'll give her a ring and arrange for us to meet. It'll be comforting to confide in her about my two-timing husband. She'll sympathize, since she's never liked him.*

Glenna drifted into the past, recalling how she'd chanced upon her future husband.

*****

On their visit to the Cotswolds, she and Diane had strolled through the streets of the ancient English village, admiring the thatched cottages and lovely flower gardens with vibrant roses and lilies. Then they stumbled upon a square with Morris Dancers twirling around in time to traditional British folk music. "Wow. Isn't this great?" Glenna said.

"Whoopee." Diane clapped her hands. "So glad you invited me to join you on this trip."

Andrew was one of the dancers. A handsome and talented young man, he immediately caught Glenna's eye. And when the performance ended—to her astonishment—he wandered over, introduced himself and asked, "Would you two like to join me for high tea?"

"Sure. Sounds like fun," Glenna replied, beaming.

Sitting closely together in a charming tea room, they sipped on their English tea and shared delicious currant scones lathered with clotted cream and strawberry jam. She learned Andrew was only nineteen years old—four years younger than her. Fortunately, their age difference didn't stand in the way of their strong attraction to each other.

Despite Diane's objections, Glenna invited him to move in with her for the few days they remained in his village. He lived with his parents, so his place wasn't an option. Fortunately, she and Diane had booked separate rooms at the local inn. The time with Andrew was the highlight of Glenna's visit to England—she'd been completely enraptured. It'd been difficult to leave for the next leg of their trip, but she'd already made plans to visit relatives in Scotland, the country her parents had immigrated from before she was born.

*****

The fond memory made Glenna reluctant to separate from her husband. Her son Jim wouldn't mind—he'd probably celebrate—but her daughter Emily would be heart-broken. And so would their angelic grandchildren.

I may be stupid, yet I'm not ready to give up on my marriage. But how the hell am I going to make it work? It doesn't help that Andrew is younger than me.

Today during lunch hour—despite a heavy workload—Glenna had sneaked off to the hairdresser to get rid of her invasive white strands. She'd hoped this would improve how Andrew felt about her. When she got back to work, she'd glared into the mirror at her short, bright orange hair. Her hairdresser had failed to do what she'd requested— recreate the natural ginger hair she'd inherited from her mother. *For god's sake. I don't look younger, just goofy. Oh, what does it matter?*

Glenna brushed her fingers through what earlier had been an immaculately shaped cap, not caring if she messed it up. She trembled, still upset that Andrew had failed to show up. She examined her text messages again—nothing new. And it was already seven. The sun would set in about half an hour and the park close at eight. *Where the fuck is Andrew?*

"Aw, aw, aw." Glenna popped up from the park bench. In the field across from her fluttered a murder of crows. Their nasty cries matched her mood. She nipped on over to the nearby wooden bridge. The gentle flowing creek barely rippled over the mud and glittering rocks. She leaned over the guard rail, fascinated by the racing current farther along, where the stream sloped down. But rather than continue through the open fields ahead, Glenna darted back across the bridge and turned left.It was the path Andrew took at the end of his jaunt.

She hurried down the unpaved, grassy trail, situated a short distance from the creek, and

surrounded by willow shrubs and balsam poplars. The ground was covered with large broken branches, echoing the break in her marriage.

Going this way led to the path back up the hill to where they lived. Illuminated by the fading sun—now low in the sky—some white tailed deer, often seen in this area, pranced among the trees. Another reason her husband chose this route.

Glenna halted by a clearing, where a graceful fawn nibbled on brome grass. The adorable young deer lifted his delicate head and turned innocent eyes toward her before sprinting away.

As she rustled through the fall leaves on the ground, a huge twisted dead tree trunk—bleached by the sun—caught her eye. What was that underneath? She gasped. Surely not?

Appalled, she rushed over, bent down and shrieked—the lower part of Andrew's body was tucked under the tree skeleton. His head was brutally bruised and swollen, as if it had been smashed against the large rock it was resting against. Blood dripped from small dints on the side of his head and flowed profusely out of his mouth. He appeared unconscious, his alluring blue eyes firmly closed within his pale face. She crouched down and checked his pulse. He wasn't breathing! Through her avalanche of tears, she spied some pearly white objects scattered across his chest and in the dry grass beside him. She crouched down to get a better look. Christ! Someone had yanked out Andrew's teeth and flung them onto the ground.

Suddenly she was startled by some branches shaking on an adjoining clump of balsam poplars. An arm and leg emerged from the trees. Glenna's hand flew to her mouth as she stifled a scream. Could it be...? She leapt to her feet and raced away. Anxious to leave the park as quickly as possible, she climbed up the closer but steeper path—near Annie's Cafe. After staggering up the hill, she dashed home down Parkland Boulevard.

*****

Curled up on the family room couch, snugly covered with a quilt,

Glenna brushed her wet cheeks, cradled the cell phone in her palm and called her son-in-law. Greg answered right away.

"Hello Glenna. Did Andrew turn up?"

"No, and you won't believe what I found," Glenna said, her voice broken. "He's lying under a tree trunk with his eyes shut, and I couldn't find a pulse." Someone likely killed him. Otherwise why would his teeth have been extracted and discarded? But she didn't tell Greg this detail because she wanted him to be the one to come, not a bunch of strangers if she called 911.

"Oh my god! Are you home now?" Greg asked.

"Yes, I am."

"So I'll contact my sergeant, and we'll pick you up so you can show us where to find Andrew."

"Okay, but you'll have to arrange access to the park. The gates will be locked by eight."

"No problem, I'll take care of that. And don't worry. We'll be there right away."

An incessant howl sounded. Glenna rushed to the back entrance. Rufus, his matted fur covered with dirt and leaves, bounced up and pushed his paws against her. Glenna stroked his shaggy white and black head. "Poor, poor boy. Come in and I'll feed you."

Too bad Rufus couldn't speak—he'd probably witnessed Andrew's slaughter. "Wow. Wow," he howled as if agreeing.

After she fed Rufus, Glenna stretched out on her couch again, swigging another glass of wine. Mourning the loss of her husband, she flashed back to memories of their life together.

*****

After returning home from that life-changing trip to England, Glenna had regularly exchanged letters with her British lover. And after Andrew completed his Bachelors of Science degree a few years later, he came to Canada to be with her. They lived together that first summer, but Andrew was determined to become a dentist, his long-time dream. Unfortunately, this meant going to the University of Alberta in

Edmonton. Glenna had once more to endure a long distance relationship. At least Edmonton was close enough that they were able to get together occasionally. After his graduation, he moved back to Calgary and they were married.

Andrew opened his own dental practice, leaving them well off, particularly since Glenna was also working. They were able to purchase this two storey dream house with its amazing view of Fish Creek. And soon they had two lovely children—first Jim then Emily. And in recent years they'd created her precious grandchildren—Bonnie and Dougie.

*****

Now with their renewed separation, by his death, Andrew would never be back. Glenna clasped her aching chest.

When the bell pealed, she hauled herself off the couch and hurried to the front door. It was her daughter's husband Greg with a fellow officer, both in uniform. He rushed in and stroked her arm. "Hi Glenna. Emily sends her love. She wanted to come with me, but Bonnie was napping, and she shouldn't have brought her anyway. And after you show Mike and I where Andrew is, I'll take you straight back home."

"Okay. Let's go."

*****

Her heart racing, Glenna stood beside Greg and his sergeant and stared down with trepidation at her husband's body, still partially buried under the tree trunk. They both wore gloves and booties and had made her don them as well.

His forehead deeply furrowed, Greg bent over Andrew and checked his pulse. "I'm sorry Glenna, but I'm afraid he's dead." Greg scanned the leaf and tooth-covered ground surrounding the body. "Were his teeth removed when you found him?"

"Yes. Sorry, I was too upset to tell you."

"Well, obviously he didn't pull out his own teeth."

I'll never see my husband alive again. Despite our faltering marriage, this is a horrible way for it to end—and forever.

"I didn't stay with him, because someone was coming through the trees. And I thought whoever attacked him may be returning."

"What did this person look like?"

"Don't know. All I saw was an arm and a leg before running away." Tears streamed down her cheeks.

Greg strode over and wrapped his arms around her. "Hang in there my dear. I need to seal off the crime area before I take you home. We'll call the Ident team right away, and after we leave, they'll come gather evidence and take photos." He unravelled the yellow tape he held in his hand.

"Surely Andrew's body won't be abandoned here all night?" Glenna wrung her hands.

"Of course not. When the Ident team are done, they'll contact the medical investigator who'll take his body to the morgue." Greg tied one end of the police tape to a tree then extended it to block off the area where Andrew was killed. "And why don't you spend tonight with us?"

*****

After Greg dropped her off, and Glenna was back lying on the couch, she felt under siege. But staying with her daughter didn't appeal to her. She wanted to remain in her own home. *Maybe I should call Diane?* She poked the contact link on her cell.

Her friend answered immediately. "Hi Glenna," said Diane. "Haven't heard from you in ages. What's up?"

"You won't believe this, but Andrew was murdered this afternoon." Glenna sobbed.

"This must be extremely difficult for you. Do you know who did it?"

Why didn't Diane sound more surprised about Andrew's death? "No, the police are investigating. But the reason I'm calling is I wondered if you might come and spend the night with me." Oh please, let Diane agree.

"Sure, I can do that. Anything you need me to bring?"

"Just yourself. Thank you Diane. Means a lot to me."

"First I'll need to pack an overnight bag, but I should be there in less than an hour."

Thank goodness. It'll definitely help to have Diane here. Now I should phone Jim and tell him about his father's death. I do hope he won't be glad about it—that'd make me feel even more wretched. She tapped in his number.

"That you Mom?"

"Yes. I'm afraid I've some very bad news. Somebody killed your father while he was walking Rufus in Fish Creek Park."

"How awful for you. Do you want me to come over?"

"No thanks. My friend Diane has agreed to spend the night."

"Well at least I won't have to deal with Dad ordering me about all the time. And over lunch yesterday, he threatened to disinherit me. But I doubt he had time to change his will."

"I'll be in touch when I find out more." Glenna clicked off her phone.

Soon she found Greg stationed on her front steps. "So want to come with us?"

Glenna shook her head. "No thanks. Diane is going to stay with me."

"Then why don't I bring Emily over in the morning?"

"That would be great."

"Okay. I'll drop her off before joining the other homicide detectives in the door-to-door investigation, assuming Mom will look after Bonnie."

"Will you let the clinic know about Andrew's death, or do I have to?"

"I can stop by first thing in the morning." Greg kissed Glenna on the cheek. "Take care."

"Thanks. See you tomorrow."

Glenna unlocked the door for Diane and traipsed back to the family room to lie down while she waited. She clutched the quilt snugly around her neck. *Fuck. I'm a widow.*

"Woo, woo." Rufus jumped up and snuggled down beside her, rubbing his furry paws on her arm. He'd miss Andrew even more than she would. She ruffled the fur on his pointed white and black head.

With his dark almond-shaped eyes, Rufus gazed back at her affectionately. Andrew's special pal will be shattered when he never shows up again.

In a few minutes, Diane rushed into the house with a backpack strapped to her shoulders.

"I'm so sorry about Andrew," she said, hugging Glenna who'd pulled herself off the couch.

"Really appreciate you coming. Let's put your bag in the guest room. Then I've some chilled Riesling for us to drink."

"Terrific. My favourite wine."

Glenna's shoulders slumped. "I'm exhausted—I won't be able to stay up for long. And I'm too queasy to eat anything, but I can get you some chips and salsa if you like."

She nodded. "Thanks." Glenna brought the snacks and wine to the family room. Diane joined her after dropping off her bag. "So tell me some more about what happened."

"Andrew went missing after work. I went looking for him in the Bow Valley Ranche,

where he always takes Rufus for his walk, and found his head bashed in and his teeth spread out on the ground."

"Horrific! Poor you." Diane took a sip of her wine. "Do you have to work tomorrow?"

"Hope not. I'm going to phone the office in the morning and ask for some time off."

After Glenna visited with Diane for a while and drained her wine glass, she headed to the bedroom to try and sleep. "Thanks for coming."

"Glad to be here for you. Goodnight."

Tucked into their king-sized bed without Andrew was like being stranded on a desert island. Chances that she'd manage to doze off were slim.

*****

In the morning, after a miserable night, Glenna called the office then joined Diane for breakfast. "I'm devastated. But at least I don't need to go into work this week."

"But Andrew was repeatedly unfaithful," Diane said. "So you're well rid of him, aren't you? I'm surprised you didn't leave him years ago."

"Well, he's the father of my children. And despite his lapses, I couldn't imagine living without him. There'd be no fun in my life." *Having never married, Diane doesn't realize what a disaster this is for me.*

Diane shook her head and shortly afterwards went to work.

Alone at the kitchen table, wearing her pyjamas and housecoat, Glenna lingered over a second cup of coffee. *How ghastly that the last memory of my husband is when I told him to leave and never come back.*

"Ding, dong. Ding dong." Rufus trotted into the kitchen, yelping to announce a visitor. Who's here now? It's too early to be Greg. She patted Rufus' hairy head to calm him down then went and found Jim hovering in the entrance, attired in his royal blue work coveralls and orange safety vest. She had mixed feelings about seeing him.

"Hi Mom. I'm on my way to the construction site, but first I wanted to see how you were doing. Losing my Dad must be very hard on you." Jim wandered inside and took her in his arms. He resembled Andrew, having the same special green eyes as well as thick and curly dark hair. Jim, his three year old son Dougie—named after Glenna's father— Emily and her daughter Bonnie were all the immediate family that remained. Her parents had died years ago.

"Why don't you stop and have a cup of coffee?"

"Sure, but can't stay long. Don't want to get in trouble with my boss." He followed Glenna into the kitchen where she poured him a coffee, adding cream and sugar, the way he liked it.

Sitting across from him, she asked, "Were you working yesterday afternoon?"

Jim scowled at her. "No, I had the day off. But surely you don't think..."

"I'm sure the police will ask the same question. It'd help for you to be prepared."

Jim glanced at his watch and finished his coffee. "I've got to go. Want me to stop by this evening?"

"My plans are up in the air at the moment. Greg is bringing Emily over this afternoon, but I'm not sure about tonight. I'll give you a call."

"Sounds good." He got up, kissed her on the cheek, hurried to the exit, turned around and waved. "Bye now."

After Glenna showered and dressed, she scrutinized the contents of her fridge, trying to figure out what she might manage to eat. The door's ringer interrupted. It was Greg. "Come on in. And thanks for bringing Emily."

Her daughter ran up and embraced Glenna. "Poor Dad, poor Mom."

"Greg, did you go to the clinic and tell the staff about Andrew?"

"Yes. Not only were they shattered by the death of their boss, but they knew the clinic would likely have to close, and they'd lose their jobs."

Glenna's voice quavered. "How did the dental hygienist Jody react?"

"She wasn't there. Apparently starting yesterday afternoon, she's taken a couple of days off. The receptionist will phone and let her know about Andrew."

She will no longer be able to steal my husband.

"And I've learned that Andrew left work early yesterday, which is what you suspected."

"Why did he leave early? Did they tell you?"

Greg shook his head. "And I convinced my boss to let me take part in the door-to-door investigation with the rest of the homicide team, since they're short staffed. But unfortunately, after today I'm off the case because I'm related to the victim."

"That's too bad," said Glenna, frowning.

"But normal. And since Mom can look after Bonnie only until suppertime, I'll be back before then to pick up Emily." He waved to his wife. "Good-bye sweetie."

Glenna was back in her reclining chair reading her mystery book, while Emily lay on the couch, watching a Netflix movie. "How's my precious granddaughter doing?" she asked.

"Bonnie's fine. And I pumped some breast milk, so that Greg's Mom can feed her."

"Good for you. I'll go now and make us some lunch."

Although not eating, Glenna sat at the kitchen table with Emily who was munching on some pancakes and bacon. She dropped her fork and her lower lip trembled. "Poor Daddy! What a horrible way for his life to end. I can't believe I'll never see him again."

"It's terrible alright. But nothing we can do about it." Glenna's phone sounded its usual night owl notification. "Need to take this call, but I won't be long. Stay and finish your lunch."

"Not sure I can eat much more, but you go ahead."

Glenna scuttled to the family room and answered her phone. "Hello."

"Hi. How are you doing Mom?"

"Not well Jim, but that's to be expected. At least I have Emily here for support."

"Have you made any plans yet? Do you want me to stop by after work?"

"Probably not, because I'd like to go see Bonnie. But I've been thinking. Shouldn't I be worried that I may be a suspect in your father's death? It's no secret that we didn't get along."

"No, I don't think so," Jim scoffed. "No one would believe you capable of murder. And I'm a more likely suspect. Dad and I were always at each other's throats."

Surely it'd be possible for someone to imagine that Andrew's repeated betrayals would have tempted me to get rid of him.

"I've got to go. We're having lunch. Thanks for calling." Glenna put down her phone.

Back in the kitchen, Emily was clearing the table with Rufus at her heels. Her lush ginger copper hair cascaded down her back. *Such a beautiful daughter. And she somewhat resembles me thirty years ago when I was her age.* "Thanks dear. You want some blueberries and ice cream?"

"Maybe later. I'm full. And my breasts are engorged and hurt. Fortunately, I brought the breast pump with me. How about after I use it, I take Rufus for a walk?"

"Sure, that would help. Hardly slept last night, so I could use a nap. But make sure to be back by four. You don't want to keep Greg waiting."

Returning from the bathroom, Emily fetched her jacket and hooked Rufus onto his leash.

"See you later."

"Woof, woof."

While Glenna was forcing herself to eat a bit of lunch, someone rang the doorbell. What the hell? Who could that be?

On the steps stood her neighbour Karen, frowning. "What's the matter?" Glenna asked.

"Your son-in-law came by and told me about Andrew—I'm so sorry. Greg wanted to know if I'd seen him yesterday. Since I had no choice but to tell him, I thought I should come over and fill you in as well. About four yesterday afternoon, when I was raking the front yard, Andrew drove up, parked on the street and went in to fetch Rufus. Meanwhile, a young woman with long blonde hair pulled up behind his car, got out and joined them. Then they made their way to the path leading down to the park."

Glenna swept her hands over her mouth. "Oh my god, I know who that must have been."

"Sorry to have to tell you this Glenna."

"Not to worry. I'm sure Greg would have told me anyway."

"I know how difficult it is to lose a husband. But how Andrew died was so dreadful compared to my elderly husband's death from a heart attack. But remember, I'm here for you."

Karen scrambled down the steps and trudged to her house.

Back in bed with the duvet tucked under her chin, Glenna couldn't help dwelling on what

Karen had told her. *Yuck. I hate to have my neighbour know about my husband's infidelity. At least now they'll have to bring Jody in for questioning. But why would she have murdered Andrew? I imagine it will be difficult for the police to understand that as well. It would make more sense if she'd killed me.*

Glenna gave up trying to nap, slid out from under the covers, slipped on her moccasins and made her way to the chair where she'd draped her jeans and hoodie. After she'd dressed and grabbed another glass of wine, she went back to reading her mystery. She hoped the story would distract her from her grief.

A howl signaled Emily's return. Her daughter and Rufus joined Glenna in the family room. She checked her watch—it was already four.

Soon Greg showed up. "Done for the day. Need to go home and relieve my Mom."

"Would you like a drink before you go? Karen came over and told me that yesterday she saw Andrew with a young blonde, who I'm sure must have been Jody, leave for the park. I'd like to know what you think."

Greg plunked himself down on an armchair in the living room. "Would love a beer."

Glenna went and fetched her son-in-law a Big Rock Trad. Emily was in the kitchen eating blueberries and ice cream while Rufus rubbed against her legs. "Greg's here. When you finish your dessert, you should get ready to go home."

"How about I feed the dog first?"

"Sure. Thanks Emily."

Glenna handed Greg his beer. "What are you going to do about Jody?"

"Being off the case, I can't do anything. But I did let the head of the homicide team know about what Karen saw, and he's interrogated Jody."

Glenna pursed her lips. "Did she confess?"

"No. I understand she admitted they were in the park but claimed she departed before Andrew did, and when she left him, he was fine. But my boss believes there's lots more that she hasn't told him. He's ordered her to come to the station in the morning to make a formal statement and answer more questions."

"She's a suspect then?"

"Yep. But why don't you come to our place? Bonnie would love to see you."

"Thanks Greg, but I need to be here. I haven't yet written Andrew's obituary."

Emily strode into the living room, wearing her coat and grabbed her handbag. "I'm ready. Coming with us Mom?"

"No, sorry dear. But thanks for your company today."

Emily draped her arms around Glenna's shoulders. "If we leave you here on your own, I'm going to worry about you."

"I've barely slept in the last twenty-four hours, so I'm too exhausted to go anywhere. And you're better off without me."

"Okay. Bye Mom. Hope to see you soon."

After they'd gone, Glenna returned to the kitchen, then the family room, where she watched the local news while chewing on her supper— a piece of toast and cheese. At least she was now able to eat a little. To her astonishment, Andrew's killing was one of the top news stories. Now everyone would know her husband had been murdered. She'd better check her texts and emails to see if anyone was trying to reach her.

"Oh my god!" She found an email Andrew sent yesterday that she'd overlooked. Usually he only texted her, and that's how she communicated with him. But on the rare occasion, when his phone's battery gave out, he'd email her from his office computer. Glenna clutched her cell phone and read the missed message:

> *Hi Glenna. Want you to know that*
> *I'm breaking up with Jody. Will tell her by*
> *the end of the day that it's over. And I hope*
> *then I can return home to my precious wife.*

*Sorry. Promise it won't happen again. And
I'll make it up to you. Maybe we can
celebrate tonight. Love, Andrew.*

So he'd loved her after all. But she'd lost him anyway. Glenna
sobbed. And Jody did have a motive. Glenna decided to go to bed early
and try to catch up on her sleep. Tomorrow she'd write the obituary
and start planning Andrew's funeral.

In the morning, Glenna got a call from Greg. "Okay if I stop by?
Need to talk to you."

"Sure. I've discovered something the police need to know." She
hoped it'd help hold that slut responsible for Andrew's death.
Perspiration covered Glenna's brow as she waited for Greg.

When he knocked, she let him in. "Glad you're here."

Sitting in the kitchen with a coffee, Greg reached over, patted her
arm and spilled the news. "I don't have all the details, because I wasn't
allowed to interrogate her myself. But my boss told me he believes it
was Jody who shoved Andrew onto the ground where he smashed his
head on the rock. They've charged her with murder." Greg rubbed his
hands together.

"The bitch!"

"Removing his teeth and not calling an ambulance confirms it wasn't
an accident—Jody clearly wanted him dead. And we did speculate
earlier that whoever extracted his teeth would likely have a dental
background."

"Well, I found an email from Andrew that explains why she did it.
He was going to break up with her."

Greg clapped his hands. "Do phone the homicide department and
let them know. That will help convict her."

"Have they arrested her?"

"Of course. And the Ident team found a dental pick at the murder
site. It was likely what was used to make the bleeding indentations on
Andrew's head and would have helped Jody remove his teeth. They
found Jody's fingerprints on it, so the evidence is solid. I suspect she

returned to retrieve her tool when you found Andrew's body but took off when she spied you."

Glenna shuddered. "Thanks for letting me know. If it's okay, I'll come see Bonnie another day. I need some time to recover."

Greg stroked her shoulder. "Glad to update you, but please keep it to yourself. Would get me into serious trouble if my boss knew I'd told you. I'm sure he'll contact you before the charges are made public, but I wanted to tell you myself."

"Not to worry. It's our secret."

*****

After work that afternoon, Jim dropped by. "Hi. If you like, I could go with you to take Rufus for his walk."

At least now Glenna didn't have to worry about her son having killed his father. "Okay, it'd be nice to have you along. But let's take a different route than Andrew. Going back to the Bow Valley Ranche area of the park where he was killed would be unbearable."

"Why don't we drive to Hulls Woods then? It's close enough, and we can stroll along the Bow River." Rufus came bounding over and flopped his head on Jim's knees.

"Okay. Come have a drink first if you like, while I get ready. And I'd like you to have a look at the obituary I wrote."

"Sure."

Glenna brought the draft to her son while he downed his beer. Rufus growled by his side, pining for a walk.

When she returned from the bedroom and grabbed her jacket off the chair, Jim handed her back the obituary. "Looks good to me."

"Thanks Jim for being here for me." She hooked Rufus up to his leash, and Jim led him outside. Glenna locked up and followed. When she thought about this being Andrew's beloved daily task, sorrow overwhelmed her. They settled into Jim's old Honda Civic. In the back seat, anxious to get out, Rufus whined. As they drove off, Glenna told Jim about Jody being charged.

He grimaced. "Jesus! Dad was having an affair?"

"I'm afraid so." As they travelled farther, she dwelled with despair on her loss. When they entered the park, Glenna gazed out the car window at the golden leaves fluttering in the breeze. They reminded her of a Tom Thomson autumn painting.

"How's my grandson Dougie?" she asked.

"Fine but he misses you. I'll bring him over to see you this weekend if you like.

"Nice. It'll give me something to look forward to."

"Woof. Woof."

"And as we walk Rufus, let's discuss the funeral details."

"Okay," he said.

When they reached Hull's Wood, Jim got out of the car and let the dog out. Glenna joined them and they sauntered down the path toward the river. As they moseyed along, she reflected on her future.

I'm going to have to get used to being alone. This spring Andrew and I would have celebrated our thirtieth wedding anniversary. Now that will never happen. It's going to be a struggle to not give up on life. But I want to be there for my children and grandchildren.

She imagined Dougie skipping down this treed path behind Rufus. And Emily pushing sweet Bonnie, tucked in her stroller and cuddling her baby blanket. Both her grandchildren were so adorable.

I'm sorry you're gone Andrew. You may have been a cheater, but I miss you anyway.

Have You Seen Rebecca?
Joyce Bingham

"Please come home Rebecca. If you don't feel safe contact the police and they will talk you through the next steps. Mum and I really want you back with us. Please forgive us for not believing you, we understand now." His voice was steady, he looked directly at the camera, she gripped his arm, her knuckles white, eyes downturned.

The interview ended and an advert for online gambling chimed its jaunty tune. I restarted the clip and paused to show Rebecca's mother and father again, their faces haggard in the harsh light of the police briefing. Her mother was pale, withdrawn, and would hang herself two months after this was recorded. He was craggy, all headteacher corduroy and swagger.

He knew where my Rebecca was, I could see it in his eyes. Peering at the screen, I enlarged the image until it pixilated. His pupils were dark, spotted with the flashes and beams of media lights. He lied. Rebecca was mine before, she can be mine again, not his.

I heaved the spade from the boot and pulled out the large suitcase, it was heavy, who knew dead dogs weighed so much, or took so much poison to kill. It was a vicious breed, trained to fight, not like Rebecca's soft Labrador, Honey. Trundling the case along the path took time, I had to pause to scatter the tracks. At a clearing beside the river bank, I lifted the suitcase over the edge of the path. Staggering I dragged it over the ground as the wheels embedded and the soft clay demanded to make the suitcase its own. The hole filled with water as I dug, all the better to suck down the carcase of the dog. I sobbed as I covered it, his guard dog, but never Rebecca's, her beloved Honey died years ago.

Her father's house was on the edge of the estate, a sought-after corner plot but now overgrown with trees and bushes. All the better to watch from the woods behind it. Rebecca's mother must have been the gardener, he had left it to grow wild, with one single well-kept bed of roses. The scraggy lawn was patchy with dog pee marks. He'd been out looking for the dog for days now, distracted and worn out with shouting. *Here Sheila.* Calling the dog after your dead wife was disrespectful. The human Shelia had been delightful, warm-hearted and I could see how well Rebecca would age, their similar gestures, the way they both angled their heads when listening intently. He must have killed her, made it look like suicide.

The door to the kitchen was unlocked in his distraction or maybe he was showing his age, so tantalising, so enticing. You'd have thought he'd have a sophisticated alarm system after the events of 2009, but you needed to switch it on for it to work.

I'd been watching him for so long I knew when he woke, slept, ate and shit. Today was like any other, he wandered downstairs, I heard him call the dog, and he sat on doorstep and cried when there was no answering bark. I howled and screamed when Rebecca did not come home, he deserved to suffer, all he could manage was a few crocodile tears.

He went about his usual day, the grocery van delivered, he collected the rattling whisky bottles, in his dressing gown, dirty slippers over his blue veined feet. Bacon for lunch, the smell drifted out to my hideaway to make my stomach rumble. Dressed in stained clothes, he wandered around the garden, paused to tend his roses and sat again on the doorstep and smoked a cigarette. All the time I seethed; my finger itched to pull the trigger of a gun, but I had only my cunning. I'd waited all this time, a few more hours would only serve to make my longing warmer and sweeter.

The moon was swallowed by ponderous black clouds, the darkness of the trees leaned closer to the house. I paused to put on plastic gloves. The balaclava revealed my eyes, hid my mouth and nose, and kept any stray hairs from falling to betray my presence in this house. After exploring his shed, I tucked his axe into my belt, it might come in handy to open anything locked. The back door was still open and I walked into the kitchen. The fridge hummed and the dishwasher sloshed its way through a cycle.

I'd been here before with Rebecca, we'd come for dinner, to tell them about our love, our hopes for the future. They didn't trust me, claimed I had bewitched her, turned her against them, they wanted a son-in-law not a daughter-in-law. The smell of Rebecca, vanilla and amber, was long gone from this house, replaced by musky dog, whisky and the dust of age. The house was silent and in darkness, the timed lights had gone off half an hour ago.

Evidence remained of the dog, its bed in the corner, deep scratch marks on the sides of furniture. A clean dog bowl waited as if for the soft tread of a new puppy all fur and wet nose. He wasn't fit to own a dog, I'd seen him kick the vicious dog, maybe that's how Honey the Labrador died. He will never know where his dog went, as I was bereft of Rebecca, so he too was snarled up in the unknowing wilderness of heartbreak.

I opened the fridge, I took off my mask and gloves and helped myself to some food, the makings of a sandwich but crammed into my mouth in the order I found them. Washed down with milk my stomach felt full, so comfortable. Then I remembered fingerprints and I washed the fridge door down with the washcloth. The water was warm and I rinsed my hands under the luxury of the hot water, letting it flow down the drain, his money, his problem.

I left the sitting room door open as I explored the bureau, listening for any stray noise. I opened each drawer, meticulously returned items to their original positions. It was a tidy space, pencils lined up and an expensive fountain pen rested on the pristine polished surface. I longed to crush papers, snap the precise tips of the pencils. I did not find what I needed. I did not expect to, he was too careful. This was a blank charade, another lie.

He'd spoken of forgiveness from his serpent's tongue, it dripped acid. The police listened to him; he poisoned them against me. The police hounded me, as if had been the guilty one, not him. They'd ransacked and plundered our home, taking precious photographs and gifts as evidence. He owed me so much after all the recriminations, I saw no understanding in his eyes, no softening of his lips. Each dawn brought another day without her, another day of yearning and pain. Another day on the run, living in my car, career destroyed, he needed to pay.

There was a change in the air in the hallway, a click and a door opened on the floor above. The unwashed smell of bedclothes, wrinkled and sleep soaked, his whisky breath, slipped out of his bedroom and fell in aromatic folds down the stairs. I closed my eyes, counted to ten, relaxed my shoulders, controlled my breath. It was not yet time to confront him.

I heard the creak on the landing, the light flickered in the bathroom, ping-ting, ping-ting. I moved to the first step and listened for more, leaned the axe against the tread. The toilet flushed, the shuffle back to his room was lumbering, each floorboard sang as the wood joists wore against each other. My teeth ached with the creaks; the noise made me shiver.

The bookcase in the dining room drew me to it. The higgledy-piggledy books and papers were unlike the bureau. This was not his to tidy it was her mothers. A book slipped from my fingers. It fell in slow motion, pages flutter-flying like the wings of a dove. Before it touched the wooden floor, I'd caught it, my clumsy fingers wrinkled pages and turned corners. I clutched it to my chest, holding my breath waiting on the floorboards to creak. All was quiet.

A soft leaf of paper, as light as a dried rose petal lay on my shoe. It was Rebecca's handwriting, an address, a phone number. I caressed it, tried to smell her, feel the cells she left behind on the paper, but it was too long ago.

I slipped back out into the garden and in the shadow of the trees I called the number on my burner phone. It rang, once, twice. My lungs wanted to burst; I heaved in a breath as a voice answered.

"Hello? Who is this? Rebecca, is that you?"

The voice was old, querulous, shaking. One of her mother's friends, I guessed. I hung up, cut off further words. Why did I think this was a lead? There were no more words to say, no more crying to be done.

Returning to the bookcase, I noticed the layer of dust, the tips of my gloves fuzzy with the detritus of years of abandonment. He never looked at this, never touched anything, it was unnecessary to search, I would find nothing incriminating.

This was too long a task. My teeth hurt as I clenched them, I pulled up the balaclava and rubbed my hands over my face, pinched the top of my nose, keeping tears at bay. I needed to interrogate him, confront him. The cable ties were in my pocket, it was time. The lead feeling in my guts had begun to fire up, anger pulsed through my veins.

At the bottom of the stairs, I listened, breathed silent gasps. The clock behind me ticked, ticked. A car passed its headlights created a wide arc of light through a chink in the curtain. I waited. Picking up the axe from where I'd left it, I took the stairs one step at a time, pausing to listen.

The boards creaked, just as they had for him. Will the noise wake an old man? Each grinding squeak was like a clap of thunder echoing through the hallway. There was no stirring from the bedroom above.

I clicked off my torch and pushed the bedroom door open. There was no resistance. The room was in darkness. My heart thumped against my ribs, Rebecca, Rebecca. The old man smell was cloying with an underlying stink of disease. I reached out to grab him, to pin him to the fetid bed. There was bare mattress, cold to the touch.

He was behind me; the stale whisky smell and the ammonia of dried urine made me gag. I turned and swung the axe at him. His bony fingers caught my wrist and squeezed hard, my bones ground together. I dropped the torch and threw the axe towards his shadow figure, aiming for his face. I heard a crunch and a spurt of blood hit me.

"Bitch, I'll bury you bloodied and scarred, and I will dance a jig on your grave," he spat the words at me.

"You killed her," I cried, sobs began to rise up in my throat.

A rush of air as he threw himself on me, I was tossed back onto the mattress.

"I've been waiting years for you. We made sure she didn't love you back. We buried her in our rose garden, adored all these years, while you marinaded in your own misery." he said as he sat on me, squashing my lungs.

"Good to see the gloves, I will have less cleaning up to do, no fingerprints, and kind of you to wear the balaclava," he said, as he ripped it off, he took a fist full of my hair and yanked it back, my scalp on fire.

"Watch my face as you die," he screamed, his hands were around my neck.

Rebecca, Rebecca, I called her name as lights flashed in my eyes. I could no longer hear, no longer see, no longer feel.

Teeth Can Hardly Stand
Jeff Somers

Winter always depressed him. It had been many months since he'd been able to jump and run and hunt birds, but that had once been his passion and primary hobby; The People had often chastised him for bringing dead and dying birds into the house, but he had never taken their shouting and cavorting seriously. Birds were dirty scavengers, and he had delighted in abridging their reign of terror by leaping, suddenly and from a well-chosen hiding place, and lancing them with his outstretched claws.

Once, a disgusting bird had its final revenge by giving him worms. He'd gloried in the kill, toying with the horrible thing and imagining its terrible fate would be legend among its own, and would perhaps teach the birds to behave better, to reform. This had been the work of cats for eternity, and Pierre felt part of an unbroken line when he hunted. But then he'd experienced a bloated feeling a few days later, and his trips to the litter box had been unsuccessful, prompting the People to take him to the Dreaded Place, where he was humiliated and terrified as usual. Back home, he'd attempted to hide in the deepest, darkest places in order to convey his displeasure, but the People had found him and dragged him into the light in order to feed him awful things, and then he'd had the terrifying experience of expelling worms in huge, alarming clumps.

All because of a bird. Which just proved how terrible they were, how deserving of their fate.

Even though it had been some time since he'd been capable of the hunt, Pierre still found winter depressing because it meant cold and snow and few opportunities to chase something, to luxuriate in his ability to sail through the air. Winter meant being inside, and being cold. And his first memory was of being cold, so cold, unable to make his own body heat and shivering endlessly in the dark before the People.

He sat, now, on the shelf built next to the big picture window looking out into the garden, watching the first hesitant flakes of snow fall. It wouldn't amount to much, he didn't think, but he found himself feeling small and tired as he watched it.

A small, reddish form suddenly appeared next to him, sitting down without even a feint at asking permission.

"I can't wait for snow," Prince Harry said. "You can really dive into it and roll around and get it *everywhere* and then you come in and warm up and it just melts away like it was never there. It's so much fun."

Pierre said nothing. Harry was a kitten, still, not quite a year old and recently rescued from certain death, and so had a surfeit of confidence. Pierre remembered that feeling of euphoria, of living in darkness and cold, hungry and alone, and then being plucked from doom by The People and brought to live in a palace. It made a cat feel like they were the chosen creature of the world, secure and safe from any possible harm.

The tragedy was, the feeling faded. Pierre felt the ache in his joints and mourned just how quickly it faded.

"Have you seen my gray mouse?" Harry demanded fiercely. "I had it in the corner in the room downstairs with all the cushions and left it there and today it's gone and no one will admit they took it. It's just the right amount of broken-in, and I almost have the tail off and if I have to start on a fresh one it'll take *days* and then one of you will probably just steal it again."

Pierre pondered the fact that he'd saved Harry, and questioned his own judgment. The little ginger cat never shut up.

"Coco snores. A lot. You'd think it would be adorable since she's so tiny, but it's super annoying. I crawl into the back of the closet upstairs to get away from it. Is she really your wife? She tells everyone she's your wife."

Pierre sighed.

"You have a very pink nose. *I* have a pink nose. Spartacus has a red nose. Otto, Coco, and The Beast have black noses. Do we smell things differently? Do we smell in *pink*? Is that why The Beast smells so *bad*?"

The sound of claws clicking on the floor behind them was a welcome distraction. Pierre turned and found a large, muscular black cat sitting like a recently erected statue.

"Hello, I am Otto," the black cat said. "The Phantom has asked if you would join him upstairs."

"Really?" Harry said, leaping over Pierre in an alarming display of dexterity. He trotted over to Otto and sat down in the same chest-forward pose. "What does he want? Did he say? Did he mention a gray mouse? I've lost a gray mouse. Maybe Spartacus took it. Why do we call him the Phantom? Why is his fur so long? Is *that* why?"

Otto stared at Harry for a moment, then looked back at Pierre. "Not him. You."

Then Otto turned and walked away, claws clicking. Harry sat for a moment, then bounded after him.

"Did you know your sister snores?"

Pierre paused to groom his front paw, waiting until Harry was out of range before stepping off the shelf and making his way to the stairs. He took them slowly, one paw at a time, and found Spartacus, aka The Phantom, sitting as usual on the shelf attached to the windows overlooking the gardens. The small, skinny cat with the flowing cinnamon fur spent most of his time in the third floor bedroom, looking out the windows, and saw everything.

"Winter," Spartacus said, sounding dismal.

"Winter." Pierre agreed.

"There is a dead cat in a yard two houses down."

Pierre turned his head and peered out the window. The Phantom sat here most of the day, every day, watching. Things might be happening in the street in the front of the house that The Phantom did not know about, but in the yards behind the houses he saw everything.

At first Pierre couldn't see anything, but then he picked out the small, brown form in the midst of a messy, weedy garden. A pang of horror went through him; dying was terrible. He'd seen old Blue, his mentor in the house, at the end. After a long, good life, the end had come suddenly. Pierre remembered being frightened, because old Blue, who had so often licked his head and batted his ears, simply stared through him, breathing rapidly, all his sense of place and purpose sapped from him. And then the People had taken Blue away, and never explained where they'd taken him. Pierre would have liked to visit where he was, if only to know.

"I'll see to it," Pierre said, jumping down and making his way back downstairs. He went out into the garden, and used a complicated series of small jumps to gain the low wall between his garden and the next. A similar set of leaps got him into the next garden over, where the corpse lay in the midst of the yellowed weeds.

Before Pierre could walk over to the body, two dogs scrambled over the garden wall, barking and snapping. Pierre scrambled back, hissing, and soon found himself trapped in the corner, his legs too shaky to make the jump back onto the wall leading to safety. He pulled himself into a tight crouch and bared his teeth. Dogs, he knew, were savage, and poorly behaved.

"Little cat?"

Pierre hesitated, then raised his head up. "Begby?"

He moved slowly, belly low, emerging from the plants ready to bolt. Begby flattened his ears, and then suddenly sat forward, huge pink tongue flopping out to lick his snout. "Oh, it's you."

The other dog, leaped forward, snarling, and Pierre compacted himself into a ball. A second later Begby was between them, snarling back, his fur raised in tufts.

"He is a friend!" he roared. "He is under my *protection*!"

The second dog was black with a white muzzle, somewhere in-between small and large. He slinked backwards, teeth bared. "If you say so," he growled.

Begby turned to Pierre. "I am sorry. My friend Bear is a little excitable."

Pierre slowly expanded, resuming his normal shape and posture. He watched Bear carefully as the dog paced back and forth behind Begby, offering zero reassurance.

"Hello Begby," Pierre said, shaking himself. He eyed the black dog distrustfully. "How are you?"

"Well. Who is your friend?"

Begby licked his nose and sat down. The black dog prowled behind him, moving restlessly back and forth. "His name is Bear. He has no People."

Pierre considered the way Begby was always befriending the animals that lived outside, and raised his estimation of Begby and dogs in general by the tiniest of margins. He flared his nostrils and took in the rank, damp smell of this new dog. He liked nothing about it. "Hello," he said. "I will remember your scent."

Bear kept prowling. "What do you know of this, cat?"

Pierre glanced at the body. "We saw him from the window. I came to investigate."

"Pierre is very good at investigations," Begby said, tongue lolling.

"Did you know him?" Pierre asked politely.

Bear growled, low in his throat. "She had no People, like me. We met from time to time, in the gardens. She was … kind." He finally stopped prowling. "She and often kept each other warm."

Pierre squinted, lowering his snout in respect. "I am sorry. What was she called."

Bear sat down, scowling. After a moment he snorted. "Valentine."

Pierre rotated his ears. "I am sorry."

Bear leaped up and pawed at the ground, tail thrashing. "Someone has murdered her. *Look* at her! Look what they have done!"

Pierre hesitated, then crept forward, giving Bear a wide berth. He picked his way carefully to the body, the smell of death rising up around him like a terrifying wave. The cat was a small cinnamon-colored shorthair, not young, with a white bely yellowed by years outdoors. Her paws were rough, her claws broken and ragged. She had been terribly bloodied, a rash of deep wounds on her belly and back, angry welts, deep and scabbed over.

Pierre paused for a moment to imagine Valentine's last moments, and a wave of sadness washed through him. He thought of Blue, he thought of Begby's friend Ivory. There was, he concluded, no *good* way to die, and he resolved to stop pretending to himself that he would pass away in a warm bed, with a full belly, with Coco pressed against him while the People scratched his ears and cooed at him. This, he decided, was fantasy. Death was violent. Death was involuntary. Death ripped everything from you when you were least prepared to fight it off.

He took a deep breath, filling himself with Valentine's rotting scent. There was something else underneath the death something sweet and artificial, something that seemed familiar, but he couldn't place it. "There are no claw marks."

Bear growled again, but Begby stood and padded over, pushing his nose close to the small cat's body. "Yes," he said.

Pierre pushed his snout in close to her neck. "The attack occurred elsewhere, not here. There is no blood."

Begby flared his nostrils. "Yes."

Pierre steeled himself and pushed his nose into the dead cat's fur. He startled and straightened up. "Water. She's ... wet. Soaked."

"It didn't rain last night," Begby said, his tail thumping the ground in agitation.

"Drowned," Pierre said, horrified. Death was terrible. Murder was worse. But murder by drowning? He despised water. The few times in his life that he'd gotten wet had been terrifying experiences that left him miserable. To die like that was the worst thing he could imagine.

"The moving of the body," Bear said with a low growl, "makes it murder."

Pierre was about to argue the point, but Begby twitched his snout, letting out what sounded like a wet sneeze. "We should ask the triplets."

Pierre followed the dog's gaze to the large picture window

overlooking the garden. Three small black cats were framed in the glass, skinny and short-haired, their noses pressed against the window as they strained forward to see what was happening.

As he studied them, the three cats began to sing in unison.

Poor smol Moll, poor smol Moll

She was very brave but very small

Pierre examined the terrain near the window, and bounded up onto a plastic barrel, then onto the wound-up garden hose hanging from the side of the wall. This put him more or less on the same level as the three cats, who peered out at him with wide eyes. They sang a single, sustained note of wonder. He could see they were well off, sitting on a downy bed that had been installed on the seat of the window—exclusively for their use, he assumed.

"Do you know what happened to her?"

The three cats conferred with each other through glances, then pushed their bodies together again to sing.

Moll in our yard, Moll in our yard,

Had a nice house but staying inside's hard

She liked to explore she was very brave

She told us about sleeping in the White Cave

Pierre sniffed the air. "The White Cave! What's that?"

The three shrugged in unison, eyes wide again.

Pierre considered. "What house? Whose were her People?"

The three cats shrugged again, pent up behind glass. Pierre wondered if they had ever sniffed fresh air.

He turned and jumped stiffly back down. Bear and Begby were sitting next to each other, a study in contrasts.

"What on earth could the White Cave be?" Begby wondered.

Pierre's ears rotated around, seeking new and interesting sounds. "I have no idea, but it sounds ominous."

*****

Pierre was depressed all evening and the next day. He nibbled his dinner and breakfast and stayed in his old, tattered black bed, head in his paws. He knew if he kept it up much longer the People would lure him into the plastic box and take him to the Dread Place that smelled like illness and blood, but he found himself unable to shake the sense of doom that came in the wake of Moll the cat's untimely death. Sometimes it seemed as if all of existence was just the random luck of existence, a gift that could never last for very long.

At one point he heard the soft tap of claws on the floor, and opened one eye to find Coco sitting next to his bed.

"Husband," she said. "You are ill."

He closed his eyes. "No. I am thinking." He opened his eyes again. "And I am not your husband."

Late at night, when the People had gone to sleep, he made his way quietly to the bedroom on the third floor, and found Spartacus, their Phantom, sitting in the front window instead of the back. Amidst the light snoring and restless shifting of the People, he joined the smaller cat on the sill.

"Look," Spartacus said.

Pierre looked out onto the street below them. It was a scene he'd studied many times, and a new detail immediately caught his attention. Someone had pasted a large poster on a tree with some writing and a photo of Moll.

"What does it say?"

Spartacus flicked his bushy tale about. "I cannot be certain, but People put these up when they search for one of us when we are lost."

Pierre considered this. "Where did she live?"

"Six houses down," Spartacus said. "A family. Children."

Pierre's ears flattened slightly. "We cannot tell Begby."

They sat in silence for a moment.

"How did she die?" Spartacus asked.

Pierre hesitated. "Drowned. Beaten, all over her body. No wounds. A strange smell." His rear paws extended, gouging into the wood of the sill. "Cats who interacted with her on her travels told me she would often speak of the White Cave."

"I see."

Pierre let Spartacus be; he had experience with the cat and knew he often fell into brown studies, emerging with sudden epiphanies.

"Was it sweet?"

Pierre blinked slowly. "What?"

"The odd smell on Moll. Sweet?"

Pierre conjured the scent. "Yes. Floral, but not real."

Spartacus nodded. "Come."

Pierre was surprised when the other act leaped down onto the floor and walked towards the stairs. The Phantom never left the bedroom, as far as Pierre knew—*had* never left the bedroom. Moving with graceful, mincing steps, tail in the air, Spartacus walked quickly down the stairs, however. Pierre followed stiffly, slowly. The Phantom led him just a few feet from the stairs and sat down, looking up. Pierre sat down next to him and stared up at the washer, a white cube the People fed things to, making it hum and slosh as it digested them. Its front was dominated by a large glass circle, like an eye. It was one of the many strange things the People did.

"Soap," Spartacus said quietly. He lifted his snout at the washer. "The smell you described. Old Blue, who you might remember, told me that when he was a kitten, he would often climb inside. He learned to pull open the door, and said it was dark, and quiet inside." He turned to Pierre. "Soap. I give you the White Cave."

*****

It took him almost an hour to make his way, post-breakfast, to the garden behind the sixth house over; a high wall between the fourth and fifth spaces presented a challenge to his aging joints, and required some brainpower to overcome. When he descended into the sixth garden, he found Begby and Bear waiting.

Begby glanced at him and looked away. Bear growled, lips skinning back from his teeth.

"Cat," Begby said.

"What is happening?" Pierre asked, sitting and curling his tail around himself, aware of his escape route.

"They did this to her," Begby said. "The *children*." He snorted and shifted his weight. "Children are terrible."

"The *brutality*," Bear growled. "They will feel it as well."

Pierre's eyes widened. "No! The children did not do this!"

Bear growled again, more loudly, but Begby turned his head. "How do you know this?"

"The posters," Pierre said quickly. "The People came to our house this morning. They told our People it was an accident. Moll crawled into the White Cave to nap. She had done it before, but The People weren't aware—they fed the machine, and it digested Moll. They couldn't bear to *tell* the children, and so they took her away, and pretended she was lost." He struggled to contain his emotions. "They thought it was better for the children to think her alive, and lost, than ... dead like that."

Like that, he thought, with a shudder. He could so easily imagine it: A fine, quiet place to hide. And then, it floods, and begins to move, and you are trapped and no one comes to save you.

No one comes.

"So they *leave* her?" Bear demanded. "They *leave* her out there, like *trash*?"

Pierre bristled. "I—"

"She was one of you!" bear growled. "One of your own! *Cats*," he spat, leaning down, baring his teeth. "*Cats*."

"Bear!" Begby barked, standing up and stepping between them. "Go!"

Bear growled again, a long, steady rumble, his snout wrinkled and his ears flat, and for a moment Pierre thought the two dogs were going to fight each other. Then Bear reared back and lifted his snout and howled. It was a piercing, disturbing sound, and Pierre flinched from it, narrowing his eyes and flattening his own ears.

"Bear," Begby said, more softly. "Go."

Bear snarled, then turned and in a flash had bounded up over the far wall and disappeared beyond. For a moment, Begby stared after him, ears forward. Pierre relaxed slightly, and realized his tail was three times its normal size.

"You defend all the People," Begby said quietly. "You own, I understand. My People are wonderful. I would die to protect them. And they for me. But others?" The dog turned his head and looked back at Pierre, his eyes sad. "You have seen what other People can do. They abuse us, torture us, kill us. And move on with their lives. Yet you excuse them." He turned to face the wall. "Children especially."

The dog trotted over to the wall and leaped over it, effortlessly. Pierre sat for a moment in the garden, alone.

Yes, he thought, turning to begin the struggle home. *Children especially.*

It's Twelve Midnight at Haley's Diner
Glenn Francis Faelnar

"Indulge me for a minute here Chris. Imagine a diner, like this one. It's midnight. The waitresses are clearing tables. The cashier is ringing up someone's order. Another waitress is pouring coffee for this lone man who's sitting in a stool by the counter." Arty gestured his hands to every part he mentioned while he had his eyes closed.

"Wait, I'm sorry. Is this for a movie?" Chris said.

Arty opened his eyes, annoyed by his friend's question.

"Yes Chris. It's a movie that I'm writing." Arty said.

"Oh...." Chris said.

"Oh? What's that supposed to mean?" Arty said.

"Well, it's just that I thought you would give yourself time to rest and regroup after your last movie." Chris said.

"Fuck you Chris. I stand by that movie. I know the production was troubling but I still think it was a success." Arty said with pride.

"Dude, you had a meltdown all through production and the movie was panned by the critics. And didn't it lose money at the box office?" Chris said.

"I'm not saying that it was a financial success. I meant that it was a success from a creative standpoint. I like to think I inspired a lot of people." Arty said.

"I'm sure you did buddy." Chris said. He took a sip of his coffee and was silent for a while.

"Now that I think about it, I never asked you what you thought about the movie." Arty said.

"We don't need to talk about that." Chris said.

"Sure we do. I want to know what my best friend thought about my movie. So come on, tell me what you thought about my movie." Arty said.

"Okay, fine. I thought it…sucked." Chris said with a pained expression on his face. He felt guilty letting his best friend know the truth.

Arty was silent. The whole diner was silent and the only sound Chris heard was Arty tapping his fingers on his mug.

"You know what Chris, you're a shitty friend and that's a shitty thing to say to your best friend." Arty said.

"Look, I'm sorry Arty. But I don't think lying to you would've been better." Chris said.

"Fuck you, man. I invited you to the premiere. You got to meet celebrities." Arty said accusingly.

"And I will always thank you for that. But you got to admit, it was a little overindulgent." Chris said.

Arty glared at Chris. His own best friend thought that his movie was overindulgent. But Chris was being honest. He realized that he would rather have an honest best friend than a liar who's was only trying to ride his coat tails.

"Fine. But you're fucking listening to this new idea. Now close your eyes." Arty said.

"Do I really have to close my eyes?" Chris said.

Arty just stared at him. His eyes were accusing Chris of being a really shitty best friend.

Chris surrendered and said "Fine. Go ahead."

"It was a quiet night like this one. All of a sudden, a man walks in. He makes his way to the counter and stops to look at the menu board. He orders eggs and juice. The cashier asks him to take a seat. The man nods and then proceeds to walk up to the man who was sitting alone. The man who sat alone by the counter was puzzled as to why some strange guy was standing in front of him. The strange man then reaches for his back pocket and then pulls out a gun. Before the man who was sitting could plead for mercy, the strange man shoots him in the head, instantly killing him. Blood splatters everywhere. Every one screams and runs out the diner. The man asks for his eggs and juice. The scared waitress serves him his meal. The man enjoys his eggs and juice as if nothing happened." Arty said.

There was a long pause after that. Chris wondered why. He opened his eyes and saw Arty with his arms raised triumphantly.

"Is that it?" Chris said.

Arty opened his eyes and placed his arms down. "Yes. That's all I have for now."

"That sounded great buddy." Chris said.

"I know, right? It just came to me one night." Arty said.

"What's it called?" Chris said.

"I don't know yet. The title's a work in progress for now." Arty said.

"Oh, okay. But that was really good. And I really mean that buddy. I think that was a good opening to the movie." Chris said.

"That was actually the ending scene of the movie." Arty said.

"What? Why would you make that the ending scene?" Chris said.

"It works as a really good ending." Arty Said.

"No it doesn't. It works better as a cold open. It sets up the whole mystery of the movie." Chris said.

"Hey, this is my movie. If I say it works, then you just have to trust me. I'm also not about to take notes from an accountant who can't even ask his co-worker out on a date." Arty said.

"Fuck you. What does that have to do with anything?" Chris said.

Both of them started arguing over the scene and where it works best. Chris explained his point to Arty, who wasn't giving in and was adamant that his creative vision was better than his friend's. Their argument came to a sudden halt when the door swung open and Arty saw a man walk in the diner. Chris tried to talk but Arty shushed him silent. Chris saw that Arty had his eyes fixated on something so he said "What are you looking at?"

Chris looked over and saw a man. The man had just walked in the diner and stood in front of the counter with his eyes focused on the menu board. Chris immediately realized that this was eerily similar to the scene that Arty had described for his movie.

"Art, this is just like—"

Arty cut him off and said "I know, now shut up. I want to see what he's going to do next."

Both of them watched with anticipation as the man ordered. The cashier rang up his order and the man moved to the side. Much like the scene that Arty had described, there was also a man who sat alone at the edge of the counter focused on his meal and coffee. They wondered if it would play out the same way. It would be crazy if it did.

The man kept walking to the side of the counter. Then he stopped and sat on a stool three chairs away from the man who sat alone eating. As soon as they saw this, both of them let out a sigh of disappointment.

"I really thought that it was going to go the same way your scene did." Chris said.

"I know. It's a shame. It would've been amazing." Arty said.

The doors opened again and that drew their attention. Arty's eyes widened when he saw who just came into the diner.

"Art, is that Shirley?" Chris said in a hushed tone.

Arty was slightly annoyed at Chris for stating the obvious. It was Shirley. She was clearly on duty because she wore her police uniform. He felt weird because this was the first time he saw Shirley after they broke up. He saw Shirley look his way and their eyes locked. He averted his gaze immediately and stared at his cup instead.

"Shirley incoming, brace yourself buddy." Chris jokingly said then took a sip of his coffee as Shirley made her way to their table.

"Hey Art." Shirley said.

Arty was startled. His hands shook and spilled some of his coffee on the table. He moved his cup away and wiped his hands with a napkin. He looked up at Shirley and said "Hi Shirley. It's been awhile."

Shirley stood in front of their table. Her hands were firmly on her waist. Her eyes were locked on to Arty. "I guess it has been a while."

Chris felt every bit of awkwardness that was in the air at that moment. He wanted to go out and wrap a cord around his neck and tie it to a truck and let it drag him across the country. He could only imagine how Arty and Shirley felt.

"Look, I know things didn't end well between us. I just wanted you to know that I have no ill feelings towards you whatsoever." Shirley said.

It took a moment for Arty to respond.

"Of course. I feel the same way. How's it going?" Arty said.

"I'm doing well, you?" Shirley said.

"I'm doing great." Arty said.

There was a long pause between them. The dead air was like nails on a chalkboard. It was unbearable.

Finally, Shirley said "Well, it was nice seeing you again. Good luck on your movies."

"Thanks. Good luck with your policing." Arty said.

Chris shook his head because he knew it wasn't a good response. Arty knew it too. And on some level, Shirley knew it as well.

Shirley walked away and made her way to the counter to order. Arty breathed a sigh of relief. Chris was glad the whole interaction was over. He considered throwing his hot coffee on his face just to relieve the awkwardness of the situation.

"Are you okay buddy?" Chris said.

"Of course. I'm fine as a daisy." Arty said.

Chris knew that Arty clearly wasn't okay. Arty was caught off guard. Arty wasn't expecting to meet his ex at that diner that night. Arty knew that he was going to bump into her someday after they broke up and he had this whole picture in his head about how it was going to go down. But what transpired earlier was far from what he had imagined.

Arty began tapping his fingers on the table. He kept looking over to where Shirley was sitting. He was uneasy. Chris felt like he was about to see his best friend explode.

"She's seeing someone." Arty said, out of nowhere.

"What?" Chris said.

"She's dating someone new." Arty said.

"What makes you say that?" Chris said.

"It's pretty obvious buddy. I mean, why else would she tell me she was doing well? You know what that means right? That means that she's moved on. She might not have said it but that's exactly what she wanted me to understand." Arty said.

"Okay. Calm down Art. You're starting to sound crazy. Well, crazier than usual." Chris said.

"You know what? I'm going to show her that I'm doing well, really well." Arty said.

Arty suddenly stood up with a determined look on his face. Chris saw his face and knew that this wasn't going to end well.

"Where are you going?" Chris said.

"I'm going to get my typewriter." Arty said.

"You brought a typewriter?" Chris said.

"I did. And I'm going to show her that, not only am I a successful director, I'm a successful writer too." Arty said.

Arty walked out and made his way outside the diner.

Arty walked over to the parking lot to where his car was. He always brought his typewriter with him all the time because you never know when inspiration would hit you. Having a typewriter ensures that he had the opportunity to write it all down.

Arty went and opened the trunk of his car. That's where he placed his typewriter. He fished his keys out from his pocket. He inserted the key and turned it then the trunk popped open. He was shocked to find what was inside. His typewriter was gone and the only thing left in his trunk was a dead body.

*****

Arty panicked and immediately slammed the trunk close. "Shit" was the first thing that came out of his mouth. He looked around and checked if there was anyone near. Luckily, there was no one around.

Arty backed away slowly then immediately stopped when a thought came to him. He wondered if it was actually his car. Maybe he opened the wrong trunk. And his typewriter wasn't there so it clearly wasn't his. All he needed to do was check the plates. He bent over and checked. He ran to the front of the car and checked. "Fuck" was the first thing that came out of his mouth when he realized that the car was his.

Arty calmly went back inside and made his way back to his table. He walked casually and tried to show that he was relaxed. He wanted to avoid any suspicion from anyone who was at the diner that night. He slid back in his chair and gave Chris a nod.

"Where's your typewriter?" Chris said.

"Oh, It's at my apartment. I used it earlier today and I forgot to bring back to my car." Arty said.

Chris began to notice that something was off with Arty.

"Art, are you okay?" Chris said.

"Of course. I'm always okay." Arty said. He tried to take a sip of his drink but his hand shook too much.

Arty became jittery, almost paranoid, as the night went on. He kept looking out the window of the diner. He kept moving in his seat. He was the least relaxed person in that diner. This was starting to bother Chris.

Arty kept moving in his seat for the nth time and Chris had enough of it.

"Dude, what the fuck is going on?" Chris said.

Arty stopped. He looked at Chris, his best friend, and contemplated whether he should tell him or not. He didn't want his friend to get roped into whatever it was that happened but he had no choice. He was the only person he could trust to help him.

"Okay. I'll tell you. But promise me you won't freak out." Arty said.

"Okay." Chris said.

"I'm serious. I need you to swear it." Arty said.

"For fuck's sake. Fine, I swear." Chris said.

"Okay. Shit. I don't think you're even going to believe me." Arty said.

"Just spit it out, Art." Chris said.

"Fine. So, I went to my car to get my typewriter. And when I opened the trunk, there was a dead body inside." Arty said.

There was a pause between them.

Chris stared at Arty. He examined him. He wanted to know if he was serious or if he was just fucking with him.

"Are you still mad at me for saying your movie sucked?" Chris said.

"What?" Arty said.

"Look, I told you that I was sorry for what I said." Chris said.

"I'm not fucking around with you Chris. I'm serious. There's actually a dead body in my trunk." Arty said in a hushed voice.

"You seriously want me to believe that you found a dead body in the trunk of your car that we both rode in to the diner together? You're not fucking with me for saying your movie sucked." Chris said.

"Fuck you, Chris. If you don't want to believe me, fine. Go see it for yourself." Arty said. He slid the key over to Chris.

Chris cupped it when it reached his side of the table. He took one last look at his friend to see if he was serious. He did seem unusually rattled when he got back from the parking lot. Maybe it was worth checking out.

"Fine, I'll check it out." Chris said.

Chris got up off the table and made his way to the parking lot. A single lamppost was lighting the entire parking lot and the light was a little dim. The light was just enough for you to see where you parked your car. He got to Arty's car and opened the trunk. As soon as he opened the trunk, a man in blood-soaked clothes with his limbs folded into positions it wasn't meant to, revealed himself to him. He immediately closed the trunk and vomited. Seeing things like that in movies was one thing. It was more gruesome in real life. After he finished puking everything he ate that night, he pulled himself together and went back inside the diner.

Arty saw Chris and was certain that there was no doubt in his mind that his friend knew was telling the truth. He saw that Chris was visibly shaken. He had never seen his friend like that before. He felt guilty for letting him see it but he had no choice. It was the only way for Chris to believe him.

"What the fuck?" Chris said, as soon as he sat down.

"Now you know why I felt freaking paranoid earlier." Arty said.

"We need to call the cops." Chris said.

"What? No. We are not calling the cops." Arty said.

"Are you kidding me? There's a dead guy inside your trunk." Chris said.

"Keep your voice down, you idiot." Arty said.

"If you won't do it, I will." Chris said. He got his phone out and started dialing. Arty immediately took his phone out of his hands.

"Call the cops and say what Chris? Hey officers, we suddenly found a dead body in the trunk of my car. They're never going to believe that. Calling them only ends with me in jail for murder." Arty said.

"Fuck. What should we do?" Chris said.

"I don't know." Arty said.

"Wait, we could tell Shirley." Chris said.

"No way. I'm not telling my ex that there's a dead body inside my trunk. She'll never believe me." Arty said.

"Fuck. Did you at least recognize the guy?" Chris said.

There was a pause. Arty didn't answer.

"What?" Chris said.

"I didn't actually get a good look at his face." Arty said.

"What?" Chris said.

"I panicked and closed the trunk." Arty said.

"Shit. Well, we need to check at least." Chris said.

Arty was silent, contemplating if it was the right thing to do.

"Alright. Let's do it." Arty said.

They made their way back to the parking lot. Arty slowly opened the trunk but not all the way. They opened it just enough for them to see the dead man's face.

"Shit." Arty said.

Arty closed the trunk and walked back to the diner.

Chris chased after him and said "What? Did you recognize the guy?"

"This is bad." Arty said.

"What? Why is it bad? Who was in your trunk?" Chris said.

Arty stopped and sighed. Then he said "The dead guy in my trunk was my landlord."

*****

They were back in their booth. Chris looked at Arty and waited with anticipation. He was curious as to why it was bad that it was Arty's landlord. Arty remained silent. He tapped his finger on the table. Arty saw the curiosity in Chris' eyes. His friend wanted answers and Arty knew that he needed to tell him.

"I know you're wondering why it's bad." Arty said.

"Fuck yes. So, why is it?" Chris said.

"My landlord and I, we're not exactly on good terms." Arty said.

"A lot of people aren't exactly friends with their landlords. I hardly think that's enough reason for you to actually stuff him in your trunk." Chris said.

"Well, we kind of have screaming matches almost every time we see each other." Arty said.

"Did it ever get violent?" Chris said.

"Well…" Arty said. He grimaced, unwilling to share what happened.

"What the fuck did you do Arty?" Chris said.

"It was the last time I saw him. We had one of our usual screaming matches. Only this time, it got physical. We never threw hands at each other. I guess he was in a pretty bad mood that day. He hit me right across my jaw." Arty said.

"Jesus Christ. Did you hit back?" Chris said.

"No. I still had my self-control. I did say something to him, though." Arty said.

"What did you say?" Chris said.

"I might've said that I hope he dies stuffed in a trunk where no one will find him." Arty said.

"Fuck." Chris said. He dropped his head and had his forehead against the table. "Why would you say something like that? And why was it so specific?"

"I might've gotten it from an episode of a crime documentary. But how was I supposed to know that he was going to end up that way anyway?" Arty said.

"Why were you both in screaming matches all the time anyway?" Chris said.

"I might've been late with the rent but not always. It's just on occasion. You know how it is." Arty said.

"Arty?" Chris said.

"Okay. Okay. I was late with my rent all the time. Happy?" Arty said.

"For fuck's sake. Why are you late with your rent anyway?" Chris said.

"Hey, I'm a struggling director and rent is part of that struggle." Arty said.

"Bullshit. You bought a typewriter." Chris said.

"Don't talk about my typewriter, okay? It's still fucked up that it was gone." Arty said.

"What's fucked up is that you're landlord, who you threatened, ended exactly as you said he would. And it was not even on a random trunk. He ended up stuffed in your trunk for God's sake." Chris said.

"I'm going to jail, am I? Fuck." Arty slammed both hands on the table. "Wait. You know what it is? Someone's trying to frame me. They want me to take the fall for the murder they committed."

"No shit Arty. Of course you're being framed. You didn't exactly go out of your way to exact revenge on your landlord by stuffing him in your trunk." Chris said.

"But who would be jealous enough to frame me? It must be a rival director, someone who couldn't stand my creative presence." Arty said.

Arty started contemplating as to who might be the potential suspect who wanted to frame him. Meanwhile, Chris was left staring at Arty wondering how much of an idiot his friend was.

"Wait." Arty said.

"What? You finally realized no one's jealous of you?" Chris said.

"Fuck you, Chris. I realized something else. The person who wanted to frame me would've used my car. There's no way he would've killed and stuffed my landlord in my trunk out there in the parking lot. He must've driven my car somewhere." Arty said.

"Where are you going with this Art?" Chris said.

"I'm saying, if he used my car, then he might've left something inside. It could lead us to whoever killed my landlord." Arty said.

"How sure are you that whoever the suspect was left something in your car?" Chris said.

"It happens all the time. It was mentioned in a documentary series I saw a few days ago." Arty said.

Chris wasn't sold on the plausibility that the suspect made a mistake and that Arty was sure of this because he saw it on a documentary. But they had no other choice. So, Chris reluctantly agreed.

"Okay, fine. Let's go check it out." Chris said.

They got up and left their table. They made their way to the parking lot again.

*****

Both of them searched for any item that might've belonged to the suspect who was trying to frame Arty. Chris took the back of the car while Arty looked around in the front. Chris found nothing in the backseat other than some empty wrappers.

"There's nothing here Art." Chris said.

"There's got to be something there. Keep looking." Arty said.

"I'm telling you, I've looked everywhere. There's nothing but trash here in your backseat." Chris said.

Arty was too busy looking for anything he could find in the front seat to respond to Chris.

"Maybe the whoever framed you didn't make a mistake. Maybe he was just that good." Chris said.

Chris got inside and sat on the backseat. He felt pity for his friend as he watched him frantically looking for any evidence he could find like a madman.

"Let's just call the cops and explain everything to them. I'm sure they will understand." Chris said.

Chris was about to reach out to Arty when Arty suddenly sprung out from under the front passengers seat.

"Aha. I knew I was right. No one's that good." Arty said.

Arty held a leather wallet, with some of its skin peeled off, and showed it to Chris.

"Holy shit Art." Chris said.

"I knew that asshole would screw up. Crime documentaries are never wrong." Arty said.

Arty opened the wallet and looked through its contents. He took out the driver's license and it was addressed to a William Gardner.

"What the fuck?" Arty said.

"What?" Chris said.

"It's just some random guy I don't even know." Arty said.

"So?" Chris said.

"Well, I was kind of hoping it would be a rival director, someone who hated me so much and was jealous of me. Instead, it's just some guy I don't even know." Arty said.

"So what if it wasn't who you expected? We found evidence and now we can call the cops or go to Shirley." Chris said.

"I know. I was just disappointed, that's all." Arty said.

"Well, get over it. Let's call the cops so we can be done with this." Chris said.

Arty suddenly felt something pushed up against his hip. He didn't know what it was so he called out to Chris. He didn't get a response. He started getting nervous because the thing that was rubbing up against the side of his hip felt like a gun.

"Don't do anything stupid. Just slowly get out of the vehicle with the wallet." A voice said.

Arty noticed that it was a man's voice.

"Okay." Arty said. He gripped the wallet in his hand and slowly got out of the vehicle. He straightened his posture. He had his back turned with his hands up from his would be assailant.

"Now, turn around slowly." The voice said.

Arty slowly turned around and saw that the man in front of him was pointing a gun at him. He looked around and saw that Chris also had his hands up and was equally as scared as he was.

"Now, give me the wallet." The man said.

Arty extended his arm. He arms shook as he slowly gave him the wallet.

"Are you this William guy's partner or something?" Arty said.

The man was puzzled by his question as if he didn't understand it.

"What are you talking about?" The man said.

"I'm just asking if you're partners with William Gardner." Arty said.

"No, you idiot. I am William Gardner." William Gardner said.

Arty was surprised at how different he looked in person compared to his photo from his license.

"You look really different, almost unrecognizable, from your license photo." Arty said.

"Well, the DMV takes shitty pictures." William Gardner said.

"You were a little skinnier in your photo too." Arty said.

"Fuck you, man. I've been stress eating, okay?" William Gardner said.

"Okay. Okay. I'm sorry." Arty said.

"Now, here's what's going to happen. Both of you are going to come with me and we're going to take a walk out in the woods." William Gardner said.

"Please man. We gave you back your wallet. Can't you just let us go? We promise not to tell anyone." Chris said.

"Hey, fuck you Chris. Are you trying to get me arrested?" Arty said.

"It's better than being dead, Arty." Chris said.

"Fuck you. I'm not going to jail for this guy. I don't even know him." Arty said.

"Shut the fuck up." William Gardner said.

Chris and Arty, with their hands up, stopped arguing and focused their sights on William Gardner.

"Now, let's get going." William Gardner said.

*****

They all walked deep into the woods. Arty and Chris were both distraught at the situation they were in. William Gardner became increasingly paranoid that someone was following them as they kept walking. With every twig snap and every rustle they heard, he ordered them to stop and he looked around to see if there was anyone there. This made Arty and Chris uneasy because there was a good chance that one of them was going to get accidentally shot by the idiot William Gardner.

To distract William Gardner from the paranoia he felt, Chris said "How did you know that we were looking for your wallet? Fuck, how did you know we were at that diner in the first place?"

"That's a dumb question. I followed you to the diner. I stole his car and did the deed. Then when I returned it, I got hungry. So, I came in to get something to eat." William Gardner said.

"Wait. Were you the guy that just came in when I started telling Chris the ending for my movie?" Arty said.

"I keep telling you Art. It works better as a cold open to a movie." Chris said.

"Oh, here he is again ladies and gentlemen. My friend, Chris, who thinks he knows better than me, an actual director." Arty said.

Chris rolled his eyes when heard what Arty said.

"Okay. If you're such a good director as you claim to be, let's get a second opinion. William, you've heard of him right?" Chris said.

"Of course, I've heard of him." William Gardner said.

"Well, what did you think of his last movie?" Chris said.

"Come on, he's probably never seen it." Arty said.

"No, I've seen it." William Gardner said.

"So, what did you think of his apparent masterpiece?" Chris said.

"I thought it sucked. I thought it was pretentious." William Gardner said.

"Fuck you, man. I don't want to hear that from someone who screwed up framing someone by leaving his wallet." Arty said.

"Fuck you, asshole. I only noticed that I forgot my wallet when I was about to leave and had to pay for my meal. I'm glad I did anyway because I found you idiots there." William Gardner said.

William Gardner looked around and decided that they were far enough from the diner.

"I guess here's fine. Both of you get on your knees right now." William Gardner said.

"Look man, maybe we can work something out. Do you want money? We can give you money. We don't have a lot but we can give you what you need, right Arty?" Chris said.

Chris looked over at Arty and saw that his friend was completely frozen. Arty stood there unmoving and silent.

"Shut up. I don't want your money. Now, get on your knees or I'll shoot your kneecaps off." William Gardner said.

Chris knelt and kept his eyes on Arty, who knelt slowly as well but appeared to be on autopilot.

"Please man, I've got kids." Chris said. He wasn't sure if that would work but fishing for William Gardner's compassion was worth a shot.

"Shut up. I don't care." William Gardner said.

The disappointment Chris felt was clear from the look on his face.

William Gardner pointed his gun at Arty, its tip almost kissing Arty's forehead and said "I'll start with you Mr. Director, any last words?" William said.

There no response from Arty. It was dead silent in the forest. They could hear the rustling of the leaves.

"No, words then? Okay. That's fine by me." William Gardner said.

Before William Gardner could pull the trigger, Arty said "I'm a fraud."

"What?" William Gardner said.

"I'm a fraud. I'm a hack." Arty said.

"Arty, I don't think this is the time to have an existential crisis."

Chris said.

Arty wasn't listening.

"Chris, I know you said my new story was great but the truth is, it wasn't my idea." Arty said

"What do you mean?" Chris said.

"I mean, I didn't come up with that scene. I took it from someone else." Arty said.

"Whose idea was it?" Chris said.

"It was from my assistant, Jacob." Arty said.

Arty started sobbing, uncontrollably.

"It was a few weeks after the movie came out. We were panned by the critics. Some of them were even in our payroll. Ungrateful little shits. Jacob and I got high at my apartment. We got to talking about movies and then he started spewing something about an idea he had for a movie. We both thought it was good. I even told him he should write and direct it. I was going to bring it up to him and ask him if I could make it the next day but he completely forgot about it. He had smoked too much. I was the only one who remembered every word he said. I guess I wasn't that high. So, I took it for my own. I wasn't worried because he would never know." Arty said.

"Jesus Christ Arty." Chris said.

"That's a shitty thing to do man." William Gardner said.

"That's not even the worst part." Arty said. "The worst part is that my movie flopping and getting panned, completely broke my ego. I even spent my last paycheck on that stupid typewriter. I thought it would make me feel better. I thought it would make me seem authentic to prying eyes and producers when they see my script. And for a moment, it did make me feel better. But I'm completely broke. The only reason I even invited you to dinner was so I could eat. I was so hungry for real food."

"But you said it was your treat." Chris said.

"I lied. I was going to pretend I left my wallet at home and make you pay for my meal. I'm sorry, Chris." Arty said.

"Look, I'm sorry that you're broke man. But I still have to kill you." William Gardner said.

William Gardner was getting ready to shoot when he heard a noise coming from behind them. He turned around and said "Come out. Show yourself or I'll blow this man's brains out."

Out of the shadows, Shirley appeared with her gun pointed at William Gardner.

"Sir, I'm going to need you to put down your weapon. You don't want to do this." Shirley said.

Chris felt a sense of relief. There lives were going to be saved. Arty, on the other hand, only felt shame. His shame was amplified when he saw Shirley. He knew she heard all of it.

"Sir, lower your weapon now." Shirley said.

William Gardner uneasily looked at Arty then looked back at Shirley and said "You first."

William Gardner pointed his gun at Shirley and was about to shoot. Without even thinking, Arty lunged forward and tackled William Gardner by the knees. The shot went off but missed Shirley and hit a tree instead. William Gardner fell to the ground and dropped his gun. Chris lunged forward and lay on top of him and grabbed his hands, preventing him from grabbing his gun. Shirley ran towards them. She placed her gun back in its holster and took out her handcuffs. Arty and Chris moved out of the way and let Shirley do her job.

*****

They all went over to the precinct. William Gardner was booked and charged with murder. Arty and Chris were also asked to recount what happened that night. Both of them told the officers what happened the same way. Arty kept looking around and tried to get a feel for what it was like being a cop. He even went up to one and got to ask him a few questions before the officer excused himself because he was busy.

"He probably just wanted to be somewhere else." Arty said. He sat down beside Chris and waited patiently for Shirley. She was going to give them a ride back to Haley's. When Shirley finally came back, she told them what happened.

It turns out that William Gardner was Arty's neighbor. He lived just one floor above where Arty was living. Like Arty, he also didn't have a good relationship with their landlord. But their strained relationship wasn't because of late payments like Arty. No. They didn't have a good relationship because he was dating his landlord's daughter. And it wasn't just a fling or fooling around. They were madly in love with each other. At least, that's what William Gardner said. The tipping point in William Gardner's hateful relationship with his landlord was when his landlord shipped his daughter off to Los Angeles to live with her grandparents. When he went to his landlord to confront him, his landlord told him that he knew their secret. His landlord knew that his daughter was pregnant and that they were going run away together. They were never going to get his approval.

"I'm sorry Shirl. This is all sad and depressing but how does any of it relate to me getting framed? I didn't even know he had a daughter." Arty said.

"We're getting there Art." Shirley said.

"Just shut up and let her finish." Chris said.

"Okay." Arty said. Arty threw his hands up in surrender.

Shirley continued.

William Gardner was furious that he was never going to see the love of his life and their child again. A few weeks after the landlord's daughter left, he planned to murder his landlord. He didn't have a plan that allowed him to avoid getting caught. That was until he heard Arty and his landlord on one of their screaming matches. It was the argument where Arty described how his landlord would die right to his face. When William Gardner heard that, a light bulb went off in his brain and he now had a solid plan.

"Fuck. So, I practically gave him the idea." Arty said.

"See, I told you your insult was too specific." Chris said.

Shirley looked annoyed at both of them. They saw that she was and immediately shut their mouths. This allowed Shirley to continue.

William Gardner had planned to frame Arty for the murder of their landlord. Their constant argument and what he said would immediately be seen as motive. He was going to kill their landlord the way Arty described it to hammer home the possibility that Arty would indeed murder their landlord because he described it. To do that, he needed a key to Arty's car. He planned to break in to Arty's apartment and steal his key. But as luck would have it, Arty came to the fancy restaurant where he worked as a valet.

"Shit. He works at Visage." Arty said.

"Visage? You mean that five star, expensive as shit, restaurant that's always fully booked?" Chris said.

"That's the one." Shirley said.

"Wait. I thought you were broke? How can you afford to eat there?" Chris said.

"I didn't eat there per se." Arty said.

"What the fuck does that mean?" Chris said.

"I needed to keep up appearances, okay? I wasn't going to let my rivals know that I'm broke. They'll have a field day. So, I made a reservation. I got one. It was one of the perks of being a director every one knows. But I didn't eat there. I just hung out at the bar. I got a few complementary drinks from some rich fans that saw me. We took a few pictures and then I left." Arty said.

"And those photos were proof?" Chris said.

"Yes." Arty said.

"Can I finish telling you what happened?" Shirley said.

They both apologized and asked Shirley to continue.

William Gardner made a duplicate of Arty's keys. He followed Arty and Chris to the diner, stole Arty's car, then proceeded to murder their landlord and stuff him in Arty's trunk. Then he drove back to the diner and was lucky enough that the spot where the car was parked before was still empty. He parked the car then went into the diner.

"I think both of you know the rest. So, that's it. You're all caught up." Shirley said.

"Did he mention a typewriter?" Arty said.

"Jesus Christ, Art." Chris said.

"Fuck you Chris. That's the only possession I have." Arty said.

Chris sighed.

"So, did he mention a typewriter? It was in my trunk." Arty said.

"He did, actually. He said he used it to bash your landlords head until his skull caved in then threw it away." Shirley said.

"Fuck." Arty said. He let out a deep sigh, filled with pain and sorrow. "If you find it, will I get it back?"

"I'm sorry but you're typewriter is now evidence in a murder. You're never getting it back." Shirley said.

It was quiet for a while. None of them had anything to say.

Shirley broke the silence and said "Okay. Let's get you boys back to the diner."

Both Arty and Chris gave her a nod.

They followed Shirley to her car and they drove back to the diner.

*****

Shirley dropped them off and then bid them farewell before she drove back to the precinct. Arty and Chris stood there in the front of the diner.

"Wait. Why did we ask Shirley to drive us back here to the diner?" Chris said.

"What do you mean?" Arty said.

"How are we supposed to go home? The cops took your car." Chris said.

"Oh, that's right. They did." Arty said.

Both of them stood there silent. The sounds of crickets were the only thing that echoed in the dead of night.

Chris checked his watch and saw that it was already midnight. "Shit. We're never going to find a bus at this time of night."

Arty wasn't listening to Chris.

"You know, with all the stuff that happened tonight, the murder and all that, I'm actually a little hungry." Arty said.

Arty looked at Chris. Chris glared back at him because he knows what he wanted. It was dead silent between them. No one said anything. Until, Chris relented and said "Fine. But you can't order too much."

"You are a good friend Chris." Arty said.

"Shut up. I hate that you're fucking broke." Chris said.

They went inside and sat at the counter. They order food. Chris made sure to limit Arty's orders. While waiting for their order, Arty told Chris that he had another great idea for a movie. Chris sighed and dropped his head on the table. Arty ignored his reaction and told him anyway.

Trophy Wife
Douglas Soesbe

The first text came as he was about to leave the office.

Hi! Remember me?

Bart stared at the phone number. He didn't recognize it. The 609 area code meant New Jersey, but you couldn't tell anymore; the caller could be anywhere. Even though he'd lived in New York City for ten years, his own area code was still Los Angeles.

He was exhausted, irritable, a long day of calls and confrontation.

He typed angrily:

Who is this?

There was no response, and after a minute Bart decided it was a wrong number. He started out of his office, high atop the Carmody Bank Building. His assistant had already gone home. He felt smug as he walked across the empty floor, expensive loafers tapping at polished tile, a chorus of echoes reminding him he was the last one there. How about that? Am I your best employee or not? At thirty-two, he felt he was inching toward a V.P. slot. He made sure his boss, CEO Daniel Lane, knew how late he stayed.

"I'm watching you," Lane had told him a while back.

Bart was glad. He wanted that promotion.

He got in the elevator, hit the first floor button and felt the smooth whine of machinery, that little lurch in his stomach as it delivered him to the lobby. When the door opened, he heard the ping of another text.

You should know who it is.

He stepped out of the elevator and felt a flush of paranoia.

I asked who this is – I don't play games.

When nothing appeared on the screen he hurried to the train that would carry him from midtown to Briarwood in Queens and the house he shared with wife Claire. He wondered what sort of mood she'd be in. Things had been strained lately. They'd been married almost five years. He needed her. CEO Lane himself had told him how beautiful Bart's wife was. Bart decided that Claire, both attractive and stylish, was the perfect woman to have on his arm when he made it big. It's the reason he chose her.

He heard the ping and looked at his phone.

What do you mean you don't play games? We
played a lot of games together.

Stop texting me!

He went through his contacts, trying to find the number, but it wasn't there.

They got to his stop, he stepped off the train, and had walked only a few steps when another text arrived.

I miss you. We had so much fun. Did your wife find out?

And then he knew. He came to a dead stop. He felt the lurch in his stomach again, but this time it wasn't the elevator.

Is this Cheryl?

Hours seemed to pass.

Yes.

What do you want?

I'll tell you later.

Bart fumbled with the phone, as if he could will her to answer, but the screen was blank and the phone silent. He should have known it was Cheryl Rhodes. The affair was ill-advised, he knew. She was a temp secretary, an actress wannabe from an agency. He took her out for drinks one night, and it wasn't long until he took her to a hotel. After a few more secret meetings, they fell out of contact. He hadn't seen or thought about her in months.

How stupid could he be? This could torpedo his promotion. CEO Lane was a widower. His marriage had been happy. He liked his V.P.'s happily married, too.

"Of the three candidates, your marriage seems the most stable," CEO Lane had told him.

Bart reached his townhouse. They'd bought it three years ago, a bargain, and they'd been happy there, a cozy nest that throbbed with mounting equity, but he knew they'd have to buy something better when he got his promotion. After all, a V.P. needed better digs.

He went inside.

"Claire?"

"In here," she called from the kitchen.

He already smelled the aroma of something delicious. His wife was an excellent cook, too. Everything about her was perfect. He thought of that phrase again, "trophy wife." How could he have endangered it so?

He walked to a hall mirror. He straightened his hair, and at the same time tried to adjust his mood. He didn't want Claire to see how anxious he was.

Claire was at the stove, stirring a pot.

"Your mom's spaghetti sauce?"

"That's right," she said.

Bart put his arms around her from behind, enveloping the petite body, slender and always fit. Her skin was olive, smooth, her black hair a gift from her Italian heritage. He wondered again how he could be so lucky. How could a kid from L.A. who'd graduated from a nothing college end up with a great job in New York City and a perfect wife?

"Almost ready," she said, pulling away gently, walking to the refrigerator.

Bart turned away with the dutiful moves of a cooperative husband and went upstairs. As he did, he peeked again at his phone. No messages. He changed into jeans and a pullover. Washing his face, he tried to convince himself the texts were a mistake.

But she'd said her name was Cheryl!

He pictured her face, the way he'd usually seen it, softly lit in that little bar over on 57th. He remembered the night she agreed so readily to go to a hotel with him. All that sweet surrender now felt like a crime.

Stupid! Stupid!

It had gone on for over a month. And the texts were correct. They had played a lot. That is, if playing is what one chose to call it.

"You coming down?" Claire called to him.

"Right away, honey," he said, and he heard the fake good cheer in his tone. Would she see right through it?

Bart hurried down the stairs, as if a prompt arrival at the dinner table would absolve his guilt. He ate his dinner with gusto, complimenting his wife with every bite. He helped with the dishes; they watched a little TV and then went to bed. All the time, he kept checking his phone.

"Work?" she asked when she noticed his preoccupation.

"Always," he said with a shrug, and then put the phone away. He didn't want to arouse suspicion. He slept fitfully that night, the phone turned off. At just after five, he slipped out of bed.

"You okay?" Claire mumbled beside him.

"Thought I'd get an early start," he said.

He entered the bathroom and turned on the phone. There were several messages.

> *Where are you?*
> *Are you avoiding me?*
> *Think you can just ignore me?*
> *I suppose you're with her!*

The final one scared him.

> *What do you think she'd do if she knew about us?*

Once he'd left the house, he typed.

> *This is Cheryl, right?*
>> *Cheryl? Is that who I am?*
> *Stop playing games!*
>> *Such a nervous boy. Okay, you're right. This is Cheryl.*
> *I thought so.*
>> *Wow. It didn't occur to you right away? How*

many affairs have you had?

What do you want?

The screen went blank again. He waited a few minutes, but when no message appeared, he headed for his train.

Bart's early rise paid off when he got to the office. CEO Lane was in his office. Bart waved at him as he passed the glass enclosure. Lane signaled him to enter.

"You really do come in early, don't you?"

"Yes, Sir," he said, adding, "I was the last to leave yesterday, too."

"Very good."

CEO Lane was in his late sixties. He was a slender man, not unhandsome. The expensive grey suit lent him an additional air of distinction.

"I'm getting close to a decision," Lane said.

"I appreciate that, Sir."

"It's you, Philips, or Bryer."

Bart quickly pictured his two rivals, hating them both for their competition.

Lane shook his head. "There's a problem with Bryer, though."

"Oh?"

"Yes," Lane said, sitting back, his delicate hands forming a steeple before him. "I understand there's trouble with his marriage."

"I'm sorry to hear that."

"I am too," Lane said. He leaned forward. "Grace and I were married for thirty-six years," he said, "most of them happily."

"That's impressive, Sir."

"Not impressive. It's the way it should be. If she hadn't passed, we'd still be happily married. You see, I believe a man's marriage is a reflection of his character. A successfully managed marriage is the sign of a successfully managed career."

Bart nodded dutifully.

Lane smiled. "I'm fond of your wife… Claire, isn't it?"

"Claire. Yes."

"A fine lady, I'm sure."

"She is."

Bart felt a damp rise of sweat along his forehead as he made his way to the coffee room. He flicked on a light, poured grounds into a paper cone, placed it in the coffee maker, waiting for it to finish. He felt the lack of sleep. He needed the jolt.

He checked his phone as he entered his office.

Nothing.

A part of him wanted to pretend that it wasn't happening, that it was a wrong number, a kid's prank, but as he sat at his desk, firing up his computer, he knew it was real. He checked his emails, shocked to find one from Cheryl.

> *Thought you'd like a relief from the phone. Did you think I'd gone away?*

How did you get my email address?

> *I'm resourceful.*

Bart took a deep breath.

Okay. What do you want?

> *What I always wanted. You!*

That's impossible. You know I'm married.

> *Didn't seem to bother you when we spent time at the hotel.*

Why now?

> *Why not?*

He slid his phone across the desk, so that he couldn't see the screen. He finished his coffee and went for another. When he returned he saw that his assistant, Diane, an efficient woman in her fifties, was at her carrel.

"You're early," she said.

"I've been here two hours."

"I see you already have coffee," she said

"Yes."

"Did you want to roll calls?"

"Later," Bart said, more curtly than he intended. He caught Diane's look of hurt, but he couldn't be bothered. He entered his office, shut the door and sat at his desk. He took a large gulp of coffee. He grabbed the phone and typed.

Let's cut the nonsense. What do you really want?

I told you.

Let's get real.

You shouldn't have dropped me.

Nobody dropped anybody.

That's not what I felt.

Money? Is that what you want?

Money's nice, but no.

You implied you were going to tell my wife.

I've thought about it.

What good would it do?

A long time passed, and then:

It would show everyone the kind of person you really are.

Bart felt that lurch again, only this time it was like falling fourteen floors without the benefit of an elevator.

Bart typed:

Where do you live?

That's right. You never knew.

You never told me.

Would you have cared?

I guess not.

Why do you want to know?

Bart was careful with the next message. He tried not to sound angry.

I thought maybe we should talk.

About what?

Us.

Is there an us?

That's why we should talk.

Her answer took a moment.

As long as "us" doesn't include Claire.

Bart startled:

How did you know my wife's name?

You told me.

Bart thought about the times they had seen each other. Had he? He couldn't remember.

I need to see you.

Got you scared, huh?

Confused maybe.

Talk to you later.

The screen went blank. He buzzed Diane.

"Let's roll those calls," he said to her.

Bart spent the next few hours on business. There were no more texts. He felt a new confidence as he left the office that evening, once again the last to leave. Once home, he greeted Claire with cheer. This time she broiled two thick steaks, serving them with baked potatoes and asparagus. They chatted as they dined, managing a laugh or two, and Bart, as he sliced off a final delicious bite of sirloin, was as relaxed as he'd been since Cheryl's first text.

But then:

"Oh," Claire said, "do you know someone named Cheryl?"

Bart tried his best not to choke on a hunk of asparagus. He lay down his fork, and looked Claire in the eye. He measured her suspicion, and then managed a shrug.

"Cheryl? I don't think I know a Cheryl. Why?"

"I got a weird text today."

"Oh?"

"Yes. It said, you don't know me but my name is Cheryl."

Bart swallowed hard. "That's strange." he said.

"Yeah," she said, delivering a small piece of steak to her mouth.

"So, um, what did you do?"

"I texted back, asking who she was, but that was it. Nothing more."

Bart wanted to feel relieved, but he knew there was nothing to feel relieved about. Cheryl was intensifying her game.

"Oh, well," he managed, "probably just a wrong number." He affected a nonchalant laugh. "I've done that before…"

"What?"

"Sent a wrong text."

He noted her puzzled expression.

"Sent a text to the wrong person, I mean."

"Oh."

They ate their remaining dinner in silence. Bart helped her with the dishes, as he always did, eager to be cooperative. It was important now to stress their partnership. But as he stacked the last plate in the dishwasher, he excused himself and went upstairs. He carried his phone into the bathroom, locking the door behind him.

Why did you text my wife? What are you up to? What do you want?

Bart waited there amidst the sparkling spotlessness of the bathroom, another example of Claire's perfection. They lived in a perfect world. He must be careful not to destroy it.

Bart flushed the toilet for effect and went downstairs. He was careful to add bounce to his steps. Claire knew him well. She could read his mood by the way he walked -- slow, fast, or with a lazy, morbid shuffle. She had told him such before.

He found her in the den. The TV was tuned to a documentary.

"Wonderful dinner," he said, passing her chair. He sat in one of his own. "I've been meaning to watch this documentary," he said, having no idea what it was. His aim was to please her.

"A gorilla sanctuary," she said. "Isn't it wonderful how they're trying to preserve them?"

"Oh, yes," he said, fearing his eagerness to agree was too contrived.

Bart fixed his gaze on the TV. He tried to concentrate. He was eager for distraction. But as he watched a gorilla pound its chest, a gesture of intimidation, he could not help but impose Cheryl 's face upon the confident beast.

Bart had difficulty sleeping. He kept the phone off, not wanting the ping of another text to awaken Claire. In the morning, as he readied himself for work, he saw there were no new messages.

He worried now what Cheryl's next move would be. He had wanted to peek at Claire's phone to see if Cheryl had contacted her again, but he didn't find the opportunity. Claire had a habit of going to sleep with her phone beside her in the bed, beneath the covers.

Diane greeted Bart at the office with a chipper attitude and he tried to be chipper back. He felt anything but chipper as she went over the call sheet with him. For the next few hours he lost himself in the urgency of financial deals. All the while, he texted Cheryl.

What are you doing? Why did you contact my wife?

The screen stayed blank.

He went to lunch by himself, a rarity. He chose an out of the way sandwich shop on Columbus. He needed to be alone. He ordered a large pastrami sandwich with coleslaw and fries. He hadn't thought he was hungry but he devoured it ravenously. The pleasure of eating distracted him, but only briefly. He sipped a bottled beer and wondered what he should do. He thought of telling Claire the whole story, but if she walked out on him, his promotion would be in jeopardy.

He felt better as he walked back to the office. The air was clear, the sky blue, and the sun felt good upon his face, but the pleasant mood vanished as he grew closer to his office. In the elevator, riding up to his floor, popping a breath mint, he decided there could be a way out. If Cheryl no longer existed, the problem didn't exist. He thought again of the gorilla, pounding its chest, asserting its superiority.

Bart hurried past his assistant Diane, worried she'd smell the beer on his breath. He shut the door and sat at his desk. Diane buzzed and read off his call sheet. He made the calls dutifully, as if to prove he was an executive worthy of promotion.

Still no texts from Cheryl.

Once the calls were finished, he typed:

Where are you?

The answer came so quickly it startled him.

Right here! Where else would I be?

I asked you what you wanted. And don't say it's 'me.'

Can we cut to the chase?

She offered a smiley emoticon:

> ☺ *Cut to the chase! You always used that expression. What was I? The chase? Was that it? Cut to the chase when you're tired of your wife?*

Bart kept his temper.

I'd like to see you.

> *Really?*

Yes.

> *Why?*

To talk. What else?

> *About what?*

Stop playing games! You know what!

Another angry emoticon.

> 😾

Sorry. I'm just frustrated.

> *I'll bet you are.*

Why don't I come to your place?

A long pause.

> *All right.*

Where do you live?

> *I'll get back to you.*

When?

A blank screen.

> *Are you there?*

He waited a few minutes, but she was gone again.

He needed to get away and think. He thought of telling Diane he wasn't feeling well, but perfect attendance was another diamond he'd been polishing for CEO Lane. The perfect, dependable employee. Never late. Never absent.

That night, he caught his train on time, wishing the trip were longer, as he cherished the moments alone. He needed time to think. He didn't want to ruminate in front of Claire, because she'd know something was up. She hated it when he was preoccupied. He imagined she saw it as disinterest. He couldn't blame her, really, because it often was.

Bart clenched his fists, and as he did he felt the strength of his hands. They were large hands, not used to hard labor, but they were strong nonetheless.

Maybe they could be of use.

The next two days passed as if all were normal. There were no more texts. When he couldn't stand it any longer, he typed:

What's going on? Why the silence?

Surprisingly her text came at once.

You sound upset.

Of course I'm upset.

Not sure I'd like to be around you right now.

I'm not that upset.

You sound like it.

Who wouldn't be?

I mean, I'm not sure I'd be safe around you.

The response startled him.

That's absurd.

Is it?

Of course. I mean, you think I'd harm you?

He waited a long time, staring at the blank screen.

A response came:

Okay. Maybe we should meet. Decide what to do.

Weekends are best.

And they were. Not only was it not a work day, but Claire always spent Sunday afternoon with a friend.

Sunday, late morning, to be specific. Maybe around eleven.

A long pause, then:

Okay.

I'll need your address.

The address was a condo on East 57th. Bart felt at ease now that they'd made arrangements to meet. It gave him the feeling he was on the way to solving the problem. He was cheerful that evening with Claire.

"You seem in a good mood," she said after they'd finished another of her magazine-cover dinners.

"Because I'm with you," he said as she closed the dishwasher and he brought her into his arms. He felt resistance, and he worried he was overdoing it.

There were no texts that evening, yet he couldn't sleep. It was two days until Sunday and he lay there scripting in his head what he would say to Cheryl. Claire slept soundly beside him. He found comfort in the easy, steady rhythm of her breathing. Things would be all right: He could keep his trophy wife.

As he got out of the shower the following morning, he looked at his phone on the bathroom counter. A text had arrived.

He picked up the phone:

I'll see you in forty-eight hours.
Don't text me when I'm at home with Claire.
You're lucky I don't text her directly.
If you do, you'll be sorry.
Don't threaten me!

Bart clicked off the phone, got dressed, and went downstairs.

"You want breakfast?" Claire asked.

"I'll be fine," he said. "Running late."

She was seated at the kitchen table, still in pajamas and robe. He leaned down to kiss her on the forehead.

"Bye," she said.

Bart's anger with Cheryl festered the whole way to the office. It persisted through the day, and although he kept up with his calls and was even-tempered with Diane, he felt a gathering rage. Not hungry, he skipped lunch, occupying the afternoon with yet more calls. Always at the back of his mind was how much he hated this woman for interfering with his life. He had to do something.

Maybe something desperate.

He stayed in his office late again, certain everyone had gone. Once he left the building, he found his way to the address he'd located on Google. The shop's name GUN was as simple and brutal as its product. He hesitated before going in. He didn't know much about guns, but he did know that in New York a permit was needed before buying one. That was too long of a wait, he knew. He looked in the large glass window. The guns he saw displayed on a back wall seemed glorious but out of reach. He imagined a bright flash, an explosion of powder, a rush of blood as Cheryl fell to the floor. He was about to enter the store when it occurred to him what a foolish move it was. Even if he had a license, buying a gun two days before his mistress was murdered? Not smart.

He tried to relax once he was on the train, but he was far too distracted. His mind raced with scenarios of what might happen at Cheryl's. What would she want? Money? A job? A wish to continue the relationship? The possibilities angered him. He clenched his fists. Again and again. And as he did, he studied them. His hands were strong. Very strong.

They might come in handy.

Sunday came quickly, or at least it seemed that way to Bart. On one hand he looked forward; on the other he dreaded it. There had been no more texts.

As was her weekly custom, Claire dressed in a simple but elegant black cocktail dress, did her make-up and readied for her weekly lunch with her best friend Nikki.

"Where are you two having lunch today?" Bart asked. He hoped it wasn't anywhere near Cheryl's apartment.

"Torchia's," she said.

Bart nodded. "Very nice," he said, knowing that the cozy little Italian restaurant was many blocks away from Cheryl's apartment.

"You look lovely," he said.

"Thank you."

And he meant it. At moments such as this he couldn't believe his good fortune. He led her to the front door, kissed her, and sent her on her way.

Now that he was alone, just two hours before his appointment, he felt a strength he hadn't felt in days. He was about to take care of business.

He would end this ridiculous obstacle to his dream of a perfect life.

A cab would have been easier, but Bart didn't want a witness to his whereabouts. This required walking a long way after getting off the train, but he didn't mind. The day was sunny but a snap of cold air pursued him as he hurried toward his destination.

He reached Cheryl's condo, a venerable old building that nonetheless had fallen into neglect. He waited outside the entrance for someone to exit the main door, entering swiftly, keeping his head down. Once in the lobby, he reached in his pockets and pulled out leather gloves.

The elevator was slow and noisy, lurching all the way to the fourth floor. The doors shuddered open as if they might not make it, so Bart helped them along by pulling them apart with his gloved hands.

Cheryl lived in 418. He walked down the dimly lit hallway, hoping no one else would happen by. The hallway was grim and exuded the odor of disinfectant that barely covered a stench of old decay.

With each step down the hallway he felt stronger, ready, and almost sexy, as if some other being were taking hold of him. He clenched his fists again, measuring their strength.

He reached her door. He was about to knock when he saw that the door was open just a crack. A jolt of surprise threatened his resolve, but he took a deep breath. He rapped knuckles lightly against the old door. He didn't call out her name because he didn't want neighbors to hear his voice. After a moment, he pushed the door open gently. He took a step inside. The living room smelled as bad as the hallway. A pall of medicinal scent pushed up his nose, as if someone had forced it there. The room was decorated too neatly for the building. It didn't match.

He called out in a low voice. "Cheryl?"

The rooms stayed silent and cold.

He looked into the tiny kitchen. The counters were neat, almost empty. There was a tiny stove and refrigerator. The room spoke to him of a loneliness that felt closer to panic.

He stepped carefully, not wanting to be heard in the unit below. He crossed into a hallway. There was a bedroom to his left, a bathroom to his right. He stepped into it. And it was then he saw Cheryl. She lay sprawled on the bathroom floor. He heard himself gasp, but it could have been someone else he heard. He did not feel as though he existed in this moment.

He stepped closer. It was obvious she was dead, and the closer he got, it was clear to him by the red marks on her throat, the twist of her mouth, slightly open, that someone had done what he had intended to do himself.

Bart stood in shock, and as he raised his hands in the air to touch his face, he wondered crazily if he had done the deed and had somehow forgotten, as if there had been a section cut out of his life, as though a splice in a film.

But he knew he hadn't. And he knew he had to run.

Bart stumbled his way to the living room. He waited at the door, pushed it open gently, checking that the hallway was empty. When he saw it was clear he ran. He avoided the elevator and went down the stairs, taking two or three at a time, nearly falling. He dreaded running into someone, but his luck held. It was if this old building were empty of everything except the strangled corpse of Cheryl Rhodes.

His luck held as he ran through the lobby, but when he got to the front entrance he saw the red and blue flash of police vehicles.

They must be here for something else he thought. How could they have been alerted so fast? And who would have called them?

He continued out the door. He nearly fell as he made a sharp turn, running away from the police cars. He had not run so fast since his teenage days. And although he kept up the speed, he felt how much it taxed him now that he was older. His throat burned with the fast intake of air. His feet hurt. His knees hurt.

But he kept on running.

He knew the city. He knew it well enough to know where Torchia's was, the restaurant where Claire had met her friend for lunch.

What would he say when he got there?

With brisk air pushing against his face as he ran he decided he'd tell her he'd gotten bored, that he thought he'd surprise her for lunch. He knew she would find it odd, out of character, but perhaps it might do some good in warming up their cooling relationship.

He ran across intersections, not caring about traffic. He hopped out of the way of honking cars and cabs, nearly knocked down a woman who held a bundle of packages, hearing her angry cries of protest as he advanced down the sidewalk, finding his way through the snaking phalanx of people.

At last he figured he was close to Torchia's. He saw its red and green sign down the block. Almost there. Almost there.

He realized he was sweating. He stopped as he approached the restaurant, patting at his shirt, which was soaked through. He wiped his face the best he could with his hands, but it did little good.

He got to the entrance door and pushed it open.

A startled maître d' noticed his condition as he ran inside.

"May I help you, Sir?"

He was so out of breath he could barely speak. "I think my wife is here."

Bart looked around the crowded restaurant.

And he saw her. Way at the back.

"There she is," he said to the maître d', and he started toward her.

As he got closer he saw that she hadn't noticed him yet.

But who was that sitting opposite her?

It wasn't her girlfriend Nikki. It was a man.

He stopped a few feet back. Claire saw him, and even from several feet away he could see how she sat back in surprise. Her lips moved, but he could not tell what she said. The man who sat across from her turned to look.

Bart's mouth opened in shock when he saw that the man was CEO Lane.

Bart thought he must be in some kind of mad, crazy dream, a nightmare that had begun the moment he had entered Cheryl's apartment.

He heard sounds behind him, but before he could turn to see who it was he heard a loud male voice.

"Hands over your head."

Bart did as instructed. He knew who it was. The police had caught up with him. In a strange way he preferred this outcome than going to the table where his wife inexplicably sat with his boss.

Two policemen turned him around and cuffed him. They led him out of the restaurant, passing by the worried maître d', the tables of patrons looking in his direction.

Claire turned to CEO Lane.

"What in the world?"

He shrugged shoulders beneath the silk fabric of his expensive suit.

"I'd better go see what's going on," she said.

"I understand."

She reached across the table and touched his hand. "I'm sorry he had to find out this way."

"I have a feeling that's the least of his worries," CEO Lane said. He started to get up. "I'll get my car."

"Better I get a cab," she said. "I need to go find out what's going on."

Claire raced out of the restaurant, and as she did CEO Lane watched her. He was sorry the way things had worked out. He would have preferred a better outcome. His affair with Bart's wife Claire had gone so well until now. It was only a matter of time before Bart found out.

He turned back to his plate, a generous serving of fettuccine alfredo. There was no use letting it go to waste.

The maître d' hurried over to him. "I'm so sorry about the

disturbance, Mr. Lane. We'll gladly comp your lunch."

"Not to worry. I'm fine."

The maître d' thanked him and scurried away, making apologies to other tables.

And as CEO Lane resumed eating his meal he truly did feel that things were fine. Long before he had taken up with Claire he had succumbed to the charms of Cheryl Rhodes. But once he threw her over for Claire her texts became a nuisance. Dangerous. Cheryl had threatened to complain to the board. They didn't take kindly in these MeToo days to what she would claim was sexual harassment.

A luscious strand of fettucine worked through his mouth and down his throat.

He felt the burner phone in his pocket. The one he intended upon tossing into the East River after lunch. The one he had used to text Bart. He had merely followed the script that Cheryl had written, sending Bart the same texts that she had sent to him, adlibbing the rest according to Bart's responses.

It had gone as planned. He had managed to work Bart into the same frenzy that Cheryl had worked CEO Lane into. He knew from Bart's text that he was going to Cheryl's at eleven. Lane got there first, did what needed to be done, yet still had time to meet Claire for their weekly lunch. It had all gone well.

CEO Lane gripped his wine glass.

His hands were strong, too.

When he finished his wine he would go to the police station and comfort Claire, the woman who would become his trophy wife.

Skin Deep
Carol Goodman Kaufman

The room would be dreary even without knowing its purpose. Bare pea-green walls surround me. Minimal natural light sneaks through a slit of a window; the majority of light comes from fluorescent bulbs blazing overhead. Cinderblock walls section off about a dozen small cubicles, and glass windows over dull metal counters separate visitors from the prisoners. My nostrils tingle with the sharp smell of industrial cleanser. A uniformed guard stands in each corner. After all, this is the maximum security jail, where Worcester County's most dangerous criminals await trial.

I wait for him, my hands in my lap, fiddling with my wedding ring. I touch the heavy plate glass that will keep me from touching him. Keep him from touching me. The telephone attached to the concrete wall will be my only access to him.

I catch a reflection in the glass: a woman with perfect features. High cheekbones, flawless complexion, smooth brow, dimpled chin, bright eyes. That reflection is me. Perfect me. Stunning me. I straighten, correcting my posture.

He comes through the door. I note that he's lost weight and his once thick and wavy hair is now shorn and streaked with silver. I feel a momentary pang of regret.

We pick up the telephone handsets on either side of the glass.

*****

In honor of my 40th birthday, Gabe had made dinner reservations at our favorite bistro, Ciao Bella. I was really looking forward to a quiet, romantic evening, just the two of us. But that was not to be. Friends and family had gathered in the back room and jumped out, shouting, "Surprise!"

I had to hand it to Gabe, he really did surprise me, but I wondered if I was being selfish to want some time alone with him. He travels so much for work, and when he is home, we focus on the kids.

While I greeted the friends who had come out from behind the curtain hiding them, my sister Meg ran up and threw her arms around me.

"Happy birthday, little sister!" she exclaimed.

"I can't believe Gabe pulled this off," I said. "We know how bad you are at keeping secrets."

"He didn't tell me until Wednesday. It's a good thing I was free."

"Who are you kidding? You never miss a party."

"True enough, Leni." We laughed.

Gabe's sister Tracy sidled up to us.

"Happy birthday, Lenore," she said.

"Tracy, you look fantastic," Meg said.

"Think so?" she asked with a sly smile.

"New haircut?"

"I've had some work done."

"Plastic surgery? What did you do?" I asked, stunned I hadn't known, and a bit hurt she hadn't told me.

"My chin. It was really starting to droop."

"So that's where you've been for the past few weeks?"

"I had the surgery while Hank was away on his annual fishing trip with his brothers. He never even knew about it."

"What did he say when he saw you?" Meg asked.

Tracy frowned. "He never actually said anything. I'm not sure he even noticed." Then, changing her mood, "The doctor did a fabulous job, didn't he?"

Poor Tracy. The harder she tries, the less satisfaction she gets.

"It does look natural," Meg said.

"You know, Lenore, maybe you should think about paying my

doctor a visit," Tracy said.

Meg and I exchanged glances. Tracy was in her own little world of spas and lunch dates.

Tracy didn't let up. "That's right. Honey, you're forty years old. Gabe is …"

I bristled. "Gabe is what?"

Tracy began to count off on her perfectly manicured fingers. "My brother is a red-blooded American guy, and you have to admit there's a lot of temptation out there. Young, supple, fit temptation. He travels a lot. And you're not getting any younger."

"But …" I figured I'd better stop her before she got to the fingers on the other hand.

"But nothing. You pay lots of attention to the way you design your clients' homes and, I suppose, even your own. Maybe you should pay more attention to your body."

Meg's eyes widened as she mouthed the words "don't react."

What a bitch Tracy. I'm a really good designer. And in good shape. Pretty good shape.

"Trust me," Tracy said. "This guy's great. And he's really easy on the eyes."

At that last, she raised an eyebrow and, with an inscrutable grin, she turned on her heel and made her way to the bar.

Meg snorted. "She's just jealous, Leni."

"Of what?"

"You have a wonderful family life. A wonderful life altogether."

"You're right. I do."

And there was the proof, right across the room: My two fabulous kids, Jacob and Ella, were batting balloons back and forth. I was indeed blessed to have such children.

If only Gabe were around more often. And present when he was here. On that thought, I scanned the crowd. And, of course, there he was in the corner, huddled behind a towering ficus, on the phone.

*****

That night, as Gabe brushed his teeth, I went into the bathroom and sat down on the side of the tub. I waited for him to notice me as he scrolled through his phone messages.

"Honey, you asked me what I wanted as a birthday gift. Well, I've decided. I'd like a small cosmetic procedure."

Gabe rinsed, spit, and wiped his mouth with a towel. "A what? Why?"

"Just to freshen up a bit."

"But, Leni, you're beautiful. I love you just the way you are. Besides, there's a risk in surgery. Are you willing to die for a firm chin?"

"So you noticed Tracy's chin?"

"My narcissistic, image-conscious sister pointed it out rather forcefully when I didn't say anything."

"Anyway, sweetie, it's not surgery. I just want a microdermabrasion to clear up my skin. There's no anesthesia involved at all."

"None?"

"No. Really. And no incisions. I've been reading up on the procedure."

"What brought this on all of a sudden? Did she make some nasty comment?"

I ignored the question. "You have to admit, Tracy does look great."

"Yes she does, but look at her personal life. It's a disaster."

I couldn't argue that point. Gabe was right. Tracy was already on husband number three and her kids were all in therapy. Her tennis serve and her tan, however, were fantastic.

"I'm not looking for anything drastic," I said. "Just a facial peel. It would get rid of my scars and bumps and …" I'm ashamed to admit that Tracy's comments had, in fact, hit their mark. We had all heard stories about traveling husbands.

Gabe put his arms around me and whispered, "Okay. If that's what you want for your birthday, then that's what you'll get." At that, he immediately returned to his cell phone.

*****

The next morning, alone in the bathroom, I stripped down and stood in front of the floor-to-ceiling mirror. Under the bright makeup lights, I could see laugh wrinkles, stretch marks, sagging breasts, and incipient jowls. My neck was beginning to show horizontal lines that a scarf or a turtleneck could disguise only in cold weather. At least my teeth are good, I thought.

I'm only forty, and I'm already starting to look like Aunt Masie. Of course, Masie was probably forty when I thought she was old. Maybe there's something to what Tracy said.

I groaned.

*****

The waiting room was gorgeous, and I wondered who among my competitors had designed it. No white walls and plastic chairs here. The carpets were a deep forest green, and café au lait walls were adorned with colorful lithographs signed by artists one would see in an art history survey course. Chagall, Mondrian, Klee. *He must have one heck of a security system if these are in the waiting room.*

I was looking intently at one of the pictures when a nurse called me in. As she led me down a hallway, I hoped to get a peek into his office, but the door was closed. *Darn. Maybe another time.*

*****

The moment he came through the door of the exam room, I could see why Tracy thought Dr. Scott Allen was "easy on the eyes." Tall and lanky, with wavy-bordering-on-curly blue-black hair that snuck over the collar of his white lab coat. Ice blue eyes. Yep, definitely Tracy's type. I went more toward the outdoorsy, L.L. Bean kinda guy. Like Gabe.

"Ms. Franklin, how nice to meet you." He approached me with arm extended and took my hand in both of his. They were warm and soft. He sat. "So, what can I do for you?"

"My sister-in-law, Tracy Madison, suggested I come to see you. She spoke highly of your skill."

"What did I do for her?"

"Her chin. It looks absolutely natural." *Boy, would Tracy be furious to know he didn't remember her.*

"I pride myself on making every patient look as fresh and natural as possible." He took a deep breath. "So tell me. What bothers you? Of all your features, what makes you cringe?"

"I'd really just like to feel fresher," I said. "My business puts me out in front of people who want their homes to look beautiful, so I want to look well-maintained. Perhaps a facial peel?"

He clapped his hands and smiled. "Okay, then, we'll start there." My ears should have pricked up at the word "start."

The telephone on the wall of the examination room rang, and he turned to answer it. As he talked, I picked up an issue of *Art News* magazine from the rack on the wall and began to read an article about underrated artists.

The doctor hung up the phone and turned to face me.

"Do you like art?" he asked.

"I actually studied art history in college. By the way, the lithographs you have in your waiting room are amazing."

"If you think those are nice, I have other collections you might enjoy."

I guess there's a lot of money in cosmetic surgery.

He went to a cabinet and pulled out a pair of examination gloves. When he turned back to me, he gently took my chin in his gloved hand and turned my head from side to side. Scrupulous about germs. Good sign. I didn't need any infections.

"Your skin is in pretty good shape for your age, although I do see a few spots that could use some help. Some fine lines, wrinkles, age spots, sun damage, uneven pigmentation, clogged pores. Do you use sunscreen?"

"Every day."

"Good. I think you can get away with a microdermabrasion."

"What's involved with that?"

"It's actually my preferred method for skin like yours. It's a noninvasive procedure that uses a spray of aluminum oxide microcrystals to exfoliate the skin. In other words, it removes the outermost layer of dry, dead skin cells. While that's going on, a mild suction removes the skin debris and crystals. I really like it because it eliminates any problem with chemical sensitivity. The microcrystals I use are hypoallergenic."

"How long a procedure is it? What's the recovery like?"

"One of the main reasons microdermabrasion is so super popular is that it's almost painless, and each session takes less than an hour. There's virtually no downtime. That's why it's called a 'lunch hour' procedure."

"So, one and done?"

He shook his head. "No. You'll need between five and twelve treatments spaced two to three weeks apart."

"That's a lot of treatments," I said, thinking that maybe I should just forget it.

"Well, multiple treatments are critical because they encourage the production of a new layer of skin cells with higher levels of collagen and elastin."

"How much does all this cost?"

"It's two hundred dollars a session. It does cost much less than other cosmetic procedures. And you probably won't need all twelve. As I said, your skin is in pretty good shape. Some patients get by with as few as five."

"I assume that my health insurance won't cover this, right?"

He smiled and nodded. Long dark eyelashes contrasted nicely with the light of his eyes. I mulled it over for a minute. Twelve sessions at most, at two hundred bucks a pop. I couldn't ask Gabe to pay for all that. I had a decent income from my business. I could cover it. I just wouldn't tell him how much it cost.

"Do you have any other questions?"

"Actually, I do. Have you had any cosmetic procedures, Doctor?"

"I have indeed. Growing up, my ears were so big, the kids called me Dumbo, so I had them pinned back. That's probably why I chose this specialty. Nobody should have to go through life being teased about the way they look."

Honest and empathetic. And careful about cleanliness. "Okay. I'll do it."

"My receptionist can help you set up an appointment."

*****

Six months later, I stood in the doorway of the bedroom and watched as Gabe packed a suitcase, preparing for a month-long trip to Southeast Asia. He was so used to travel that he had one bag with all his toiletries ready to go, and just needed to get his clothes in order.

"Gabe, I need to talk with you before you go."

"Sure, babe," he mumbled. "What is it?"

"I'm having some pain in my legs. I'm going to see a doctor about it."

Gabe barely looked up. "Of course you should take care of it."

"I have an appointment tomorrow."

"Mmm," he mumbled as he continued to fold shirts.

Was he even paying attention?

"I'll have the procedure done while you're away."

"Mmm."

*****

"Ms. Franklin, how nice to see you after all this time." Dr. Allen washed and dried his hands at the sink, donned gloves, and then made his way across the exam room, a look of concern creasing his forehead. "I hope you're not unhappy with your microdermabrasion?"

He lifted my chin with his hand and turned my face left and right. Even gloved, his hands felt good on my face.

"I must say your skin looks great. I don't see a problem."

"No, no. There's no problem. I'm really happy with the results. I feel fresh and clear, and it was so easy to do. I came to talk about having another procedure."

"What were you thinking about?"

"I'm getting varicose veins on my legs."

"Okay. Hop up on the table and we'll see what's what."

Wrapping the johnny tightly around myself, I got up. The doctor pulled the extension out from the foot of the table, and began to examine my legs. His fingers tickled a bit.

"Most of these are simple spider veins, but you do have the beginnings of what might be a swollen varicosity forming here," he said while pointing to the side of my right leg.

"Can you do something about them?"

"Of course, and it can all be done right here in the office. I'll just inject saline solution into the veins."

"How long is the recovery? I want to do this while my husband is away on business."

Dr. Allen frowned. "Does he know you're doing this?"

I hesitated. "Yes. No. I'm not actually sure. He was preoccupied while I was telling him, getting ready for a business trip. I promised him I wouldn't do surgery, but this isn't real surgery, is it?"

"No, but it is a medical procedure."

Conservative. Looking out for me. I liked that.

"So, how long?"

"Within a week, all dressings will be gone. You can walk for exercise, but need to be careful about squatting or heavy lifting. Within a month, most bruising will be gone. You must, however, wear support hose for up to six weeks."

I did the math in my head. It's winter now, I thought. Nobody will see the support hose under my jeans.

*****

A few weeks later, I was back in Dr. Allen's office for my follow-up visit.

He came in with that dazzling smile and got right down to business. When he was done with his examination, he sat down, placed his hands on his thighs, and said, "You've got to be the best patient I've ever had. I can see you have been following my instructions faithfully."

I blushed. Competitive by nature, I liked being his best patient.

"But, I do have a concern."

My heart thudded. "What's that?"

"I'm concerned about your eyelids. When you first came to me, your makeup camouflaged your eyes, but when I had you in the OR, I could see them. It would be unethical not to warn you about a potentially serious problem. Do you feel your eyes getting heavy at any time? Not counting bedtime, of course."

I thought for a moment. "I suppose I do get drowsy in the afternoon. But, doesn't everybody?"

"Yes, a certain amount of drowsiness does occur in the afternoon, but I'm looking at your eyelids. I think they're okay now, but I can see a problem just a little down the road. They'll be getting so heavy that they will interfere with your daily functioning."

"What are you proposing?"

"I think you should consider blepharoplasty."

I must have looked alarmed, because his eyes softened. "It's a fairly simple procedure, but it does require a recuperation period of a few weeks."

I didn't respond right away. He was talking about actual surgery, the one thing I had promised Gabe not to do. Of course, this was a health related issue, so maybe he'd be okay with it. Of course he would. He'd only want the best for me, wouldn't he?

Then, as if he had been reading my thoughts, Dr. Allen said, "I know you don't want your husband to be worried about surgery, but this is not simply a cosmetic procedure for the sake of vanity. It will affect how you live your life."

"I'll need to talk with him about this."

He nodded. "Of course. Just let me know what you decide. This procedure should be done as soon as possible, before the problem becomes too extensive."

That night, as we were washing the dinner dishes, I started to broach the subject with Gabe, but Tracy showed up at the kitchen door in one of her all-too-frequent visits to complain about her latest husband. After she finally left, I made an unfortunate comment about her behavior that triggered an argument. Gabe and I didn't argue often. After all, he's not around that much. But when we did, it could get loud. The next day Gabe left on yet another business trip. We never discussed the surgery.

In retrospect, I definitely should have told Gabe about it. If there had been a real medical reason to do surgery, he would have understood. By that point, however, I admit that I had become a bit infatuated with Dr. Allen and those warm, smooth hands. And more than a bit frustrated with Gabe's absence while present.

*****

I called Meg first thing next morning and set up a lunch date. As soon as we sat down, I launched into my plan to have my eyelids done.

"Are you sure you want to do this, Leni? This is real surgery. You'll be out of commission for at least a month, right?"

"I am sure. Dr. Allen was really concerned about my eyes."

"What did Gabe say?"

I hesitated. "He didn't. I never got the chance to tell him. We got into a big fight last night, and then he left for a business trip this morning."

"What happened?"

"I made a comment about Tracy, and …"

"What did you say?"

"Nothing he himself hadn't said a hundred times before, but I must have really hit a nerve."

"I don't like it, Leni. Gabe's going to be furious that you went behind his back. You have to tell him. For something this big, he needs to be on board."

"I'll do it when he gets back."

"No. You'll do it today. In fact, call him now before his plane takes off and tell him. He's going to want to be there for you. At least, he will if it's really a medical issue."

I sighed. "I suppose you're right."

"You might consider apologizing for dissing his sister, too," she muttered as I stood.

"I heard that."

I picked up my cell phone and walked to a quiet hallway near the restrooms to make the call.

Gabe didn't pick up. I checked the time. He should be at the gate, waiting to board. Had he seen my number and declined to answer?

*****

I woke up in a haze. It was silent in the room except for the whir of a fan blowing cool air. Thick bandages were wrapped not just around my eyes but around my entire head. My mouth tasted like dirty socks. I needed water. I groped around for a call button and found it clipped to the blanket. I pressed it.

While I waited, I tried to shake the wooziness from my head by sitting up, but a sharp pain slammed me back down. I could feel the tube from an intravenous drip bag tethering me to the bed and I started to wonder if having my eyelids done had actually been a good idea.

The door opened and Dr. Allen entered.

"How are we doing?" he asked.

My mouth was so dry I had trouble answering. From a pitcher somewhere in the room he poured me a glass of water. I could hear him unwrap a straw to put into it. Then he sat down gently on the side of the bed and propped me up, holding the cup and straw at an angle. I sucked until I heard the burbling sound of air. He poured more and, from the sound of it, placed it on a nightstand next to my bed.

"I don't know how I am. I'm still too groggy."

"That will pass in a few hours, but I can tell you that you did great. Your procedure went off like clockwork and I think you'll be very pleased with the results."

"Thank you, Doctor Allen."

"I think you've earned the right to call me Scott."

My drugged laugh was more like a gargle. I had become a frequent flier with Scott Allen Airways.

"When will you take off the bandages?" I asked.

"It will be a while. I don't want you touching your face while you're sleeping. That could cause permanent injury. As for the eyes, there are just some tiny steri-strips holding the sutures in place."

I nodded my understanding, as hazy as it was.

"You'll have complete support here during your recovery. Your job is to rest, but we must get you up and walking every hour. If you need to use the bathroom, please use the call button. I'll escort you. I don't want you falling. In a few days I'll remove the stitches from your eyes."

"Why you, and not your nurse?"

"Sandra's gone on her vacation. I'm afraid you'll have to endure me." I could feel that brilliant smile through the bandages.

"When can I go home?"

"Not yet. You told me that your husband is away. I want to keep an eye on you."

Yet again, I was touched by his concern.

"I'm having some pain," I said.

"As I explained in the office and in the brochure I gave you, that's normal after surgery. We'll get you a small dose of oxycodone and some ice packs to help with the swelling. That and the redness will fade with time. But it will take time. You must have patience."

"Patience is not my strong suit, I'm afraid."

"Well then, you'll have lots of practice getting there. Plus, you told me that your husband is away on business for the entire month and your kids are at summer camp, right? You're free as a bird."

"That's true."

"You can watch television or read, but mostly I want you to relax and heal."

"Absolutely. And I can talk to my sister and Gabe, and text the kids at camp."

"For the first week or so, you should not use the phone. I don't want to risk infection."

Free as a bird? A caged bird, more like it, as I was soon to learn.

*****

About a week later, Dr. Allen, er, Scott came into the room and his soft, warm hands got to work removing the gauze from my eyes. The bandages finally gone, I looked around. Rather, I tried to. Although it was very dim, the light was too much for me to keep my eyes open for any length of time. Plus, I was still a bit wobbly. Probably from the painkillers I had been taking.

The room was not at all like a typical hospital recovery room: stark white and gray steel under glaring fluorescent lights. Instead, it looked more like a professionally designed boudoir. A lushly upholstered chaise longue sat in one corner of the large rectangular room. The bed and drapes were of a different pattern, but all complemented the deep eggplant walls. A Prairie style lamp cast a soft amber circle on a dresser that looked to be made of an exotic wood. Cocbolo maybe? I'd used it in a house I'd worked on a few years ago. Gorgeous.

"Can I look in the mirror?"

"That might not be such a good idea yet. Your face is very red and swollen now."

"My face?" I lifted my right hand to my cheek and realized that there was still gauze all over my face. How could I have missed that?

"Yes. I made a little surprise for you."

Surprise? A tiny shiver ran up my spine. I loved surprises. "What kind of surprise?"

"You'll see," he said with a sly grin, then turned and left the room.

*****

Scott came into the room just as I was waking from a nap.

"We need to get you up and moving a bit. Would you like to see my art collection?"

"I'd love to."

He opened the door and brought me into a large great room. It was only then that I understood. The reason the recovery room was so beautiful was that it wasn't in his clinic downtown. It was in his house. How I had ended up there I had no idea, but I was still a bit woozy and didn't really focus on the logistics.

At strategic points around the room stood magnificent pieces of sculpture on simple wooden pedestals. Giacometti, Calder, Brancusi, Arp. My head was spinning, and not from the drugs.

"This is one of my favorites," he said, bringing me to a bronze nude. "The workmanship, the grace, the beautiful face, and the perfect patina makes this one quite special," he said as he ran his hands over the curves of the bronze. "Are you familiar with Jaeger?"

"Just from books, I'm afraid. This is the first time I've seen one up close."

"His work is perfection. My goal in collecting is to obtain the most beautiful things."

I shuddered, but I wasn't sure why.

*****

A few days later, Dr. Allen — Scott — plopped a large sunhat onto my head and handed me a long-sleeved jacket to wear over my t-shirt. He took my arm and brought me for a stroll outdoors. From the confines of the house, I hadn't realized just how much of the mountain he owned.

"This is a beautiful piece of property," I gushed. "What a fabulous view. Is that Mount Wachusett?"

"Yes. I see you have good sense of direction."

The yard featured a fountain and more sculpture, including a large Henry Moore. As we reached a far corner of the yard I spotted through a gap in the trees a ten-foot high chain link fence.

"That's an enormous fence," I said.

"I'm afraid I've had some problems with burglary. We're rather isolated up here on the mountain, and some of my more unscrupulous neighbors seem to think that my possessions would bring a high price on the black market. Of course, they'd be right."

"How horrible to be so vulnerable," I said.

"I'm okay. That and the security system make me feel very safe."

"You do have an impressive art collection."

"Thank you. One of the things I liked about you from the start was that you took an interest in art. You're curious. I noticed that the first time you were in my office, you chose *Art News* magazine instead of *People*. Then, here, the first book you picked up from my library was Andre Malraux's *The Voices of Silence*. That said something about you."

My face reddened. "Malraux is a classic. Still, to have to barricade your home like this …"

Little did I know then that fences can keep people in as well as out.

*****

"I think the swelling has gone down. When can I look in the mirror?" I asked. "I can't wait to see the surprise."

"Well, you have been very patient. But be prepared. It's not really ready yet."

I agreed. I really was like a kid on Christmas morning.

Scott went into a cabinet and retrieved a hand mirror. His eyes were glistening. Were those tears in his eyes? I took the mirror and, for the first time in weeks, saw my reflection.

Had there not been bone and skin holding it inside my body, I think my heart would have leapt from my chest.

I stared into the mirror, my chest constricting. What had I gotten myself into?

"I've given you a complete facelift. My compliments."

*****

"I need to lie down," I said. "I feel a bit queasy." That was only half true. I needed some time to think. Alone.

"Of course. I did warn you that it would be a shock."

I just nodded, mute, and shuffled to my room. He followed me and settled me into the bed. Before turning the light off, he whispered, "Take it easy. You'll feel better soon. I promise. You're going to be perfect." Then he left, closing the door behind him.

I began to sob into my pillow, but the salty tears hurt the open wounds on my face, so I forced myself to stop. How could I have risked my life for this?

What a fool I had been. "Perfect," he had said. What was he up to?

Was I just another one of his collection? A memory of his hand caressing the nude bronze woman flashed before me. What would he do with me once I was perfect?

I needed to get out of there. Fast. I opened the drawer in the nightstand to retrieve my cell phone and call for help.

It was gone.

*****

I thought my chest would explode. I was sure I had put the phone in the nightstand drawer for safekeeping. Had I been so drugged that I had forgotten? Then it dawned on me that I hadn't heard the phone buzz indicating that I had a text or a call.

I got up and frantically searched the room. Suitcase, toiletry bag, pockets of every item of clothing, drawers. Nothing.

Twenty minutes later, I came to the stunning realization: Dr. Allen had taken it.

I collapsed onto the bed, my heart pounding with equal parts fear and fury. My kids would be expecting me at camp visiting day. What would they think? That I had forgotten them? I hadn't texted in days. And Gabe and I hadn't parted on the best of terms. What would he think when I didn't answer his calls?

I knew I had to plan my escape, and it wouldn't be easy. But, before doing anything, I knew I had to slow my racing mind and outline a strategy. I closed my eyes and began to do some breathing exercises remembered from a long-ago meditation class. Once I had calmed down enough, I resolved to look at the house in a way I hadn't thought to do before.

*****

The situation was pretty dire. My cell phone had mysteriously disappeared, and Dr. Allen — no more "Scott" for me — had no landline in the house. His office door was locked, so getting to a computer was impossible. Anyway, it was probably password protected. The biggest challenge: every exit door was locked with a double-key deadbolt, and he kept his keys close at all times. I was willing to bet he slept with them under his pillow.

My first strategy: drug him. From now on, every time he handed me a painkiller, I would palm it and start a stockpile. If I could somehow get the pills into his food or drink, I could find his keys, open the door, and run like hell when he passed out.

The next day, I launched my plan. Before he left for work, I said, "You know, Scott, I feel so useless here. You've been beyond hospitable and I'm really feeling fine. Won't you let me make dinner tonight? I'm a really good cook."

"There will be plenty of time for that after you've fully recovered, but right now I don't want you lifting anything. I'll bring dinner. You just relax, but remember to walk around every hour. Tonight, we can talk about art. I think you'd enjoy hearing about a paper I'm writing. I'd like your feedback."

"That sounds wonderful," I said, hoping the smile on my face looked sincere.

What did he mean, there would be plenty of time to prepare dinner "after you've fully recovered?" Wouldn't I be going home?

As Dr. Allen loaded papers into his briefcase, he said, "You know, I didn't like the way you got so pale yesterday after the big reveal. Your recovery is going so well I don't think you need the oxycodone any longer. After all, we don't want to start an addiction. If you need anything for the pain, I think we'll stick with acetaminophen from now on."

My chest tightened in panic. Had he read my mind? Of course not. I'd better get a grip. And a Plan B.

But what would that look like?

*****

I decided that I really needed to play up to Dr. Allen and make him think I was totally in his thrall. After all, I'm ashamed to say that until the moment I looked in that mirror, I had admired him. I had thought he was attractive. My skin crawled in anticipation of the things I might have to do to make him believe I was under his thumb.

I waited a few days to work out any kinks in my plan. I would climb the fence. Ten feet wasn't so high, and I had small feet that could easily fit into the chain link. And there might even be a ladder somewhere. That would make it even easier.

While he was putting his breakfast dishes into the dishwasher, I said, "I know you're concerned about my overdoing, and that is so sweet, but I do get so antsy sitting around the house all day waiting for you to take me out for our nightly walk. If I promise not to exert myself, I'd love to walk in the backyard today."

"That's a good idea. Just remember to cover up."

I should have known it wouldn't be that easy. That fence around the property? It was topped with barbed wire. Invented in Worcester, Mass, my hometown. The moment I saw it, I went into the house and headed straight to the basement door. Locked. Damn.

I went outside and began to case the house, looking at the windows lining the foundation wall. One by one, I pushed the wood frames until, miracle of miracles, I found a loose one. I pushed it open and, thanking my lucky genes for a petite body, slipped through the opening and onto a heavy industrial metal shelving unit. I lowered myself onto the floor and searched every inch of that basement for wire cutters. Nothing. And no ladder, either.

I had to get out of there and back to my children.

*****

That night, Dr. Allen closed himself in his office, supposedly to read journals, but I could hear voices coming from inside. I tiptoed up to the door to see if I could make out anything. The familiar voice of a Channel Five News reporter came through.

"Lenore Franklin, 40, of Worcester, has been reported missing since Sunday. Her sister has told authorities that she went for a medical procedure, but hasn't heard from her for several days. Her husband, learning of her disappearance, is flying back from China, where he has been on a business trip."

They're looking for me! Thank God I told Meg my plans. And then

I heard her voice. It was choked with fear.

"My sister went to a clinic to have a procedure on her eyes. She and I talked or texted every day until a few days ago. Then nothing. She hasn't answered my calls. It's not like her."

The reporter took over. "The clinic at which Ms. Franklin is supposed to have undergone the surgery has no record of her having been there recently. In fact, at the time her sister claims she was having her surgery, the clinic was closed for vacation."

Of course they had no record of me! Kidnappers don't leave records. My stomach churned and my eyes filled with tears as the reporter concluded.

"Anybody with information that can help with the police investigation is urged to call the number on the screen."

The news anchor then went onto another story about an unsavory building contractor.

And then it hit me. The nurse, Sandra, wasn't there the morning I came in for the eyelift, nor was the receptionist. The doctor himself came out to greet me. It was so early in the morning – 6 a.m. – that I had just assumed they hadn't yet come in for the day.

And Dr. Allen had made the appointment for me. I saw him at the computer and, again, assumed that he had entered my name into the schedule. *Never assume, doofus.*

Suddenly, the sound of a squeaking chair startled me. I scooted over the carpet to the kitchen as quickly and quietly as I could, where I placed my hands on the counter and took a few deep, cleansing breaths to steady myself. The cool granite was soothing. Then I busied myself filling a kettle. Just as I opened the cabinet door to pull out a mug, Dr. Allen walked in.

"There you are. Make some for me, too?" he asked.

I turned and smiled. "Of course. Regular or herbal?" If only I had some rat poison to add to it.

*****

More than a month had passed, and I was no closer to getting out of this prison than ever. Gabe would have returned from Asia, and the kids would be home from camp and getting ready to go back to school. I was getting more and more depressed. And desperate.

It was around noon on a very hot Wednesday, and I was sitting on the sofa in the air conditioned great room reading a book when the roar of a lawnmower startled me. It occurred to me that, over the many weeks I had been here, this was the first time I had seen the gardeners. The property was meticulously maintained, so they had to have been here on a weekly basis. And then it struck me. Every Wednesday, on his day off, Dr. Allen would take me on a picnic in the woods. He wasn't taking any chances that I would get out from his clutches.

But this morning, he had received a call about an emergency with one of his patients, and he had left in a hurry. I ran to the sliding glass door, excited to finally get help, but it was locked.

I banged on the glass and shouted, but the noise of the equipment was too much to overcome, so I decided to wait until they were done. When all was quiet, I would bang and shout again. They were sure to hear me. They were sure to help me.

I waited for about an hour, and the moment the roar of the motor stopped, I ran up to the door. Just as I lifted my arm to begin banging on the glass, Dr. Allen walked in with an enormous bag from a local cafe.

"Picnic!" he announced.

*****

If I were a superstitious person, I would have seen the glorious rainbow outside as an omen that something good was about to happen. As it was, I was simply going through the motions of a day just like all the others since I had fallen into my real-life nightmare. And, miracle of miracles, Dr. Allen had become complacent. I was now just another object in his collection. He didn't even have to dust me.

I was sitting on the chaise longue in my room reading an article in *National Geographic* magazine when he came in.

"Good morning," he said as he crossed the room. When he reached me, he leaned over to kiss the top of my head. I tried to control my repulsion and play the part I needed to play if I was ever going to get out of there.

"Good morning to you," I said in what I hoped was a cheerful voice.

"I must be off. Lots of patients today. I'll see you tonight."

I stood and walked with him to the bedroom door. He turned, smiled and kissed me again. I put my arms around him and hugged him close. Pretend, pretend, pretend was my mantra. Thank God he never seemed to want me for sex. But, of course, I wasn't perfect yet. My stomach roiled as I realized that he must have more surgery planned.

Once he had left, I took my magazine into the great room and put my feet up on the sofa. Before too long, I fell asleep. About ten minutes into my nap I jerked awake. It struck me that I hadn't heard the metallic thunk of a bolt sliding into place. Had he remembered to lock the door? Had my loving goodbye somehow distracted him from the critical task of locking me in? I jumped up from the sofa so fast I got lightheaded, and cursed myself as I sank into the cushions and put my head between my knees. I didn't have a moment to waste, I thought. Once I felt steady, I got up and rushed to the door and put my hand on the knob.

It turned!

*****

I couldn't believe this day had finally come. I had no idea where exactly I was, but just ran. At the end of the driveway I hesitated for a second. Which way to go? I turned left and headed downhill. I walked for miles and miles, keeping well off the shoulder of the narrow, twisting mountain road to avoid being seen. I didn't care how long I'd have to walk. I was going back to my family.

I was terrified that Dr. Allen would suddenly remember that he hadn't locked the door. He would come driving up the road, find me, and drag me back to his lair. I was also afraid to hitchhike, not that many cars were driving on this very remote road. God only knew what kind of creep might pick me up. That would be going from the frying pan into the fire, right? But then again, no creep would be as bad as Dr.

Allen.

After what seemed like hours, I spied a wooden sign with faded lettering that announced "Jake's Garage." Under it was a rural still life. Old fashioned gas pumps sported blistering red paint. A Coke machine that would have been retro if it hadn't been legitimately old stood to one side of the office door, and a pay phone hung on the other.

I limped over the blacktop, spiky weeds pushing up through the cracks and brushing my calves. My feet were blistered and bleeding, and I cursed my flimsy sandals that were in no way made for long walks. When I reached the office I fell into an ancient plastic chair. The cracked seat pinched the back of my thighs and I sat up to adjust myself. Jake, or a man I assumed was Jake, stared at me through a haze of cigarette smoke, his brow furrowed.

"I need help. Please, may I use your phone?"

He squinted through the smoke and nodded toward the pay phone.

"I don't have any money. I'm sorry, but I really need to call the police."

The man finally spoke. "911 calls are free," he said.

My eyes filled with tears as I lurched toward the phone and my deliverance.

*****

I let the EMTs examine me but refused a trip to the hospital. After all, what if Dr. Allen were there? I didn't want to take the risk of his seeing me. Until, of course, I would be testifying against him in court. In my panic I didn't consider that, as a plastic surgeon, he wouldn't have been anywhere near the emergency department.

A young uniformed officer brought me in his cruiser to police headquarters and escorted me inside, where I told the whole sordid story to a detective while drinking greedily from a bottle of water he had brought me. He listened with a look that was a mix of horror and disbelief, but he was kind enough not to judge. I was exhausted and beyond thirsty from the long walk to the garage, and my feet were bloody and filthy. My face was beet red — both from shame and a bad sunburn. Exposure to sun was the first of Dr. Allen's many rules I had broken. But I knew that, at this point, my embarrassment had to take a back seat to getting away from this madman and back home where I belonged.

*****

After telling my story, the detective brought me to an empty desk in the detectives' area and gave me a magazine to read while I waited for Gabe. I almost laughed. It was the same issue of *National Geographic* that I had been looking at this morning. As I read an article about ice hotels in Mongolia, my eyes got heavy. I nodded off until a commotion in the detectives' room woke me.

It was Gabe's voice. "Where's my wife?" he cried.

"She's right here, Mr. Franklin," he said, "She's all right, but you need to be prepared. She's not what you expect. She's been through an awful lot."

I stepped out from behind the office partition.

Gabe rounded the corner and stopped suddenly. He shook his head, his expression changing from anxious to confused. "This isn't my wife."

"Yes, it's me, Gabe."

He stared at me. I was a stranger to him.

"It's true. I know you don't recognize me. The doctor kidnapped me and did so much surgery ..." Tears filled my eyes and my throat became so tight that words couldn't escape.

"Is this really you?" Gabe said as he inched toward me.

I nodded. "I've been so stupid."

At that, He put his arms around me and held me until I calmed down.

"It's okay. Thank God you're safe now."

It felt so good to be in his arms that I broke down and sobbed.

"Tell me what happened."

I related the entire story, from beginning to end. When I finished, I hiccupped and he wrapped me in his arms and didn't say a word.

After a few minutes, he spoke. "You never mentioned the surgery at any point. Why didn't you tell me?"

"I called you at the airport to apologize about the fight we had, and to tell you about the surgery. You didn't answer."

Gabe took a deep breath. "I know. That was wrong."

"And then you never called me after that. Why? I must have texted you a dozen times."

He extended his arms until he held me at arm's length, and looked at me as if I were a stranger. I suppose I was.

"Why didn't you try again? I've been frantic."

"He took my phone! Didn't you talk to Meg? You know that she and I talk every day, so when I didn't call, she knew something was wrong. She went to the police. Didn't you talk to her?"

"Meg called me back from China, hysterical that she couldn't reach you. And when I got home, your suitcase was gone. I was sure you had left us."

"But she knew I hadn't. You had to know I wouldn't do that."

"I wasn't so sure. I thought you might have given up on me when I didn't return your calls."

And then Gabe changed the subject. "You promised me you weren't going to do any surgery."

"I didn't have any. At first. And I only did the second thing, my varicose veins — also not surgery–when you were away in Hong Kong so you wouldn't have to see the bandages and the bruises. But I did tell you about that. You just ignored me. But again, it wasn't surgery. Just an office visit."

Gabe pulled over an office chair and sank into it, his eyes not leaving me. Was he trying to remember my old face?

"The doctor told me that I had a problem with my eyelids. Not a cosmetic thing but a problem that was going to interfere with my vision. He said it needed an operation to fix it."

"So you just went ahead and did it? Without discussing it with me?"

"No. Yes. I told you, I tried to talk to you about it. Anyway, when I woke up from the surgery, I discovered that he had done a complete facelift and he insisted I stay in the clinic until he cleared me to go home."

"Then why didn't you just pick up and leave?"

"Because it turned out I wasn't even in the clinic. He somehow got me to his house, out in the country."

Gabe interrupted. "This sounds more like a movie script than real life, Leni."

"I know it does. But it's all true. He wouldn't let me go. I was trapped."

"And you didn't try to get out? You didn't try to call for help?"

Was he really listening to me? Or was his mind on business, as usual?

"Until the surgery, I was talking to Meg every day. I didn't realize until the bandages were removed that he had taken my phone and that I was being held prisoner.

"And I did try to escape, several times. But he had this enormous fence with barbed wire along the top."

"Leni." He let out one long controlled breath and said the words that shattered my already bruised heart. "How can I let you back into my life when you showed so little trust in me? And the kids? To have left us in the dark for so long?"

How could I confess to my husband that I had trusted this doctor? That I had actually admired him. That he seemed to listen to me, unlike absent-while-present Gabe.

And then it was my turn to get angry. "What are you talking about? I couldn't get away from him. I was locked in his freaking house. What kind of person do you think I am? Did you really think I would leave you and our children?"

"What kind of person? A person who would go behind her family's back to have cosmetic surgery."

I was speechless. I had no defense.

He spoke again. "But you did manage to get out."

"Only because he got complacent. I had to figure out how to get him to let his guard down. That took time. Don't you see?"

"I see that you were so vain that you had to expose yourself to danger."

"How was I supposed to know he was dangerous? He convinced me that the surgery was medically necessary. Besides, Tracy recommended him."

"You believed my self-absorbed sister? But when *I* told you I loved the way you were, that you were beautiful, *that* you wouldn't believe."

Now it was my turn to change the subject. "Where are the kids?"

"They should be home from school now. Tracy is there with them."

I stood. "I want to see them."

"I'm not sure they'll want to see you."

*****

Tracy was already talking as she opened the front door. "I heard the car drive up." Then her eyes widened.

"Tracy, it's me, Leni. This is what happened when your adored Dr. Allen got a hold of me."

"Oh my God, Lenore. You look fantastic."

"Shut up, Tracy," Gabe said and pushed his way past her into the foyer.

I followed. My house looked strange to me, even though I could see that nothing had changed. My chest hurt. Then, I heard the kids shouting "Mom" as they ran from the family room at the back of the house. When they got to the foyer, they stopped in their tracks, goggle-eyed.

"Jacob! Ella!" Then I broke down and sobbed. "Come here and let me hug you. I've missed you so much."

They stood still. "You're not our mother," Ella said. "Who are you?"

"No, really. I am. Please believe me. Gabe, tell them."

He was silent and stone-faced.

Desperate, I began to sing.

"Little Ella, my sweet little girl,

Has blue eyes and a big blond curl.

I love her so much, yes I do,

I'll give her hugs and kisses, too."

"Do you remember that song, sweetie? I used to sing it to you every night when you were little."

Ella began to scream. "How did you get that song? What did you do to my mother?"

"I am Mummy! Ask me anything! I'll prove it!"

Jacob put his hand on Ella's arm, leaned over, and whispered something in her ear. She nodded.

"What was the name of my favorite stuffed animal?" she asked.

"You called your bear Bluebeary." Then I added, "Monkeybar was a close second."

Ella narrowed her eyes.

Then it was Jacob's turn. "Why didn't you come to my ninth grade soccer championship game?"

I smiled. "I *was* at the ninth grade championship game. I had the flu for the eighth grade game." I'm ashamed to admit that I succumbed to snarkiness when I took a deep breath and added, "Dad was in Switzerland that week." *Yeah, guys, who's been there for you?*

The two kids moved into the living room for a huddle, leaving me alone in the foyer. I tried to listen in, but was only able to pick out a few words of their muted conversation. Tracy sat in an armchair and stared at me, running a finger over her chin. Was she admiring my new face, or was she envious of it? Gabe sat on the staircase, staring at his clasped hands. Could I ever earn his trust again? Would they let me back into the family?

*****

"What are you doing here?" Dr. Allen asks. The orange prison jumpsuit hangs on him. He's lost weight.

"I wanted to see you and let you know how you've destroyed my life. My husband and kids don't recognize me. According to them, I've made up this whole story. I'm some crazy, evil woman who's come to take Leni's place. They think I've tortured her for bits of information about the family. And my husband feels betrayed. He believes I brought this on myself." I stopped and blew out a breath. "Maybe I did."

"I'm sorry to hear that."

"Are you? What am I supposed to do now? Where am I supposed to go?"

"Well, I certainly can't help you. I'm in here and will probably be here for some time."

"Confess. Save us all the agony of a trial."

"Confess to what? I made you beautiful. I took care of you. I expanded your world."

The room began to spin. Expanded my world, my ass. Had I been delusional, thinking that he would admit to his deeds? This man saw himself as Professor Higgins. He was actually Dr. Frankenstein, except that the monster he made was absolutely gorgeous. But like that monster, I will wreak havoc.

I stood, putting my hands on the counter and leaned toward the glass partition separating me from pure evil. Gripping the handset so tightly my fingers were white, I hissed, "I promise you that I will dedicate my life to making sure that you are convicted and sent to a place where your good looks will make you very popular. And you won't get out 'til they carry you out on a slab."

At that, I stood and left the jail. The taxi was waiting where I had left it. I got in and asked the driver to take me to the place where I hoped what Robert Frost said was true: "Home is the place where, when you have to go there, they have to take you in."

How Easily Things Can Explode
Daniel C. Bartlett

Nolan knew they'd come for him soon enough.

So he was nervous, of course, but not surprised when the two detectives found him in his back yard among the paths and planting beds and pond where he spent most of his evenings. Just some routine questions, they said. Due diligence.

The male detective had the heft of a former athlete who'd gone to flab in his middle years, his belly bulging over his slacks and his sport coat a bit too tight. He said, "If you were truly a suspect, you'd be having this talk in an interview room with the feds. You understand? Be glad it's us visiting you and not them." That fake smile people give before they come out with the ugly truth they really mean. "A lot of people, Nolan, they know the stories about you. The *incident* back in high school. So, situation like this, people might have suspicions."

"It wasn't like that. Not like they say," Nolan said quietly. He didn't say that high school was over twenty years ago anyway. And he didn't ask when people would let go of the rumors that were lies to begin with.

He recognized the detective as a guy who'd been a year behind him in school. Darryl Hebert. Detective Hebert now.

"Look, Nolan," Hebert said. "You probably don't understand all that's going on. People are going crazy here. We've got angry crowds, protests, fights. Add these bomb threats to it all."

That was it right there. People always thought he didn't understand. They saw how he didn't quite meet their gaze with his own, his uneasiness around people. They saw his general inwardness and took him as *off*.

But he knew. He'd heard the news reports. Someone making bomb threats on the south end of town. Sending taunting letters to the police and the media. Handwritten notes saying, "*people need to know there place*" and "*illegals get out*" and "*this land is my land.*" Two bombs had already been found, fortunately without having gone off. One in a trash can outside of a café called Grandma's Soul Food, another in a dumpster outside of Hernandez Mexican Market.

Nolan also understood that next Tuesday was election day, an ugly contentious one that had people worked up and at each other's throats.

And a few days away, this Friday was the cross-town rivalry football game. Cross-City Insanity, they called it. The more affluent, mostly White north end school versus the much less well-off, largely Black and Hispanic south end school. For decades the game meant pranks between the rival schools, but in recent years those pranks had escalated to a level bordering on malicious.

Nolan knew all those things and how the lines were getting blurred between them, but he knew better than to try explaining himself.

Instead he looked around at the cobblestone paths, the wooden deck with chairs and bistro tables. Oak and pecan trees filtered the evening light, dappling the paths and planting beds. Placed among the plantings were items he'd salvaged on his garbage route—broken wheelbarrows he'd fixed up as planters flowing over with petunia blooms, a bed headboard he'd repurposed as a trellis for jasmine vines, and old door he'd painted turquoise and decorated with a mosaic of stones and glass. Colorful koi shimmered in clear water beneath waterlilies.

He saw how Detective Hebert shifted impatiently. "Nolan, you hearing me?"

He saw the female detective place her hand on Hebert's arm. A signal to let her take the lead. Lopez was her name. Detective Lopez. Nolan hadn't gotten her first name. She was compact with short brown hair and strong-looking arms.

She followed his gaze, then said, "It's beautiful. You do all this yourself? Must be great for parties."

Nolan watched the koi swirl and mouth the surface of the water. Truth was there were no parties here.

"Fish are hungry, huh?" Lopez said.

"Some people say koi know their owner by their footsteps," Nolan said.

"Really? Isn't that something," she said and nodded. Then, "All right, Mr. Delacroix, how about we get these questions out of the way. We need to account for your activity over the past week. We want to be able to say we cleared you. Head off the suspicions might come your way."

*****

His phone rang early. Middle-of-the-night early.

"We got a situation," his boss from the City Sanitation department said. "Need all hands on deck. Get on down to the bend on Old River Road. You'll see the spot."

Old River Road ran north-south through town, winding along-side the Old River through ancient oak trees with sprawling limbs that dangled Spanish moss. It was one of the main routes to the industrial zone on the south end, where the shipping channel gave access to the port, petrochemical plants, and refineries. The bend was a section that ran between drainage basins and channels, fenced-off pastures, and wild sections of trees overgrown with vines. Here and there along the route were shambling neighborhoods made up mostly of poor day laborers and recent immigrants.

From his home in the mid-town area, it took Nolan fifteen minutes to find the scene. Flashing lights strobed the blocked off roadway. A firetruck, an ambulance, several police cars. Uniformed responders moved around in a low ground fog. Refinery flare towers hissed in the distance beyond the trees and a sulphuric smell lingered in the air.

And milling about the curve in the road, dozens of cows loose from a pasture on one side of the road.

On the other side of the road, the taillights of a car that had careened off the pavement, gone through the road-side ravine, and crashed to a stop upside down in the trees near the river.

Some of his co-workers from City Sanitation were trying to coral the cows while cops gathered at the gate, shining flashlights at tire treads in the grass and dirt. Nolan kept an eye out for the detectives, Hebert and Lopez, but didn't see them.

Nolan wandered among the scene. He passed a group of cops talking and pointing. Picked up snippets of their discussion—terms like *accident, prank, vandalism,* and *hate crime.* Stated as possibilities more than facts. What was certain was that the lock on the gate had been cut. So, not entirely an accident. They glanced his direction, noted his sanitation uniform, and kept chatting. Nolan passed close enough to hear them discuss checking security cameras at a gas station, a bank, other businesses down the road. Try to get a record of traffic in the area. As he walked on he heard them asking each other if there'd ever been any cases of cattle rustling around here. And if that was still a thing anywhere.

He found his boss, a broad-chested big-bellied man with very dark skin. "Nolan. Emergency services already stretched thin, so we got to help get these cows rounded up ASAP. Soon as the cops give the go-ahead, help get the cows back through that gate."

"Yes sir," Nolan said. "We know what happened?"

"Someone cut the lock on the gate. Guy heading home from the late shift comes around the corner, it's foggy, there's a herd of cattle in the road." He gestured toward the flipped car, the emergency personnel gathered around it. "Don't know if he's gonna make it. Why would someone do this? Shit. You watch, there's gonna be some kind of hell erupts from this."

There's already some kind of hell erupting, Nolan thought. This is just part of it.

But he didn't say that. He kept his mouth shut.

*****

After the cops gave them the go-ahead and they got the cows corralled back into the pasture, the crew gathered in "The Barn," what they called the large metal building where the sanitation crew kept their equipment and loaded onto the garbage trucks early each morning. "Gather the cows, head to the barn," the guys joked. They were all young, half Nolan's age. Some of them barely out of high school. Most guys started here and either screwed up and got fired or moved on to better positions with better pay and more responsibility. Nolan didn't want more responsibility. He was fine riding the back of the truck, jumping off at each pile of trash and hefting bags and boxes and whatever else people threw out.

Most mornings they went about their business, the trucks rumbling to life with diesel fumes and squealing brakes as everyone climbed into position. This morning, though, the supervisor stood before the gathered workers, dispensing warnings. Daylight was coming up now, pinkish-orange hues in the dissipating mist.

"You're on the front lines. Keep your eyes open. You see something don't look right, call it in. The two bombs they found was in the trash. Another thing, people are losing their shit right now. Fights breaking out at grocery stores. Mobs screaming at each other downtown. So I'm telling y'all, keep your mouths shut and do your work. I better not see none of y'all sounding off online. And don't be out marching and demonstrating. You can have your freedom of speech or you can have your job."

Nolan wasn't one to sound off online and crowds made him feel like he could barely breathe, so he certainly wasn't one to join mobs. All the same he felt his supervisor's firm gaze on him. He knew what it meant. People are worked up, looking for the worst, looking for easy targets.

Nolan knew what it was to be an easy target.

*****

That thought rang in his head as they made their rounds.

He should have been able to relax. The bomb threats had all targeted the south side. Today his truck's route was on the northwest side of town. A wealthy, conservative area. The properties here were pristine as opposed to the south end with its yards often strewn with junk and weeds and dogs on chains and rusted out cars. In this neighborhood people parked their cars in the garages. Here the professionally landscaped lawns displayed signs pushing politics and school spirit. A common one lately read, "I vote red, I bleed maroon and gold." Politics, school colors. Many homes here displayed large proud signs touting football players or cheerleaders or band members who lived there. On the south side the few signs he might see were paper banners that shredded and blew in the wind, wrapping around trees and sticking in the ditches and weeds.

Riding around like this, collecting the trash, Nolan saw how people lived, what they bought, what they threw out. Or what they didn't. On the north side, people tossed perfectly good stuff all the time, high dollar stuff. On the south end, decent stuff was almost never tossed out, and broken crap stayed on people's porches indefinitely or until it was stolen. It rarely ended up in the garbage heap at the street's edge.

Nolan liked the rhythm of the job, the way his mind was free to roam. Hop off the truck when it slowed, grab and toss the trash, hop back on the truck as it moved on. A nice flow. He liked occasionally finding items he could use in his yard. Furniture, tools, outdoor equipment.

Sometimes he found laptops or tablets or phones. Usually dead or locked so they couldn't be accessed, but sometimes working and accessible. Valuables like that they usually turned in back at "the Barn" in case someone came asking about an item accidentally tossed out, but it wasn't unheard of for one of the guys to hold onto something useful.

Today, though, he wasn't looking for useful items. Instead he found himself approaching each pick-up with anxiety. Not for fear of setting off a bomb, but for fear of finding one. Nolan wasn't sure why it worried him so much. Was it because he was afraid of being blamed? Or because he didn't want the responsibility of reporting it?

*****

That evening, Nolan signed in at the front desk to visit his mother at Willow Glen Nursing Home. The staff had recently started limiting guests to two per visit due to increasing incidents of arguments and fights breaking out when crowds gathered. The restriction made no difference to Nolan. He was always alone.

He made his way down the quiet hallway with floral patterns in the carpet. He carried real flowers cut from his garden. A nurse came out of a resident's room and nodded a tight smile at him. He knew the nurses and aides whispered about him. Whether he was a dutiful son regularly seeing to his mother or a weirdo loner who still lived in his parents' house. The truth was he was both.

In fact, he still slept in his childhood room, leaving his parents' master bedroom empty. His father had died years earlier, his lungs rotten black from decades working in a butadiene plant. His mother now lay withering in bed with late-stage Alzheimer's. When he entered her room, her eyes fluttered open and her lips moved in what might have been a smile, though not so much of recognition as of acknowledgment of someone speaking to her.

"Got some azalea blooms and some Chinese lanterns," he said. "Couple white roses. And look at this. Would you believe the hibiscuses are blooming this late in the year? Been a warm fall." He set the blooms on the bedside table, their stems too short to be set in water. He'd bundled the flowers into a nice bouquet wound in twist-ties. They'd dry out within a day or so, but he'd bring fresh ones.

She looked at him, her forehead furrowing like she was working out a problem. Then she turned her attention to the TV mounted on the wall.

Nolan settled in a chair beside her bed. He told her about the cows on the road. But not about the accident they caused. He told it like a humorous anecdote, just a wild thing that happened at work. He also did not tell her about the cops visiting him. After that they sat in silence. She dozed off and he watched the local news, the TV volume turned low. They talked of the election next week, then locally the bomb threats, the growing protests, the wreck and the man lying in ICU, the investigation into the incident. They showed a picture of a smiling Black man wearing the blue Nomex uniform of one of the refineries. His name was Larry Harold. Then they showed shots of boarded up businesses downtown, broken windows, graffiti. There was talk of whether to postpone or even cancel Friday's Cross City Insanity game. The news station had done a poll asking people their opinions—the overwhelming majority dismissing the risk and saying that the game was too important for the community, that it had to go on. The school district had released a statement that they were working with authorities to ensure a safe environment. The news ended and a game show started.

Nolan found himself thinking about that visit from the cops. It wasn't like they implied, the *incident* back in high school. He'd let himself be talked into going to a school dance with his childhood friend Sarah Bullard, his cousin Matt, and a few of their friends. Matt and Sarah were two of the very few people he interacted with. High school dances weren't Nolan's scene, but at lunch one day Matt had pushed and said it would be fun, and when Sarah chimed in leaning her head on his shoulder and squeezing an arm around him, Nolan agreed to go. Of course he was in love with Sarah. He had been since fifth grade. She was just about the only person he felt comfortable being that kind of close to.

But at the dance, the music thumped loudly and the lights strobed and the crowd pressed in. Sarah was taken up by one dance request after another from a seemingly endless line of guys. Matt went off to find one girl or another. And after being jostled by the crowd even as he stood pressed against the wall, Nolan retreated to the walkway outside the gymnasium. He'd just wanted to lay low and collect himself, but he was spotted by a group of big shot football players huddled in the shadows sneaking smokes.

One of them called to Nolan, "What's the matter? That hotty don't want to hang with a retard?"

Someone else quietly said the guy's name, "Heath."

"No, man, I mean it. He follows her around like a damned dog, sniffing at her ass all the time." Then to Nolan again, "Hey, Delacroix, you think Sarah Bullard's your speed? Go back to the special ed room."

Nolan wasn't in special ed. In fact, he sat right behind Sarah in English and beside her in History.

When Nolan didn't reply, Heath stepped closer so he loomed over Nolan. "What, freakshow? You want to say something?"

To this day Nolan could still smell the musky cologne Heath wore. The football team had lost the night before and was out of the playoffs. Nolan knew that Heath needed someone to lord his superiority over, to reassure himself. Nolan started to turn away, to walk back inside, but Heath grabbed his arm with a hard grip, squeezing, trying to make Nolan cry out. Nolan couldn't pull away.

Out of instinctual fear Nolan found himself saying, "Let go or I'll blow your ass up." It was just something he'd heard on TV. Imitating a tough guy threat against a bully. He hardly knew what it meant and certainly had no way of backing it up.

Things could have gone so many ways. Heath could have decked Nolan. His pals could have jumped in. Everyone could have laughed and let the whole thing go as a joke. But no.

Instead, Heath stepped back and nearly yelled, "What'd you say? Jesus, he threatened to blow up the school. He said he's going to bomb the school."

Murmurs spread from that, and teachers who of course weren't around moments before quickly showed up.

There was zero tolerance about threats like that, and there was an investigation, though there wasn't anything to find. Still Nolan spent the rest of that year as well as his senior year at the alternative school where they hid away the "troubled" kids.

If he hadn't already been marked, he was after that.

*****

The next day at work his crew was assigned to help the school custodians prep and clean the stadium. It was not lost on him that in the past decades he'd apparently proven trustworthy enough to clean trash at the school before the big game, but not to move past the false accusations of his childhood when others needed a convenient scapegoat.

He spent the morning picking up loose debris around campus, working his way to an alley between the stadium and the school building. He was reaching for trash wedged between the brick wall of the school and one of the huge green dumpsters when he heard a whispered conversation at a back door that opened onto the alley. He figured that students might use the stoop outside that door as a place to hide for a private conversation, or maybe to sneak a smoke or vape. From his place behind the dumpster, he couldn't see the kids and knew they couldn't see him. He didn't intend to eavesdrop. But their whispers carried in the concrete and brick alley, and the desperate, near-tears tone made him freeze. He heard snippets, but not every word.

"…keep thinking about that guy…in the hospital…"

"I know but . . . keep cool"

"I … didn't mean … happen like that . . . couldn't stop them…"

"Dillon, come on … was an accident … you didn't…"

"Only supposed to … a prank….going to release … cows on the Sabine South field …now the police…"

"Talk to your grandfather … maybe he could… make it go away."

"Yeah, maybe. He's . . . city council… maybe mayor soon."

The sniff of muffled crying. Then the squeak of the door widening open and shoes shuffling like the kids were heading back inside.

Nolan straightened up, and his toe nudged a Coke can that clattered along the concrete. He moved to pick it up and noticed in his peripheral vision the school door still in the process of closing and the shadowed movement of someone going inside, but not quite there yet. Nolan paused for the briefest moment. The student at the door flinched and looked toward him, but Nolan kept about his business as though unaware of anyone there.

Because he knew who the kid was, and he wished he didn't, and he didn't want to look up but he had to because he hoped to prove himself wrong. He glanced up and saw the kid and the kid saw him, and with a sick feeling in his gut Nolan knew he was right.

He made a show of going about his work. When he looked toward the door again, Sarah Bullard's son had gone inside.

*****

Despite his discomfort in crowds and despite the warnings at work, he needed to see what was happening for himself.

In the graying late afternoon light he went downtown, where hundreds of people gathered in the blocks between City Hall and St. Mary's Hospital. Some appeared to be holding vigil outside of the hospital, while others yelled slogans and held signs reading, "Justice for Larry Harold" and "No justice, No Peace" and "Stop the Hate." Others appeared to be counter-protesting, yelling at people to go home. Inside the hospital, Larry Harold, the man injured when he veered to avoid the loose cows, lay in the ICU.

Nolan kept his distance from the fray as he wandered along the sidewalks and streets where the crowd thinned. No one paid him much attention. Those who glanced at him looked him over and quickly dismissed him. Because he was able to wander without notice, he overheard pieces of conversations. Plans to protest Friday night, references to a "show of force" and "making them pay."

He felt anger surging through the crowd in a way the TV news didn't convey. Felt it trembling like the lid on a pot of boiling water. He understood that Larry Harold was becoming a symbol for people tired of being targets and victims. And he understood that hopelessness. He knew what it was to be marginalized, targeted. He didn't know the racial side of it, but he knew it personally.

*****

That evening Nolan hunched over a plate of seafood nachos, a pile of tortilla chips with crab, shrimp, and crawfish slathered with queso. Across the table sat his cousin Matt. Matt watched him, leaned back and hooked his arm over the back of his chair. He looked toward a nearby table of five middle-aged women, all nicely dressed, drinking, laughing among themselves, looking around to see who noticed them and who was worth noticing.

"Those women are on the prowl," Matt said. "They have grown or nearly grown kids and fat, obnoxious husbands who haven't satisfied them in years. Or they're divorced already and looking for the next conquest. Look dude, their expectations are already low. They'd love to break you out of your shell."

Nolan picked at his food, gave a half-smile. They were at The Riverside, a restaurant with a large patio overlooking the river. The place had a stage for live bands, a palapas bar, and tables situated under umbrellas and strings of outdoor lights.

"You can't just putter around the yard," Matt went on. "When's the last time you had anyone to your house? Who even sees that garden you spend so much time on?"

Nolan shrugged. "You don't have to babysit me," he said. "I'm sure Liz would prefer you at home with her and the kids."

"They're at her parents'," Matt said. He waved his hand dismissively, then smiled. "Believe it or not, you're my better option."

Nolan and Matt had a standing weekly dinner. Sometimes Matt's wife and two kids came. Sometimes Nolan went to their place. He knew Matt did it partly as some obligation to watch out for Nolan, and Nolan had long ago accepted that it was easier to keep the weekly dinner rather than beg off and have to face his cousin's intense pestering. Tonight Nolan actually wanted to talk to Matt. He just didn't know how to say what was on his mind. If he said the wrong thing, he might make things much worse.

"Hey, I'm kidding. Don't sweat it," Matt was saying.

Across the patio a conversation back and forth between a few separate tables grew louder, agitated. Chairs scraped the ground as people jostled to stand. Other voices rose, demanding that everyone settle down.

"What's going on?" Matt said. "You've been quieter than usual today."

Nolan put down his fork. "The game Friday night," he said. "Will they cancel or postpone if the bomber hasn't been caught by then?" He didn't say it, but he hoped they didn't catch the bomber before the game, so the game would be postponed, if not outright cancelled.

"They don't want to cancel or postpone," Matt said. He was a vice-principal at Northside High, so he was in the loop. "Obviously if there's a credible threat, yeah. But the game's a significant event for the kids and the community. Like confirmation that life's normal."

"Life's not normal," Nolan said.

Matt shrugged. "You think they won't have the stadium covered in security?"

"It's bigger than that," Nolan said. "Regardless of the bomber, people are already amped up. Looking to take out their anger on others. The stadium will be packed. Thousands of people. It's a tinderbox, Matt."

Across the patio, the argument was heating up again. The women at the table near Nolan and Matt got up and left. Matt gestured for the waitress to bring the bill.

"That wreck, the cows," Nolan said. "People are saying it's a hate crime. Come on, it doesn't make sense. Who releases cows as a terrorist act?"

"There's the old Black cemetery nearby. The Hispanic Heritage Center just down Old River Road. Maybe those were targets. Think of the damage a herd of cattle could do if they stampeded all over the place. Look at what happened."

"Matt, it was a prank that got out of hand."

"Maybe. What makes you so sure? And why are you so worked up about it?"

Nolan was looking at his plate when he quietly said, "What if I heard something, something that might hurt a friend if I told anyone? But if I don't say something, things could get really bad for a lot of other people."

"A friend? You don't have friends. You barely talk to me and you've known me all your life." Matt tilted his head and squinted a scrutinizing look at Nolan. "This doesn't have anything to do with Sarah, does it? Aww, Nolan. I see it on your face. Do y'all even talk?"

Nolan shook his head. "No."

"Look, I know she's getting divorced, right? So maybe you've got ideas about you and her."

"It's not like that."

"Just keep your head down and stay out of stuff you don't get. This'll blow over. The hype of the moment's fostering unusual behavior in people."

"I don't think it's unusual behavior at all," Nolan said. "I think people are revealing their true selves."

"Nolan, you're a lot smarter than most people realize. But let's face it, you're not necessarily great at understanding people. Or social situations."

But Nolan did understand. He knew that people needed scapegoats. He knew they'd crucify Sarah's son and anyone who was with him if they were identified for causing the wreck, even inadvertently. Nolan also understood that if people didn't see that it was a prank gone wrong and not a deliberate act of hate, tensions would continue to escalate until they exploded. There were enough true acts of hate to fuel everyone's rage. They didn't need a falsified, misunderstood one.

Across the patio the argument among several tables erupted into a scuffle. Chairs overturned. Glasses fell. People scattered as a few red-faced, large-bellied men converged. Heated voices yelled, "You don't like it here, you can leave," and "I'll help you pack your shit," and "Come on, let's do it, come on."

Matt stood to leave, and Nolan followed suit. He'd gotten the response that he'd expected. It left him feeling all the more like he was helplessly witnessing something terrible unfolding.

*****

The next day, after another anxious but ultimately uneventful shift at work, Nolan found himself sitting in his truck across the street from Sarah's house. He wasn't entirely sure what he wanted here. He wanted to ask about her son. Feel out whether or not she knew. He hadn't spoken to her in years, though, and it troubled him that maybe Matt was right that Nolan had ideas about Sarah. The more he thought about it, the more he recognized that in some way he simply wanted to be close to her. He'd been sitting there for half an hour trying to work up the nerve to go to the door.

He watched the house. It was in a north end neighborhood with large brick and stone homes. Sarah's was two stories with faux-balconies and decorative ironwork extending off the second-story windows. Nothing like the security bars on so many places on the other end of town. There was also a three-car garage with carriage-style doors. In the front yard was an elaborately hand-painted sign in the school colors and the shape of a football helmet: Dillon, #18.

Over the years they'd crossed paths a few times, passing from a distance at a grocery store or a restaurant. She was always with her family or friends, moving away, but Nolan thought he saw her give a brief, sad smile in his direction. Mostly he'd kept up with Sarah from a distance. They were "friends" online. So, yes, he knew she was going through a divorce. He'd noticed her soon-to-be-ex-husband's absence. How Sarah's son Dillon often missed bringing out the trash on time. Sometimes, Nolan drove by after work in his own truck and grabbed the trash still sitting out so it wouldn't fester there for days until the next pick-up. He felt gratified to help her, even without her knowing.

Nolan opened his car door, then closed it again. His heart thumped so hard he felt it in his stomach. Whether it was uncertainty, nerves, or just a bad feeling about things, Nolan started his truck and eased away. He felt relieved to escape facing what he'd been thinking about but also sickened at himself. At, frankly, his cowardice.

As he pulled away, a black Mercedes passed him, slowed, turned into Sarah's driveway. Nolan knew the car, of course, and knew the face turning to look at him. Kenneth Bullard. Sarah's father, a leading figure on the city council and frontrunner to be the next mayor. Sarah's father had always been against Nolan and Sarah's friendship. More than once when they were kids Bullard had pulled Nolan aside at some school event and warned him not to get the wrong idea about Sarah, that he wasn't the right material for her. After Nolan's incident in high school, Sarah's father forbade her from hanging with him at all.

*****

One thing Nolan knew for sure, when someone comes looking for you early, it's not good.

Kenneth Bullard came into the service barn the next morning while the crews were prepping. The morning sky was gray, the pavement dew-slick. Bullard parked his Mercedes in front of the open oversized garage doors as if to block anyone's escape. Then he strode inside, his crisp gray suit and tie nearly the same color as the morning air. At seventy, Bullard was tall and lean with a full head of salt-and-pepper hair and a neatly trimmed beard. He carried himself in the manner of someone used to commanding deference.

From the far side of the garage, Nolan saw his supervisor bow slightly, saying, "Yes sir, of course, right over there." Pointing in Nolan's direction. The other guys busied themselves, keeping their distance but staying in view either so they could see or be seen for their diligence.

Bullard didn't walk over to Nolan. Instead he clicked in his shiny shoes on out the back of the barn to the gravel parking lot where the garbage trucks idled. He flicked two fingers in a gesture calling for Nolan to follow him.

"Care to explain yourself," Bullard said when Nolan stepped before him. He spoke in a low tone barely audible over the trucks' idling engines.

Nolan wasn't sure what to say. He shuffled on the gravel.

"Let me try it this way," Bullard said. "Why did I see you pulling away from in front of my daughter's home yesterday? Surely you won't try denying it was you."

Nolan wanted to explain. To ask if Bullard knew about his grandson Dillon. If Dillon had gone to him yet. Nolan wanted to explain that he was terrified of what might happen, that he had no idea what to do about it. That he knew Bullard had never liked him but that maybe they were on the same side here. But Nolan wasn't sure what the sides were.

Bullard pointed a long finger toward Nolan. "Whatever you have in mind, forget it. Despite Sarah's marital problems, you have no place in her life. You understand me? There is no reason in the world for you to be near her home unless you're on one of these trucks picking up garbage. If this happens again you'll be looking for a new job. At the least."

Nolan toed a divot in the gravel and nodded.

*****

Late that afternoon, a device hidden in the shrubs beside the front door of Our Lady of Guadalupe Church exploded. The door to the church was ripped away and several windows shattered. Nobody was nearby at the time, although not a hundred yards away the school affiliated with the church had recently dismissed for the day.

One of the local news stations received and released a handwritten note reading, "*south Port Sabine used to be a nice place. Look at the FILTH its become. Don't you know your NOT welcome here! If the police didn't agree with me I'd already be in custody!*"

Nolan felt compelled to check the pulse of the crowds downtown. A light drizzle was falling and people huddled there as dusk settled in and the streetlights came on. It was hard to tell who was holding vigil, who was protesting, and who was counter-protesting. Nolan wandered just close enough to feel the foreboding calm that had descended. Like people were steeling themselves for what would come next.

In spite of that, Nolan felt a glimmer of hope. Certainly they'd have to cancel the game now. Certainly they would.

*****

That evening Nolan brought his mother roses cut fresh from his yard.

He found himself at a loss for what to tell her. He couldn't think of any amusing anecdotes, and frankly he wondered if it was worth bothering anyway. Did she even understand what he said?

He slouched in the bedside chair barely paying attention to the game show on TV when the local news cut in with Breaking Updates. The suspected bomber had been arrested. On TV were shots of a pudgy pale man with a goatee, hunched with a windbreaker pulled over his head as federal agents and police led him from a normal-looking ranch home in what might be any working-class neighborhood in the city. The news anchor reported that investigators were looking into possible accomplices though it was likely that the *alleged* bomber had worked alone. The anchor announced that in tonight's ten o'clock broadcast they'd provide further information … but Nolan had tuned out.

He felt a wave of nausea come over him. The bomber being caught should be a good thing, he knew. And he wondered at the state of the world when the capture of a dangerous lunatic did nothing to improve matters. When in fact it might make matters worse.

*****

Nolan had missed only three days of work in his entire career, but he called in sick on Friday morning. As the light of day grew, he walked the paths of his yard, here and there clipping an overgrown limb or pulling an errant weed, unsure if he was working up his nerve or simply coming to accept what he had to do. Once the regular business hours of the day began, he swallowed the queasiness growing in his stomach and got to it.

Nolan didn't find what he was looking for outside City Hall, so he drove by the office for Bullard & Associates Accounting in a business park of mostly law firms, insurance agencies, and accountants on the city's north side. He found the black Mercedes parked in the prime spot front and center before the gleaming glass face of the office.

Inside he told the receptionist he was there to see Mr. Bullard. He said that he was there on behalf of Mr. Bullard's grandson Dillon. Within ten minutes he was escorted to Bullard's office. Leather chairs before a mahogany desk. Bookshelves along one wall. Windows along another. Bullard sat behind the desk, pen grasped in his hand, papers stacked neatly before him, squinting at his computer monitor. He didn't acknowledge Nolan except to point with the pen toward one of the chairs. He wore a suit only a shade different from the one he'd worn yesterday, the jacket hanging from a rack in the corner.

Once the receptionist left, Bullard looked from his monitor to Nolan but still said nothing. He scrutinized Nolan as though trying to work out some new and puzzling insight. Finally he put down his pen with a thunk and took in a long, slow breath. Bullard started to speak, but Nolan suddenly spit out the words he was afraid might abandon him entirely if he didn't say them right then.

"I think it would help calm people down if they knew the accident that injured Larry Harold wasn't a hate crime. That it was a prank that went wrong. Especially now that the bomber's been caught. Maybe people would ease up a bit if they knew the truth."

Bullard blinked.

Outside the windows was a view of sidewalks leading to picnic tables and gazebos among small grassy hills—an attempt to make the business park look inviting, though it didn't appear that anyone was utilizing the tables or gazebos.

"Why are you coming to me about this?" Bullard finally said, noticeably collecting himself.

Nolan continued looking past Bullard, out the windows. "You're in a position to do something to help. A unique position."

"Look at me, son. Look me in the eyes."

Slowly, Nolan shifted his gaze toward Bullard's.

"You mentioned my grandson's name to get in here."

Nolan held still. Bullard studied him.

"You know what happened," Bullard said.

Nolan nodded.

"How do you know?"

Nolan shrugged.

"Is there a video? Something like that?"

Again Nolan shrugged. Let the old man believe what he would. No benefit in telling him otherwise.

"Dillon came to me. He told me what happened," Bullard said. "He's torn up about it. You don't understand the complexity here. His intention was simply to load up a few of the cattle and set them loose on the Sabine South practice field. I'd told him about the year we dumped loads of manure all over their field. It's all part of the rivalry."

Nolan remained silent.

"What is it you think I'll do?" Bullard said. "You can't honestly believe I'll ruin my grandson's life by, what? Bringing him forward?"

Before he even thought about it, Nolan said, "Or maybe ruin your shot at being mayor?"

Bullard stood. They looked at one another, both surprised at Nolan's audacity.

Bullard placed his hands flat on his desk, leaned forward with a hard glare at Nolan. "Before you get any grand ideas, ask yourself this. How do you think Sarah will feel about someone threatening her son's future?" There was a tremor in his voice.

This wasn't what Nolan had intended. He hadn't come here to coerce Bullard. He'd come for help, hadn't he? Nolan stood up. He started to apologize but stopped himself.

Bullard's shoulders rose and fell with his breaths. He looked as though he might come over the desk at Nolan.

"Everyone always tells me I don't understand. You said it yourself just a minute ago," Nolan started, stopped, then began again, "But I understand that there are no good options here. People are going to get hurt. It's only a matter of how many and how badly."

"And who," Bullard said. "It's also a matter of who."

Nolan turned and walked to the door. He'd crossed the room and reached the handle when Bullard spoke again.

"Maybe I've been a bit harsh with you," Bullard said. "I didn't think it was in Sarah's best interest to be close with you when y'all were younger. It's possible you could be a good friend to her now, though. This divorce is difficult for her."

Nolan heard the desperation in Bullard's voice. He also recognized it in himself when he paused with his hand on the door handle. There it was. The prospect of being close to Sarah again. But no, that wasn't something Bullard could offer. That was strictly between Sarah and himself. So why did he feel…what? Enticed?

And simultaneously disgusted.

He opened the door and walked out, focusing all he had on staying upright on hollow legs.

*****

A few hours later, Larry Harold died due to injuries from his accident.

News spread quickly and crowds downtown swelled. A "March for Justice" formed but encountered rioters who flooded the streets, throwing bricks and bottles, breaking windows. Counter-protesters wearing militia gear and carrying AR-15s engaged the crowds. Enough law enforcement arrived on scene fast enough to disperse the crowds and prevent an all-out riot.

Nolan watched clips of the eruption on one of the local news sites, and he knew it was far from over.

*****

He didn't give himself the chance to back out. He parked in the driveway and went to the front door and rang the bell. When Sarah opened the door he was dumbstruck by the reality of being in her presence again. He'd missed her. And he realized that he'd always expected to be close to her again, that he'd maybe even lived every day waiting for that to happen.

She was beautiful. The years had lightened the color of her hair but her eyes still had the intense blue-gray brilliance he remembered. She was dressed for the game in jeans and a maroon and gold jersey with "Dillon #18's Mom" emblazoned on it. Nolan knew he was shaking as he watched her expression go from curiosity to recognition to surprise.

"Nolan?" she said. A smile that broke his heart spread on her face. She blinked and tilted her head. "Wow. What's…how are you?"

He shuffled. Wanted to turn and run. Wanted just as much to go inside, sit across from her, just be there with her and forget about everything else.

Behind her, a young man's voice was saying, "Mom, is my gear bag in the washroom? I have to get to the field house."

Nolan saw Dillon coming down the staircase behind Sarah, and at the same time Dillon saw Nolan. He stopped, recognition and understanding forming on his face. A face that Nolan saw his old childhood friend in. Nolan forced himself to hold his gaze steady.

Dillon stood still for a moment, then crumbled. He dropped heavily onto the stair-step behind him and sobbed.

Nolan saw Sarah's smile fade. Saw the pained, questioning look she gave him. Saw her entire presence dissolve into anxiety as she turned to look at her son.

"Mom," Dillon was crying. "Oh God, Mom."

Nolan still had not said a word.

"Granddad said …" Dillon was saying through heaving gasps, "not to tell…"

"What?" Sarah said. "What is this?"

"But that man…" Dillon was saying, "he died, didn't he?" He looked at Nolan, his face a bawling mess.

Nolan nodded yes.

By then Sarah had turned away from him entirely. She started up the stairs toward her son. Nolan felt the trembling fear in her, the terrible realization of something unbearable. And he knew he'd brought this to her.

"I'm so sorry," he said, backing away. "I didn't know what else to do. I didn't want any of this."

*****

He didn't know what he'd accomplished. The game was still on. The city was willing to overlook the turmoil so they could have the reassurance of their traditions.

He waited until it would be too late to thoroughly check the stadium, but before the gathering crowds waiting to enter grew too large. He wanted people turned away before the numbers surged and things would so easily get out of hand. He drove to the outskirts of town so when they pinged the call it wouldn't trace to anywhere he'd be found.

He used a pre-paid cell phone he'd found one day on his work route.

He called in a bomb threat at the stadium.

Then he threw the phone into a drainage canal and drove home.

Nolan knew he couldn't eliminate the inevitable conflict. It was the nature of things. But maybe he could buy some time. Maybe the best anyone could do was stave off imminent disasters. Diminish the damage. People thought he didn't understand. But what Nolan knew maybe better than anyone was how easily things can get distorted, blown out of proportion. How easily things can explode.

At home he walked the paths of his yard. He didn't think anyone would come for him. He'd already been cleared, after all. The dusk air had a purple hue and held the scent of night-blooming jasmine. The blooms on his shrubs rustled in the breeze. All this beauty he so painstakingly nurtured. He'd never before felt lonely. Hadn't until now understood what that meant.

Let My Pistol Decide My Fate
Richard J. O'Brien

The dead man had no past. He carried no identification. His fingerprints did not show up in any of the regular databases. It was as if he had just fallen out of the sky.

I had a friend in the FBI. We did each other favors. Actually, she did me more favors than I did for her. The agent's name was Claudia Rankin. We'd been a thing once. Not anymore. After she joined the Bureau, we became a thing of the past. I sent her the prints from the dead man.

Claudia had access to databases that tracked people with super top-secret clearances, the kind of people who were out in the world working clandestine operations for CIA, DIA, or what have you. If it turned out to be one of those people, an alert popped up. The whole system was automated. In theory, the group to which the person belonged would take over at that point and deal with local law enforcement directly. In my career, I had never dealt with anything like that. And I was grateful. It made life simple. A couple of days after I sent her the dead man's prints Claudia got back to me. She had come up with nothing.

"Not a single match?" I asked Claudia over the phone.

"Noah," she said. "The very definition of the word 'nothing' implies—"

"Sure," I told her. "Listen, thanks. I got to go. Call me when you're in town."

"Drop dead," she replied by way of goodbye.

Ten years is never enough to get over heartbreak. When couples break up things have already gone bad. Everyone knows that. Yet, people used to say of Claudia and me: *I didn't know you were having problems?* Our problems were so bad that Claudia applied for the FBI while still working the larceny beat with me in Philadelphia. She never said a word. Sometimes it felt like our time together wasn't real, as if those memories belonged to someone else. It ended like this: one day I woke up alone and found a note on the kitchen counter. *Off to Quantico*, it read. I knew she had applied. A couple of FBI agents came around on my day off nearly a year before Claudia left. At first I thought they were Internal Affairs. They just wanted to know the nature of my relationship with Claudia. I was honest. It was contentious at best. What I never counted on was Claudia keeping her acceptance a secret. When I found that note I was plenty sore about it.

"Sergeant Detective Brennan," my commander Captain Brodsky called out from his office when I was on my way to roll call that day. "A word, please."

He proceeded to tell me about how Claudia made it her express wish that I be kept out of the loop. Her father had been a cop. He and Brodsky went all the way back to the days when Frank Rizzo was mayor, and the two men were just rookies. Brodsky should have retired long ago, but he was afraid of suffering a heart attack or stroke the way some guys did right after they left the job.

Anyway, the dead man was found one morning in Rittenhouse Square by some citizens on their way to work. We might have chalked it up to natural causes save for the bones of the dead man's body. Nearly all of them were broken. The shape of the dead man's head shifted and sagged some when the medical examiners finally placed his corpse in a body bag.

*****

The Philadelphia County Medical Examiner's Office was a place I dreaded. You'd think that a homicide detective would get used to being around dead people, but the truth was you never did. I've seen the toughest bastards crack when faced with dead infants that had been starved for months. Life as a homicide detective gnawed at you. No one was immune.

The medical examiner who went over the autopsy report with me was named Samson. Abraham Samson. He was a wiry-haired, barrel-chested Jew with a Santa Claus beard. His permanent smirk hinted that he knew something no one else did, and he wasn't telling.

"Abe," I said.

"Noah," he pumped my hand when I offered it. He kept on shaking it as if he were grateful just to be in the presence of someone alive. "How have you been?"

"Working a lot of hours—" I started to say.

"This one is fascinating," he cut me off. Good old Abe Samson. He wasn't interested at all in other people's lives. He always said that the dead told better stories. "You'll read in the report I prepared that the decedent's injuries are consistent with someone falling from a high altitude."

"He wasn't near any of the high-rises around the square," I told him.

"I know," he said. "I read your report. Even if he were found on the front drive of the Rittenhouse Hotel I'd still rule out our John Doe being a jumper."

"Why would you do that?"

"Because his injuries are more consistent with someone whose parachute failed to open," Samson announced.

"He wasn't wearing a chute," I said. "And I'm fairly certain that skydiving into Center City Philly is against the law."

"Maybe he fell out of a helicopter."

"How far do you think the fall was?"

"That I don't know," Samson informed me. "The human body is remarkable in keeping itself in one piece after a high fall, but after a certain distance the chances lessen."

"You mean like when a body pops open?" I asked.

"Stop watching movies, Noah," he advised.

"Fine," I said. Then, "What should I be looking for? Foul play in the skies over Philly?"

"Nothing like that, I'm afraid," he said. "I found no evidence of bodily trauma that occurred before the fall. If your John Doe was roughed up and thrown from an aircraft, the party responsible took great pains to hide it."

"So, what? We got a guy who committed suicide? What did he do? Jump from his aircraft? If he did, where is it?"

"I suppose," Samson said, "that's not the kind of thing people tend to miss."

"A deranged angel of mercy flying around and letting terminal patients jump from his plane or helicopter sans parachute?"

"That's for a detective like you to figure out, Noah," he told me. "But I can tell you that this gentleman was in perfect health before he met his end."

By the time I left the ME's office, I had more questions than answers.

*****

I spent the following day and a good part of the evening interviewing radar operators at the Philadelphia International Airport. I contacted New Jersey State Police, and they had a couple of detectives canvas the two closest regional airports on the New Jersey side of the Delaware River. As I suspected, there was nothing strange or otherwise untowardly going on in the skies over Philadelphia the night John Doe died.

After a fourteen-hour shift, I called it a night and went to Monk's Café, my favorite center city watering hole. Depending on the hour, I usually got a seat at the bar. When it was crowded I sometimes left my jacket open. Often enough, the sight of my holstered service pistol under my arm and my badge on my belt was enough for someone to abandon their bar stool. It was a dick move, but I wasn't out to impress anyone. Likewise, I didn't want to meet anyone new. Most strangers I met were dull, as if they were background characters in someone else's story.

Ever since Claudia and I split, I never made time for another relationship. I didn't take a vow of chastity. Far from it. The truth was

I was a saboteur when it came to relationships of any length. Sometimes I didn't call when I said I would, a hazard of police work. Sorry baby. I was tied up working on a case. Other times women made themselves scarce. It was not uncommon to discover that they had changed their phone numbers. One day, years after Claudia's departure, I woke up and realized my forty-fifth birthday had already passed. My only lasting accomplishment thus far had been not getting shot and killed on the job.

That night at Monk's I got a seat at the bar. One of my favorite things to do was to eavesdrop on conversations. I didn't do it as a cop. I used to kid Claudia that if I hadn't been in law enforcement I would have been a therapist. I was good at listening to people. So, I sat there trying my best not to look too much like a plainclothes cop which, after fifteen years as a detective, was next to impossible.

"So what did you do?" the bartender asked a patron seated to my left.

"I called the cops," said the patron. He was a short, nervous guy in a wrinkled dark blue shirt. "They were no help."

"But someone stole personal property from you?"

"Pages from a novel manuscript," the short man said. "It's not like you can put a monetary value on them."

"Do you know Noah?" the bartender said, pointing at me.

Shit, I thought. Some days listening to people bitch about the police was enough to make me quit. I wasn't in the mood.

"J.D. Clark," the short man extended his right hand.

"Like the writer?" I shook his hand.

"Guilty," said Clark.

I didn't read much, but a guy on my squad had turned me on to J.D. Clark's books a few years ago. Clark wrote police procedural books with a supernatural twist. He was a regular face around various precincts when he was performing research for his novels. Thus far, I hadn't been tapped to help the Philadelphia native in a professional capacity.

"What does J.D. stand for?" I asked.

"The answer to that I will share," he told me, "if you can name one book of mine you've read."

"The Iron Widow's Prayer," I replied.

"Impressive," he said. "You didn't even have to think about it."

"My buddy got me onto your books. *The Iron Widow's Prayer* was my favorite."

"Jericho David," Clark announced. "That my parents were into the bible would be a gross understatement."

"Mine were only vaguely familiar with it, I'm afraid," I mumbled.

Clark found this hysterical. Before he guffawed loud enough for everyone around us to hear I was ready to write him off as a stuffed shirt. His laughter was high-pitched, infectious to the point that other people, including the bartender, chuckled even though they didn't hear the joke.

"Call me Jerry," he said.

We chatted about *The Iron Widow's Prayer*. I learned all about Clark's background, which was oddly enough parallel to mine. He grew up in Northeast Philadelphia, spent his summers with family at the New Jersey Shore, and attended Philadelphia Community College. He went to Temple University after that, the same as I did, but here our paths no longer mirrored each other's. I finished my degree: criminal justice. Clark dropped out in the spring semester of his second year when his first novel was published. *The Alley of Memory.* He was twenty years old.

"My advance on the hardback was hardly enough to live on," Clark informed me, "much to my parents' chagrin. But the paperback rights afforded me the chance to find my own place. It helped that I had an agent who got me a three-book deal."

The conversation drifted away from all things literary. I wanted to ask him about how pages from his current work in progress came to be missing. I didn't get the chance.

Just after midnight, four young women entered Monk's Café. They forced their way against the bar the way college girls do in all of their vibrant, fearless allure. Their presence gave the room a renewed sense of hope, a second wind, a promise of light in the dark.

I would be remiss if I said I didn't find them beautiful. At twice their age, however, I did not delude myself into thinking I had a shot at bedding any of them. For one, I didn't speak their language. When they looked at a guy like me they didn't see a mysterious, experienced man. They saw their fathers. I was left with no choice but to honor societal boundaries.

Jerry Clark was hewn from a different grain. He managed to work into the first five minutes of conversation with the girls that he was a writer. It became abundantly clear that none of them had heard of him. Clark played it cool. He knew his audience. Judging from what he told them about his life, he had to be in his mid-fifties. That didn't stop him from flirting like a boy a fraction of his age. I had to hand it to him. He was fearless. The tide turned after he asked one of the girls to share her name again.

"Miriam Chastain," she said.

The young woman said it so matter-of-factly. There was a distinct absence of suspicion. Miriam, like her friends, was confident and comfortable in Clark's presence. He did not represent a threat. By all appearances, he did not seem like one of those louts with hidden and perverted ulterior motives.

"Want to get out of here?" Clark asked. "We can have drinks at my place."

"No," Miriam said, flatly.

The color of Clark's face changed. He got off his bar stool and shuffled toward the door.

I followed him outside.

"Are you all right?" I asked as we stood on 16th Street.

"Sure," he said. "Sometimes things get weird. It wasn't supposed to go that way. I must be losing my touch."

Some guys could never accept rejection. I was not immune, but it had been years since I felt anything close to confidence where the opposite sex was concerned.

Clark didn't look visibly drunk. Drugs? I wondered. He wouldn't have been the first writer in history to make a living doing what he loves while in the throes of addiction.

"She's one girl," I attempted to console him.

"You would think I'm crazy if I told you," said Clark.

"Tell me about it, Jerry," I said.

"The novel I'm working on," he explained. "One of the female characters I named Miriam."

"It's not an uncommon name."

"Miriam Chastain *is* the character's name," he replied. "Do you know what the statistical possibility is for something like this to happen?"

"Sometimes coincidence is stronger than we think," I said.

Clark looked at me. He offered a nervous laugh.

"In the pages I reported missing to the police," he said, "Miriam was first introduced."

"You saved it on a computer, I'm sure," I offered.

His expression soured.

"I type first drafts using an old manual typewriter," he told me. "An Underwood. The very one I used to type my first novel. So, no. I can't print it out again. I know it sounds stupid, my not using computers to back up my work. I eventually use them after I revise the first typed draft. I must sound like a crazy man."

"Not at all," I said, ignorant of how the writing game worked.

"Writers are a superstitious lot," Clark informed me. "I am more superstitious than most. There are certain practices and traditions I abide by for fear of screwing up the works, if that makes sense."

Clark looked south along 16th Street, waved down a taxi as it approached. When the taxi came to a stop at the curb Clark jumped inside without saying another word.

*****

I had a friend in the burglary division. I told him the particulars of Jerry Clark's complaint. Eric Stokes, my friend in the burglary division, wasn't much of a reader. He didn't know J.D. Clark. Stokes looked up the complaint by Clark's last name. He put me in touch with a detective in the sixth district. Clark, I discovered with Stokes's help, lived in Society Hill on Washington Square.

I paid a visit to the 6th District Precinct. I spoke to the guy Stokes had told me about. Roland Lapland was his name. He was on his way out to follow up on an unrelated case. I walked with him to the parking lot.

"Yeah man," Lapland from the 6th precinct said, "I remember him. Snobby son of a bitch. He wanted to know what we are doing about his missing pages. I told him, 'Hey, if you backed up your work in the cloud—"

"He uses a typewriter first," I explained.

"How the hell do you know that?" Lapland asked.

I explained that I had met the writer recently. I lied, telling Lapland that I knew Clark from community college and recently saw him at a book signing near Lower Merion. The missing pages of his book came up. I told Lapland that Clark was just baffled.

"I never handled a case like this," the detective told me.

"Me neither," I assured him.

"Missing manuscript pages," he scowled. "What's next? Investigating stolen pencils? Bad reviews?"

"Were there any signs of forced entry?"

"The guy lives at Hopkinson House on Washington Square," said Hopper. "On the twentieth floor overlooking the park. You got to get past a doorman and a security guard in the lobby before you get onto the resident floors."

"Did he have any work done in his place?" I asked.

"Look, Brennan," he said, puffing up his chest. "I've been around just like you. I know how to do my damned job."

"I am not disputing that," I assured him. "I'm just trying to help an old friend."

Lapland deflated a bit after that.

"Nobody's been to his place," he said. "No utility workers. No cable television repairmen. No contractors. No one. The doorman says Clark rarely goes out. He says that Clark even gets his groceries delivered."

"That sounds like a promising lead," I said.

"Save it," countered Lapland. "We checked it out already. Clark always has the groceries left in the lobby with a concierge. Apparently, your writer friend is paranoid about people being in his apartment."

"Working from home is harder than we think," I said.

"Writers," Lapland said, with certain contempt. He spat on the sidewalk as we stood outside there by his car. Then, "No offense, but the guy's a loon."

I thanked him and we shook hands.

When I pulled away from the building on 11th Street I didn't make it a block before my police radio came to life. Another body: female in her twenties. Cause of death undetermined. This time the dead was found at a residential building on Green Street in the Spring Garden section of the city. It was two o'clock in the afternoon. My shift was only two hours old.

*****

In every detective's career, there's a case that, at first, defies all reason. The new case turned out to be almost as baffling as the man who had fallen out of the air into Rittenhouse Square.

By the time I arrived at the city's Spring Garden section, Green Street looked like a block party for uniformed officers. The supervisor on the scene was Sergeant Lou Stanovich. Everyone in the district called him Sergeant Stosh.

"Sergeant Brennan," the uniformed sergeant said when he spotted me. "I didn't know this one was ruled a homicide sight unseen."

He was tall, thin, and balding. His wrinkled uniform shirts leveled a permanent mark against law enforcement couture.

Stosh smiled often, like a village idiot who didn't know better. It gave him a chance to proudly display his two missing front teeth, a job-related injury from years ago during the Republican National Convention. He got caught up against a gang of young animal rights activists breaking storefront windows along Walnut Street.

The tide of young anarchic bodies proved too much for Stosh that day. He ended up on his back. Like any officer outnumbered by assailants, he feared that he would be stripped of his firearm, and that the weapon would be used against him. Stosh held fast to his weapon, even when one of the protesters stomped his face with the heel of his boot. A cop of a lesser mettle would have fired on his assailants. Not Stosh. He did mace the lot of them and, once he got to his feet again, beat them bloody with his nightstick.

If you asked Stosh why he never got his missing teeth replaced, he'd tell you that a '*thiggerette*' wouldn't fit so well in his mouth. Ditto for drinking '*th-trawth*.' The truth of the matter was that he was just too cheap. His co-pay for partials would have cost less than a weekend in Atlantic City.

"Nice to see you, Stosh," I said. "Where's the body?"

"All business," he said, butchering the latter word due to his missing teeth.

He sounded a little like Daffy Duck, the way his tongue inadvertently slipped into the space his missing teeth had created and all of the S sounds he muttered ended up sounding like the 'th' in the word 'three.' The poor bastard. It was all I could do to keep a straight face.

"She's on the roof," said Stosh. "We can do the stairs inside or go around to the alley and use the fire escape."

I chose the stairs. The building was a four-story walk-up. Tenants hung around in their apartment doorways. Uniformed officers were stationed on each floor by the stairs to keep people from trying to gain access to the roof.

"We canvassed the tenants," Stosh said with labored breath as we climbed the stairs. He instinctively reached for the cigarettes in his shirt pocket but thought better of it while he was indoors. "Nobody knows the decedent."

The roof had been retro-fitted with a deck made from pressure-treated wood. A privacy fence of considerable height bordered the deck to make would-be suicide attempts work harder before completing their mission. A propane grill stood bolted to the deck. There were benches and a long table, also bolted down, that provided a seating area. Mismatched beach chairs stood along one stretch of the privacy fence. A sign had been bolted to the fence that read: *Please don't throw beach chairs into the street below.*

Privacy barriers bearing the Philadelphia PD logo had already been placed around the body located at the far end of the long picnic table.

"Forensics is already doing their thing," Stosh advised me.

I slipped behind the barrier. The dead girl, clothed, lay on her back as if napping. Her head looked misshapen. Even so, there was no way to mistake her identity.

"There's no identification on her," Stosh said as he stood behind me.

"Miriam Chastain," I told him.

"You knew her?"

It put me in a bad position. Not telling would put me in a worse place later on.

"Not really," I said. "I met her at Monk's Café last night. She had two or three girlfriends with her."

"Did you take her home?" Stosh asked.

I turned on him. He backed up a few feet and put his hands up.

"No, Stosh," I told him. "I did not. I'm old enough to be her father, for Christ's sake."

"More's the pity," he mumbled.

A forensics officer's radio came to life. She answered it briefly and stood up from where she had been kneeling beside the body.

"ME's on his way up," she said. "We're done here. He can do the transport."

The flap on the privacy barrier flew open and Abe Samson came through along with an assistant. He left the assistant to push the stretcher laden with spare body bags.

"Jeez Louise," Abe gasped. "Why can't people die on the street like good citizens?"

"Not funny, Abe," the forensics officer said before she slipped past him.

Abe nodded at the flap after the forensics squad member exited.

"She loves me," he said, fitting a beard net over his Santa beard. Then, looking me over, he asked, "What's gotten into you?"

I gave him the twenty-five-words-or-less version of meeting Miriam Chastain the previous evening.

"It's a small city," came Abe's reply. Then, thrusting the index finger on his right hand into the loosely closed fist of his left a few times, he asked, "Did you...?"

"Like I was telling Stosh just now," I said. "No, I did not."

"Oh, I wish I could meet someone young."

"Abe, you're married."

"Thirty-two years," he said.

"I don't recommend you start cheating now," I advised him.

"You're right," said Abe. "Besides, who would toast my Pop-tarts and tie my shoes in the morning?"

He winked at me.

I let him and his assistant get to work.

*****

Everything moved fast after that.

For starters, Abe Samson informed me that Miriam Chastain had died from injuries identical to the John Doe found in Rittenhouse Square. I wanted it to be something else, anything, but wishes carried little weight in police work.

The other thing I had to contend with in the immediate days following the discovery of Miriam Chastain's body was a formal interview with investigators from Internal Affairs. On television those guys are always portrayed as sanctimonious jerk-offs. In real life they were anything but that. For starters, IA investigators had to be smarter than everyone else. They also needed to gain the confidence of the individual being investigated by not flaunting their intelligence. I didn't envy them. Ninety-six hours after my interview I was cleared.

It turned out that the bartender at Monk's Café had informed the police that he saw Miriam leave the bar with a young guy. The person last seen with Miriam, Tad Bircher, told police that they fooled around at his place near 17th and South Streets, but Miriam had left sometime around four in the morning. Abe Samson confirmed the kid's story after the autopsy had been completed.

"It's like an X-Files episode," Abe told me when I paid him a visit the day after Internal Affairs cleared me of any wrongdoing. "Two people with wounds consistent with falling from a great height, but not high enough to cause their bodies to break apart. When I tell you I have not seen anything like this in my career, that's not hyperbole."

It gnawed at me, especially the John Doe. At least Miriam Chastain had a name. The problem was there was no next of kin to notify. Tad Bircher told detectives in his interview that he had met Miriam in his chemistry class at Drexel University. They had eaten lunch after class a dozen times, flirted at parties that semester, but never got together until the night he met up with her at Monk's.

In the interim, I had one more case that week. It was an open and shut one involving a jilted husband who shot his wife after he found out she had been sleeping with his brother. He was sixty-three years old. His wife had been the same age.

A week later, I decided to call it an early day, even though it was already seven o'clock in the evening. Some days you felt like that. Everyone needed to recharge. When I was a young officer, I never thought that way. I was too concerned with making a good impression.

When I knocked off that night my first thought was dinner. I had avoided Monk's since the discovery of Miriam Chastain's body. I wanted to avoid all the inane questions that would come my way if anyone there had heard the story in the news or knew the young woman personally. I was bent on getting a fine dinner. A good meal, after all, can often be the best medicine. First, though, I had to make a pitstop.

*****

The guard on duty that night was a retired badge. His name was Olson.

I never got his first name, but I remembered him from the district before he was transferred. We talked shop for a few minutes before I got around to telling him that I was there to see J.D. Clark. Olson had me sign in when I told him the purpose of my visit.

"All visitors must be announced first, detective," he said, lifting the telephone receiver at his console.

Two minutes later, I rode the elevator to Clark's floor. There was a mirror on the wall just outside the elevator. I stopped for a moment to look at myself. When does it happen, I wondered, that we wake up looking more like our fathers each day? In truth, I could no longer remember what he looked like, but I was sure I resembled him. I stood there until the non-descript satin-finish stainless steel elevator doors closed behind me.

At the end of the hall I knocked on Clark's door. No sooner than I did, a door directly across from Clark's unit opened a few inches. An elderly woman with a full head of long white hair, intense blue eyes, and a hawkish nose stared at me over a door chain. I only saw her for an instant before Clark opened his door.

"Detective Brennan," said Clark. He looked past me at the old woman across the hall. "It's ok, Mrs. Schlesinger."

The old woman shut her door.

"I hope I'm not disturbing you," I said.

"Not at all," he replied. "I do most of my writing early on in the day. It used to not be that way. But my habits have changed over time. I'm getting older. You know how it—"

"The reason I came by," I said, "is to ask some routine questions."

"Oh? About what?" he asked. Then, "Don't tell me you want to get into the writing game?"

"No, nothing like that," I assured him. "I wanted to talk to you about Miriam Chastain."

"The character from my book?"

"The young woman from Monk's Café."

"I saw on the news what happened to her," said Clark. "A terrible thing."

"Are you still discovering missing pages in your novel?"

"You think they're related?"

"I'll ask the questions, Mr. Clark," I told him.

"Well, no," he said. "With regard to pages turning up missing. That hasn't happened since the police came that one day."

"That night at Monk's when I met you," I said, "you mentioned that Miriam Chastain was the name of a character in your novel."

"I did," he said. "I remember telling you it was weird. Actually, I often run into people in the city with the names of characters from my books. I tell them, 'I made you.' And they look at me like I'm insane."

"Do you remember what you wrote about the character named Miriam?"

"How does this help your investigation?"

"Look, Mr. Clark," I said. "We can do this here or we can take a ride to finish the interview at the precinct."

"The news didn't say how Ms. Chastain died," he said. "Will you tell me?"

"That's part of an ongoing investigation," I told him.

"Almost as if she was dropped from a prop engine airplane or a helicopter, right?"

No one in the department had made Miriam Chastain's cause of death public. The press release gave her name and stated that foul play was suspected in her death. Police aren't giving any more information at the present time. Relatives are asked to contact Philadelphia Police. That sort of thing.

"Maybe it's time we take that ride," I announced.

Clark nodded. "Do I need a lawyer?"

"You're not under arrest."

"I know my rights, Detective Brennan," he said. "I don't have to go at all."

"I can come back later with a search warrant," I told him, "and have a half-dozen detectives flip your entire apartment, if you like."

Clark weighed his options. He pointed at an open door visible in the hallway outside the living room.

"I need to lock that door," he said.

"It'll be fine," I told him.

"No, it will not. I secure my office now when I am out," he said. "Next week I am having a key card lock installed. It will keep a record of every time the lock is accessed."

"You can never be too careful."

He locked his office door.

Downstairs, on the way out of the lobby, I waved at Olson when Clark and I exited the building. He gave me a knowing nod.

*****

Hank Fallon was a detective who worked the night shift with me. He was broad-shouldered and bull-necked. Forty years of smoking had turned the skin on his face to that of a fresh cadaver. He still sported the same haircut he had back when he was in the Marine Corps as a young man. Fallon was the perfect guy to counter my good cop routine.

It turned out Clark knew a few of the other detectives. They had taken him on ride-alongs over the years for Clark's research. I didn't give the author any time to chat with those detectives. Instead, I shuffled him straight into an interview room.

"Wait here," I told him.

I found Fallon at his desk. He was drinking coffee and going over a report. I told him the particulars about Clark and the Miriam Chastain case. Fallon was familiar with Clark's books. He offered to use that to our advantage. Clearly, I didn't think that Clark could fly a plane or a helicopter *and* throw someone out at the same time. But, I told Fallon, I had a gut feeling that Clark knew more than he was letting on.

"Twenty minutes," I told him. "Then I will come out and you can go in."

"I'm going out for a smoke," said Fallon. "See you then."

The thing with police interviews is not to make the person of interest nervous. They already know something is up if they find themselves in an interview room inside a police building. The important thing was to make sure they didn't clam up. Once they did, lawyers were soon to follow.

Clark was good. He admitted straight off that he had attended a Wicklander-Zulawski course on criminal interview and interrogation and the advanced seminar as well. His novel *The Bookie's Sonata* portrayed police interrogations in several chapters. I had read the book. Personally, I thought those scenes detracted from the plot. But I wasn't there that night to review books.

By the end of the first twenty minutes, Clark acted even more smug than when I first brought him in that night. He rolled his eyes and giggled a lot, like it was all a game to him.

"Let's go back to the details left out of the news," I said. "The one you knew even though the police never disclosed Miriam Chastain's cause of death."

Clark shrugged. "When you know, you know," he said.

"If I arrest you for suspicion of murder," I warned him, "that's what you are going before the judge with?"

"It's hard to explain,' he went on.

"Now would be a good time to try."

He pursed his lips and looked toward the ceiling, as if he were carefully plotting what he would say next.

"The novel I'm working on," said Clark, "includes a killer in it that mangles his victims and leaves them in public to be found. You don't strike me as much of a reader, though you claimed to have read my first book, so I'll spare you having to go through the pain of getting any search warrants. The killer in my book uses a hydraulic press. It's an old one in an abandoned workshop his family owns along with everything inside."

"Excuse me, Jerry," I said, gathering up my notebook and the file on the Miriam Chastain case. "Duty calls."

Outside the interview room, Hank Fallon took the file and notebook from me. When he entered the room he made a big show of slamming the file down on the table where Clark sat.

I watched and listened from behind a two-way mirror. Fallon worked Clark over, figuratively speaking, for thirty minutes. He pulled no punches, so to speak.

Twenty minutes later, Fallon gave me my notepad and file back outside the interview room.

"Little bastard sure is cocky," Fallon said.

"What do you think?" I asked.

"The hydraulic press thing was interesting," he said. "I'd chalk that up to fiction; yet we have Chastain and the John Doe, both of whom died in a similar fashion."

"Maybe I should have dug deeper about his past," I said, "before bringing him in."

"But that's not what's bothering you."

"You're right. I don't see how a little guy like him can pull off killing someone in a hydraulic press," I said, "without his victim fighting back, maybe overpowering him."

"Ever hear of Pee Wee Gaskins?"

"Should I have?"

"Born David Henry Parrot in South Carolina, 1933," Fallon said. "This guy was so neglected the first time he heard his name was when it was read in court when Gaskins was a juvenile. That's how much his momma loved him. Anyway, this Pee Wee Gaskins guy was a textbook bad seed. Robbery, assault, he was even accused of participating in a gang rape. Later on, he killed a girl with a hammer. Other murders followed, including one while he was already in prison. Ultimately, Gaskins was charged with the murders of eight people, including a niece, though he had claimed eighty or ninety victims he had killed between the late 1960s and 1975. After killing another guy in prison, Gaskins earned the title 'The Meanest Man in America.' The reason I'm telling you all this is because Gaskins stood five feet four, maybe five inches tall and weighed less than one hundred forty pounds."

"Jesus, Hank," I said. "You've been reading behind my back."

"My point," he said, sourly, "is never underestimate a man because of his size."

It was time to let Clark go, as much as it dismayed me to do so. He didn't seem like much of a flight risk. I got him out of the interview room and had the desk sergeant on duty call Clark a taxi.

*****

I didn't want to go to Monk's anymore, but that night I felt like I needed a drink, a strong drink, and to have regular people around me. I settled for The Pillbox, a former windowless bank near Graduate Hospital. The place was crammed with Penn students and local miscreants of every stripe. I was the oldest guy in the place, and I felt alive again.

My euphoria didn't last long, however. My pager went off. It was already one in the morning.

I showed my badge to the bartender.

"May I use your phone?" I asked her.

She looked at me like I had just time-warped from another decade.

"There used to be a pay phone by the restrooms," the bartender told me, "but they took that out long ago."

"Is there a manager's office or something?"

"The owner had the phone turned off," she said. "Sorry. There are pay phones in the lobby of the hospital."

I walked a half-block to Graduate Hospital. Hospital security gave me the once over. I didn't blame them. I was pretty much inebriated.

"This is Brennan," I said when a detective on-duty answered.

The voice on the other end belonged to a young guy named Marple. He'd just made detective grade six months prior. Sure, he had to man a desk some nights, but even that was better than walking a beat.

"You better get over here to the precinct," Marple instructed me. "Something's happened to Detective Fallon."

Shit, I thought. I could barely remember where I had parked.

*****

When one of your own goes down on the job, it turns into a who's who of police brass and internal affairs. The former wants to make sure the right optics are being put forth; the latter needs to figure out if another cop had anything to do with the dead cop's demise. We're supposed to figure out what happened, and maybe in our own special way mourn the loss of a friend, but then the circus arrives and then everything goes to hell.

It didn't take long to find the crime scene inside the precinct. I only had to follow the smell of cigarettes and regret.

"Brennan," Captain Brodsky approached me and braced my shoulders.

The hallway outside the men's locker room was crowded. Captain Brodsky wore a suit and a wrinkled shirt. Despite his best effort, he looked like he'd just crawled out of bed.

"You been drinking?" Brodsky asked.

"I was off-duty," I told him.

"So was Fallon," he nodded at the locker room door.

"I heard you brought in that writer fella?"

"Earlier this evening, sure. He knew about—"

"Well, it's turned into a shit show."

"You mean bigger than one of our own getting killed inside the police precinct?"

"The guy you brought in?" said Brodsky. "It turns out he knows just about everyone and their brother."

"Do any of them fly prop planes or helicopters?"

"Yes," he replied. "The governor has a pilot's license for small aircraft. You want to bring him in for questioning too?"

"I was out of line."

"Worse," Brodsky told me. "You had no probable cause."

"He knew the manner in which Miriam Chastain and our John Doe died," I told him.

"He's got contacts on the inside," he countered. "This guy could have gotten that from any number of the cops he worked with for research. You know the department. It leaks like a sieve."

"I'd like to go see my old friend now," I said.

Brodsky stepped aside. There was a lot of chatter in the hall that night. A uniform stood post at the door looking nervous in such close proximity to all the men and women of rank who could make or break his career.

"I need to get inside," I told him, looking at his name tag, "Officer Pinter."

He looked past my left shoulder at one of the other captains. Several members of the brass gave the nod at once. Pinter stepped aside to let me pass.

*****

Abe Samson had on sweatpants, slippers, and his ME Office windbreaker. His white hair stood up like the Heat Miser's from that television Christmas movie.

"They got you out of bed for this one?" Samson asked. "Good."

"Not exactly," I told him.

The locker room looked different. The dull green walls I had been used to were now painted sky blue.

"Noah," Samson said. "Are you all right?"

"I was out when I got the call," I said.

"Obviously, we'll know more after the autopsy," said the medical examiner, "but preliminary findings indicate that Hank Fallon suffered the same fate as Ms. Chastain and the John Doe from Rittenhouse Square. You want to see him before we bag him?"

I nodded. Samson led the way. I tried not to look at the walls. I was drunk, sure, but what I experienced during those moments was something else. My reality appeared altered. I wasn't sure if Abe Samson noticed, or anyone else.

Fallon's body was located near his locker toward the back of the room. A few uniformed officers and a couple of young detectives stood in a semi-circle around the space where Fallon lay. One uniformed officer held prayer beads in her right hand.

Hank Fallon's eyes were still open, staring up at the place where the living world and the next place converged. Like the John Doe from

Rittenhouse Square, his head looked slightly misshapen. His hands lay palms down on the floor. They looked odd, as if someone had tried to fashion Fallon's hands out of pancake batter.

I looked around the room. Detective Marple was making his way toward the urinals. I pushed past the others and stopped him.

"What time was he found?" I asked Marple.

"About ten minutes before I called you," he said. "A uniform named Rodriguez found him."

"Where's Rodriguez now?"

"I.A.'s got him," he replied.

Goddamn Internal Affairs, I thought. "When you go back out," I told Marple, "tell Captain Brodsky to tell someone far enough up the food chain that Rodriquez had nothing to do with it."

"You know nobody tells I.A. what to—"

"Just tell him," I said before I walked away.

A transfer board had already been placed on the floor beside Fallon. Samson was busy getting someone with rank to clear the locker room. I wanted to stay with my old friend. Samson had other ideas.

"You don't need to see this," he assured me.

"I've seen worse," I told him.

"Not like this," said Samson. "Please, I am asking as a friend."

I didn't have any fight left in me. Not that I would have gone against old Abe. I did glimpse his two technicians move Fallon's corpse onto the transfer board. When they tried to tilt my dead friend's body onto his right side to fit the board beneath him, all the shattered bones in his body shifted. It reminded me of a bag of rock salt being turned over.

*****

I waited until my old friend Hank Fallon was buried before I went around to pay a visit to J.D. Clark again. Captain Brodsky gave me specific orders to stay away from the guy. I spent a career following such mandates. This one time it had to be different.

Olson wasn't on-duty that night, so I returned to Hopkinson House. The guard was a young woman. She was all business, standing up a little straighter when I showed her my badge. I didn't have time to make small talk. Otherwise, I would have given her the pitch to join the force. Her name tag read: Ruiz. When she called up Clark to announce me, her expression changed. I couldn't hear him on the phone, but I could imagine the dressing down he gave her. Ruiz mentioned obstruction of justice, a phrase I did not utter that night. After that she hung up and pointed to the elevators.

When I got off on Clark's floor I looked at myself once more in the hallway mirror. I looked even worse than the last time I'd been there. Something was different about the elevator doors in the mirror's reflection. The doors were stainless steel with an art deco style border etched on to it.

The carpet was different too. The recessed lighting in the ceiling cast a different glow.

No sooner than I knocked on Clark's door another one across the hall opened. A woman peeked out, a chain lock stretched between the door jamb and the door. I was expecting to see the elderly resident, Mrs. Schlesinger, staring out at me. The face that showed behind the chain lock was considerably younger than the one I expected to see. She looked to be forty or fifty years old with a short bob of dark hair and large brown eyes that stared at me.

Just then Clark opened his door. He offered me a nod.

"Detective Brennan," he said.

"Mr. Clark," I offered.

"It's ok Mrs. Schlesinger," he said to his neighbor.

The woman withdrew and shut her door.

Clark waved me into his unit. I motioned for him to retreat into the apartment first. He shrugged and obliged me. I felt anxious, nauseous, as if someone had rearranged my world without telling me.

"Is that the old woman's daughter-in-law?" I asked him.

"You're very astute, detective," he said. "But no. I changed her."

"I beg your pardon?"

"Mrs. Schlesinger. I didn't like the old one in my story," the writer said, "so I changed her. Sure, she's still nosy. I liked that about her, but I saw no reason for having to gaze upon such an old face every time someone came calling."

He's insane, I thought.

"Is that what you did with detective Fallon?" I asked. "You *wrote* him out of your *story*?"

"And Ms. Chastain, don't forget," Clark told me as he headed for his office. "I did the same for her."

"Did you do the same with our John Doe in Rittenhouse Square?" I followed him as he walked backward now.

"A superfluous character," he said. "A false start to a narrative that took a different direction. I didn't need him anymore."

Clark had reached the open door. I whipped my suit jacket back and placed my right hand on my holstered pistol.

"Stop," I advised him.

"I surrender," Clark said, putting his hands in the air. Then, "Do you really think I'm going for a weapon in my office, detective?"

"Stop moving."

"You should come look at my typewriter," he said. "It's a beauty."

"I'm bringing you in," I said. "You are under arrest."

"What's the charge?" he asked. "Revising a story?"

He took one more step backward. I pulled out my pistol and pointed it at him.

"I said stop," I warned him. "Get down on your knees—"

"No, no," said Clark. "This isn't how the story goes."

"Get down on the floor."

"Do you like old things?" he asked. "I have this old-fashioned stapler I found at a flea mart. It's got to weigh a pound—"

"I won't say it again," I told him. "Get down on your knees now."

"There's a page in my office," he said. "All I need to do is crumple it up and throw it away. If I do, your life will be over just like the others. But first let me show you this."

Clark reached past the jamb of the open doorway. When his hand showed again he held something black and metallic in it.

I fired twice, shooting him in the chest.

Clark fell backward into his office.

I advanced with my weapon trained on him. Clark lay on his back, his arms spread out as he stared at the ceiling. A few inches from his left hand was an antique stapler made from black metal.

I kneeled and felt Clark's neck. He had no pulse. The two rounds I fired had pierced his sternum. I harbored no doubts that bone and bullet fragments shredded his heart to ribbons.

After I radioed in the incident, I waited for the show to arrive. Crime scene investigators would be crawling all over the apartment in no time. Ditto for Internal Affairs once they caught wind of my shooting a civilian armed with a stapler. I had maybe ten minutes before the cavalry arrived.

Clark's writing desk was located just past where his head came to rest. A black mesh waste basket stood beside the desk. It was filled with balled up pieces of typing paper. I fished out a few of the pages from the top. The third one I retrieved had a page-long paragraph detailing Hank Fallon in the police locker room at the precinct. A little further down I found a page Clark had typed showing Miriam Chastain on her roof deck.

My attention turned to Clark's desk. Next to the old typewriter a manuscript in progress several inches thick lay face down.

I picked up the last page and turned it over to read it. An unfinished passage ended like this:

Brennan's attention turned to Clark's desk. Next to the old typewriter a manuscript in progress several inches thick lay face down.

The detective picked up the last page and turned it over to read it. An unfinished passage ended like this:

The rest of the page was blank. I put it back where I found it and exited Clark's office.

In his living room I paced the floor, waiting for the calvary to arrive. Five minutes passed. Then it was ten minutes. I sat down on the sofa.

After another thirty minutes had gone by, I used Clark's phone to call in the situation a second time. A desk sergeant taking calls told me that responding units were already at the apartment inside Hopkinson House.

"But I am here and no one else is," I told him.

"Apartment 2007, right?" the desk sergeant said.

"Yes."

"They're there now," he replied. "Hold please."

A minute later, the desk sergeant got back on the line. He told me to stand by while he patched through one of the responding detectives.

"Hello?" I said through the static.

"Brennan?" a voice asked. "This is Tully. Ed Tully. Are you sure you're not in 1907 or 2107?"

"J.D. Clark lives in 2007," I said. "I'm sure of it. There's a woman across the hall in 2006. Her last name is—"

"Schlesinger," said Tully. "We spoke to her already. Listen, I got officers going floor to floor now checking—"

Static blocked everything else. I hung up the phone. When I picked it up again there was no dial tone.

I went to the door. When I opened it, I stood facing a dark void's deafening rush. I closed the door and locked it.

In the days after I became stuck in Clark's apartment, I read the entirety of Clark's latest manuscript. It was nearly finished when I killed him. The tale was a long and complicated one, a work that served as a departure from everything else he'd written. I was in it, so was Hank Fallon, Captain Brodsky, and all the other cops I knew. I found no reference to John Doe or Miriam Chastain. It began familiarly enough, a police procedural that followed all the norms within the genre, but half-way through he took another direction. It happened at the point where Clark figured out just how much power he had in creating a real life.

I tried hard not to think too much about that new reality, about how the writer created me. I felt like more than words on a page. I felt like flesh and blood. God knows I had more than enough emotional baggage the way human beings often did. But God was not my creator. Clark was.

When I consider how my life was spent, I understand that free will was foreign to me. Clark made sure of it. Every move and every decision I made came from him. It made me wish I hadn't shown up at Hopkinson House, even though I was destined to do that once Clark wrote himself into his own book. If I had left Clark alone would my life have gone on? Maybe, provided he did not revise the story and ball up the page I existed on.

Three days after I shot him I dragged Clark's body through the living room and deposited him in the void outside his apartment. I kept the drapes in his living room closed after glimpsing only nothingness beyond the floor-to-ceiling windows.

I tried writing my own exit from Clark's apartment on his old typewriter and adding to his unfinished manuscript. It didn't work. The void outside his apartment door remained.

There is no day or night anymore. There is no way of knowing how time passes in this place of Clark's creation. My cell phone no longer works, and Clark never kept a clock in his apartment. I have eaten all the edible food in his refrigerator and his cupboards. I miss the job. I miss the city at night. My hope is that one day someone finds these pages I have written. I will let my pistol decide my fate. With Clark no longer around to dictate my life I harbor no doubt that I can end my story.

Ledger

David Bradley

"It's pure genius, if you think about it." How many times had I heard that? Every time Marty had an idea, he thought it was pure genius.

"There's got to be more to it than that," I said.

"Not a thing," Marty said. "'The definition of genius is taking the complex and making it simple.'" He took his eyes off the game for the first time in an hour. Looked at me like I was the idiot. "Einstein said that."

"Tell me again," I said. "I'm not seeing the genius part of it."

He took his time this time. Sat his recliner up. Walked out to the kitchen. Opened the refrigerator. Came back with two cans of beer. Set one on the coffee table in front of me. Flopped back into his chair. Reclined. Opened his beer. Put his eyes back on the TV. "You just use their gun," he said. "That's all there is to it."

"That's too simple," I said.

"You're not listening. It *is* simple. That's what makes it genius. 'The definition of genius—'"

"Is making it simple," I said. "I heard you the first time. But this is ridiculous. It doesn't make any sense. How would it even work?"

"There's nothing more to explain," Marty said. "It's the simplest concept in the world. You gonna shoot somebody, use their own gun. That's all there is to it." He settled deeper into his chair. Took a long swig off his beer. "Look at this damn game. Twenty minutes ago the Eagles were up thirteen. Now it's three points and they can't cover anybody. Everybody's open."

"How would you use their gun on them? How would you even get it? Wouldn't *they* have their own gun?"

"I don't know. You be patient, I guess." He thought about being annoyed, but liked that I was interested. "It couldn't be a heat of the moment type of situation. A crime of passion or whatever. Those guys always get caught. You'd have to think things through. Ad-lib it. You keep your eyes open. You find their gun. Find out where they keep it. When the moment comes, you take it. And when you leave, you leave the gun behind. Just throw it down next to the guy." He spread his hands in front of him. "That simple."

I opened my beer. "I don't get it. What am I missing? Where's the genius part come in?" Commercials now. Two-minute warning.

"You're trying too hard. There's no trick to it. It just is what it is. As soon as the cops find the gun, that's all they see. They're blind to everything else. When they find out it's the guy's own gun, first thing they think is, suicide. If they rule that out — and probably they don't, they want to clear this thing off their desk, they get five of these a month, they've got work to do — but if they rule out suicide, they look at that gun, the guy's own gun, and they think wife, or girlfriend, or kid. Business partner, maybe. Whatever. Somebody close to the guy."

"Because only somebody close would be able to get the guy's gun."

"Bingo," Marty said. "That simple. Now they're thinking crime of passion, which I just made clear you don't do. Use that gun and they keep looking away from you. You're practically invisible." He took a long, sloppy pull off his beer. There was a scrum at midfield. The ball was stripped, lay on the turf for a second, and was scooped up by an Eagles linebacker. Marty lurched forward in his chair, screaming.

Time was running out. The Eagles were up by three. The linebacker stepped out of bounds at the thirty.

"Son of a *bitch*," Marty said. "It was open field."

"That's the play. Avoid another turnover. How much it cost you?"

"I had seven and a half points. All he had to do was keep running."

"How much?" I asked again.

"Five hundred."

"What're you, crazy? You're betting five hundred a game now?"

"Five hundred on this game, yeah. How could they miss with seven and a half points?"

"C'mon, it's the Eagles. How could they do anything *but* miss?" He threw himself back into his chair. "How're you going to pay five hundred?"

"I don't want to talk about it," Marty said. He stabbed the remote at the TV, switching to the four o'clock pre-game. We sat in silence until the next commercial break.

"What if they don't have a gun?"

"Everybody in this town's got a gun," he said.

"And the cops just see the gun and that's the end of it?"

Now he was annoyed. "You can't be stupid," he said. "There can't be any witnesses. You don't leave prints on the gun. All the rest of it. But they're not going to turn over every rock looking for someone if you hand them the answer they want in the first place. They're trying to clear cases. You use the guy's own gun, you're doing their work for them. Let 'em get home for dinner on time."

"Seems too simple."

"'Course it's 'too simple,'" Marty said. "That's why it would work."

"Einstein. I know."

"So, there you go. Now shut up." He pointed at the TV. "I've got a hundred on the over-under and a hundred on the Steelers and three and a half."

*****

"You're late," Maxine said, even before I was up the porch steps. "Game ended forty minutes ago. We're supposed to have a deal," She picked up her pocketbook and cigarettes from the kitchen table and had a hand on the screen door before it closed. "You don't keep up your end, we don't have a deal anymore."

"We've still got a deal," I said, pulling thirty dollars from my wallet. "I'll pay you the extra hour."

"You let me smoke in the house, wouldn't be such a big deal," she said. She lit a cigarette on the porch and blew the smoke away from the house. She stood there, one hand on her hip, making that wilted sundress work like a power suit. She talked to me through the screen. "They ate good. Took their baths. Watching their shows." From where I stood I could see into the living room, dark except for the pulsing light of the TV. Janice filled the big chair, a book in her lap, Anthony wedged in beside her.

"Looks like they're asleep already."

"Big day. This warm weather, they stayed outside most of the afternoon. Sure you don't need me this week?"

"No, thanks, I'm on straight time the rest of the month."

"It ain't good for them kids to come home to an empty house every day."

"It's only for ninety minutes and then I'll be here," I said. "Every kid on the block does the same thing."

"That don't make it any easier on them," she said. She flicked her butt into the azaleas. "I'm right down the street."

"That's not our deal. But I'll see you Sunday, right?"

"Not if I see you first," Maxine said. She lit another cigarette before she got to the gate.

Janice woke up when I turned the TV off. She held my hand as I carried Anthony down the hall to bed. Kissed me on the cheek when I tucked her in.

In the morning, she pretended she didn't remember me coming home.

"You were really late," she said as she ate her cereal.

"It was midnight," Anthony said.

"It wasn't even ten," I said. "And you two should've been in bed anyway. Maxine spoils you."

"It wasn't even dark yet," Anthony said.

"You just said it was midnight," Janice said.

"So?"

"If it wasn't dark yet, it couldn't be midnight. You were asleep when daddy got home."

"Was not." He turned the cereal box so he could read the back and tuned us out.

"Did Uncle Marty win?"

"Time for school," I said. "Dishes in the sink. Let's go."

"You're late."

"I'm late. Move it."

*****

When I got to work, the corrugating machines were already running. I could hear them even with the car windows up and the radio loud. I put earplugs in as I crossed the gravel parking lot. Inside the Quonset hut two machines were roaring. Men stood at the end of each machine, lifting the aluminum sheets off the conveyer belts and stacking them on wooden pallets. The place smelled of gasoline and bleach and sweat. Tommy and a couple other guys were standing by the coffee pot. They looked like they'd already had a good going over. Tommy leaned in when I got close, yelling over Classic Rock blasting through the speakers and aluminum twisting through the machines. "Nate's on fire this morning," he said. "Wants to see you right away." He pointed a thumb at the closed office door. I gave a nod to the other guys, poured myself a cup of coffee and walked to Nate's office, removing one ear plug as I shut the door behind me.

"Ritchie," Nate said. "You're late." It wasn't even nine and he'd already sweated through his shirt. He looked like he'd been up all night. At some point he'd put on a suit, but now the jacket was hanging over the back of his chair, his sleeves were rolled up, and he'd loosened his tie. There was a thick stack of twenties on his desk, like he'd just counted them. A big metal desk, beaten and scratched, like it'd been through a war, covered with invoices and porn magazines and coffee cups, and right in the middle of the mess, maybe a thousand dollars in twenties. "Tough weekend?"

"The usual."

"Yeah, I notice you're coming in late most Mondays lately. Tuesdays, too. You and your brother staying up late?" The walls of his office were covered with pegboard, and there were things hanging everywhere: order forms, business permits, faded centerfolds. The first dollar he ever made, in a five-dollar frame from Wal-Mart. A picture of a thinner Nate and a guy who'd been an alderman twenty years ago, shaking hands in front of the shop. Another picture, of Nate and some professional wrestler. Another picture, of Nate and some woman with too much make-up, a stripper he said, on the boardwalk at Atlantic City. Behind his desk, a trio of mounted hunting trophies staring down. "I get it. Your marriage on the rocks, his marriage on the rocks. You got to keep each other company. Watch a game, have a few beers."

"I've got to get the kids to school in the morning now. Gets me here a few minutes late sometimes. I make it up at the end of the day."

"I know you're good for the time. I'm not worried about that," Nate said. "How's your brother doing?"

"Marty's doing alright."

"He working?"

"Still on disability," I said.

"Six more months?"

"Something like that."

"Then what?"

"Look, Nate, I know what this is about. He owes you five hundred off the Eagles yesterday—"

"Yeah, that was a tough break all around. Kid had an open field."

"But Marty caught the over-under, could've been—"

"Over-under's a woman's bet," Nate said. The good mood was gone. "I'm cutting him off until he pays down his debt."

"I'd appreciate it," I said. "Many more games like that and he'd be in over his head."

"He's in over his head already," Nate said. "That's why I'm cutting him off. I just found out I'm not the only one he owes. That crew over in Gainesville too. Maybe more." It was the first I'd heard of that.

"How much?"

"To them? I don't know yet. But that's how it starts. Guy knows he's tapping out at one place he tries his luck somewhere else. Thinks he'll be able to pay me off with what he wins there. Before you know it, he has to move on to another place. Meantime, he loses my phone number. Like I'll forget about it." He was looking me straight in the face. "I can't just let it go."

"What's he into you for?"

"Twelve thousand five hundred after yesterday," he said. "That's more than I normally let anybody carry. Tell the truth, he went from dead even to twelve thousand so quick it caught me by surprise. And I don't normally charge points. This is a cash and carry type of operation. You bet with me this weekend, we even up by Wednesday morning, latest. But Marty's been betting with me a long time. I know you a long time. I know he's cashing the disability checks. I figure, what've I got to lose? He's good for it, right?"

"He's good for it," I said. It was a reflex. I knew there was no way Marty could pay that money back.

"Between the two of you I don't see how he's good for it," Nate said. "He signs those disability checks over to me, straight up, it'd still take him months to get even. But the guy's got to eat, right? Got to pay his rent? You got two kids on your hands, and I pay you every week, so I know that's a dry well. He's not signing those checks over to me."

"So what do we do?"

"No idea," Marty said. He looked genuinely concerned. Worried for Marty. Worried for me. Mostly worried about himself. "This isn't a movie, Ritch. I'm not a hard ass, breaking legs and all that. Taking bets is a side business for me. But it's still a *business*, and floating this kind of debt isn't good for business. I've got business partners. You understand? People who finance this operation. That game yesterday, your brother wasn't the only one got bent out of shape by the Eagles."

"What are you telling me?"

"This is getting too serious for me. I can't hurt you guys, even for twelve thousand."

"I know," I said. "This is just you and me talking here. We work this out, we're all good."

"I know you know. That's the problem. You know I can't hurt you. Marty knows I can't hurt him. So, why's he pay me? He goes to those other guys, they don't know him, they can hurt him—so he'll pay them. See what I'm saying? I take his action all this time, but when push comes to shove, I'm going to be last on his list. Calls me his friend, but I'm the one he's going to screw over." I saw where he was going with it. "I just want to get my kids through college. Pay off the boat. I don't want to get involved in any gangster shit. But if it comes down to telling my business partners that I'm coming up short, or telling them the truth, that it's your brother who's in for twelve thousand five hundred? I'm not going to throw myself under the bus."

I wasn't believing what I was hearing. "What're you saying?"

Nate crossed his arms. He was looking at the twenties on his desk.

"I owe people, too. Business is business, and bills are bills. Everybody's got to pay what they owe for this thing to work. You tell Marty I won't take his action on the game tonight, or any other game, until he pays down his debt. Ten thousand at least by the end of the week, and the rest next week. And I better not hear any more about him betting with anybody else, either."

"Or what?"

A muscle in Nate's jaw flexed, like he was biting down on a leather strap.

"Or what, Nate?"

His teeth cut through the strap.

"He owes me money," he spat. "I'm not getting in trouble because Marty got in over his head. Right now, this is just you and me talking. But I can't keep it off the books forever. He pays me this week, Ritchie, or I have to send his account to the collection agency." He looked me in the eye. "You understand what I'm saying?"

I worked hard like it was a normal morning. Kept my mouth shut and my head down. Easy enough in a place like that on a Monday. The machines screamed and the aluminum crashed and the music roared. Nate came out of his office after about an hour. He said something to Tommy and headed for the door. Gave me a nod. I couldn't tell what it meant.

At noon they shut off both machines and I slipped my earplugs into my pocket. The guys grumbled and joked about the usual things as they went to the break room. I stayed out front. They were pushing buttons on the microwave and buying Cokes from the vending machine. Someone was hitting ping-pong balls against the wall, warming up for a game.

I went outside. Stood next to my car. Called Marty. Sounded like I woke him up.

"You didn't tell me how deep in you are," I said.

"Nate needs to shut his mouth," Marty said. "That's nobody's business."

"He doesn't think you're going to pay him his money," I said. Tommy stepped outside. Lit a cigarette and leaned against the Quonset hut. Pretended he wasn't watching me.

"I'll get back on top tonight," Marty said. "The Seahawks never fail me."

"You can't bet the game tonight," I said. I turned away from Tommy, leaning on the car, keeping my voice low and steady as I could. "Nate's cutting you off."

"There's other places to play."

"That's all over too. He knows you've been going to Gainesville. Where else? Word gets around, nobody's going to take your action."

"Somebody'll take it."

"Nobody's going to touch it. He probably got the word out already. You can't bet your way out of this."

"You're overreacting."

"I'm not," I said. "You're in really deep. Marty says twelve thousand five hundred, just to him. You didn't tell me twelve thousand five hundred. What about these other guys? What do you owe them?" It got quiet at his end. I could picture him sitting on the edge of his bed, the place a mess. Terri gone. Nothing in the refrigerator. The GMC stuck in the carport, the hood up, a patch of dirty oil spread across the cement. I heard mattress springs straining or a screen door scraping. "You there?"

"What am I going to do?" He didn't sound so pissy now.

"He wants his money by the end of the week."

"I can't get it. I can't."

"Nate wants his money first. They're all going to want theirs first. What've you got to sell?"

"Just the Sierra."

"You call a wrecker and have that thing towed to a junkyard for whatever they'll give you for it. You get up in the attic and take everything to the pawn shop on East Market Street and you take whatever they'll give you for it. All of it. Everything."

He moaned at the other end of the phone. "I don't have anything," he said. Sounded like he was going to cry. Tommy finished his cigarette, made a show of grinding the butt into the ground.

"Doesn't matter," I said. "You do whatever you can to get as much cash as you can. I know you can't pay it all back right away. But you need to show a good will effort. Give him enough that he believes you'll pay it all at some point. That you're done fucking up."

"Maybe Nate'll loan me the money. To pay off these other guys."

"Are you crazy? He's not going to loan you money. You're already into him more than he can carry. He wants what you owe him."

"These other guys are serious, Ritch."

"Nate's serious, too," I said. "You don't get it. You owe him so much that he's into other guys the same way you're into him. He's worried he won't be able to pay his own bills. He's scared. You're driving him under."

"All the action he takes? He's got nothing to worry about."

Or maybe, I thought, Nate wasn't worried about his business partners. Maybe he didn't even have business partners. He never mentioned business partners until that day. Maybe that was just a line. He was bluffing. Made them up to put a scare into me, so I'd put a scare into Marty. Maybe, if he'd found out about Gainesville, they'd found out about him, too. Maybe they found out about him first. Maybe what spooked Nate was somebody finding out about the side business he'd been playing out of the back of his redneck Quonset hut by the side of the road. Wondering if maybe they'd decide the easiest way to collect on their debts was to take over his debts, and everything that went with them.

"How much action you think Nate takes on a Sunday?"

"You kidding? Everybody in town," Marty said.

Everybody in town? A thousand dollars on his desk Monday morning before he'd even seen most guys. And Marty owed twelve thousand five hundred? Maybe our problem wasn't paying Nate what Marty owed. Maybe it was just about paying his Gainesville nut. After that, who'd be asking any questions?

"I'll talk to Nate, see if I can buy you some time," I said. "He was pretty hot this morning. I'll try to catch him in a better mood later."

"Get a few drinks in him. He'll lighten up."

"Don't bet on it. He's in a hard place too. Don't depend on me to talk you out of this. Scrape together what you can."

I worked with my head down after lunch. Not sure what was coming next. Nate came back late afternoon. Straight to his office. Slammed the door and didn't come back out.

End of the day, I left the same time as everybody else. Headed home same way as always. Six of us, Tommy fourth, me fifth, all driving along the country two-lane, one after the other, same as any other day. Got to the light, two went left, one went straight, three of us pulled into the 7-11. Me, Tommy, another guy. Twelve-pack Coors Light, twelve-pack Bud Light, twelve-pack Miller Lite, all of us reaching into the coolers at the same time. Some joke about Mondays, everybody laughed. Held the cooler door for them so I'd be last at the register.

Pulled around to the gas pumps. Topped off my tank, watching the road to make sure Tommy'd gone home. Pulled out of the parking lot, drove a half-mile toward home, watching the mirrors. U-turned in the kids' school parking lot.

Lights were still on in the shop and music was still blaring. Nate jumped when I stepped into his office. "Scared the hell out of me," he said.

There was a TV in the corner. Sports Center with the sound off. Nate pulled a bottle of Jim Beam out of his desk drawer and poured three fingers on ice. I said no thanks when he offered one to me. The stack of twenties was still on his desk, tied with a rubber band, and now there was another pile, this one crumpled fives and tens and twenties. "Sons-a-bitches'd pay in pennies if I let them," he said. He took his first drink of the night. "You here about Marty's tab?"

"Between Marty and me, we'll get you your money," I said. "You know we're good for it."

"How do I know that?"

"When've we ever not paid what we owed?"

"When've you ever owed this much?" He drained his glass and poured another.

"I never have."

"But we're talking about Marty. Marty's the one that owes me twelve and a half."

"He's working on it. He's going to do the right thing here. He's out selling his car right now. And I'm going to help him."

"Where's Terri in all this?"

"She's out of the picture."

"Alimony?"

"Not yet. His lease is paid through the end of next month, then he'll move in with me if he's still under. Disability checks'll cover most of what he owes, after he takes out enough to live on."

"I'm going to have to charge him points," Nate said. His voice softened. "I don't charge points. I'm not really set up for points. I don't even keep a ledger. If I don't know you, you don't bet with me." He pulled an ashtray closer to him. Sipped his drink, slower this time.

"You're going to have to give me something by Friday. I can't float you guys forever."

"Marty'll get it together," I said. I didn't have any idea how Marty could pay what he owed. But I didn't want to close the door Nate had opened for me. "You know Marty. He's always got an idea cooking."

"Ain't that the truth? Guy thinks outside the box," Nate said. "I'll give him that. I feel bad closing him out. I don't want to be the bad guy here. But I've got to cover my nut, just like anybody else." For a minute, he lost himself in the TV. He propped one elbow on his desk, rested his chin on his hand. He was having trouble keeping his eyes open.

"You okay?"

"Eagles fucked me yesterday," he said. "I didn't get to bed last night trying to track down what I need to cover tonight. Marty's not the only one in over his head." The edge was back in his voice. "You tell Marty I need at least half what he owes me by Friday."

"I don't think he can get six thousand this week," I said. Nate's eyes jabbed me across the desk. He grabbed his lighter and squeezed it like a roach. "He's had a tough year—"

"We've all had a tough year," Nate muttered. "I told you where I am on this. I like Marty fine, but I'm in a bind here. I need six thousand by Friday or I'm going to have to get this off my desk."

"What's that mean?"

He yanked open the top drawer on his desk. Everything in it rattled to the front. I watched his hand scrabble like a crab in a boil pot.

Paper clips.

Ballpoint pens.

Spare keys.

A loose cigar.

A silver plate pistol.

Nate tore the cellophane off the cigar and crammed it into his mouth. He saw my eyes stuck on the gun. "Nice, huh?" He picked it up. Waved it around, pointing it at the fluorescent tubes in the ceiling. At the TV. At my face. Something in his eyes went dark. "Six thousand by

Friday, Ritchie. Understand? I got no wiggle room on this." We stared at each other across the desk. Along the barrel of the gun. Until the light in his eyes came back on.

Nate laughed. "Relax. It's a replica. Just for show. Colt Hammerless .32. Won it in a raffle in Atlantic City a few years ago. Keep meaning to mount it on the wall." He tossed it back into the metal drawer. The gun and all the other junk banged like the end of the world.

There was a newspaper on the corner of his desk, nearest me. Wilted, food stained. Nate pointed at it with his eyes. "Pick it up," he said. I didn't understand. "Go ahead," he said. "Pick up the newspaper."

Underneath it was a flat-black revolver with a short barrel. Nate's eyes were locked on mine. "That's the real one," Nate said. "That's a Rock Island .38."

The grip was in my hand before Nate made his move. The gun was lighter than I expected. His drink shook in his hand.

Who's Moz?

Kamal M

The humidity was infernal. A mortuary grayness hung over the bay of Algiers. The mid-June gloomy weather fell upon me like a curse. I was hoping for the summer sun and its obliterating light when I parted the curtains this morning. I needed it. Instead I got this drab burnt sky. The dismal conclusion of my last case was still hurting but I had to go forward. I never thought that being in the police for only seven years would take such a toll on me. For months, nervous breakdown was showing its taunting face.

I drank a fresh coffee brewed by my mother and ate her exquisite butter biscuits. It was hot outside despite the heavy clouds. Walking to the car, my clothes already began to stick to my sweaty skin despite the morning cold shower. Inspector Abbas called me yesterday and asked me if I was ready to go to war with him after months of me shunning him in the hallways of the cop's Lair (that's how some of us called our station). What a character! Always so quirky and colorful in his early sixties, after decades of crimes, riots, hierarchical backstabbing, terrorist attacks and political turmoil. Almost became crazy during the 90s black decade. He saw it all. He was a true inspiration in a sense but he sometimes had this unsettling and uneasy vibe. I was shunning his piercing stare and destabilizing inquiries.

I started the car and turned on the radio. A stupid pop song blasted through the speakers. I scrolled through the FM stations. A piece of 90s alternative rock caught my ears. I thought "perfect!". Spectral voices and sharp guitars assaulted the car interior. Dilapidated alleys and decrepit walls flowed for quite a while behind the windshield.

I arrived at the police station mentally drained. The streets were busy and the clouds were still menacing.

I greeted everyone as I entered the cop's Lair. Inspector Abbas's voice boomed from the top of the stairs: "Moz! Need to talk to you! Now!" He was standing nervously, his usual angry mask on his face, his confusing blue eyes reaching something deep inside you. An intense stare softened by his droopy eyebrows.

I hurried up the stairs and followed him into his office, quite curious about the topic he wanted to discuss with me. There's always a "topic" with Inspector Abbas. Always a way of putting words together that makes you feel like the perfect culprit for something wrong you didn't know you did. Always acting like the tough boss, the warlord of the Lair, while, basically, spouting laughable pseudo sophisticated reasoning. He was such a weirdo weirdly turned cop in the eighties. Everyone here knew it. He was a fan of The Smiths. One of the five or six fans of The Smiths in the whole country. He told me the first time I met him that I had the same awkward vibe as his idol Morrissey, the singer/songwriter of The Smiths. Checked the band on Spotify and never liked their music. Too snobbish and too British, which is for me one and the same. I like hip-hop and heavy metal. "You're a Barbarian", he told me, "and barbarism begins at home". He's the only one to ever call me "Moz", which means bittersweet in Arabic. Later I came to know that Moz is also the abbreviation used to call Morrissey. I should have guessed it since his pronunciation was not that Arabic. My real name is Djamel and everyone here except him calls me Djamel. I can't remember the last time Inspector Abbas called me by my real name or if he ever did since I got to know him.

His office never changed a bit: boxes, papers and messy files scattered on the desk, the chairs and the coffee table, photos stuck all over the place with a piece of tape, some nice pictures framed on the wall. We could see the bay of Algiers, its old districts, him as a young officer. His vintage eighties boombox was always on the shelves with a bunch of cassette tapes.

I sat down on a chair in front of him. He cleared a tiny space on his desk and leaned on it.

"Moz! We have to interrogate a suspect! Someone that won't willingly come here for a chatter."

I nodded.

The suspect allegedly stole a bag from a lady in her early forties. It contained a smartphone, some cash and many other personal effects. Happened two days ago at around 8:30 pm in a narrow alley near a flea market. She resisted him and tightly grabbed her bag. He severely punched her in the face. Inspector Abbas spoke at length about the thug. He didn't like him at all. He never seemed to like anyone anyway. But then again, it was always difficult with him to differentiate between the posture and the true feeling.

"The woman is not afraid to confront that scumbag. I mobilize two or three agents, he's rarely alone during the day, and we bring him down here to interrogate him... do you hear me or am I talking to myself?"

I was depressed. I needed to cheer myself up.

"We trap that bastard whenever you want, Inspector!"

*****

He was there chatting with two big men while sipping tea on a sunny terrace. His days always begin there, around ten. The thug is in his early thirties, slim, clean-shaven, gel-shiny hair, rather well dressed.

We discreetly took a seat on the café's terrace, me and the Inspector. Inspector Abbas did not go unnoticed with his full well-groomed gray mustache, his penetrating steel blue eyes, his strange exotic allure. Our prey spotted us right away. We then acted as if nothing had happened. We got up and walked across the terrace. I stood there at the entrance as Abbas quietly went to drag out our thug to the sidewalk. Two of our officers were waiting for us in a vehicle nearby. The Inspector walked slowly towards him. All the customers were looking at the scene. He spoke softly in his ear, then took him by the arm and asked him to stand up. Which he did without a fuss. I was watching the entrance to the café. Sleazy boys were vegetating there with their heads on the screens of their smartphones. Abbas pretended to know the man well enough, which was true in a way. They both headed for the sidewalk. I thought we should be able to bring the punk to the station without much trouble. We were going to stuff him gently in the back seat and head for the station. I really thought so. Two meters from me, the thug, acting like one, violently pushed Inspector Abbas on a table, causing panic among customers. In a matter of seconds it's chaos in the *caoua*. I immediately jumped on the punk but could only grab the back of his jacket with my fingertips. He easily escaped me and fetched a knife from his pocket. I lost balance avoiding his stab and found myself on the greasy and dusty floor, with hot tea on my face. He jumped over the fence and ran away. I got up, grabbed my gun and looked around for the Inspector. He was already running after the thug with our other two guys who jumped from the vehicle. "Over there, over there... run! Run!" I followed them as close as possible. We left a weak legged and breathless Inspector far behind us.

After a small sprint, we managed to neutralize the confused bastard. He'd wanted to try an escape through the narrow streets of the city center. A dense and compact crowd formed around us handcuffing him. We copiously insulted him while dragging him to the vehicle and his entire family tree went through it. The people around us were laughing, frightened and strangely entertained. The onlookers suddenly began to insult the punk, picking from their anthology of razor-sharp insults. Names rained down on him like blows from a lynching mob. On our way to the vehicle we came across another excited crowd of screaming kids. "The blonde mustache... he's going to die!" We ran to dispel the crowd and found Inspector Abbas on the floor, his hand clenched to his chest, panting heavily. I ordered the officers to quickly call an ambulance. He mumbled a word or two, something totally incomprehensible.

"What?" I asked him.

Suddenly, a gunshot thundered behind us. The crowd dispersed in a monstrous mess. Screeching screams and stampedes ensued. We were flat on our stomachs, me on Inspector Abbas, who uttered in a death rattle like voice: "my gun!"

Almost all of us were running away or lying down on the ground except for a livid kid, frozen by fear, stunned by the shockwave of his gunshot. He was holding the Beretta, too heavy and bulky for his frail limbs, with a trembling hand. I stood up gently and walked over to him with slow, measured steps.

"It's okay, boy! No one will hurt you. Now give me the gun and we'll just forget about it!" Until the last second I was afraid the kid would do something stupid for the second time.

He handed me the Beretta with a shaking hand and bulging eyes. He took several steps back.

"I... I hurt someone!" He told me with a frightened, hesitant voice.

With a flickering finger, vanishing into a narrow alley, he pointed to another kid his age, lying on the floor at the entrance of a clothing store, marinating in his own blood.

*****

The ambulance came fast, lights flashing and sirens roaring. The paramedics quickly took care of the kid. Soaked in blood, left shoulder tattered, but still breathing. Inspector Abbas was on his feet when they arrived, chest pain almost entirely gone. Me behind the wheels, Inspector Abbas on the passenger seat and our agents holding the handcuffed thug huddled together on the back seat, we were clearing a path for the ambulance, ripping through the dense traffic.

At the crossroads, just before the slope leading to the hospital, we were blocked by a huge traffic jam. I was exhausted and ready to do anything to shake up this steaming heap of iron junk blocking access to the emergency. I started yelling and honking like an unhinged maniac. A complete anarchy ensued to clear a passage for us. Cars escalated the sidewalk, almost bumping into pedestrians. Car horns, police and ambulance sirens, forming a demonic choir. Somehow a very narrow passage was arranged for the ambulance. Five minutes later we were in the hospital parking lot. We haphazardly parked the car and followed the badly injured kid to the emergency room. We dragged the thug around. We released our nerves and tension on the punk. He received everything converted into kicks, slaps and insults. He was petrified. "You'll pay for all of this, you big piece of shit!"

*****

Later on that evening the Inspector was examined. His wife was by his side. It was the first time I ever saw her. She was a gracefully aging woman. Maybe in her late fifties. Grizzling hair at the roots, sloppily worn headscarf and floral patterned ample outfits. Didn't even know who called her. The doctor told us that there was nothing to specifically worry about, but still recommended tests and consultations to get an accurate health assessment. She listened intently to the doctor. The kid, on the other hand, was in a much more worrying condition.

The Chief came in late. Confused and fulminating. He spoke to us harshly with a patronizing tone. He always cared about keeping a distance but we all felt the heat that evening. Abbas was boiling inside but he didn't utter a word. The Chief, not unlike Abbas, was just a surly man who could only express himself through cold, manly protocol. They were from the same mold, but the Inspector was an anarchist character.

The boy's family was shocked and distressed. Tension spread among them when told of eventual complications. The mother was ceaselessly weeping. The father showed up later, angry, screaming at us, trying to corner Inspector Abbas. He was threatening to press charges against the Inspector for negligence. He was furious. Paramedics tried to placate him. The Chief was flushed with anger. He warned us: there will be consequences.

I returned home at around 6:00 pm. My mother was dozing on the sofa with the TV at a very low volume. She slightly swung her face at me when I closed the door. She could not see the dried blood stains on my clothes in the dark TV lit living room.

After a good bath, I was on my bed. I turned on the TV and started pushing buttons on the remote control like a zombie. Everything on the screen seemed bland, stupid, boring and, most evidently, unreal. I was in the mood for nothing. I felt some anguish slowly building upon me. Later I barely touched my dinner. Back in my room I couldn't find sleep. Images of the kid in blood and Inspector Abbas in pain clogged my mind. I also remembered some of our past long conversations with Abbas. He once said to me that not having any children was one of his deepest regrets. I told him there's no regrets to have because it was beyond his will. He looked at me with his unfathomable stare and replied: "the fury at our crushing fate! It's the primal anger!"

After many position changes, I desperately fell asleep to an ambient music playlist on Spotify.

*****

In the morning when I parked at the station, I checked my face in the car's mirror. A real zombie with dark circles around volcano-red eyes. I took a deep breath then got out of the car.

The Lair was quiet and deceitfully serene. The thug was sleeping in his cell like a baby. I dawdled a bit in the hallways with a steaming cup of coffee in my hand, anguished at the thought of running into the Chief. When the agent at the entrance called me downstairs, I yelled at him to leave me alone. I had to write the report on yesterday's events. The agent insisted. I growled back. He replied in a frightening tone: "It's urgent Djamel! I am not kidding!" Something was seriously wrong. I quickly went downstairs and picked up the phone he handed me. I was very surprised to hear the voice of the Chief.

"Djamel, Inspector Abbas is dead! You hear me? He's dead!"

"How? How this..."

"When she woke up, his wife found him lifeless on a sofa in the living room! She called us right away. Apparently it's a cardiac arrest. We're at his flat."

I was shocked and confused.

"Come here, we're waiting for you!"

He hung up the phone. I was breathing heavily. The entry agent handed me a chair, but it was not necessary. I headed for the parking lot.

I was driving like a freak to the Inspector's apartment. My brain was running wild. The warning signs of impending heart failure were quite obvious yesterday during our calamitous chase after that disgusting thief. The doctor didn't see anything coming. Doctors rarely do anyway.

The apartment transformed into a crime scene was stifling. Police officers, forensics and what seemed like male family members were occupying the living room where the Inspector was found dead. There was a heavy atmosphere and the sadness was palpable. Inspector Abbas was just a corpse and his face was chalky. No serenity or peace or any other mystic feature. Plain cold dumb death. The Chief walked up to me as soon as he saw me.

"Quickly offer your condolences to his widow and family. They are in shock. We all are. Hurry, I have to talk to you." he said to me pointing with his finger to a room at the end of the corridor.

Inspector Abbas's widow had apparently recognized me according to the stare she gave me; or is it the circumstantial gaze of all widows!

"May Allah grant him His Mercy!"

In the midst of veiled women maintaining a tearful atmosphere, I declaimed the commonly used words then immediately joined the Chief. He was standing in the living-room like a totem. His stony face looking at the cold corpse of Inspector Abbas. Hidden under the impassive demeanor, there was a perceptible sadness for those who knew him well.

"He was a good copper. I appreciated all these years working with him. Saw him dealing with really tough situations and he always delivered. Sure some of those situations could have been handled differently…"

He sighed.

"Why was he always calling you Moz?"

"It's the nickname of one of his favorite singers!"

"A singer? He always had strange tastes. He was a pseudo punk in the eighties. A punk in the Casbah! May God forgive him!"

Something remotely resembling an emotional vulnerability finally permeated through the Chief.

"The forensics expert is adamant, it's just a cardiac arrest like millions of other cardiac arrests that send every year millions of men straight to the grave. What will you do now?"

"Go to the hospital. Check on the kid."

*****

When I got to the hospital, soaked in sweat, I pulled out my badge and asked to see the doctor in charge. Absently the nurse consulted her register then told me to wait a few minutes. Two minutes later, when I was thinking of having my third morning coffee, the doctor showed up, excited and shouting at me.

"It's a miracle! The kid recovered so quickly! He's alive and well. Miraculously well given the circumstances."

"Can I see him?"

"Of course you can! He's with his mom!"

*****

He looked quite good, everything considered. Tired, lanky, but his eyes were full of vitality. That was almost disturbing. The kid took a bullet less than 24 hours ago. His mom was smiling. She said that the recovery was a miracle. Probably the words of the doctor. Or not.

"How are you, brave boy?"

"I'm great. Alhamdoulillah!"

Something was off in the way he stared at me. Something taunting and daunting.

"In two or three days at most he'll be home!" Mommy said to me with wet eyes. "Who's Moz?" she asked abruptly.

"I am Moz! Who told you about this nickname? There's only one person who calls me Moz! Well… there was!"

She just smiled and rolled her almond eyes toward her son.

"See! I told you he would come!" the kid said, keeping his strange eyes on me.

A strange and yet so familiar gaze. Back from the dead.

*****

I received a call from the Chief as I dipped my lips into a hot coffee taken at a stand just outside the hospital. I told him about my strange and short meeting with the boy. It made me so uncomfortable. What I had to say about the conversation with the kid and his strange demeanor sounded to me completely surreal and out of place as it unfolded word by word with my own voice.

"I think you need some rest, Djamel. Take some days off. It can't hurt you."

My hand slightly trembling, I took a sip of the dense and bitter coffee. The city was awfully vivid.

The Usual Unusual Suspects

Laurie Stevens is a 2nd generation Los Angeles native who writes crime fiction based mostly in California. Her *Gabriel McRay* novels have won twelve awards, including *Kirkus Reviews Best of 2011* and a Random House Editors' *Book of the Month*. In regards to writing thrillers, *Suspense Magazine* says Laurie is "the leader of the pack," while *International Thriller Writers* claims she's "cracked the code" of writing psychological suspense.

For more of Laurie's story visit: http://www.lauriestevensbooks.com

Jesse Aaron served as a police officer in New York City and Connecticut for over five years and also worked in the field of private security/investigations. His first novel, *Shafer City Stories* is available on Amazon.com (https://www.amazon.com/Shafer-City-Stories-Tales-NYPD-Harlem/dp/1518853137/). Jesse's short story *The Leaky Faucet* was featured in *Crimeucopia – It's Always Raining in Noir City* and *The Gathering Puddle* in *Crimeucopia — One More Thing To Worry About.* Jesse has two more short stories on the way to publication and is currently at work on his upcoming serial killer thriller *Harlem Hipster Homicides.* Jesse's style is dark and gritty, and his stories focus on the underside of the police and private detective worlds. Jesse has a love of all things Noir, Science Fiction, and Fantasy.

Patrick Ambrose lives in North Carolina with his partner Kim and their three cats, Ashton, Shelton and Monster. His work has appeared in *Mysterical-E, Timber Creek Review, The Morning News, Creative Loafing,* and other print and online publications.

Stephen D. Rogers is the author of *Shot to Death* and more than 800 shorter works. His website, www.StephenDRogers.com includes a list of new and upcoming titles as well as other timely information.

Wendy Harrison is a retired prosecutor who turned to short mystery fiction during the pandemic. Her stories have been published in numerous anthologies including *Peace, Love & Crime, Autumn Noir, Crimeucopias —Tales from the Back Porch* – and – *One More Thing To worry About, The Big Fang, Gargoylicon,* and *Death of a Bad Neighbour* as well as in *Shotgun Honey*. When Hurricane Ian destroyed her home in Florida, she moved to Washington State, as far from Florida as she could get.

Jan Glaz From 2011 to 2022 she was employed as a full time newspaper reporter/writer for *Village View Publications, Inc.*, located in Chicago IL. Since 2016, she has published, sold, and continues to sell, on *Amazon* a wide range of best-selling, top reviewed fiction, non-fiction, and children's books.

Brandon Doughty lives in Austin, Texas with his wife Janna and their two children. His stories have been published in magazines like *Black Petals, Yellow Mama Webzine,* and *Aethlon: Journal of Sports Literature.* By day he maintains his fake identity managing a team in supply chain operations while secretly writing his first novel in the wee hours each night. When not working you can find him reading or in a theatre watching every movie possible, regardless of genre.

Elena Schacherl was born in Trieste, Italy, then immigrated to Canada as a young child. She lives in Calgary, Alberta and for several years held the position of Executive Director of Friends of Fish Creek Park where her mystery story primarily takes place. She has an Honors B.A. with distinction from the University of Saskatchewan and studied post-graduate English at the University of Calgary. Elena's a member of the

Writers' Guild of Alberta, the Calgary Crime Writers' group, the East Village Writers' Circle and the *Alexandra Writer's Centre* where she took creative writing classes and served on their board. She has published several short stories including *Swimming with Sharks* in the Canada Council funded *Printed Word* on permanent exhibit at the main branch of the Calgary Public Library. And her novel *Beach of the Dead* was published in December 2021.

Joyce Bingham is a Scottish writer who enjoys writing short fiction with pieces published by *Molotov Cocktail, Ellipsis Zine, Noctivalant Press, Funny Pearls* and *Free Flash Fiction*. She lives in the North of England where she makes up stories and tells tall tales. When not writing she puts her green fingers to use as a plant whisperer and Venus fly trap wrangler. @JoyceBingham10

Jeff Somers has published over 20 short stories in various magazines, most notably *Another Chicago Magazine, The Portland Review,* and *Brutarian.* His *Ringing the Changes* (*Danger City* anthology from Contemporary Press) was chosen to appear in *The Best American Mystery Stories 2006*, and his *sift, almost invisible, through* was included in the anthology *Crimes by Moonlight* edited by Charlaine Harris. His first novel, *Lifers,* was published in 2001 and was reviewed favorably in The New York Times Book Review. Since then he has published 8 more, including the *Avery Cates* series of Noir SF novels, *Chum* (Tyrus Books), and *The Ustari Cycle* series (Pocket Gallery). In May 2018 *Writer's Digest Books* published his *Writing Without Rules.* His recent short works include *The Company I Keep* (in *Life is Short and Then You Die*, edited by Kelley Armstrong) *Zilla, 2015* (in the *Lascaux Review*), and *The Little Birds,* set in the same universe as *Teeth Can Hardly Stand* (in *Alfred Hitchcock's Mystery Magazine.*)

Glenn Francis Faelnar is a writer from Cebu in the Philippines, who has been writing fiction for the last 8 years. His recent work has appeared in such diverse places as *Storyberries* and *Daily Science Fiction*. He is looking to hopefully have more of his stories published.

Douglas Soesbe is originally from Portland, Oregon, where he received a Master's Degree in Playwriting from Portland State University. He taught Theatre Arts at the university, also directing several plays. He established a one-act theatre company in Portland, where some of his original plays were performed.

In Los Angeles, he worked as feature film Story Editor for Universal Pictures, later moving to Tri-Star Pictures, where he was also Story Editor. He was eventually given a three-picture writing deal at Tri-Star, doing uncredited rewrites on such films as Chances Are and Blind Fury.

He returned to Universal in 1997, remaining there until his retirement in 2019.

His published work includes two novels, Children in a Burning House (Knight's Press), and Scream Play, a horror novel published by Berkeley.

Televison-wise, he has worked on various productions, including CBS Tuesday Night Movie, Hearst Entertainment, ABC Family and, at the time of writing, Look Again (starring Morena Baccarin) is currently on Lifetime.

He also has a feature film writing credit for Boulevard, the last on-screen performance by Robin Williams.

Soesbe was recently named as one of ten finalists in a screenplay competition sponsored by writer/director Francis Ford Coppola and Zoetrope. Soesbe's script, Tender Outcast, was one of ten chosen from over 2,000 entries.

Currently residing in Palm Springs, Soesbe is working on a new mystery novel, The Miracle Murders.

In a prior life ***Carol Goodman Kaufman*** was a psychologist and criminologist who reached her limit on writing about abuse and violent extremism. She now writes about happier subjects such as food history and travel, but when she decided to take the plunge into fiction, she chose to write mysteries, quite often of the murder variety. Ironic, huh? But not totally out of character. Since her first encounters with *The Happy Hollisters* and *Nancy Drew*, her guilty pleasure has been curling up with a good whodunit.

Daniel C. Bartlett's fiction has appeared or is forthcoming in *Ellery Queen Mystery Magazine, Mystery Tribune, Mystery Magazine, Thrill Ride: The Magazine, Yellow Mama, Mysterical-e, descant, Iron Horse Literary Review, Chiron Review, 3:AM Magazine* and *Crab Creek Review*, among others. His work was recently shortlisted among "Distinguished Mystery and Suspense" in *The Best American Mystery and Suspense 2023*. He teaches writing and literature at Lamar University in Beaumont, Texas, and is currently working on a P.I. crime/thriller series. To find out more about the author, go to: https://www.facebook.com/DanielCBartlett.writer

Richard J. O'Brien has, over the years, had fiction appear in *Pulp Literature, The Del Sol Review, Dark Moon Digest,* and other publications. His novels include *The Last Days of Iggy Scanlon* and *Rejoice for the Dead*. At present he lives in New Jersey, where he teaches part-time at Stockton University. In 2022, Requia Studios optioned his feature thriller *The 9th Messiah* and a horror/sci-fi limited series entitled *Red Lake*.

David Bradley spent a dozen years as a newspaper reporter and columnist in Northern Virginia before turning to fiction full-time – having also written the non-fiction Human Rights work *The Historic Murder Trial of George Crawford* (McFarland & Co.) His short fiction and poetry has appeared in *Broken Pencil, The Adirondack Review, Down in the Dirt, Main Street Rag, The South Carolina Review, Pennsylvania English* and others.

Kamal M was born in Algiers in 1979 and works in the fields of advertising and lately animated films production.

He wrote in French some bad poetry in his youth and some unfruitful noir novel attempts in his adult years. Who's Moz is his first short story written in English. Unless the ghosts of Shakespeare, Agatha Christie and John le Carré decide to gang up to prevent it, he firmly intends to commit his future literary misdeeds in English as well.

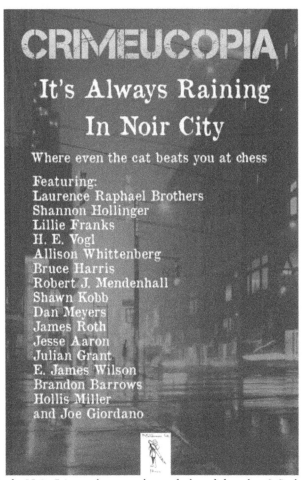

CRIMEUCOPIA

It's Always Raining In Noir City

Where even the cat beats you at chess

Featuring:
Laurence Raphael Brothers
Shannon Hollinger
Lillie Franks
H. E. Vogl
Allison Whittenberg
Bruce Harris
Robert J. Mendenhall
Shawn Kobb
Dan Meyers
James Roth
Jesse Aaron
Julian Grant
E. James Wilson
Brandon Barrows
Hollis Miller
and Joe Giordano

Is the Noir Crime sub-genre always dark and downbeat? Is there a time when Bad has a change of conscience, flips sides and takes on the Good role?

Noir is almost always a dish served up raw and bloody - Fiction bleu if you will. So maybe this is a chance to see if Noir can be served sunny side up - with the aid of these fifteen short order authors.

All fifteen give us dark tales from the stormy side of life - which is probably why it's *always* raining in Noir City....

Paperback Edition ISBN: 9781909498341
eBook Edition ISBN: 9781909498358

CRIMEUCOPIA

WE'LL BE RIGHT BACK -
- AFTER THIS!

FEATURING:
JIM GUIGLI, GLEN BUSH, EDWARD LODI, CATE MOYLE,
JAY ANDREW CONNOR, BOB RITCHIE, MICHELE BAZAN REED
EVE FISHER, MICHAEL WILEY, JOAN HALL HOVEY, J. T. SEATE,
AND MADELEINE MCDONALD

This is the first of several 'Free 4 All' collections that was supposed to be themeless. However, with the number of submissions that came in, it seems that this could be called an *Angels & Devils* collection, mixing PI & Police alongside tales from the Devil's dining table. Mind you, that's not to say that all the PIs & Police are on the side of the Angels....

Also this time around has not only seen a move to a larger paperback format size, but also in regard to the length of the fiction as well. Followers of the somewhat bent and twisted Crimeucopia path will know that although we don't deal with Flash fiction as a rule, it is a rule that we have sometimes broken. And let's face it, if you cannot break your own rules now and again, whose rules can you break?

Oh, wait, isn't breaking the rules the foundation of the crime fiction genre?

Oh dear....

With 16 vibrant authors, a wraparound paperback cover, and pages full of crime fiction in some of its many guises, what's not to like?
So if you enjoy tales spun by
Anthony Diesso, Brandon Barrows, E. James Wilson, James Roth,
Jesse Aaron, Jim Guigli, John M. Floyd, Kevin R. Tipple, Maddi Davidson,
Michael Grimala, Robert Petyo, Shannon Hollinger, Tom Sheehan,
Wil A. Emerson, Peter Trelay, and Philip Pak
then you'd better get
CRIMEUCOPIA - Strictly Off The record
by the sound of it!

CRIMEU C PIA

BoomSHAKALAKiNG!

Modern Crimes for Modern Times

Featuring: Scott Talbot Evans, Edward Sheehy,
Robb T. White, Robert Petyo, Brian R. Quinn,
Orca Green, Robert Parker, Brandon Barrows,
S. E. Bailey, Edward St. Boniface, Dan A. Cardoza,
Sean Marciniak, Lynn Hesse and Hernán Salvarezza

Boomshakalaking is a variant of the expression Boomshakalaka, currently recognised as a boastful, teasingly hostile exclamation that follows a noteworthy achievement or an impressive stunt — the meaning similar to *in your face!*

Which is why this anthology is subtitled *Modern Crimes for Modern Times*, because most, if not all, are not your 'regular' crime fiction pieces — in fact some quite happily dance along the edges of multiple genres and styles, while others skew it like it is.

Of the 14 who appear in this anthology, 8 are new Crimeucopians, and even we have to admit that this is one of the most diverse Crimeucopia anthologies so far, and still sits under the umbrella of Crime Fiction.

As with all of these anthologies, we hope you'll find something that you immediately like, as well as something that takes you out of your comfort zone – and puts you into a completely new one.

In other words, in the spirit of the Murderous Ink Press motto:

You never know what you like until you read it.

Just An Eight Banger With Big Baloneys

To honour motor transportation in some of its many roles in the crime fiction genre, we have gathered together a fine collection of short pieces that we feel, in one way or another, will crank up your adrenaline and get your emotions racing without making you blow a gasket or strip a gear.

Featuring: Ed Teja, John A. Connor, Ruth Morgan, Jesse Aaron, Scotch Rutherford, Billie Livingston, Robert Petyo, John Elliott, M.E. Proctor, William Kitcher, R. M. Linning, Annie Reed, Wil A. Emerson, Dan A. Cardoza, Alan J. Wahnefried, Sam Wiebe, Jon Fain, and Mark James McDonough

We hope you'll find something that you immediately like, as well as something that takes you out of your regular racing line comfort zone — and puts you into a completely new one.

In other words, in the spirit of the Murderous Ink Press motto:
You never know what you like until you read it.

Paperback ISBN: 9781909498525 eBook ISBN: 9781909498532

Milton Keynes UK
Ingram Content Group UK Ltd.
UKHW042146160324
439502UK00005B/201

9 781909 498563